Brad Linaweaver lives in Clarkston, Georgia. The short story that was the genesis of this novel, also called 'Moon of Ice', was a Nebula Award nominee.

BRAD LINAWEAVER

Moon of Ice

GRAFTON BOOKS

A Division of the Collins Publishing Group

LONDON GLASGOW
TORONTO SYDNEY AUCKLAND

Grafton Books
A Division of the Collins Publishing Group
8 Grafton Street, London W1X 3LA

A Grafton UK Paperback Original 1989

ISBN 0-586-20359-1

Printed and bound in Great Britain by
Collins, Glasgow

Set in Times

Moon of Ice appeared as a novella, 'Moon of Ice',
in *Amazing* © 1982, and in *Hitler Victorious* © 1986.

To the Mad Gang, my old group of friends, with a special nod to Bill Ritch.

To three editors who helped my story through its gestation: Elinor Mavor the first time out, Gregory Benford the second time, and David Hartwell for making the novel possible.

To my agent, Cherry Weiner, and my wife, Cari.

And finally to the Sense of Wonder that makes our field notable.

Acknowledgements

With a book as controversial as this may prove to be, acknowledgements should come with a disclaimer. Everyone listed below either contributed encouragement or suggestions (and in some cases both). When they see this page, they will also be encountering the final form of the novel for the first time. Omitted are names more prominently displayed in the dedication. Wendayne and Forrest J Ackerman; Robert Adams, Clifton Amsbury, Jimmy Arthur, Isaac Asimov, Robert Bloch, Berl Boykin, Ray Bradbury, David Brin, William F. Buckley, Jr, John F. Carr, Joe Celko, Gordon B. Chamberlain, Chauntecleer Michael, Comrade Wally, Marion Crowder, Earl Davis, Martin H. Greenberg, Paul Greiman, Craig Halstead, Big Lee Haslup, Robert A. Heinlein, Gail Higgins, Arthur Hlavaty, Phil Klass (William Tenn), Victor Koman, Samuel Edward Konkin III, Kerry Kyle, Robert LeFevre, Rebecca Leggett (Aunt Becky), June and Melville Linaweaver (my parents), David T. Lindsay, Alex Lucyshyn, Sandi March, Dr Bill Martin, Michael Medved, Chesley V. Morton, André Norton, Alex Nunan, Michael Ogden, Gerald W. Page, Jerry Pournelle, Dr Steven S. Reily, Leland Sapiro, J. Neil Schulman, Cary Ser, Michael Shaara, Robert Shea, Joe D. Siclari, Charles T. Smith, L. Neil Smith, Norman Spinrad, Mark Stanfill, Edie Stern, James L. Sutherland, Wilson 'Bob' Tucker, Dr James Whittemore, Warren Williams, Robert Anton Wilson, and Zolton Zucco, Jr.

Prologue

He who controls the past controls information.
He who controls information controls decisions.
He who controls decisions controls the future.

– George Orwell, *1984*

They took him out under the stars of Burgundy, and they laid him upon the damp grass. The women had implements of marking, and these they used to write a secret language upon his forehead. Behind them stood the flagellomaniac, his muscles grown hard and lean from the use of his whip – and trembling in anticipation should need arise to punish the chosen one.

'Behold the heavens, behold the eternal enemy,' intoned an elderly man, his voice muffled by the deerskin hood he wore. 'Tell us what you see.'

The chosen one did not hesitate: 'Above is an eternity of ice.'

'Tell us the answer to our dilemma,' demanded the voice.

'Only through fire do we hold back the ice; only the flame melts the dagger that would freeze our souls.'

The whip cracked through the still, summer air, leaving a red welt above the right pectoral muscle of the chosen one – who felt the pain as an electric shock, followed by a dull ache. A sudden tightening in the stomach made him glad that he had only eaten a plain potato before the ceremony. Through gritted teeth, he corrected his error: 'The dagger would freeze the Folk Spirit that underlies

7

the Aryan Soul, and we who are of the *Völk* must stand as one.'

The man in the deerskin hood took no notice of the interruption, but he continued in the same even tone of voice. 'What is that?' he asked, as he pointed to a bright dot of light in the east.

'The space station.'

'What does it portend?'

'It is an assault on the Eternal Ice; it would bring on us a judgement that might quench the flame.'

'What must be done?'

'The station must fall. It must burn. It must be given to the flame.'

The man in the hood nodded to the women, and the younger came forward carrying a small, black cylinder. 'Are you prepared to receive the vision?' she asked.

'I am.'

The cylinder had a small suction cup on one end, and by this means was it attached to a spot on the chosen one's forehead that had been marked with a polygon. Immediately the night sky above the chosen one disappeared, to be replaced by roiling clouds at midday . . . but it was a darksome daylight that gave the impression of night.

He got to his feet, but with some difficulty because of heavy armor that he now wore. He could smell his own sweat and cursed the strain on his legs. But there was no more pain from the welt; it was as if he had never been whipped.

In his hand was a weapon unlike any he had ever seen. Four oddly shaped blades rotated slowly above a handgrip that seemed almost an extension of his mailed fist. Somewhere deep inside, there was knowledge whispering to the chosen one: 'This weapon is of the people and of the soil; it is the *Völk* weapon. It can only serve if you obey!'

8

Behind him was a great throng of beautiful women and handsome youths. They all looked to him. Then they looked beyond, and he felt a compulsion to follow their gaze. What he saw made him tremble.

Giants loomed on the horizon, dark as the hills whence they came. They had sloping features and little pig's eyes that glittered with a deep malice. And they were on the march. Raising his weapon, the chosen one sought to engage the foe, but again his secret voice spoke to him: 'There can be no defense unless the Folk Spirit is pure. One there is among you who corrupts the rest.'

Yes, it was true – he could find one who didn't belong. The face did not have the fine features of its companions, nor was it bestial like the giants. The face was an unnatural amalgam of the attractive and the repulsive. And the owner of that face knew he was found out the moment the chosen one caught his glance.

Now did the blades of the weapon begin to spin, faster and faster, until they were a blur of motion. The weapon pulled his arm toward the fleeing form of the enemy . . . and then, despite the weight of the armor, he was flying, lightly and quickly and with joy. He marveled at the surgical precision by which the traitor's head was separated from his ungainly body.

Although the blades still spun madly, he could see a stain of red to mark their work. And now the weapon lifted him straight up into the purple vault of the heavens . . . and he felt himself thrown at the bovine faces of the giants, so brutish that they did not even show surprise. Expressionless they had lived; expressionless they died.

When the sanguinary work was finished, the chosen one stood in a lake of blood. The people cheered and loved him. He was complete. Then did the people point to the sky, where far away to the east glimmered a sickly,

9

yellow light. There would he attend to his most important task.

The blades were at rest. Gazing at them, he was grateful that so long as he wielded such a weapon, nothing could withstand his might. Not even the stars were safe from the man who held the shining power of the Swastika.

Chapter One

In the twentieth century there will be an extraordinary nation
. . . And that nation will be called Europe.

– Victor Hugo,
Preface to *Paris-Guide*

New York

'You're damned lucky, young man, that you're not speaking German today!' The speaker was an elderly man.
Although dressed conservatively, there was something
incongruous about the delicate rose tattooed on his left
cheek – a concession, no doubt, to popular taste, an
eccentricity of the professional reactionary.

'Excuse me, sir, but I *do* speak German, along with
Japanese, Russian, Yiddish, and, of course, the King's
English, not to mention American.' Alan Whittmore was
used to this sort of abuse and had gotten to the point
where he had a number of set answers. As editor of the
latest incarnation of *The American Mercury*, it was par
for the course.

A new voice joined the chorus: 'Your hero Mencken
would have sold us down the river, you dead-ed. If it
hadn't been for FDR, God bless 'im, we'd be a German
colony today, all rightso.' The speaker was a Townie,
dressed in camo jungle gear and wearing a pink top hat.
Judging from the glazed condition of his eyes, he was high
on Speck, but that in no way diminished his desire to
participate. 'Trouble with you dead-eds is you got no grip
on harsh realities, dig?'

'Pardon me, but I'd very much enjoy having my lunch in peace. If you wish to engage in badinage, you'll have to be civil, or we'll continue the discussion outside, once we find a witness – perhaps this gentleman who was here first – and I claim first choice of weapons.' If he read his man right, that would be the end of it.

'Dampen down,' said the Townie, retreating those few crucial steps, before departing altogether, leaving the floor to the old man.

'Do I know you?' asked Whittmore, affecting a smile.

'I'm Dr Evans. Why don't you ever publish my letters to the editor?'

So that was it! Whittmore's memory was suitably jogged. 'You are premature, sir. Your most recent missive has been selected to lead off next issue. I must say that you put the Revisionist case as well as can be expected. As you are familiar with my editorials, you know that I'm sticking with the majority view on this issue. I still believe it was for the best that Roosevelt was impeached. But please join me.'

'Thank you,' said Evans, settling himself with great care into the seat opposite.

'Health troubles?' asked Whittmore politely.

'Bursitis. Made the mistake of trying the Manchurian method, but now it's worse. My wife warned me against Chinese superstitions, but I didn't listen. God rest her, I've been falling apart since she passed away.'

'Perhaps you will allow me to minister to your needs. A drink?'

'A Berlin Blockbuster if you please.'

'You won't even know you have any pain after that.' Opportunities such as this should not be wasted. It was all too easy to become complacent in one's weltanschauung. Opposing views could be made into a tonic, provided they came in a polite package.

'Sorry about the kid,' said Evans, noting that the Townie had merged with his gang, now congregated about the blind man's bluff game. Their occasional shouted imprecations were their sole contribution to the serious matter of barroom debate. 'He seems erudite for a young hoodlum. Followed me over. He probably recognized your picture from the papers.'

'I've been getting a lot of publicity since Hilda Goebbels signed with me.'

A nude waitress glided over on roller skates, flashing a wide grin at them and depositing the drink for Evans, without losing either momentum or a drop of the amber liquid. 'I always tip her extravagantly,' Alan explained.

'I'm not from the boonies, even if this is my first trip to New York.' It was common knowledge, even in Idaho (the good doctor's address, as Whittmore recalled), that in cosmopolitan places the bigger the tip, the less attire was worn by the waiter or waitress who was out to cultivate repeat business. A whole industry had cropped up, producing apparel that could be quickly donned or shed as custom dictated.

'You're here about your book,' said Whittmore. Once his memory had been triggered, he was good at detail.

'Thank you for remembering my letter. Vineyard Publishing has agreed to bring it out, even though my thesis is unpopular.'

'More power to you, then. Perhaps you don't know this, but I first came to H. L. Mencken's attention in a fight against local censorship. If he hadn't given himself one last editorial fling in the sixties, I doubt I'd hold the position I do today. Anyway, I live by Voltaire's maxim about defending to the death an opponent's right to be heard.'

'I know, I know.' Evans sounded irritated. 'You people use the First Amendment, and the Fourth as well, to

13

undermine any hope for social justice.' Evans took his stand: 'I am not a Libertarian.'

'Obviously the case, but do you have a label you wear in public, other than the one on your suit?'

'Sir, I fought in the Second World War.'

'So did my father, and he became a Libertarian.'

'Well then, I used to be a New Dealer, but today I think of myself as a traditionalist conservative.'

'At least you've remained consistent over the years. But tell me, do you begrudge us our success?'

The old man had been around. He knew when to make a tactical retreat. 'I would never dream of interfering with free speech.'

'Good man! We'll radicalize you yet.'

Evans was having none of it: 'Not so long as there is the social injustice of the flat tax, sir.' Half the Berlin Blockbuster was gone, apparently inhaled. Whittmore noticed that the more the man drank, the more he peppered his conversation with 'sirs' . . . as though he had at some time ingested Boswell's *Life of Johnson*, surely the final word in terminal pomposity. Worse than that, the old man was adopting an annoying familiarity: 'Listen here, young fella, you've been decent to me and I want to return the favor. There's a change of mood in the country. This business of normalizing relations with the Greater Reich is not going over. The American people won't stand for it.'

A number of quips, courtesy of Mencken's influence, flitted through Whittmore's mind, but he restrained himself. The old man saw himself as a conduit through which flowed the popular will; and if what he had to say just happened to contradict the latest TVotes poll, Whittmore was not about to disabuse him of his notion. The teenage Alan had elected to be a high-church agnostic rather than a fire-and-brimstone atheist. When people claimed to

14

know either the will of God or the will of the people, Whittmore might first think of Adolf Hitler as the patent model for such absurdity, but that was no reason for being insensitive to the vigorously self-deluded. And so: 'Perhaps they are not sure what they want. It is not the American government that is having relations with anyone. Remember that as we limit the power of our own state, private individuals are free to deal with whomever they please. If one American corporation finds itself fighting a skirmish with Nazis in South America on Monday, that's no reason another outfit may not open shop in Europe on Tuesday. The National Socialists have so bungled Europe's economy that they have no choice but to let in entrepreneurs.'

Dr Evans was shaking his head, presenting himself with a problem as he was trying to swallow the last of his drink simultaneously. 'We're doomed, doomed. Cultural exchanges are bad enough, but the trading of technology will do us in. You speak of opening markets, but all I see is a black abyss.'

'A line from your book?'

'A new dawn is coming. The nuclear stalemate won't last forever. I tell you that the Nazis are evil and must be destroyed.' Here was a man for whom the war had never ended. Perhaps he was one of those oddballs who contined to refer to sauerkraut as liberty cabbage.

There was no levity in Whittmore's voice as he said, 'I agree that the Nazis are evil, but no more so than the Communists they tried and executed at the war crimes trials.'

'Ha, you opposed those trials in one of your first editorials, sir!'

What an inconvenience! Here was Whittmore, minding his own business, having a peaceful lunch at Oscar's, when out of nowhere materialized a loyal reader of his words. 'Yes, I did, but only because of a moral insight

15

that I cannot claim to be original with me: two wrongs don't make a right.'

It went on in this vein for some time. At one point, Evans went so far as to argue that Lord Halifax was innocent of having contributed to the distrust and paranoia that made World War II inevitable. Whittmore told him that his opinion was shockingly uninformed. Then the dialogue degenerated into the sort of rhetoric one hears on a school playground: of the 'is so/is not' variety. By some miracle of grace, they managed to avoid the topic of Pearl Harbor. Even so, there was no longer communication worth the name. They were bouncing slogans off each other, and Whittmore didn't even have a drink of his own.

'One day America will pay for its treatment of Roosevelt, our last great president!' declaimed Evans, his face positively livid with passion.

Whittmore's response was equally windy: 'Dewey and Taft helped undo the damage; and those who followed put America back on the road to sanity.' Although Evans would grant a kind word for the last Republican presidents, he had nothing but scorn for those who had followed, and their parties, from the America Firsters to the Liberty party. Whittmore got Evans to admit that he saw no value in any of the presidents who had served since the failure of the military coup in 1952. That there had been a proliferation of new political parties did not seem to him an acceptable outcome; he would have preferred a return to the old two-party monopoly, a return to 'normalcy,' and two chickens in the imaginary pot of the Good Old Days.

'It's true that I was taken in by the scare stories of a Nazi sneak attack,' said Evans, 'but the conspirators would never have gone to such lengths if the first Liberty

16

party president, crazy Rothbard, hadn't driven them to it. It's a wonder we weren't invaded!'

'The defense of the country was never in doubt – and this was proved by the calm response of those generals who remained loyal to the president while keeping an eagle eye, if you will, on how thoroughly bogged down were the Berlin boys in their latest reconquest of the glorious Russian steppes. Were you one of the public-spirited fellows looking for Nazis under every bed back then?'

'Please don't accuse me of Roggeism, sir. If I worried about guilt by association I wouldn't be here with you.'

'My apologies, then. But I thought that careless fraternization was still cause for alarm in the Bipartisan party.'

'What makes you think I'm a member?'

'Well, aren't you?' Whittmore prided himself on his political instincts. The small, ineffectual party gave disaffected Republicans and Democrats of yore a place to congregate. This fellow was made to order as a BP delegate.

'Very well, I am. Where else is a patriot to go these days? You say that the defense of the country was never in doubt. I beg to differ. There is more to defense than just keeping the enemy out. Football coaches tell us that the best defense is a good offense, therefore the righteous must be offensive in nature. Uh, that is, I mean to suggest that our foreign policy was activist during the war. We knew what we wanted. The worst thing that could have happened was the conflict ending in stalemate. Everything had been arranged for Total Victory. Now we are passive and weak.'

'Now we are safe and strong, but only after a general housecleaning. Not all the power addicts were on the Axis side. We fixed that.'

'But surely you don't think that the fire at the State Department was a good thing. Think of what we lost!'

17

'Accidents will happen.'

'Well, no matter what you say, isolationism will destroy us in the end. There is no neutrality in this world.'

'Nonintervention opens doors that an empire would close.'

And so forth. They had raised their voices, a mistake in a restaurant flooded with Townies who were already bored with their game – a banal use of computer graphics and a cattle prod that could only engage the attention of mental children for a brief period – and were attracted to the sound of anger as if they were lawyers. The intellectual of the gang came skipping back, his top hat tilting ludicrously, as if a chimney in an earthquake. The rumbling of violence was in his manner, and his compatriots were close behind. Evans began to tremble, no doubt unused to the ways of Town No. #1.

'I hate to be surrounded before dessert,' said Whittmore.

'Still want to rip and roar outside, Herr Editor? You goddamn kraut lover. Bet you're a Slav lover, too. Let's go for broke, hey?'

The machine pistol in Whittmore's pocket was useless inside a place this crowded. He wasn't going to spend the rest of his life in insurance litigation. Trouble was that bums like this had no family ties any longer, and what passed for a community among them was not exactly awash in funds.

Whittmore's half-million-dollar insurance policy against assassination would mean that Uni-Life would receive one of their more expensive Hunt-and-Destroy licenses. Well, solvency was every American's docket. He'd be doing both Uni-Life and himself a favor if he could maneuver the Townies outside.

'Hold it!' Everyone in the restaurant knew the owner's voice. Oscar sounded like he was speaking from inside an echo chamber. He was as heavily built as his place. He'd made a name for himself as far back as the Detroit race riots. He was probably not much younger than Evans; but you'd never believe it to look at the condition of his muscles. 'Townies, I wants a word with you.'

'Ho, ho, Mistuh Sleep-and-Eat, you run the biz, but you're no scholar. Bad grammar equals big bucks, hey?' The intellectual was at it again. Alan could tell from the expression on Oscar's face that he was not inclined to dispute the Townie at the verbal level. Too bad, thought the editor; because the proprietor could express better than anybody the feeling during the times of trouble that the NRA really stood for the Negro Replacement Act. Well, the Townies were about to experience removal for reasons no man of goodwill could question.

A bald girl, who couldn't have been any older than fifteen, shrieked at her ostensible leader: 'You gootch! You gettin' us in dutch with a nigger bruiser!'

'I've got no Chinese down my back, bitch!' was his witty reply. 'Just for that, you don't get any fluid tonight.'

Unconcerned with domestic quarrels among the emotionally handicapped, Oscar headed straight for his target and lifted the Townie by the lapels of his camo jacket. 'Now lissen here, dirt-boy. I gots nothing against your money. Anytime your money wants to come into my joint, it's welcome. I has a kid studyin' to be an aerospace engineer and every cent I can spare goes to him in Florida. But when you mess with other customers, mebbe they won't let their money come visitin' next time.'

The logic of the argument was entirely lost on the Townie, whose metal equipment was otherwise engaged, to wit: 'You're tearin' the suit, coon.' Among his other virtues, Oscar inspired loyalty in his staff. Waitresses, clothed and otherwise, began skating over, each holding the most lethal weapon known to the strip: razor sharp

19

serving trays. In an amazing display of extrapolative ability, the gang broke into its constituent parts . . . and each and every mother's son and daughter of them ran for their lives. Chastened from his lack of moral support, the Townie dangling from Oscar's large, black hand attempted to be diplomatic: 'Lookie here, uh, innkeeper. We were just fraggin' around, joshin' don't you know. Jeepers creepers, there's no need to wad your panties.'

'Oscar,' said Whittmore quietly. 'I have a theory I've been wanting to put to the test.'

'What is it, Mr Whittmore?'

'I believe that the harder you shake this kid, the more English words will pour out.'

Oscar had a disarming chuckle that he now enjoyed to the limit. 'I has been feeling scientific lately.'

The experiment began: 'Now wait a mo', you gribbin'' – SHAKE – 'Uh, er, we gan glom' – SHAKE – 'Damn your blitzkriegin'' – SHAKE – 'OK, OK, stop, will you?' Oscar stopped. 'What do you want me to do?' asked the Townie.

'I understood what he said,' said Evans, getting into the spirit of the moment. It took but another moment to convince the young man to deposit his remaining gold notes on the table as restitution for any mental cruelty that Whittmore had suffered. Then the Townie left, swaying as if he were an uptown socialite. Whittmore convinced Oscar to take a sizable tip from the windfall, and the proprietor joked that he wouldn't disrobe in gratitude.

Dr Evans never did regain his belligerency of tone, but surprised Alan with: 'You would have made a good New Dealer.'

'God, you must simply love nostalgia! I guess you mean it as a compliment, in which case thanks.'

Evans didn't seem to hear. He was looking at the door where the Townie had departed the premises. 'I hate listening to a punk like that pretend at patriotism. If Oscar hadn't done it, I would have laid hands on the bum for ignorantly employing the term "jeepers creepers."'

'I'm afraid I don't understand.'

'As I mentioned earlier, I served in the Pacific. We set up signs in the jungle with an arrow pointing one way for clear paths the jeeps could use, and another arrow pointing where the creeping vines made egress impossible.'

'I've heard that phrase for years, but I had no idea what it meant.'

They began walking to the door, and Whittmore offered the old man a ride in the cab. 'No, thank you,' he replied, 'but I would like to ask you one last question. Are you really going to bring out those books by Hilda Goebbels?'

'I'm on my way to see her right now.'

'It won't be good for your country.'

The presumption of the man was too much. Whittmore might never be gracious to a stranger again. 'What the hell do you mean by that?' As he asked the question, he felt a drop of rain sting his ear.

'Why give that person an American audience?'

'Stop right there!' They had reached the curb. 'I don't like what you're implying. Nobody in the world is a more devout anti-Nazi than Hilda Goebbels.'

'That's what she *wants* us to believe. But when you consider all the things her father did – '

'Part of what we know against her father is thanks to her! And she's about to release even more information. She's a hero to the European underground. America is lucky to receive her.'

'Blood is thicker than water.'

It started to rain in earnest. For one crazy moment, Whittmore watched drops splash about the rose on Dr Evans's face, anticipating that the tattoo would wash away.

'You've asked me a lot of questions. Let me ask you another. What is the main thing you hate about the Nazis?'

Dr Evans didn't hesitate: 'They're bigots.'

Chapter Two

And many more Destructions played
In this ghastly masquerade,
All disguised, even to the eyes,
Like bishops, lawyers, peers or spies.

– Percy Bysshe Shelley,
The Mask of Anarchy

It was raining hard, and Whittmore was glad that he had
hailed a Frontier Hugger, a cab line renowned for all-
terrain wheels. He was going uptown on a street with as
many craters as the surface of the moon. He didn't like it,
but he wouldn't buy it.

Betting pools were still giving best odds against anyone
taking on the responsibility of the unowned thorough-
fares. Meanwhile, people lived by the slogan 'If you can't
make the road for the wheels, make the wheels for the
roads.' It was an obvious market solution.

As one of the curses of being an editor, Whittmore had
a good memory for statistics. There had been 900,000
miles of highway in 1940. The plans for expansion had
been on a monumental scale that, quite predictably, took
no cognizance of local economies. The New Dealers had
drawn a number of faulty parallels between the building
of the railroads and the haphazard construction of these
superhighways; and they had planned their projects to go
on and on, once the troublesome matter of World War II
had achieved its industrial objectives.

The irony was that all their dreams had come true, but
on another continent, and thanks to another kind of

public works project. Hitler had kept his promise about the autobahns for the Greater Reich. Today, superhighways stretched the length of Europe and even penetrated into the dismal Russian east, where none had ever dreamed a road could find its way. And yet the markets did not exist to support the maintenance of these vast ribbons of transport (and the promises that the roads would bring commerce in their wake had hardly lived up to the rosy projections).

Albert Speer had devised variations on every technical solution imaginable, but there were never enough marks to cover the costs. His successor, Frack, was enamored of the notion that roads could be constructed in sections, and as one piece wore out, it could be replaced by another in stock. The transport difficulties were incredible: guerrilla action soon concentrated on intercepting the giant trucks bringing the new sections and wearing out the road they traversed. Use of railroads led to even more problems. And so the National Socialists further bankrupted the Reich. In keeping with Hitler's approach to other problems, his last official order had been to start work on the greatest autobahn in the world. Half finished, overrun with weeds, the remains of this project reached half the length of Africa.

Whittmore felt a small satisfaction to know that some locally maintained US roads were superior to anything in Europe today, which proud thought neatly coincided with a jarring bump beneath him. Never one to discount an omen, Whittmore amended his position by picturing vast tracts of land that had never been graced with an American highway system. Critics of the market continually complained about wasted space and went so far as to suggest that if the city owned the road Whittmore was even now enjoying it would no longer be a surrealistic study in potholes and jagged buckling. Whittmore could not help but imagine a worse scenario: a situation in which tolls were paid on a daily basis . . . and the roads remained in a state of disrepair. A student of borough politics, he was always willing to assume the worst.

A question that had been nagging at him recently was the old thorny riddle of causation: did people determine the objects they made and used, or did the articles determine the inclinations of the people so completely that 'choice' was largely illusory? Did the road taken have to determine the outcome, when there were so many stopping places along the way? Surely all decisions resided in the individual ego, but then, there were so many egos to consider. Although an adherent to the Great Man Theory of History in his writings, Whittmore was coming to sorrowful conclusions about the ponderous weight of events in their cumulative power.

On the spur of the moment, Whittmore asked the cabbie: 'What do you think of German roads?'

The man, a chunky Russian in his mid-forties, grinned and said, 'I've never driven them, but I can tell you plenty about Hong Kong. You don't get around there without a 'copter.'

Well, if one had the stomach for it, that was probably the best way to travel. Still, Whittmore preferred wheels, even on his last trip to New Berlin. They drove like maniacs over there, as if worried they would lose their statistical distinction for highest automobile casualties in the world.

A particularly nasty bump brought Whittmore firmly back to the realities of Manhattan. His head had struck the ceiling. Such was his vanity that his primary concern was that he not appear disheveled before the woman he had wanted to meet for years: Hilda Goebbels. When she had telephoned the day before to say that she would be waiting for him in the penthouse of a swank hotel, he had felt his pulse quicken in excitement, as if he had just been granted an interview with Mata Hari in one of his favorite novels. The comparison was not inappropriate. Hilda was a remarkable woman who had lived dangerously and won battles. Her life was like something out of a romantic fantasy. Bred to be one of the aristocracy of the New Order, she had finally balked at being a Nazi Aryan princess. But it was a perilous journey to go from being a youthful rebel to underground revolutionary. Along the way, many rumors had attached themselves to her name, the worst being the charge Whittmore had just rebuffed from Dr Evans.

Other rumors had less the ring of a charge in open court than the confidential whisper of gossip in a closed bedroom. Was it true that she had had a lesbian relationship with a young Jewess? Was it true that Hitler had once tried to seduce her? Was it true that she had killed her own brother, and this after an incestuous relationship? That which titillated sold copy, but Whittmore disliked pandering to it, especially when he thought of the 'Wowsers' – Mencken's invaluable label – who would buy every detestable excess of the libeler's art, linger over every libidinous passage, then mount the public rostrum to declaim against the very thing that engaged their attention.

There was one rumor about Hilda Goebbels that fascinated Whittmore, but it was an entirely different sort of thing from the gossip mongers, If untrue, it was nonetheless born of high regard for the woman, even if it had an almost comic book quality to it. The suggestion was that she had helped to prevent World War III by thwarting a conspiracy of the SS.

No matter how fantastic the claim, if she was the subject of it the story was worth investigating. Whittmore knew for a fact that although not a scientist herself, she had helped advance the cause of medicine. She had done this by smuggling important papers about genetic research out of the Reich and into British hands. Although ostensibly allied with Europe in Mosley's postwar Fascist government, a sizable portion of the populous British Isles maintained economic ties with their North American cousins. Alfred Rosenberg could complain all he wanted to about the so-called 'brain drain' (as it was vulgarly described in what remained of London), but German discoveries, and the discoverers themselves, often found their way to American shores. In this instance, Hilda had been the transmisssion belt for what, one expert told Whittmore, was the most important theoretical work and experimental records since entering the atomic age.

The woman could have had American citizenship right then, with ribbons on it, but she chose to travel the world sans any citizenship for nearly half a decade. She had written that, as an anarchist, she saw no reason to give her sanction to any state, even one as freedom loving as the American Republic. It was hard sometimes for Whittmore, a professional advocate of limited government, to realize just how deep ran Hilda's aversion to any form of state; but, then, she had been born into the heart of Nazism.

Well, she would make a lot of people happy by her symbolic cooperation. Bio-Cure Industries was throwing a big party for her next week, and she had accepted their invitation, with the one proviso that she not be asked to say their advertising logo for the cameras: 'Splice genes and live longer.'

Since the death of her father, the notorious propaganda minister and all-around bureaucrat of the Greater Reich, Hilda had gone to elaborate lengths to secure his private papers. The cost had been high, in life as well as money, but she had achieved her purpose. Now, five years after the death of Joseph Goebbels, his apostate daughter was about to release the final entries of his world-famous diary, material that had been suppressed in Germany and all its colonies. That Alan Whittmore had become involved with the release of this material still seemed unreal to him. Hilda was going to sign an exclusive contract for both the diary entries and her own autobiography with the youthful editor who was bouncing in the back seat of a New York cab while dreaming of sitting at the wheel, if only briefly, of history's engine.

Yes, it was the biggest break Alan had had since coming to Mencken's attention in the twilight of the grand old man's life. Thank God that his father had lived to see that much. And thank God that the elder Mencken, failing badly in his sixties, had consented to try a new treatment that not only added years to his life, but gave him the stamina to return to editing for one last fling. According to legend, Mencken had had only one quibble before undergoing therapy: he wanted a written assurance that what he was about to receive was in no way a disguised form of chiropractic procedure! Whittmore doubted the veracity of the story, but he enjoyed telling it anyway. Sometimes the instinct of the journalist got in the way of the would-be historian.

There would be no room for that sort of thing with the Goebbels manuscripts. Every expert in the world (no matter his field!) would be out to challenge every line of what was printed. He'd read somewhere that paranoia was the condition of having *all* the facts. If there was any virtue to be had from the nervous habit of glancing over one's shoulder, now was the time to cultivate it!

Partly as a joke to himself, but more in the manner of a dare, Alan turned around and looked through the back window of the cab. The car immediately behind was a very well-maintained specimen of a Horch limousine. At first he was seized with admiration for the quality of maintenance on the antique, the make of which he estimated to be 1936. The rain was beading on the glossy wax finish, and as the car swayed on the unnaturally large wheels required for travel in New York City, it gave the impression of a ship at sea, weathering the storm in all its black majesty. The second feeling he had was a gentle self-mockery. The small ripple of paranoia could become a tidal wave that would engulf the last of his good sense if he didn't get hold of himself. *Just a coincidence*, he told himself, *that a sinister vehicle should be available on cue*. The damned car did give a first impression of being a hearse.

There was really no escape from worry. Those without money worried how to get it; those with it worried how to keep it; and nobody but nobody thought he had adequate security, the magic word that all too often was synonymous with power. How much of the madness in the world was the result of governmental worries? Many had thought the solution was to find the state a good therapist. Hilda was one of those who preferred giving the state over to the service represented by hearses. As for Alan, he was content with the state as an invalid, and a strong Bill of Rights as the eternal nursemaid.

Still, there were problems. Remove America's Secret Service, and watch foreign agents rush to fill the vacuum. Put some kind of Secret Service back in place – as one of the functions of a limited government – and everyone began to worry that it would be a shadow government working to return the superstate. Keep secrets from Americans, so that German intelligence would not receive bonuses from the free press across the Atlantic, and everyone would begin to suspect collusion between America's Secret Service and the Nazis. And the worst of it was

29

that whoever was spying for whatever purpose, Alan worried that they would be sure to keep an eye on him. This business with Hilda would probably make his career, but at the price of an ulcer.

It was simply too much to believe, however, that an enemy would be trailing him in a vehicle as suspicious as the anomaly closing in on his rear. No, it was probably some little old European lady who didn't trust any technological development that had come from the war or its aftermath. Sure, that was it.

No sooner did he have the thought than it became an obsession. He had to see the owner of the car!

At four in the afternoon, the traffic was nothing short of hideous in those areas reserved for private vehicles. Most inhabitants had the sense to use the extensive mass transit available in the prime business areas. As half the city streets had been sold to private owners, pedestrians had a variety of routes from which to choose, many of which took them through quaint and colorful bazaars, where they could buy anything from a drug to a gun. The Bronx had become something that had to be seen to be believed. Out of a sense of history, and an unwillingness to fix something that isn't broken, the original names for streets and avenues had been retained regardless of the new zoning for pedestrians and vehicles. New York was proud to boast one of the cleanest environments of any large metropolis in the world. Unfortunately, it also had an unacceptably high crime rate. Why, only last year there had been over one hundred murders. That might not seem like a lot by New Berlin standards, but it wouldn't do for an American.

A heterogeneous population was not the ideal mixture for tranquillity, but it did make for progress. The ideal was to allow the diverse population to move at its own varying speeds, in time with a cacophony of different drummers. Ahead, he saw that even in the rain, a goodly number of cyclists enjoyed themselves on the Oakes Bikeway, a ribbon of genteel transport arching over the motorized vehicles below as it linked First with 125th Street.

Alas, the publishing industry, preferring nostalgia and tension, operated very much out of prewar New York, and Alan Whittmore had long ago gotten over the feelings of claustrophobia he'd had when he first came to town. He'd almost come to the point where tobacco smoke in close, unventilated rooms no longer put him off, but he would never really be comfortable with the rocking motion of riding on these moon-cratered streets. He wished to hell someone would buy them! Neighborhood cooperatives owned the majority of streets, with legal control over how much traffic, and of what kind, they would allow. Business areas were paid for by businessmen, and maximum traffic was to be found there. But there were the awkward areas, the limbo regions, that provided a turf over which city government could battle. Human nature being what it is, and even more so with public servants, the residue of the old bureaucracy, smaller but still fat, was not about to cooperate with itself and set one price for all. So the battle continued, and every week there was a new proposal for how to remove the unpopular presence of local government.

Although he only had a short distance to go, it would take a long time to traverse it. At last they came to a traffic light where the taxi would turn right. Perhaps they would lose the 'hearse' here. The rain was letting up and he had a clearer view of it. The chauffeur could be seen past the slow movement of his windshield wiper. He was a big man in an outfit as anachronistic as the vehicle he drove. An old-fashioned touring cap and bug-eyed goggles made it impossible to see anything about his face other than that he was young and bearded. More than ever, Whittmore wanted to see the person in the back seat.

The light turned. They turned. The limo turned with them. Now it was a straight shot to the Isabel Paterson Hotel. He hoped he could determine whether or not he was being pursued. As the cab neared its destination and began to slow, the hearse slowed as well, but its left-turn signal was on and it was evident that the driver wished to pass a suddenly relieved young editor. Whittmore was clambering out of the cab and reaching for his wallet when the Horch glided past and he tried to catch a glimpse of the vehicle's owner. His relief burst like a bubble in a storm.

The man in the back seat had a face that would have attracted attention under any circumstances. His head was very large, and a shock of white hair extended from his scalp as if it were electricity crackling about a rheostat. His features were as angular as if they had been those of a statue; his nose was sharp as a beak, his chin as square as a building stone, his forehead as high as if he had no hair at all. These features would have surprised Alan in and of themselves, but what was unbearable was that the head was turned toward the curb. The man looked straight at Alan Whittmore . . . and he grinned. Then the long, black car pulled away and rejoined the flow of traffic. Alan continued to stare at the place where the man had been; he listened to the gentle slapping of the rain against the hotel canopy behind him. He was afraid.

'Something wrong?' asked the cabbie, still waiting for his money.

Alan said nothing as he paid, turning away before the cabbie could negotiate for some of the change that was surely too much to be an intended tip. He didn't hear another word because he was falling, falling into the face of the stranger.

Chapter Three

And ye fathers, provoke not your children to wrath.

– Ephesians 6:4

There was a carnival going on inside the hotel. At least that was the impression Whittmore received as he stepped into the lobby. Balloons and posters adorned the marble-and-wood interior with which the Paterson Hotel impressed first-time guests. The largest sign read WILD EAST CONVENTION 1975/REGISTRATION. An emaciated individual was wearing a T-shirt with the legend MUTANTS FIND ADVENTURE EAST OF THE URALS. This, Whittmore concluded, must be a science fiction fan. The culture shock of stepping into a different universe was sufficient to temporarily diminish his fear of the man outside.

Yet he couldn't help but wonder what Hilda was doing at this hotel. Surely she wasn't part of the convention! A sudden fit of dizziness seized him, and he had to sit down. As no chair was available, he found an unoccupied spot on a raised portico in the center of the lobby on which perched a statue of the American Entrepreneur, whose granite face seemed to consider Alan with a most disapproving expression. No, no, this wouldn't do at all. It made him think of the man with the white hair again. Alan got to his feet so quickly that he accidentally jostled a teenage girl who was dressed – if that was the word for it – in some ill-fitting pieces of silver suggesting a harem girl's costume. 'Excuse me,' he muttered to her disappearing back. She had not seemed to notice.

The brief interlude had helped return Alan's composure. He would think about the man later; now he must concern himself with the Goebbels manuscripts.

An officious-looking man at the desk had all the information Alan required: 'Miss Goebbels left word that she would be detained but that you should wait in her suite.' Normally, he would be annoyed at her lack of punctuality, but now he was grateful for the time alone. With the power of self-delusion most effectively employed by professional wordsmiths, he would soon have himself convinced that the man in the hearse didn't mean him any harm.

The elevator ride was uneventful.

After tipping the porter who had shown him to the room, Alan allowed himself the pleasure of a sense of proprietorship in the elegant surroundings. Whatever scent was being used gave the impression of fresh air.

And it was soothing to walk on the snow white carpet that was just plush enough to maximize comfort without turning into a trek through a dessert topping. Across this sea of carpet was a heavy rosewood table on which, propped up against a lamp in the shape of the Statue of Liberty, was a note obviously intended for him. As he went over to the table, he saw multiple versions of himself in the various mirrors set at strategic points about the suite.

'Dear Alan,' the note began, 'I have taken precautions with the final entries of my father's diaries for reasons that will become apparent when you read them. It is my sincere hope that these extraordinary steps will prove unnecessary. Will be with you as soon as possible. Please have anything in the bar, but I ask you not to use room service. The other manuscript is here.' She had signed it with her initials.

Here was an opportunity to have that drink he'd needed

34

so badly in the company of Evans, a thirst made all the more acute by the taxi ride. Running a thumb over the width of the manuscript on the table, he estimated the quantity and type of alcohol most suited to the job at hand. An inventory of the bar gave him a warm feeling about Hilda's acculturation to the American Way of Life – all his favorites were lined up, generously full bottles awaiting his inspection. Settling on a golden-hued tequila and bright green lime, he apologized to the shade of Mencken, who never approved of mixing his booze with his work, and settled into the couch by the large picture window. The feeling of unease dissipated with the first swallow of tangy, watery fire. With manuscript on his lap, he began to read the lady's memoirs:

NOTES TOWARD AN AUTOBIOGRAPHY
BY HILDA GOEBBELS
WRITTEN SOMEWHERE IN THE PACIFIC
MARCH 1970

I am no longer a European. Is this the sole requirement to become an American? I have no certainties about what to do any longer. Only yesterday I was calling myself an anarchist as a positive statement. Today it is only a negation, a way of saying that I deny the state, but what good is that if I do not know what I affirm?

They tell me that Father is dying. I wish that I could celebrate, but even this news holds no pleasure for me. Even here, cradled in the swell of open sea, I cannot escape gossip. They say that he is turning back to the Catholic church. Oh, the poor fools. The one honor I must grant my father is that he left himself no avenues of escape. He who did so much to build a hell on earth will take his medicine without begging for nectar. He took what he wanted from the Roman church – certain structures of authority – and left whatever humanity there was behind. He was a true materialist, the man who always chooses the worst and leaves the rest.

A Puerto Rican woman leaves me Catholic tracts to read. Initially she spoke to me in a rather dreadful Low German – heaven knows where she picked it up – but when I responded in passable Spanish, we got on. Her name is Maria, and I am polite to her, even though she thinks that my lack of grief for my dying parent is deeply sinful, and she peppers her speech with the German word *Sündig!* to make sure that I am not misinterpreting her strong disapproval of my indifferent attitude. What she cannot understand is that I rejected all forms of authority long ago save for the proposition of natural law.

I have learned a lot, perhaps too much, in these last few years. It amuses me that people on the outside ever thought that the Nazis wanted chaos. Their crime was the crime of authority, of order. The chaos came when others strove to be free. If there is a natural order, then leave it alone. I don't know that there is, but I do know that order cannot be imposed. If the Christians are right, then I'm sure that many Nazis are even now discovering that the Devil has some real potential for establishing new orders.

One would think that as my father nears death, I would frequently see him in my mind. I do at times; his flat, large features, high forehead and pinched mouth, gave an impression of a mummy suffering from acromegaly. But I can never retain his image for long. Even in death, his position is usurped. I see Hitler more often. Alas, in this I regret to say that I am my father's daughter.

Father lived in Hitler's shadow in life. Why should the death of either of them change anything? Memory is my curse. If I could expunge either recollection, I would rather lose my times with 'Uncle Adolf' than those spent with my twisted father.

When I was a child, I played in Hitler's sight. When I

was older, I dined with him, . . . often listening to him tell me stories about our earlier times together. Memory is insanity. Oh, to drive it away! He never tired of telling everyone about the occasion when, as an impressionable six-year-old, I had placed all my stuffed dogs outside my bedroom to guard me. An SS man had been telling me blood-curdling fairy tales about witches and ogres and other denizens of the mysterious Northern Lands. I was always able to take a hint. Uncle Adolf couldn't stop laughing over my practical response to our mythic heritage. I think what really won him over was that I trusted dogs. He often said that he only trusted dogs and the SS; and both served the same function for him.

The only forgiveness I can spare my father is that we shared the same experience of the Fuehrer Principle in action. Those who cluck their tongues about easy resistance and automatic revolution do not know what an intimate relationship with a dictator is like. Just as those who were never in a concentration camp, Axis or Allied, cannot really share in the communion of anguish. Even so, I believe that the camps provide me with an invaluable metaphor. Being in a room with Hitler was the most refined version of a concentration camp.

They say that power corrupts. An American thinker has said that immunity corrupts. In the end, I think it is hatred that corrupts. Hitler cared more for his hate than his power. With the power of empire in his hands, he laid waste whole peoples.

The most love I ever received from my father was the evening he came home and announced to the entire household that I was Hitler's favorite. This could not have come at a worse time. I had only recently made the most dangerous discovery an adolescent girl can make: I was a tease. A young girl's vanity is as cruel to others as it is satisfying to herself. My father and I became collaborators

37

in that moment. In plotting our campaigns to keep this special favoritism alive, I had my first real understanding of how my father thought. I doubt that anyone else was more qualified for the role of Reichspropagandaminister than he. The Great Reich deserved Paul Joseph Goebbels.

I was only fourteen when I was invited to dinner with Hitler and his personal filmmaker, Leni Riefenstahl. It was but a few weeks before I was to leave for Bavaria. Mother had been describing the beauties of Pathfinder's Youth Camp for years, and I was at last to begin attendance. I had been dreaming of forests and streams and mountains, and suddenly I was at dinner with the Fuehrer, and he was suggesting that I star in a movie about a young girl's odyssey to the mountaintop. Classmates had been teasing me that sooner or later my father would put me in a movie. (Father's penchant for arranging screen tests whenever he had a new mistress was Europe's most open scandal, so a nod in the direction of his family might not be judged as entirely inappropriate.) I had not expected to receive such an offer from the Fuehrer himself.

Riefenstahl said very little at first, but Hitler eventually ran down, and she took over. The story would be similar to her 1932 picture *Das blaue Licht* (The Blue Light). The high, cold mountaintop would represent the ideal to which my character would aspire. The crass villagers would interfere, out of a misguided desire to protect me. The paradox would be that only by leaving them and standing atop the mountain, alone, could I best serve them, and so serve the race. The film would end with a festival, the Fest der Völker, and the common people would be reunited with the soil. Hitler and Riefenstahl looked at me as though I were the prize jewel in someone else's collection.

It must have appeared that I was committing a crime against the state, the felony of an anticlimax. I wanted to know if the filming would interfere with summer camp. Hitler was uncharacteristically concise: 'You can't do both.' Hoping to make the best of a bad situation, I asked what mountain I would be climbing for the film. I regretted asking because no sooner were the words out of my mouth, than Hitler began to laugh. I positively detested his laugh. Then he began talking and talking and talking. He spent at least a quarter hour on the theme of 'life as art' before explaining that my scenes would be done in a studio of UFA. The actual mountain scenes, what few there were, would be done by a second unit, and a double would be used.

So that was my choice: a real mountain or an illusion. It never occurred to me that I should doubt my freedom to choose in the matter. Children of the privileged escape the daily bludgeoning in a tyranny, and thereby increase their risk. It was not until much later that I realized how remarkable it was that I survived my caprice. I turned down the offer without considering for a moment that it might be a command!

One of the perplexities of Hitler was that he would, on rare occasions, make a thoroughly pathetic attempt at persuasion. Such was my favored position – at that moment – that I received the treatment. Not all the scenes would be shot in the studio, he announced airily. There would be some on-location work for me. I would be allowed to deliver a stirring monologue in the reconstruction of his birthplace in the little town of Branau, *the* tourist attraction of what had been Austria. And if that special honor weren't enough, I'd even attend the premiere of the film in the biggest cinema palace in Vienna, the city that Hitler would never forget, and never leave alone. He would not resist boasting again of how thoroughly he had expunged the city of the pernicious influence of Sigmund Freud; and I could not resist thinking that in the fullness of time, that lovely city might be free of Hitler's influence.

When I persisted in my refusal, he became himself again. Gone was the benign façade of Uncle Adolf as a shadow crossed his face. For the first time, I really noticed his eyes. The young invariably depend on a certain amount of diplomacy from their elders. I was quickly disabused of this notion. He stood, while pointing a trembling finger at me, and I half expected a lightning bolt to leap the distance between us. He shouted that I lacked my father's will, and that any other young girl would leap at the opportunity to be a film star, and that were it not for my family, I'd end up some little linen weaver or glovemaker. As suddenly as the storm had arisen, it passed. He stood as stock still as if he were one of his statues by Arno Brecker, but without the heroic physique and poise that the sculptor was always considerate enough to add. If Hitler could be frightening in one of his rages, he was positively unnerving when he was silent in anger. It seemed to me at such times that there was a frightful vacuum at the center of the man, and if one weren't careful, one could be drawn into that vacancy.

The truth was that there was a surprising amount of leeway granted those in his private circle, provided one did not commit the unforgivable faux pas of expressing a pro-Jewish sentiment. And I suppose that my youth was a contributing factor to the granting of latitude; that, and the importance of my father to the Fuehrer. Hitler even made light of the fact that Father had never completely gotten over the way Leni was granted complete independence of his office as national minister for propaganda and the enlightenment of the people . . . and this during the period of severest censorship. Perhaps, Hitler suggested, I was helping Daddy to pay off an old score.

At the time, such considerations were the furthest thing

from my mind. I was a willful teenager, enjoying the adolescent pleasure of recalcitrance. (Thank God my life took a turning before I became a useless coquette.) Hitler resumed his seat, his damaged arm shaking slightly – always an ominous sign. He changed the subject again. I can't remember how the conversation ended, except that the ruler of Europe had retreated into a dull bourgeoise rambling, his idea of 'petit talk.'

Leni, who had not moved since the outburst – perhaps she too was unconsciously posing for one of Brecker's statues – returned to the living. I doubt very much that she had ever been enthusiastic about using me in the film anyway. The young actress she finally selected bore a striking resemblance to herself.

There was one unexpected bonus. Hitler had been too angry to entertain us with one of his impressions. He loved to do them. Mussolini still topped the list, a dubious honor that Il Duce's death had done nothing to alleviate. Friends had told me that Hitler had even perfected an impression of my father by lowering his voice to Dr Goebbels's deep bass resonances (voted most sexy voice in a poll of German fraus) and mimicking the bouncing stride that Father used to compensate for his clubfoot. I was spared ever witnessing this particular horror. I wonder why Father never consented to have an operation to correct his deformity. During the war he frequently alluded to his plans in that regard, but added that personal indulgences would have to wait until victory was ours. His master never waited when it came to amusements.

A week later, Hitler would send a bouquet of flowers, the closest he ever came to civility with anyone, but I was no longer one of his favorites. Mother took this surprisingly well. My siblings did not care. Father's silences were eloquent.

Chapter Four

Cesare! Do you hear me? It is I calling you: I, Caligari, your master. Awaken for a brief while from your dark night.

– Robert Wiene,
The Cabinet of Dr Caligari

NOTES TOWARD AN AUTOBIOGRAPHY

So I attended the youth camp. It was just outside Bamberg, interestingly enough. This was the place where Hitler had first won over Father – who up to that point had been aligned with Gregor Strasser. Father always knew when to alter his plans, something I've yet to learn, and pray I never shall.

When addressing us in formation, our troop leader, Herr Juergen, spoke with Prussian precision; but at rest, he would lapse into the friendly cadences of the Bavarian country folk. The first day, he told us about the tradition of the *Wandervoegel*, various back-to-nature youth groups of the prewar period. It was one of those clear and sunny days when you could actually see the color of the leaves and the stones and each blade of grass. There was a fresh pine smell in the air, and in the distance you could make out the snowcapped mountains as if they were made of fine crystal. We were standing in the courtyard of a well-maintained castle, a museum piece. The setting and the mood were perfect to reminisce about simpler times and easy choices. Alas, the sermon ended with the requisite dosage of propaganda. He told us that today's sense of discipline added a dimension that had been missing from the anarchic days of the 1920s. That phrase would come back to me many times . . . as I searched for an unregulated life of my own.

One thing you have to grant to the National Socialist life-style: they have more ways of reminding you of your duty than can ever be enumerated. Good old Juergen planned our schedules with care and maneuvered us where we could see the mountain from which Hitler had directed some of the war's most dangerous campaigns: high above the rocks and scars of snow lurked the gray fortress of Barbarossa. I trained myself to ignore it whenever the mountain came into view.

I have pleasant memories of that summer: the sound of running water in the clear mountain streams, the fresh aroma and satisfying flavor of cabbage and sausage, the mildly erotic pleasures of sleeping half nude on the porch of a cottage with four other girls from my troop. (Naturally they wouldn't let us live in the castle.) There was much singing, and even the tone-deaf were made to sound better through the acoustical perfection of our natural opera house. The trees were beautiful.

Father didn't believe in beauty, unless he could make a sexual object of it. I knew that much even then. If he had been there, he would have been pleased at what I found my second week: an unfortunate buck had gotten his antlers tangled in the low branches of an Aspen. There the poor animal would starve to death if no one freed him. 'There's the beauty of nature for you,' I could imagine my father saying. 'All that lives is awaiting death.'

The animal was terrified. The more it attempted to free itself, the more completely was it entrapped. None of us were tempted to draw near, at first, as the danger outweighed our charitable impulses. But at last I could stand it no longer and began slowly to descend the hill. I had no idea what to do, but I felt that I must act regardless.

43

It was late in the afternoon, the time of day when clouds have an unreal look. This was not good for shooting. Suddenly there was the sharp explosion of rifle fire, from somewhere behind and to the left of me. The buck fell dead, still attached to the tree as if he were crucified, as a number of squirrels – silent during the deer's struggles – set up a clattering of discontent.

And so I met my first lover. His name was Gunther. As he walked toward us, his eyes went straight to mine, despite the more attractive – I thought – Irena standing beside me. Throughout the skinning and gutting of the animal, he kept up a mildly ironic commentary about young women thinking themselves huntresses rather than hearth keepers. The humor would have been more to the point had any of us been carrying weapons. Gunther was a fairly simple lad, and once he fixed upon a witty observation, the facts couldn't be allowed to interfere. I was less interested in what he was saying than that he kept sneaking glances at me the whole time.

He was from Burgundy. That probably explained his interest in the occult, a subject that meant nothing to me then, but would one day make a ruin of my life. As for the moment, I was trying to remind him of the few weak double entendres that had begun our conversation, but it was too late: he had focused his mind upon Thanatos, and Eros would simply have to wait.

He began telling us how anyone who had ever set foot in Bavaria should be interested in the secret lodges of the Illuminati. Then he announced that the number 23 was of overwhelming importance to me. I would make a crucial life decision when I reached that age . . . and did I know that the year 1923 was one of the worst dates of the Depression? (The Burgundian manner of thinking was maddeningly associational, and this was my first contact with it. At the time, my sole concern was that the crazy brain was inside a magnificent, muscled body that had attracted my attention by sending a bullet whizzing past my head.)

No, I admitted that I didn't know much about dates, except the kind you eat . . . and did he have plans for supper? The ploy failed, as he continued to intrigue us (he thought) with his odd litany. He must have dragged out a dozen of his examples, but the ones I remember were: Did I also know that the year 1923 marked the failure of the original Putsch, costing many young Nazis their lives? Was I aware that the French army humiliated the Fatherland by occupying the Ruhr in that year, on the pretext of default in payments on the odious war debt? *And most astounding of all*, he assured me, it was none other than Article 231 of the Versailles Treaty that placed all the blame for the First World War on Germany, and what did I think about that?

The other girls were suffering from a severe attack of the giggles, but I seized my chance to make a conquest. With all the sincerity at my command, I assured him that what he had been saying was of the greatest possible interest to me, and I would very much enjoy learning more. Perhaps he was not as naïve as I thought him at first, but I have since revised my opinion through vanity. I was more attractive than I thought I was, and his unspoken agenda was most likely the same as mine. Teenage girls never recognize their own beauty.

We eventually worked our way deeper into the woods. The giggling was louder than ever, but we soon put the other girls at a satisfactory distance; and I made sure that we were alone before I asked him some questions. Had he ever been kissed by a girl before he kissed her? Had he ever had a girl adopt a posture that she usually reserved for saying her prayers for a less spiritual purpose? After I had kissed him and then knelt to answer the second question, he was eager to continue the instruction along any lines I thought fruitful. And it was a pure delight to see that his face was blushing a red every bit as bright as other parts of him.

Birth control was readily available for someone of my class. (The National Socialists had a use for orphans of the right racial stock, and the way to get them was through the lower classes of our supposedly classless, socialist paradise.) I assured Gunther that he need not worry about precautions because I was using the recently developed Pill (originally intended for biological control of officially designated 'inferior races'). It was my first time for many experiences. Pine needles are more uncomfortable than penetration of the hymen. As for Gunther's technique, the best that could be said was that it was there. Still, the novelty of the first time makes up for a lack of finesse, and Gunther's passion was real. I quickly climaxed. The manner in which he kept kneading my nipples made me wonder if he was looking for a secret switch that he could turn on. When his hands crept lower, he did better. For my part, I drove him wild by the simple expedient of biting his ear. He was enamored of my teeth.

When it was over, I knew more about sex, but it would take many years before I would know anything about love. The reward of the moment was that Gunther invited me to attend The Harvest Festival with him in Burgundy come autumn. Maybe it was because I'd had arguments with my younger brother, Helmuth, about Burgundy, but I quickly agreed to attend. I thought that if it turned out to be as ridiculous as I'd heard, I could talk Helmuth out of wasting his college years there. If it turned out to be better, I'd be fair about it: I'd simply avoid bringing up the subject again. Admissions of error are not meant for kid brothers.

That evening, back at the cottage, Irena crept into bed

with me so that I could whisper all the details to her about *l'amour*. Descriptions soon proved inspirational, and before I knew it, Irena was under the covers, doing for me what I had done for Gunther. I was fond of symmetry and noted that the day's triangle had consisted of one blonde, Irena, one brunet, Gunther, and myself as the redhead. All in all, it had been an educational twenty-four hours.

Nothing else that happened at Pathfinder's Youth Camp proved as interesting (not even my first attempts to climb the scenery); and it only took one day in Burgundy to overwhelm every other experience up to then. Sex is only so remarkable a discovery; but insanity encourages one to sit up and take notice. Gunther had arranged my schedule so that I wouldn't miss an annual event of the small country. As I had told Helmuth many times, Burgundy would have its silly side because it was managed by the SS. As a kid brother is wont to do, he promptly informed to Mother. This told me more about Helmuth than it did anything else. Now I was about to find out firsthand the meaning of a Burgundian ceremony.

The entire population had turned out (with rare exceptions for the ill and elderly) to join hands in a line of people of such length that it extended past the borders. Neighboring provinces of the Greater Reich were eager, if not happy, to cooperate with the SS. The only visitors who were allowed to participate were citizens – or their children – from the Greater Reich with membership in the Party. When I asked if I could merely be a spectator, the answer was a firm no. Not really aware of what was to happen, I joined hands with Gunther and the rest of Burgundy.

I looked down at my feet, where rust-colored leaves were blanketing the ground. I saw an ant bravely carrying a dead beetle three times its size across the rough surface of a large, triangular stone. The ant could have gone around the rock.

Strategically placed on small platforms were senior officials of Burgundy whose hands were apparently viewed as less crucial to the effort than their voices giving us instruction. They all had portable microphones, and loud voices to boot. At first, the exercise seemed routine (except for the hand-holding stunt) and political. It was very much a Hitler Youth kind of affair. We were told by our speaker how the Fuehrer had not yet finished teaching the enemies of the Reich their lesson. How dare Frenchmen still hold resentment against us when they had treated us so badly in the past? How dare they condemn our racial policies after the way they had exploited Africans . . . and besides, we had taught them a thing or two about anti-Semitism, for which they should be grateful. I assumed that the tirade began with the French because we were so near to them in Burgundy. The incredible hypocrisy was that he criticized them for importing colored troops to fight in the war, Berbers, Moroccans, Senegalese, and Bantu warriors. Was I the only person on line able to recognize the discrepancy between crying crocodile tears over French behaviour in Africa, immediately followed by a conventional racist harangue? The frightening answer was that I could by no means be unique in this.

Then he branched out to other nationalities. How dare Englishmen look down their long noses at our policies after the way they had treated the people of Ireland and India and so on? At the end of each little performance, the crowd would murmur assent. By the time he got to the ongoing difficulties in Russia – a new kind of weapon, the hydrogen bomb, had recently been tested on a large Slavic population in the east – the murmur of the crowd had become as loud as the sea at high tide. We were sure teaching the enemies of the Greater Reich a lesson, all right. Talk of America brought shouts of rage from some and silence from others. Talk of the Orient brought a number of hisses from those who wished to show off that they were cosmopolitan.

He got around to the Jews. Needless to say, the reaction was more negative than even the Slavs had inspired. The problem was that I had begun to wonder about the Jews. Why was it, I found myself wondering, if the Jews have been removed from the Fatherland and its territories, they continued to pose the greatest threat? It seemed that the more we were harangued to thank the Fuehrer for saving us from them, the more we were told to be on guard against them every single day. The seed of doubt had also been planted by the inexplicable behavior of my father whenever the subject was raised. He seemed coldly cynical about most of the Reich's enemies; but the mere suggestion of Jewish influence made him positively unhinged.

As I stood there, huddling in my sweater, feeling my hands become sweatier with every passing second of the enforced togetherness, I thought back to some pictures I'd seen at Pathfinder's Camp. One girl had smuggled some photographs into the cottage. They were nothing that we hadn't seen before – pitiful victims of the great upheaval, sacrifices in the name of a unified Europe. Every German coffee table had picture books of victims: victims of the saturation bombing thanks to the Americans and the British, victims of Russian sadism during the most dangerous stretch of the war, victims who had been proud Germans in the Sudetenland. These we had seen many times. Then, too, there were the books of Stalin's victims among his own people, endless pictures of starving Ukrainians from the mass slaughter of 1932 and 1933, carefully compiled during the war crimes trials, which

Hitler had used to build up morale among the subject peoples (those who had survived both the Swastika and the Hammer-and-Sickle) and to create new National Socialisms with enough sense to take their cues from German managers. Every German child grew up with images of scorched earth and wasted bodies along with his daily milk.

But I had never seen pictures of such mind-numbing atrocity as these that now passed before my eyes at summer camp. The pornographic secret of our cottage was that these were victims of Germany. I'd seen something like the radiation victims before. The government was frank about the Bomb. Whenever they released data about the atomic weapons used at the close of hostilities, the reports were accompanied with statistical projections of what German losses would have been without the weapons that, everyone agrees, saved Hitler's regime. No, the pictures that I could not stomach, that burned into my mind forever, were of children who had been operated on with a skill twisted to diabolical purpose. They were no longer human, but enough remained of the original shape to be recognized. I believe that I screamed. There is also the troubling recollection that I was the only one who cried out. Worst of all, I remember someone laughing.

There were other pictures, final statements of the art of brutality. The starved. The beaten. The diseased. These were dreadful to see, but the torture suffered by the poor wretches had not altered their human forms. Even those who were more bone than flesh at least still possessed the dignity of human bone. None presented the pure vision of the pit that blasted me from the half dozen medical photographs. The other pictures had been labeled from a number of diverse backgrounds, a last epitaph of identity for anonymous ciphers en route to a mass grave. But all the pictures of teratological nightmare were clearly labeled as Jews. Attempts had been made to render the children subhuman or nonhuman.

The face I could not forget was of a boy who could not be more than a year old. His arms and legs were indistinguishable lumps of unarticulated flesh, useless appendages on a torso that had been rendered scaly by either chemical means or radiation. To think about it was to endure a physical pain. Gazing at me was a face defined by a child's skull (the only recognizably human element) but wearing the wrinkles and sagging flesh of an ancient Methuselah. The pictures I had seen of Gandhi, taken the last year of his life, were youthful by comparison.

I could not entirely credit what I had seen at Pathfinder's Youth Camp, and yet something deep in me knew that it was true. If I had showed the evidence to my father, I'm certain he would have denied its authenticity. He would have said it was a result of trick photography and nothing of the sort had ever been done by Nazis. Perhaps I dreaded that such a statement from my father *would* remove all doubt. I had not trusted him since the time I overheard him with one of his mistresses, bragging over how simple it was to deceive Magda Goebbels.

Standing in an open field, a small link in a human chain, I listened to a Burgundian exhorting us to join in a prayer against every Jew still alive in the world . . . and I was haunted by the face. I had been turning against the official line on anti-Semitism for some time, but I could not remember the turning point. Perhaps I had never been a racist, but with that protective self-delusion enjoyed by the young, had never allowed myself to really think about a doctrine so important to National Socialism. It had been best not to think at all.

A year earlier, I had begun collecting copies of books that Father had ordered burned in the fire that proved so

51

newsworthy. My original motivation had been no more than a childish prank. The first book I had found on the list was by Moses Mendelssohn, a Jew who had been known as the German Socrates. The book was too adult to interest me then, and this was the case for most of them. When I finally got around to reading these books, I had a far better sense of what the Fatherland had lost; but nothing else would ever carry the shock of recognition that was mine upon seeing the child of the damned. It was a kind of intellectual cheating to put too much stock in the respective talents of those who had been banned and burned and murdered. A pragmatic weighing of the scales smacked too much of the way my father approached things, aside from the Jewish question, to which he had only emotional and violent answers. Only with age did I come to realize that the face haunting me cried out for all innocents butchered and forgotten, made into bloody statistics for whatever reason.

On that chill afternoon in Burgundy, I did not analyse my reaction; I merely lived it, and found myself helpless. Rage turned to fire in my veins as the spokesman, spitting out words from a pinched face sporting a pathetic duplicate of Hitler's moustache, explained the scientific basis for what we were doing. It seemed that we were standing so that we were aligned with the magnetic poles, or some such nonsense, and that a psychic cone of energy would be generated, causing distress to Orthodox, Conservative, and Reform Judaism without discrimination. That the procedure was total nonsense didn't matter. It was detestable. I wanted no part of it. Hand to hand, and hate to hate, I tried to break free of the line.

Gunther, sensing that I was pulling away, squeezed my hand so hard that it hurt. As ill fortune would have it, the man on the other side was, if anything, even more robust and indifferent than my oafish boyfriend. And so my rebellion remained largely an intellectual effort. For what it was worth, I prayed for a boomerang effect.

The most ridiculous moment came when the crowd began to hum. It sounded as if a swarm of bees had gone quite mad. At the conclusion of this, the damage was supposed to be done. The most distasteful moment came when our speaker, and his comrades obviously, called for a moment of silence in memory of Reinhard Heydrich. Accordingly, I sneezed. There were undeniable advantages to being the daughter of Dr Paul Joseph Goebbels.

After a ritual summoning of the Overman within each and every one of us – the one moment I felt in touch with my own ego – the ceremony concluded with singing the anthem for the Greater Reich. This I was willing to do. I was still very young. I enjoyed hearing about the glory of our nation, from the shining Baltic to the shining North Sea on one side; and from the shining Aegean to the shining Adriatic on the other; and nowhere was a drop of industrial pollution envisioned as marring those vast shields of open sea. (Perhaps the anthem was only appropriate in Burgundy, with their strict prohibitions on industry within the borders.)

Later I would discover that Leni had been shooting one of her documentaries that very day. I escaped being captured on her film by no more than two kilometers. Given the way I already felt about it, I counted myself lucky not to be part of the record. Father would later complain that Leni knew I was in attendance and deliberately snubbed me by not hunting the line for my beaming countenance. Thank you, Leni!

I would not make love to Gunther again, although it took a while for him to take the hint. When I went to bed that night, happily alone, I resolved to leave the next morning. Let no one doubt the woman's prerogative! An offhand comment at breakfast was sufficiently intriguing to overcome the revulsion I also felt. There was to be one more event before I'd leave this land of malevolent wonders. They were to hold a trial.

The defendants were animals. It was alleged that two goats and a pig had committed high crimes against duly constituted authority. The prosecutor was known simply as Ernest. He made a far more vivid impression than the defense, a harmless old woman who, I'm sure, was there solely as a formality. At first, I was convinced that the whole affair was a joke. But as the proceedings were cranked through the legal machine, and nobody made light of anything, I accepted the improbable reality. By an effort of will to make Nietzsche proud, I resisted laughing.

The goats had gotten loose from their owner and eaten a neighbor's beans. The pig, a fat old sow, was not guilty of trespass, but had violated Racial Law by attacking a hapless child who had fallen in the family's pigsty. Ernest reminded the good people present that Burgundy had restored medieval law as an antidote to the decadent modern ideas of criminal responsibility. The majesty of the law, so went the argument, was to ignore motives on the part of the transgressor and to remember that punishment was not for the criminal's benefit. The only reason to whip or torture or electrocute or gas or behead or shoot or fine or imprison someone was as an object lesson for the community. The opinion of the criminal mattered not in the least. Now, if even the modern-thinking judges in Munich and Hamburg and New Berlin recognized this principle to the extent of punishing the mentally defective and the insane, then all that the people of Burgundy were doing was extending the point to include animals.

The terrifying part was that I started to enjoy the logic of stupidity. The kids with whom I attended school saw nothing wrong with placing an idiot in the stocks. They'd be the first to throw rotten vegetables at the drooling target. Yet they'd laugh at the goats and pig being publicly berated. One made about as much sense as the other. Adolf Hitler had called for the New Man. Predictably, he received something as old as the blood on a caveman's spear.

When the trial was over, the goats and pig were executed. A giant of a man, wielding an axe so big that I was afraid he'd give himself a hernia despite his size, beheaded the animals. I deduced that the animals would be eaten. If the Burgundians didn't show some sense now, how could they exist at all? Sure enough, a feast was given, and lamb and pork were on the menu. Maybe this was the way officials redistributed the meat.

The barbecue went late into the night. Gunther made one last great attempt to win back my affections, but I wouldn't forgive him for what he had done on the line. My hand still ached. When he suggested that I would have gotten into serious trouble if I'd broken away, I reminded him, in my haughtiest tone, just who I was, and what I could get away with. Whatever doubts I secretly entertained contributed to a performance so self-righteous and overbearing that he pulled away from me as if I'd slapped him. One thing you can say for Nazis: they know how to be subordinate.

Gunther no longer interested me, but I was of interest to the Burgundian judge, Ernest. He took me aside to inquire about the health of my parents and provide me with an opportunity to question the events of the afternoon. I wouldn't take the bait. When someone wants to tell me something, I wait for them to do it. He finally relented and said the last thing I ever expected to hear in Burgundy.

'We are not so eccentric as we seem,' he began. 'We know that we exist on the sufferance of the Greater Reich and the goodwill of the Fuehrer. The technological achievements of Germany are the envy of the world. Only American industry is any match for it. Without the modern German military, we'd be in no position to indulge ourselves here. I myself served with a panzer division, so I know what I'm talking about.'

'Why tell me?' I asked him, with no attempt at being polite.

'You look on us with modern eyes, and in those eyes I see the same intelligence that has made your father one of the most important men in the world. A day is coming when we must all remember that National Socialism is the glue that holds us together, no matter whatever differences we might have.'

And with a sly wink, as though I were privy to some dirty little secret, he departed.

Chapter Five

To all doubts and questions, the new man of the first
German empire has only one answer: Nevertheless, I will!

– Alfred Rosenberg,
The Myth of the Twentieth Century

My years of schooling were not easy for any of us. I kept
getting into trouble and was sent to one institution after
another. By the time I was a seasoned college student,
confused and uncertain about my future, Mother began
threatening to take three of her children with her on a
trip to see the world. The honor fell to the three eldest:
my older sister, Helga; my younger brother, Helmuth;
and myself square in the middle. The younger girls, Holde
and Hedda, were spared. As I write these words, I am
overwhelmed by my family's lack of imagination, in this
case the fixation on the letter 'H'! The personality of the
Fuehrer touches us even in our sleep.

Father enthusiastically supported the expedition. The
other children would be looked after by the staff in the
villa at Schwanenwerder on the Wannsee. This would
leave him free to have an open-door policy for his
mistresses at his favorite house near the Brandenburg
Gate in New Berlin. Despite his contributions to reshap-
ing the city, he still preferred those sections retaining the
flavor of the original Berlin.

I was in hot water with Mother from the beginning. As
she was planning her itinerary, I asked that we visit the
one region she abhorred above all others. 'No,' I remember her saying, 'we will not step foot in the Wild East, as

57

you young people call it. Didn't we have enough of that in the war? Never, never!' There was no use pointing out that the Fuehrer's policy was to relocate as many German farmers as possible in the Ukraine, and that the Party's slogan remained 'Push Eastward.' But despite the hot-blooded rhetoric, the reality was that the lines were stabilized at the Urals. Beyond that was no-man's-land. After serving the required duty in one of the military branches, young men had several options. The most daring chose to prove their mettle in the frontier beyond the Urals, where brigandage was a way of life, and where the motley bands of Russians and Mongols and Chinese and Arabs and Jews and Koreans and God knows who else had no use whatsoever for the Greater Reich and its racial theories.

Screaming and kicking every step of the way, Alfred Rosenberg had had to accept the idea of a free region, an area of containment that could be used as a testing ground for people and weapons, but would not be intended for conquest and colonization. He created the *cordon sanitaire* that he had planned, but his hopes for a chain of border states, and a Caucasian federation, underwent modifications. He had learned from his previous mistakes, for there was no doubt that he was among the Party leaders who had guided the Fuehrer on a suicidal course when German divisions first rolled onto the Russian steppes. The peasants were eager to greet us as liberators. Millions were ready to join us in a war against Stalin. The practical voices of Germany called for an alliance with these people; but the mad heart of Nazism could not modify itself.

Reality had its say, and in a few years the Reich itself faced certain destruction at the hands of an enemy that should have been turned to our service instead. If we had not been granted a nuclear sword with which to lop off those hands, well, Frau Magda would not be planning a pleasure junket one fine spring day in the late 1950s.

Mother was not alone in her phobias. There were times when Hitler still winced to see a snowfall. Himmler was bothered by nearly everything. The untroubled Nazi was the anomaly. Father and Goering, different in so many ways, commanded respect by collecting artworks by their enemies. Bad associations meant nothing to them.

As a headstrong young woman, I positively lusted after the disreputable. Naturally I was excited about visiting the newly formed American Republic; but nothing could compare to the salutary chaos of the Wild East. Rosenberg's Cultural Bureaus were satisfied to leave unconquered a region that could not organize itself into an effective resistance . . . and every school child thanked God for the allure and romance of a place free of law.

Mother only wanted to travel to safe places, and it had taken a bit of doing to convince her that she wouldn't be raped in the Americas. I knew next to nothing about South America, but I'd been reading up on the United States. The very thing that made Mother afraid to travel there was, in fact, the reason we'd be let in the country.

'They have abolished most of their laws,' she said in her most worried tone. 'They were a frontier society already. They'll be turning back into the Wild West if they're not careful.'

'Mother, it's because they've opened their borders that we can go.'

'They let anyone in now, just anyone,' she answered. 'Think of all our enemies. Think of all the Jews who live in America. And they allow any kind of perverted sex there. I'm sure that they all have diseases. It's dangerous to touch a Negro, and they have so many.' I remember taking her hand and calmly saying that we wouldn't visit the US until the last leg of the trip, and we wouldn't go then unless she really wanted it. And the whole time, I was seized by the most unbearable contempt. Hitler especially admired my mother because she came from one of the better families. Here was the Fuehrer, enemy of the aristocracy . . . and a sycophant for any compliment from the class he had sworn to overturn. Worse for me was the spectacle of my mother babbling like some uncultured fishwife, afraid of anything and everything. There was nothing aristocratic about the woman.

At any rate, we reached a compromise. I promised not to press about the Wild East if she promised that when we went to France, we would avoid all things Burgundian. She couldn't understand why I hadn't enjoyed my time there and insisted on showing me the beautiful pictorial spread the quaint little country had received in *Signal*, the magazine for the masses if there ever was one. I responded by thrusting one of my lurid paperback novels at her detailing the thrills to be had on the windswept plains of Upper Mongolia. She knew when to surrender. Helmuth listened to the exchange in stony silence, no doubt plotting my downfall. He was in every way his father's son.

The trip began with a lengthy circuit of the empire. We used plane, train, and hired car. We visited France and Spain; then Italy, Yugoslavia, Rumania, Bulgaria, Greece, Turkey, and Iran. We spent a day in Afghanistan, then a week in India. Before leaving Calcutta, I made one last attempt to persuade Mother to come at least within the periphery of my beloved Wild East, by visiting our furthermost outpost within China at Manchoukuo, but that was too close to the American/Japanese zone for her, and as there was currently an altercation between an American corporation and an SS expeditionary force, she may have had a point.

We could have made plans to cross the Pacific and visit

the US beginning with California, but Mother was terrified of the thought. She was absolutely convinced that all the craziest people in the world were congregated in Los Angeles, and that we'd never get out alive. We stuck to the original travel plan, which entailed a boring trek back across Europe, and also meant that we'd only be seeing the East Coast of the US on this trip.

So we concluded the European part of our adventures with stops at Lithuania, Latvia, Estonia, Finland, Sweden, and Norway. We saw dozens of cathedrals. We saw no dwellings of the working class. We passed by many cemeteries. There was a rumor that subject countries had the highest rate of suicide in the world. Whatever the truth of that, everywhere we went we saw different peoples being Germanized, and therefore discovering a new reason to hate Germans. A least I enjoyed my time in our Swedish hotel. We had the cutest maid, and she was broadminded.

We took a boat to England and spent a murky day there before embarking on the long voyage to South America. I made a wager with Helmuth that Helga would be seasick first. He bet on Mother. I won. In retrospect, it disturbs me that the few occasions when I had a rapport with my brother was when we were indulging our malicious streaks.

The crossing was dull. Helmuth and I played a game of planning a route that would be the perfect nightmare vacation for Mother. The largest portion of the trip would be a pictorial journey through the Middle East, where a series of small wars had turned most of that inhospitable region into a free-fire zone, from Morocco to Indonesia. (Hitler had no end of fun supporting first one side, then the other.) When we presented her with the fruits of our labors, she sighed and shook her head. Helga said that we were horrid.

I was glad that I'd brought my books and tapes on English. My instructors had given me highest marks, but Konrad Obernitz had complained that I'd have trouble with those American cowboys because I had no aptitude for the vernacular. He suggested that I had a certain priggishness that biased me in favor of a more stilted speech than was popular in the States. He was one to talk, frequently insisting that his charges address him as 'Herr Doktor Doktor Obernitz,' the kind of top-heavy formality that is the curse of the German mind.

Formality was the least of our concerns when we arrived in Pernambuco to pick up our interpreter, Señor Alfredo. I'd been brushing up on my Spanish, but one exposure to the rapid-fire conversation of the locals – the verbal equivalent of a machine gun – and I longed for Europe, where the various populations diligently pursue a mastery of German. Señor Alfredo was a good interpreter, but he frequently had a repellent odor of cheap rum and cheaper cigars. Mother promised to buy him a box of the very best Cuban cigars if he acquitted himself professionally. He was deeply moved that she would offer him the flattery of a bribe. I remember that he was short and easily excited, that his white Panama suits were invariably soiled within an hour of his donning them, and that after informing me that my Spanish was awful, he afforded me an opportunity to practice English. He spoke English at half-speed. Helmuth hated him, which was another point in Alfredo's favor.

From Pernambuco, we traveled south until we arrived in Buenes Aires. Mother was especially gratified. There were quite a few Germans living in Argentina, engaging in what – our consulate would tell anyone who asked – was a friendly competition with North American businesses over markets. For the Monroe Doctrine, it was *In pace requiescat!*

Old friends of the family appeared in frightening profusion. As it rained for several days, we had to make the most of our situation. I was persuaded to wear my least favorite dress and play the hostess. We were cornered in a hotel that had never heard of modern air ventilation, and I teased Helmuth about how his Burgundian heroes should experience such heat and humidity so that they would better appreciate unadorned nature. Helga wouldn't join in our games. Her complexion was as pallid as it had been aboard ship.

Before leaving Argentina, we were exposed to a Brazilian businessman who was in town to 'purchase supplies,' but I had my doubts. I had acquired a knack for ferreting out people with an eye open to political contacts, the men who need influence to compensate for a lack of ability. This remarkably obese creature boasted that he was half German, and we should be proud of the practical reforms he had implemented in his company. His favorite German word was *Pflicht*, his gospel the duty of work. That his primary exertion was navigating his bulk through doors and up stairs I had no doubt.

Mother later told me that she couldn't stand him, especially when he leeringly told us about how he made female applicants raise their skirts so that he could see if their underskirts were clean and pressed. 'Lots of these girls would take their clothes off to get a job, if you know what I mean. I just wanted to see who was really neat and who was dirty. You never can tell with them.' He launched into a tirade against the racial hodgepodge that is Latin America. Mother listened. The price of being a Nazi. When we were alone and she complained, I hoped that she shared my revulsion over how the man was treating his employees. I should have known better. She only resented his indelicacy in discussing such things in front of fine German ladies.

63

We took a newly opened train line cross-continent and concluded our excursion among the Latins in Chile. The Pacific looked just the same as the Atlantic, although I found myself thinking of California again. I did so much want to see Hollywood. In the absence of show people and movie moguls who didn't have to take any heed of Father's aesthetic and political theories whatsoever, I settled for plain and unobtrusive reality to satisfy my taste for the unusual. The Indians lived in shacks and lean-to's that seemed insubstantial indeed against the relentless salt breezes blowing in from the sea. Perhaps as a statement about modernity, they would relieve themselves in unexpected places, such as the middle of railroad tracks. They had turned their poverty into an art. Only now, as I recollect those empty days of spoiled voyeurism, am I revolted at the young woman who observed the misery and wonder of those lives as something for her entertainment.

In our brief circuit of the Greater Reich, we had been surprised and amused by some of the folk customs that stubbornly resisted change, despite hygienic measures enforced by one of National Socialism's new departments. But our modesty and inhibitions were really put to the test by the outdoor urinals of Chile. A tiny partition was barely adequate to cover the genital region, and the rest of you was free to commune with the open sky. None of us availed ourselves of this rare opportunity, except Helmuth, who timed his release to coincide with a procession of nuns that passed close by.

We stayed in a private home atop a cliff, receiving a refreshing cool breeze from the ocean. Helga and I enjoyed standing on a small elegant patio that overlooked the surf leaving white lace patterns on the rocks below. Helga's health greatly improved. Our host was an Italian engineer who insisted on taking us, our very first night, to a German-owned restaurant specializing in steak Tartar. So I had my taste of the Wild East after all, but in the Southern Hemisphere!

The owner of the establishment was as jolly a fat man as the Brazilian had been grim, and he oversaw the serving of his favorite dish. They brought a huge platter with a mound of raw, red meat in the middle. Quantities of the finest sirloin had been finely ground no less than three times, until all the gristle was dissolved into paste. Surrounding the meat was a circle of raw eggs, peppers, and onions.

Mother beheld the vision and announced her decision: 'Never!' It was left to the next generation to uphold the family honor, but I would require liquid encouragement. Alfredo warned us off any drink laced with absinthe, a drug, he assured everyone, that was causing considerable mischief throughout the continent. As the sun follows the moon, the dinner party's discussion quickly degenerated into praise for the firm antidrug policy of National Socialist Europe (when in doubt, they eliminate the addict . . . provided he's not an official), and a forlorn hope that similarly progressive measures could be applied to the backward societies of South America. I said nothing. I did not dare let myself begin. At the suggestion from Helmuth that everyone might be forced to take urine tests to determine drug levels, I could only think that if the Nazis can't get your blood, they go after your piss.

Having settled on a potent, dark German beer, I screwed up my courage to try the steak Tartar. Selecting a piece of white bread, I put a dab of the red paste on it, as a painter might prepare his palette, carefully placed the concoction in my mouth, and hurriedly washed it down with cold beer. By the third time around, I realized that the flavor wasn't all that bad and ate more honest portions.

There had been moments of the vacation when I could temporarily forget who I was. That night, in that restaurant on a hill, I was at peace. Yet even brief moments of respite, half a world away from the iron eagle's claws, were not to last. It was as if none of us had any reality independent of the Fuehrer. Mother wouldn't eat the meal, but her comment was as predictable as I was weary of hearing the same old anecdotes: 'Hitler is a strict vegetarian. Normally I differ with him on that. He's very tolerant. But seeing this uncooked meat, well, I'd rather be a vegetarian than eat it.'

With no consideration that everyone else was dining on the subject of her ire, she was off and running. The shark-fin soup they brought her didn't even slow her down. As she told her interminable stories of Hitler's likes and dislikes, Helmuth and I exchanged glances. He had rubbed blood from the dish on his forehead and made an upside down triangle, which we both knew was the symbol for water among the ancients. Cute. My brother had his own inimitable way of fighting boredom. I passed him the water, and we waited for Mother to notice. Helga finally drew our antics to her attention. 'Helmuth!' she cried, and there was a collective sigh of relief round the table as Magda Goebbels picked a new subject.

The New England writer Edgar Allan Poe has written about the imp of the perverse, an uncontrollable desire to perpetrate something precisely because one feels it is imprudent to do so. At that moment, I had no reason in the world to make trouble, but I did.

'When it comes to uncooked flesh, I prefer sushi to steak Tartar,' I said, a trivial matter to most of the assemblage, but not to a Goebbels. Father had recently launched a series of advertisements against the Japanese dish, ostensibly for health reasons, but most informed Europeans knew that the fight was over symbolism, his guiding light in all things. The Party's current line was that the former ally must never be forgiven for the treasonable behavior of allowing itself to be conquered instead of being reduced to heroic ashes. As relations between Americans and Japanese steadily improved, the Reich suffered an increasing degree of amnesia. Since no one had responded to my endorsement for raw fish, I was foolish enough to continue. I mentioned Father's wartime articles trumpeting the astounding news that the Japanese were the Oriental analog to Aryans. This embarrassing moment in the development of Nazi ideology was not considered polite dinner conversation anywhere in the Reich. It didn't go over too well in Chile either.

Helga tensed up, Helmuth grinned, and I knew that I had done it. Mother had one of her 'heart palpitations,' and we had to make our apologies. Alfredo, ever the diplomat, attempted to save the evening, but the damage was done. Our Italian host and we returned to the villa, Mother exhausting the theme of a daughter's faithlessness every kilometer of the drive.

I wept . . . but they were tears of hatred instead of remorse. As even Rommel appreciated strategic retreats, I moved back into my shell. It was after midnight, and everyone had gone to bed except Alfredo and myself. He was a gregarious man. We sat on the patio under a gibbous moon, and we talked until dawn.

In two days, the Goebbels clan would board an experimental rocket plane and fly to our next port of call in Miami, Florida. Father's lust for publicity followed us everywhere, and this stunt was already being referred to as the Po go Stick. It was unlikely that I would see Alfredo again, but I promised him that I wouldn't let Mother forget to mail him a box of the best Havana cigars.

'*Grácias, Señorita*,' he answered, then returned to English. 'Latin America lacks unity. Is this good? Is this bad? For years and years, our politicians were bound by one passion: resentment over imperialism from the north. The only good *Yanquis* were nineteenth-century gentlemen who had opposed their country's lording it over her southern cousins – men like Godkin and Carnegie and Sumner. Their voices were drowned out by our would-be saviors. They would amputate our limbs before gangrene set in. We could not explain to the *Norteamericános* as they sawed and chopped that we had no infection and required no treatment.'

He lit one of his noxious cigars, but was thoughtful enough to sit downwind. As the smoke was dissipated on the night air, he asked: 'Are you familiar with *Luftverkehrsnetz Der Vereinigten Staaten Sud-Amerikas Hauptlinien?*' I shook my head. 'British intelligence concocted a phony map of a proposed plan Hitler had for conquering our beautiful continent. This piece of paper was used for the propaganda purposes you'd expect. It's a funny thing, but very few of us ever believed it. The United States, now there it was believed. I have a copy of the map on my wall at home. It is an inspiration to me.'

He puffed. I thought. Then, pointing the cigar at me, forgetting for the moment my aversion to smoke, he said, 'When I began my career, I noticed that the officials who were most easily bribed by the *Yanquis* were the ones who resented it so strongly, and yet bribery is a way of life here. This was a mystery to me. But now it is different. Since the USA has forsworn imperialism, the money flows in different channels. Before the war, Chile did about the same amount of business with the United States as it did with the Axis. Many other countries here did more business with Hitler than they did with Roosevelt. Now here is only the one empire, the unity of Europe. North America has been, how do you say it, Balkanized? But they are still rich, as we are still poor. Which way do we turn? Europe offers certainties. To the north, there are corporations warring among themselves. Dealing with one may mean wealth, another may mean worse poverty.'

'Take the chance,' I told him instantly. 'Choose profits.'

'You say this, you of all people?'

The conversation was frank, as befitted our mutual trust. 'The certainty offered by the Nazis will end in slavery for your continent,' I said.

'Germans treat us as fairly as anybody. They have yet to send the marines.'

'I've recently toured the part of the world where Germany has "sent the marines." They never leave. Besides, don't you trust the changes in the United States? Would you put on a new yoke the moment an old one is removed?'

The moment he laughed, I knew that I'd been right about him. 'Many think as you do, but I never expected to hear such words from a child of the elite. You must receive underground newspapers in Germany. You take a risk with me. I wouldn't have been hired as your guide if I didn't have a minimal Party association.'

'I wasn't born today. Membership alone doesn't prove much in this world.' I had gotten to the point where I could tell true believers from people in search of a job. I wasn't naïve enough to believe Alfredo's name had been drawn out of a hat. He was an honest cynic. He told me how in his youth he had been a Marxist and spoken of classes. Today, he could parrot a very similar rhetoric, only now the magic word was race instead of class. But he thought all of it was nonsense. What he believed in was the holy trinity: the US gold dollar, the German mark, and the Swiss franc. He lacked the moral courage to publicly ⟨...⟩ness to this faith. I certainly had no right to condemn him. I'd yet to discover individualism myself.

Pulling out his wallet, he peeled off two soggy bills.

They were American twenties. 'One is counterfeit. Can you tell which?' I couldn't. 'It doesn't matter in the least. They are both believed here. New dollars, old dollars, on the gold standard, off the gold standard . . . if it's US money, it will buy more than this will.' He showed me the *escudo*, Chile's national currency. 'Now this is just a piece of paper. It's all in the mind.'

He explained how smuggling was the heart of business throughout the continent. It was called *Negotio*. The customs agents were a special breed of barefoot officialdom, too corrupt to be corrupted. 'We will deal with anyone,' he concluded proudly.

'Watch out for strings attached to German goods,' I replied.

Patting me on the arm, he said, 'What a traitor you are. Let's be friends for life.'

I left Chile thinking that they might not have the political freedom that existed to the north, but compared to what I considered normal, I had felt the bracing wind of freedom among its rocky crags. I would have preferred joining Alfredo in his friend's sailplane. They were going to glide on the thermals outside Santiago, as I was thrown into the sky at a greater velocity, a speed precluding languid contemplation of the scenery.

As Mother had intended, we were behind schedule and could spend no time to speak of in the dreaded American Republic. She was afraid of assassination. My head was still spinning from the descent of the rocket plane as Mother booked passage on a ship to take us from Florida within the week.

I wouldn't come. She was at the end of her rope, because instead of arguing, she gave me funds for a few days. I stayed nearly two months, working at odd jobs, and saw a good portion of the American South. I did not loudly advertise my name.

70

In Boca Raton, I got something of a tan, improved my accent, and did my first work as a waitress. In Tampa, I became accomplished at hitchhiking and explained to one overly friendly Greek that I had received basic training in martial arts. Not everything that Father insisted upon was a bad idea. In Jacksonville, I did have to render unconscious a pimple-faced young man who wore a Swastika around his neck. If he was counting on the medallion to improve his chances as a rapist, he was in the wrong line of endeavor.

I saw a jazz festival in New Orleans and touched many black bodies without contracting diseases. I hope that I didn't give them anything. One young man touched me in a most direct and satisfying way. He was graceful, and he knew all my secret places. I loved his dark skin and his laughter and the gin and tonic on his breath. I remember the scent of his cologne. Black is beautiful.

There were odd pleasures to be found in many places. In a small town with the unlikely name of Toomsooba, I saw that a recent German horror film had arrived on American shores: *They Saved Stalin's Brain*. There was no censorship, but the American distributor had given it a classification of 'R' for racist content. My favorite scene was when the Russian mad scientist pauses in his evil scheme so that he may salute a picture of Josef Stalin hanging on the wall. The audience howled with laughter. The dubbing was perfectly terrible.

By late summer, I was in Atlanta, Georgia, the site of Mother's favorite film. But then, the Fuehrer liked *Gone with the Wind*, so as the night must follow the day . . . Atlanta made a strong impression on me. Since the wrenching changes in American life were recent history, I was sensitive to incongruities. Atlanta was a hotbed of contradictions.

For the first time since leaving Burgundy, I encountered

a follower of the Nordic cult! That the Burgundian religion could take root in America seemed impossible. A woman activist in the Liberty party who had penetrated my disguise (such as it was) cheerfully explained. The crazy young man dressed in ritual cloak and carrying a copy of a book by Professor Karl Haushofer was viewed as a harmless eccentric. If he did any violence to his neighbors because he didn't like their race or religion, then he would be punished for violating a fellow human being's rights. He would have to pay restitution, or work it off, until his debt was paid.

Knowing the pernicious doctrines of the cult all too well, I asked what would be done should the fanatic murder someone. As no amount of restitution could replace a life, the murderer would forfeit his own life. Justice would be the coin of the realm. All that sounded pretty good, but I was shocked that Americans could hold ideas inimical to their own interests. The woman from the Liberty party assured me that there was nothing uncommon about it in the least. The solution had been to remove the structures of local government that allowed one group to enforce its standards on another. The law was simple: thou shalt not initiate force or fraud.

Given my skeptical nature, I immediately wondered if a centralized government didn't pose a greater threat to freedom than the power of local authority. But the idea was an embryo then. Compared to Europe, I had discovered the promised land. In Atlanta, Georgia, there was practical freedom in an ordered, social context.

The most dramatic proof was that in a city dominated by Baptists of every hue, none of their views on alcohol or sex or observance of the Sabbath carried the weight of law. Only in America could such a miracle obtain! Protestants and Catholics, Jews and Muslims, atheists and agnostics – they all lived in peace. The lady told me that when immigrants went into the melting pot, all that was boiled away was the hate. 'Of course, confidentially,' she added, 'we do have strife with a sect of primitive Baptists who believe in holding your head under water until you agree with them. We do the best we can.'

Freedom of religion and freedom from religion was something I had never seen in practice. (With all his power, Father still kept the fact of his atheism largely a private matter.) I met a Buddhist who was very quiet. I met a Hindu who was quite noisy. I met a practitioner of Haitian Voodoo who promised to use his spells only for good. I even met a large, raw-boned woman dressed in more black leather and silver than an SS Gruppenfuehrer. She was a member of an all-woman, lesbian motorcycle gang of Orthodox Wiccans. They called themselves the Mothers. She inspired me to consider a strictly heterosexual life-style.

Although there were problems in such a diverse population, by and large they were good neighbors. I was stunned. According to the theories of Adolf Hitler, these people should have slaughtered one another. The conflicts between their values were beyond anything ever dreamed of in the Weimar Republic. If that German house could not stand under its stresses, what gave the American house its firm foundation? Throughout all the years of my education, I had been repeatedly exposed to Rosenberg's doctrine of polylogism, the notion that different peoples had different truths. Aryan logic was not the same as other logics, and so it had no choice but to conquer anything that was different. When I became hungry for freedom, I didn't know it, but I also acquired an appetite for One Logic for All.

Encountering a carnival of tolerance and freedom should have been the purest delight, and evidence that there might be one truth under which all men could live.

On one level, I was exalted. But although I'd been rejecting the Nazi philosophy, I had to admit that experiencing living proof of one's wildest speculations is unsettling.

Chapter Six

The legitimate powers of government extend only to such acts
as are injurious to others. But it does me no injury for my
neighbor to say there are twenty gods, or no God. It neither
picks my pocket nor breaks my leg.

– Thomas Jefferson,
Notes on Virginia

The one-way ticket to New Berlin reposed in my pocket,
as if it were a poisonous beetle I dare not touch. Why was
I returning home? I'd saved my money and bought the
fare. It was not a command performance, a summons sent
by special messenger. I had chosen to leave a place that
promised much, only to return to a continent of extinguished hopes. It was not that I missed my advantages: I
was certain of that. I had to return to Europe as an
enemy, but I didn't know how I would translate raging
emotions into practical action.

Late summer was a grand time to wander in the woods,
and I spent my last night so occupied. Wrestling with
ambivalence did not compare to the pleasure of turning
white sneakers red with Georgia clay. I heard singing and
followed it to a clearing. The music was coming from
beyond a lake. Vagrant night breezes picked up the notes
and carried them over a generous tangle of trees to my
ears. How relaxing to bathe in the church music and not
have to analyse the content.

It was probably some evening gathering of Baptists,
heartily singing their simple hymns, seeking to overcome
their equally simple conception of evil with the common

goodness in their laborer's traditions. The high notes were charming – the product of children searching for an elusive quality at the top of the scale. Bearing down with only an occasional false note, the organist made the best of a limited talent; and I could imagine a ramshackle wooden building as a perfect setting for the harmless performance. The hymn was every bit as clean as the Burgundian ceremony had been filthy.

A sudden caress on the face reminded me that I was still in America, tasting the subtle breezes for which her Deep South is famous. I was safe temporarily from the dark world of *Mein Kampf*. The breeze was warm and soft, and it brought a gift: an assortment of fireflies, winking their small, phosphorescent bodies in mimicry of the cold, white stars above. Holding out a hand, I saw one of the tiny creatures alight on my palm. I barely felt it. I was happy.

I went home on the largest passenger jet in the world at that time, the Hindenburg. (Germans believe if at first you go up in flames, then try, try again.) My firm resolution was to return one day and see all of America, especially the Statue of Liberty and Hollywood Boulevard. In my satchel, I carried a treasure trove of books, new titles to circulate among comrades in the Reading League. Thanks to my rating, I'd be passed through customs without the books being confiscated. Looking back, I understand that Father could have removed my classification so as to teach me a lesson. Then again, he preferred finesse where his family was concerned.

Among the books were works by the Jewish anarchist Emma Goldman. Her autobiographical *My Disillusionment with Russia* closely paralleled my own growing disenchantment with Germany, but she had lived her ideas, while I had done nothing, for good or ill. The light she had shone upon Moscow and Lenin cast shadows of discontent across the years and over New Berlin and the elderly Hitler. The similarities were pins to prick the conscience.

On the flight, I carried the day's edition of the *New York Times* with a feature story on two new appointees to the American Supreme Court, one a distinguished lay Catholic, the other a philosopher who had written a formidable essay on atheism. Such a development would have been unthinkable in the Protestant America of only a few years earlier; and the name of a brilliant Jewish legal mind was being bandied about as a possible later appointment. (Eight years later, she would indeed assume her seat on the bench.) The reaction in Europe was exactly what should have been expected. Father had already broadcast his opinion that the Americans were deliberately tweaking the nose of Nazi opinion, as if the domestic affairs of America should take heed of a foreign power's obsessions before managing its own house.

The judges who had been confirmed in their august positions were both adherents of Natural Law and interpreted the Constitution in terms of the nonaggression principle. They both read the First Amendment as an unequivocal statement against censorship, prompting the Catholic justice to say, 'Religious convictions should not be confused with secular law. For example, the Index of banned books is for the faithful. It is not a matter for the statute books.' These words demonstrated as well as anything that the United States had undergone a second revolution. Father took this as a personal slight, so committed was he to the Nazis as revolutionists, while plutocratic Americans were supposed to behave, well, properly.

There was a serious difference between the justices over abortion. One saw the fetus as a citizen. National Socialist judges never had to concern themselves over such troublesome distinctions. The Reich's policy was spelled out: Aryan abortions were discouraged; non-Aryan abortions were encouraged, outside of meeting the quota for slave labor in restricted industries.

The story devoted a paragraph to Father's outburst. I knew that he had a personal motive in objecting to the Supreme Court news. He was already using his considerable influence to insert anti-Catholic scenes in a new string of musicals being produced at UFA. (The additional footage was altered to Anglican clergy for pictures exported to the British protectorate.) I knew what had triggered this activity. The Vatican had finally gotten around to excommunicating Father, along with Hitler and Goering on the same day. Now it was one thing to put *The Myth of the Twentieth Century* on the Index in the prewar period. It was quite another to take the moral high ground in Nazi Europe.

Most of the world had nearly forgotten that these candidates for the anti-Christ (should the office be open) were still on the membership rolls of the competing firm. Cynical practitioners of Realpolitik, Nazi leaders undermined the churches while maintaining outward decorum for the *Völk* who, theoretician Rosenberg knew better than anyone, could not be weaned from their superstitions overnight. Excommunication was a symbolic rebuke, meaning nothing to Party ideologues on the personal level. But that Rome should take an action against secular power – this called for more than a symbolic response. At the very least, Bormann's campaign against the churches would be reinvigorated. On the other hand, Hitler had sworn not to make Napoleon's errors with the Holy See. Well, I had problems of my own.

Fortunate was the child who escaped *Pimpfe*, being trapped in the Hitler Youth, or the League of German Girls. These officially approved groups had the good

78

equipment and the good field trips, but what a price one paid to enjoy them. Shortly after the Jewish youth organizations were terminated, the remaining non-Nazi gatherings discovered that they weren't allowed to do much of anything. Kids will go where the action is, even Lutherans.

Father used to brag how he had adopted certain methods of the Jesuits for application in the *Kinder-Land-Verschicküng* camps and used the techniques to turn young Catholics against their own religion. I had seen how effective this could be. In no time at all, boys and girls who had been eating fish on Friday were singing, 'Der Papst ist tot' (The Pope is dead).

If certain political difficulties didn't preclude a direct strike on the Vatican, it would have been reduced to rubble long ago. I thought everyone in the world was aware of the situation. Yet while I'd been in Georgia, I'd encountered, as part of the crazy quilt of beliefs promulgated there, a fundamentalist 'Friend of Jesus' who went around babbling that the Vatican was secretly cooperating with New Berlin. He paid no heed to my assurances that a fruitful dialogue between the two parties was improbable. This person, who seemed more wild-eyed than the displaced Burgundian had been, solemnly intoned that we were in End Times. Hitler was the Beast foretold in Revelations because he had destroyed Russia and set in place a European hegemony. The sadly named 'Friend of Jesus' said that Rome was the Great Whore that would serve the Swastika and all its works. When he spoke, there was spittle on his chin afterward. The world is full of lunatics. I grow weary in the recounting.

Caring not for the company of the mad was no mood in which to greet Father. He took me aback by ascertaining the day of my return (I must have been recognized the instant I went through security), and in an action without

79

precedence, he was waiting for me. He'd only just returned from a fact-finding mission in Bohemia and Moravia, whichever facts were certain not to include the name of Czechoslovakia. His talent for euphemism was perfect.

How I longed to ask if he'd run out of girl friends in town! But I wasn't suicidal enough to do that. I'd voluntarily returned to the web. I stepped with caution, and for good reason. It was a long way from the International Desk at New Berlin's busiest airfield to the intimate discomforts of home.

When Papa was sweet, I tasted the bitter flavor of terror. Taking me by the arm, he led me to his Volkswagen touring car, and drove us to a café on the Wilhelmstrasse. En route, he chatted idly about the weather and dropped the hint that I had a treat in store if I was a good girl. We arrived. The proprietor fell over himself providing us with top service. The propaganda minister is a walking advertisement, after all. Father waited until we were seated in the privacy of a corner that had been reserved for him outside, before letting the axe fall.

'Your mother and I have had a long talk,' he began, adding cream to his coffee with slow deliberation. 'She told me about your idiotic remarks. What do you have to say for yourself?'

I believe that I prayed . . . prayed that nothing of my conversation with Alfredo was known to him. I operated on the assumption that that encounter had not been compromised. 'She was upset when I told the truth.'

'The truth! What do you know about truth? You're a young pup, playing at being the radical, lacking appreciation for the privileges you enjoy in the New Order. You're not a child any longer. What will you do with your life? You're not married, and not likely to be at this rate. You don't have a career. You majored in chemistry, but you've

80

done nothing with it . . . and believe me when I say that the Reich can always use chemists. You're a dilettante, and that's something to your credit because it's kept you out of worse trouble. Listen, Hilda, it's about time that you grew up. There's no free sauerkraut in this world. Socialism is not for children who play but for adults who serve and die, if need be. Now hop to it.' Then, without even waiting for my response, he turned his attention to the nut mousse with plums.

I was trembling with rage, but I couldn't show it, not to him. 'How am I to grow up?' I asked, barely above a whisper.

'We'll begin with your treatment of your mother. How dare you have a fit of temper in public? You didn't used to be like this.'

'When was this?'

'Helmuth and Helga were there, my dear. They saw it all.'

'But it was Mother who became angry and – '

'We needn't focus on details. I'm speaking of a general pattern. You have been sarcastic to your mother; you were even abusive! And then this nonsense about remaining in the United States to see the sights. You've caused me no end of embarrassment.'

He was holding his anger in check, and a small voice in me shrilled that my rage was but a spark against the red furnace burning in his breast. Watching his cruel mouth, I was afraid. A bad father would make a most formidable enemy even without the force of an empire behind him.

'These are difficult times,' he said, 'and our faith is sorely tested. We must extend the defense perimeter. We continue to deport enemies of the Reich from liberated territories. The number of our People's Courts expand without an upper limit. We must put enemies on trial. We

81

must make an object lesson of them. We will not forget our foes. They shall never be forgiven. Do you hear me?'

He paused, and he was trembling. Absently swirling ice cubes in my punch, I waited for the storm to pass. Suddenly he spoke in a perfectly calm voice: 'What if you had been kidnapped?'

'The thought never occurred to me.'

'Don't you read the papers? Acts of terror are committed against us by Jewish pirates the world over. You could have been held for ransom.'

'Why didn't you send SS men to bring me back?'

His eyes narrowed. 'You were watched.'

I gasped, then spoke without thinking: 'I don't believe you.'

Three beefy men walked by, unattractive in ill-fitting suits. They had Gestapo written all over them. One whistled at a pretty fraulein crossing the street. A blackbird flew overhead, screeching at other birds that were out of sight. These things happened as Father and I stared at each other, absorbed by the ticking from an ornate grandfather clock just inside the door of the café.

'Let's be off,' he said, smiling. 'Time for your surprise.'

One thought welled up to drown out the rest: say nothing more, *Dummkopf!* We drove in silence, except when he told me how he'd let his chauffeur go and that he rarely used the Mercedes-Benz any longer. The People's Car was good enough for him. Symbols. Always symbols. I noticed that he had added steel sheets to bulletproof his connection to the *Völk*. And he'd kept his car phone.

They were waiting for us at the very exclusive Otto Skorzeny Aerodrome and did everything but roll out the red carpet. Father loved his perks. They brought out one of Goering's helium planes. When I'm nervous, I get the hiccups. I probably always will. That afternoon, I had them with a vengeance. The tear-shaped aeroplane was not a mode of transportation I was inclined to try. Besides, I'd just spent most of the day in flight anyway. The conclusion was never in question: I would have to fly in the damned thing.

Maybe I was prejudiced against it because it was one of the Reichmarshal's brainchildren. This was, after all, the same man who had conceived the notion to build railroad engines out of concrete when Germany was desperate for resources late in the war. Next to that, even Himmler's plan to use dandelions for fuel seemed worthy of investigation. The nastiest military jokes are at Goering's expense to this day, largely because of his poor performance on air defense, but there was plenty of blame to go around. As for his oddball ideas, most never got off the drawing board, except as punch lines, but the helium plane was a notable exception.

They poured water down me until the hiccups were gone, and then I had my revenge. They had to wait while I repaired to the Ladies' Room. Then my time ran out. Boarding the plane, I caught the eye of the pilot, who was having difficulty squeezing his six-foot frame into the cockpit. Father and I were the only passengers.

The helium plane operates on the principle of a zeppelin and mainly was used for reconnaissance. When the pilot is over a promising spot, he redistributes the gas in the ample wings, and the aircraft descends as a leaf drifts earthward. Today this marvel of German aeronautical prowess is virtually discontinued, replaced by a new fami'; of autogyros.

Goering's toy certainly satisfied Father's purposes. 'We'll enjoy a tour of the backyard, eh, daughter?' he asked. 'You've grown up with this glory, but have you ever really seen it?' He was up to his old tricks and was going to give the show full production values. The opening chords of Wagner's *Parsifal* were piped through the speaker, as we rose above the clouds. No wonder he had been interested in the weather. Lights! Camera! Action!

'We're going to remake *Triumph of the Will*,' he said casually. 'The new capital demands it.'

'With or without Leni?' I asked. The imp of the perverse would have its way.

He was terse. 'That hasn't been decided.' He was expansive. 'Today is for you. Drink in the experience. Rediscover your heritage.'

The sunlight playing off the clouds created a jewel-box effect, a dance of colors to draw me out of myself and whisper that the works of man are ephemeral. Ghosts of the past and ghosts of the future descended with us through the eternal clouds to the vast marble mausoleum that was the giant city still under construction, and already cracking at the seams.

We came in over one of the completed sections. The wide plateau of the South Station slowly crept beneath us . . . and the monstrous cavern that was the Arch of Triumph loomed ahead. Beyond that stretched the dry riverbed of concrete that was the Grand Boulevard. Work crews were busily engaged planting one of the numerous rows of trees that would grow on the banks overlooking the vehicles that would drift by in the current.

'Notice the shadows reaching out to embrace our neighbors,' said Father. He did not even sound sarcastic.

The music was inspiring, lifting me higher and higher, swelling chords that rose to challenge the gods, but the helium plane was descending with every note. The afternoon sun put the city in the best light. But the imposing structures were dead things, designed as showpieces the functions of which could not be divined. We veered off for a close view of Goering's Palace (how Hitler had spoiled that man). This building was a perfect example of architectural window dressing. Father agreed that the Graeco-Roman motifs had been overdone, what with statues of charioteers frozen in motion, as if wishing to stampede and escape from the forest of Doric columns.

Directly across from the palace, an equally imposing and Romanesque edifice was still under construction: the Soldier's Hall. The sun glinted off more gilded pomp and grandiose colonnades. Steel girders crisscrossing next to the ancient world's splendor increased the feeling of weirdness. Small, black shapes scuttled like beetles along the lengthy base of the memorial. The Volkswagen was everywhere.

'To the heart of New Berlin!' declaimed the minister of propaganda and gauleiter of the city. His face was flushed with excitement and I wondered if he might have an orgasm. The helium plane rose several meters before the pilot kicked in the propellers, and we flew toward the recently finished Great Hall, the world's most expensive building, guaranteed never to pay for itself. The dome was 27,468,000 cubic yards and had a space reserved at the top that has since been filled by an iron eagle. 'The Fuehrer will hold a world's fair when the work is finished,' crowed Papa. I wondered how the Nazis would persuade the world to attend.

We were losing daylight by the time we banked for a final run past Hitler's Palace and the Mussolini Monument. Offices of the Reich protectors were to be found in these echoing, empty halls. The functionaries of command increased as the locusts of the Bible, each hoping that one day supreme power might be his. But Hitler lived on.

'Do you see that?' asked the extension of the Fuehrer's will who thought himself the creator of the Fuehrer. He was pointing to an ugly modern building in the distance, curiously out of place beside a gargoyle- and goddess-festooned Opera House on one side and a row of forlorn private shops on the other (the latter a concession to business amidst a jungle of public works). 'I hope that you won't force me to show you the inside.'

'I don't understand.'

'You're looking at an insane asylum. After all, one doesn't place a beloved member of the household in a work camp. It just isn't done.' He was to be commended for his candor. Day after day of suspicion without an object is tiresome. Conversations become ballets of indecision. At least Father had the virtue of detesting ambiguity.

'You would do that?' I asked. Why was it that as he threatened me, I fixated on his hair? The dye he was using was a little too black, as if it were shoe polish. When the war ended victoriously, his hair had begun turning white.

'I love you, Hilda. I care what happens to you. Now, I'm the first to admit that certain offspring of other officials are far more spoiled than you. I've always encouraged you to listen to the blood. Aryan youth of the highest caste should have the freedom to discover their duty for themselves. I've encouraged this in you. I'd hate to think that I went too far. How much longer will you be irresponsible? Don't you realize that you are part of a noble community?'

Hovering above the gray cinder block of a National Socialist madhouse, I was sane enough to discover my civic pride and to sense that patriotism is a requirement of mental health. 'I never thought of it that way,' I lied, hoping that he would stop. Hope springs eternal. Who should have known better than I that Father could match his hero's penchant for long-windedness?

And so he elaborated. It seemed that Mother had learned of my sexual egalitarianism. I couldn't believe that he would have the gall to lecture me about sex, he the great Casanova. I had not reckoned with the man who claimed to be the Voice of the People, working tirelessly to learn public sentiment, and at the same time writing: 'A government derived from the people must never tolerate a go-between 'twixt it and the people.' Hitler was his god, but hypocrisy ranked only a little further down in the pantheon. He excoriated my sexual behavior as if he were a celibate monk. But as he continued, I was relieved to note that my lesbian encounters were not mentioned. Either he was deliberately avoiding the topic, or else he didn't know. Homosexual activity could still earn the practitioner a pink triangle and free lodging in a concentration camp; although everyone knew that exceptions were made. At any rate, my boyfriends were sufficient to his purpose.

He had me all right, and he wasn't about to let it end. Not he! 'Did you know that more people died during the war from disease than from the bombings, and that's including the atomic bombs? Now don't get smart and factor in postatomic diseases. You know very well what I mean. The old-fashioned germs killed us. Don't you think sexual transmission was a big help to the Grim Reaper?'

'Father, do you want me to answer or only listen?' If he wouldn't be sarcastic, then I would.

'Listen, naturally.' He could be honest when he wished. Although I did not use it then, hanging in space and fearing accidents, I would in the next few weeks drop snippets of information leading him to an inescapable conclusion: I'd been compiling my own file about Father's indiscretions that not only matched, but probably surpassed, similar efforts by intelligence agents. Hitler had, as a useful quirk, a bourgeoise obsession with propriety – the attitude that a sadistic concentration camp commandant was a moral man if he didn't cheat on his wife. Then there were other secrets that Father had been careless in keeping from my eyes. He had enough skeletons in his closet to fill a cemetery.

Sons and daughters generally strive to make a good impression on their parents. I won Father's respect by responding to his threat in a likewise brutal fashion. I suppose that it was a rite of passage. I wasn't proud, only relieved. My motive had been survival, not angling for a berth in the family business.

We didn't speak to each other again that day. Too much had been said. He instructed the pilot to take us home. The sun was setting and we were bathed in red light that looked like blood. The city was also crimson. Recalling my impressions today, I believed that New Berlin was probably the greatest city on earth . . . but it hadn't been designed for human beings. The scale was actually malignant. Surely the staggering sum of 25 billion Reichsmarks could have been better spent.

My room had not been touched, and I gratefully locked the door so that he wouldn't see me cry. For a moment, I was so afraid that I couldn't even hear. I bit my tongue, tasted blood, and moaned. Moaning was good. It brought back the sound.

I was Papa's little girl again. He had primed me for nightmare, and the years of adolescence and young adulthood were stripped away, leaving me a doll dressed in bright peasant apron, a jewel in my parents' collection of pretty things. I was so weary that I collapsed on my bed. No tears came, but I did dream.

Childhood is when you store up all your real demons. Adult fears never replace them, but only result in their retrieval. I didn't dream of straitjackets and padded rooms and creative surgery. Far worse, I slid back in time.

When I was a girl, I barely escaped incineration in the Allied fire storm of Hamburg, the damned summer of 1943. That his own daughter should survive a tragedy that staggered the imagination was not considered acceptable propaganda that season, so Father buried the fact that I was ever there. But Hitler may have considered my survival further proof that the Goebbels family had been selected for a divine mission.

Hamburg was the fuel of my bad dreams ever after. I remember people caught in asphalt that had been suddenly rendered into a primordial tar pit by the intense heat. They could do nothing but stand and scream as a curtain of fire closed in, burning them as black as the asphalt. I remember a pregnant woman, running through the rubble, every inch of her a living torch. I will not allow myself to remember the children.

By some miracle, I was pulled into one of the shelters that did not become a tomb of living corpses, flesh roasting, lungs full of carbon monoxide. The weather must have been in an RAF uniform that night, the way the wind conspired to spread the fire storm to the broadest possible number of victims. The firefighters could do nothing against the phosphorus bombs and the tornadoes of flame.

I was glad to have survived afterward, but at the time I was too horrified to care; I only wanted to be spared further horror, which awaited me up above, amidst the steaming wreckage. A screaming man was carrying a suitcase, begging someone to tell him what to do. As he stumbled, the case fell to the ground, disgorging its contents – a shriveled brown mummy that had been his wife. I saw her face and wanted to rip my eyes out. Long afterward, when I was shown the face of the Jewish child, victim of SS scientific research, I would relive the full meaning of the Hamburg wife.

That choking night in Hamburg, I lost my belief in God. Today, I shake my head at the simplicity of youth. I pray to no deity for reasons of the intellect, but I have learned that terror does nothing to disprove God. All religions accept the reality of man's inhumanity to man. That is their starting place. It is possible that someone in Hamburg was converted to religion by encountering a brimstone punishment worthy of the Devil.

Although I reject the supernatural, my dreams take no heed of my conviction. The torments of Hamburg coalesced, that long ago summer, into one image I refer to as the Asphalt Man. Trepidation at entering an asylum was the trigger to bring back my childhood phantom in full force. I had thought myself rid of the thing, but I learned that nightmares are never banished. They are only endured.

Even now, safe on this ship on a calm Pacific, bound for Tahiti, the tall, black figure with the burning red eyes returns to haunt me. The dream has changed again, but the Asphalt Man remains. I know why the particulars are different. Burgundy is the reason . . . Burgundy and Father's dying.

Chapter Seven

Freedom is always the freedom of those who think differently.

– Rosa Luxemburg,
Letters from Prison

New York

Here the typed pages of English were interrupted by handwritten sheets in German, in the immediate tense. Alan Whittmore read several paragraphs of the new material before he realized that he had shifted languages.

The body is burning. Enshrined at the summit of the pyre, lit by the flame of the acolytes, it darkens and smokes and gives off a popping sound. The stench is terrible.

For this is a Viking's funeral, replete with the lowing sound of great horns carved from whalebone. The men blowing into the long horns appear to be northern fighting men from the twelfth century: a procession of horned helmets, leather stockings, coarse boots, and dried leather tunics. The men holding torches around the pyre are similarly attired, but the rest of the company are outfitted in twentieth-century military uniforms.

Rising from the pyre is a black monolith sweating blood, the Asphalt Man. With the advent of such a terrifying appparition, violence explodes onto the gathering. Beyond the cordon of modern soldiers and ancient warriors, a troop of guerrillas make an attack. Shouts! Gunfire! The concussion of grenades! There used to be a wall to the courtyard, but it disappears into a jagged ditch of red and brown . . . and not all the red is from the soil.

I am one of the attackers, irresistibly drawn to the funeral fire, and the demon hanging above it. My weapon is a Mauser, from the firm that also manufactures adding machines. I increase my score by taking aim at the largest of the enemy, a giant blond man who is rushing toward me. His weapon is a battleaxe, and idly wondering if brandishing such a weapon might give him a hernia, I pull the trigger. One burst and his midsection is wreathed in a garland of blood and human pulp. Into the wine of his own bowels he collapses.

The defenders have hand grenades, too. One detonates nearby, and there is a pink ball of chaos in my head and spots before my eyes as I go down. I am fortunate. I only lose a tooth. Stumbling to my feet, half running, howling, I am an animal, a wolf ravening to kill. The Asphalt Man wears a crown of flame and nods approval to each and every one of us, raving and bleeding for his amusement.

I am first to the pyre, and pull the pin on my grenade. The burning corpse is nearly consumed, and the sour odor of roasting flesh has been diminished by the charred gunpowder smell that permeates the air. But the dark shadow, ascended from the pyre, mocks me to destroy destruction. I throw the grenade up high, so that it arcs down to the top of the pyre, where it will touch the charred remains of the corpse before going off. There is maniacal laughter. It is mine.

The explosion does nothing to the Asphalt Man but make him bigger and blacker. The battle still rages. Fire raging in my veins, I rejoin the melee.

There is someone I must find: a crippled man; a man responsible in part, for the current fighting – and for long decades of dying before this day. Seeing him, my heart leaps with joy. He is lying on the ground near a broken radio, and I pray that he is not dead, as I wish very much to kill him myself.

I rush to greet my father.

The handwritten passage broke off, but Whittmore did not return to the manuscript. He stopped reading if only to catch his breath. There was something almost indecent about personal confessions. He'd not expected so much personal torment in Hilda Goebbels's writing. It made him uncomfortable.

The phone rang. He didn't answer it at first. The etiquette of the situation was elusive; but the phone kept ringing. 'Well, I'm a voyeur anyway,' he muttered and went over to answer the call. Lifting the receiver, virtually convinced that it must be Hilda inquiring after him, he felt like an idiot for not answering sooner.

'Hello,' he said. There was dead silence on the line. 'Hello?' No words, no breathing, no clicks or static. Just silence. Then, adding insult to presumption, the other, if there were another, hung up. 'You gootch!' said Whittmore to the dial tone, employing a Townie profanity. He slammed down the phone. To hell with etiquette.

He hadn't taken two steps when he heard a key turning in the lock. Now surely this was his writer at last. A smile of welcome froze on his face as the door opened, and framed in the doorway was a gaunt man with hair white as the carpet neatly combed atop a skull-like face with Mandarin cheekbones.

One second is a long time, if in that brief instant one has the illusion of complete recall. Alan's déjà vu was painful: he saw the man from the limousine entering the room. His life didn't flash before his eyes, but a catalogue of unpleasant deaths flashed by.

The next second made all the difference. It was not the stranger from the limousine, but a man to whom he had once been introduced at the Waldorf-Astoria: Harold Baerwald, author of a series of books under the pseudonym of H. Freedman. Following him into the room, tightly clasping a brown packet, was their hostess: Hilda Goebbels.

She did not show her age, but at a glance could be mistaken for her teenage self. She was one of those lucky women who as they approach middle age seem to have a second lease on youth. Alan knew that she had had a child once, but the revealing dress – transparent down the side – revealed no stretch marks; but, then, New York sold a lot of body makeup. Her hair was long and red, as she had worn it in youth, although it had lost some of its luster. This was not a woman who would use hair dye –

no chip off the old block. She had a good face with large eyes under arched eyebrows, and a strong chin, which he liked in a woman. Her cheekbones were high, but nowhere as pronounced as those of the elderly man at her side. The nose was turned up slightly, giving her expression a challenging, or haughty, aspect. But the mouth was well proportioned, the upper lip slightly extended, giving her smile a V at the center. He caught himself staring at the mouth that had kissed and tasted so many.

'I see you've made yourself at home, Alan. I remembered that you like tequila.' The voice sounded deeper than it had when he spoke to her over the phone. Her eyes were on his.

'I'm sorry. It's only that I'd been reading about how you lost a tooth. Oh, but that was a dream, wasn't it?'

'So you do read German! That dream corresponds to an event, all right.' Grinning, she showed Exhibit A. 'Top row,' she said. 'Can you tell?'

He took a quick inventory. 'No,' he admitted.

'Good. The dentist earned his marks. Although I should say gold. By that point, I only traded on the black market.'

'Hilda has one problem in an otherwise idyllic existence,' said Baerwald. 'She expends considerable energy in becoming famous; but then hopes to keep her economic transactions private.'

'Bad habits are hard to break, Harry,' said Hilda. 'Over there it was survival: but here it isn't really necessary. America is land of the brave and home of the free.'

'Well, that's land of the free and home of the brave, but close enough,' said Alan.

'Forgive me. I was thinking in terms of cause and effect. And I hope that my bad manners haven't caused you gentlemen distress. I haven't introduced you.'

94

'Haven't we met before?' Baerwald quizzed Whittmore.

'I'm flattered that you remember.' They shook hands. 'It was that fund raiser for world peace.'

'Ah, yes. I'm always willing to lend my efforts to voluntary charity for immigrants. Very soon now I'll finish my study of why the Wagner-Rogers Bill was defeated in 1939. America must never close her doors to refugees again.'

'The door is open, but they make their own beds,' said Hilda. 'We saw some newcomers living in a packing crate on the way over.'

Alan sighed and repeated a phrase that had become a litany for him: 'I'm afraid that laissez-faire capitalism has not made everyone rich.'

Baerwald cleared his throat and spoke too loudly for close quarters: 'No, but it hasn't sent anyone to concentration camps either! There are worse fates than being a beggar.'

Hilda and Alan exchanged knowing glances. They were both junior to this elderly but vigorous gentleman in the never-ending struggle for liberty. He had been a 'U-boat,' the term given to Jews who continued to live, hidden, in Berlin under the very nose of Dr Paul Joseph Goebbels at the height of World War II. He had remained 'at large' long after his lover and friends had been taken; and after the last member of his family, an older brother named Herman, had disappeared into the chaos of the New Order. The Gestapo caught him on the Potsdamer Chaussee Strass in 1944, but only because he had put himself at risk to pass crucial information to a double agent working against the National Socialists. The information concerned a certain Dr Richard Dietrich, who was supposedly nearing completion on one of the many secret weapons

Hitler kept promising to use when he tired of being 'Mr Nice Guy' (a US army joke of the time).

The agent made certain that he was not taken alive, but Baerwald was arrested. When it was determined that he was a Jew, a debate ensued. After all, there was a clearly delimited set of procedures for dealing with a spy, and another for dealing with a Jew. Here was the kind of case to give bureaucrats endless headaches. As Baerwald could not be divided in two (both components remaining alive, of course), there was nothing to do but trust that the SS would employ their typically subtle measures to insure the optimum quantity of Nazi justice. Baerwald was first sent to Sachsenhausen, a camp in the Berlin area that had been the dock for 'U-boats' before. There Baerwald received serious beatings. His wrists retained scars from occasions when his arms had been handcuffed behind him as a preliminary to hanging him from a hook, a procedure sufficient in itself to cause blackout without the beatings on which the guards never stinted.

He had been scheduled to be sent to the east, where, it was intimated, he would enjoy the hospitality of either Auschwitz or Majdanek. Of dark rumors there was no end. Even after the tortures he had endured, he could not quite bring himself to believe that human beings were capable of the evil described in frightened whispers. He only knew that his lover had been sent far away in the east to a place called Treblinka, and he'd heard nothing from her since.

Harold Baerwald never learned the truth about Auschwitz one way or the other, because he didn't arrive at his destination. In the month of July in the year 1944, the world entered the atomic age. Two human consequences were that, first, Baerwald escaped his captors, and second, Hitler's regime survived. In the chaos that ensued from the ultimate Vengeance Weapons, a train carrying prisoners east was derailed. Baerwald crawled from the wreckage and saw the sun come out at night.

A week later he was suffering the hell of radiation sickness, but he was at sea and making light of the fact that he hadn't gotten his sea legs. They loved him. A boatload of refugees, they bound each other's wounds, succored the sick and dying. They had so little – a few bandages, some quinine water – and yet there was a deep cheerfulness on that ship. To witness genuine goodwill at the rim of doom was more glorious than anything else in his life. Alive or dead, what mattered was that he was free. And so, surviving his illness, he became H. Freedman, and wrote wonderful books telling everyone that nothing is more important than liberty.

He had taken it on himself to nurse a dying man whose pride it was that he had escaped from Buchenwald. They had formed a pact that should Baerwald survive, he would tell the man's story. The testament became *To Live in Hell*, and its most famous line was 'Hier ist kein warum.' This was the motto of the camps: There is no why here. The rules changed on a daily basis. One group of inmates would be given a task that another group would be told to undo. Tortures were calculated to increase a sense of uncertainty; this was more highly prized than pain. The man said that he had begun his imprisonment under the cruel tutelage of SA guards. He thought that nothing could be worse until his jeering tormentors were replaced by young, emotionless robots of the SS. The original system appeared utopian in contrast to the new. Madness had become the order of the day, but it was scientifically applied. What preserved this one victim's sanity was his realization that nothing is done without a purpose. He had a revelation in fact: obviously Heinrich Himmler had the task of determining if the perfect slave could be created, provided that the experiment received an unlimited supply of human material. The orders were insane on the surface, but underneath they were a test of both SS robots and the prisoners who were to be made into robots. For the will of Adolf Hitler to be supreme, all other wills had to die.

Baerwald never forgot that the most wicked crimes of the Nazis were against the people they left alive. To enslave a man's soul is worse than to kill his body. As for the latter, they even took the intimacy out of murder. While others wept, Baerwald decided to understand; at all costs he would understand. The voice of H. Freedman was the perfect antidote to the voice of *Mein Kampf* . . . because Freedman did not speak in the language of fear.

Alan Whittmore was familiar with this man's work, and he was honored to be in his company. He felt a bit ashamed that his first reaction to the old man in the doorway had been one of stark terror. Hilda noticed Alan's consternation. 'Excuse me, is something wrong?' she asked.

'I guess my paranoia is showing,' he answered lamely.

'Oh, I thought that was your tie!' she replied.

They all laughed and there was a lessening of tension. Alan's tie looked as if it were a section of wallpaper with the color of a blue-green organic soup that had spawned various forms of protozoa passing themselves off as designs. The thing had been a gift from his mother-in-law, a woman who had never reconciled herself to freedom for pornographers and would have her revenge on the crazed freethinker her daughter had been so foolish as to marry.

'Your expression was murderous when I first saw you,' said Baerwald. 'I thought you might be a reviewer.'

'Let's apply our critical faculties to food,' said Hilda. 'I've made special arrangements to have a number of dishes sent up.' Alan was less impressed by the generosity than he was by the strangeness of her insistence. It had stopped raining. Later in the evening would be an ideal time to patronize one of the better restaurants. She wouldn't have it; and yet she had also asked that he not use room service earlier. Was it that she had deep-seated authoritarian tendencies that she could not relinquish?

Hilda played bartender. With a second drink expanding the warmth in his chest, Alan Whittmore relaxed into the technical side of his craft. To his first question, Hilda answered: 'The difficulty with translating German into English is that German is a more precise language. English is for poets but German is for technical manuals. Ambiguity is alien to the Teutonic mind.'

'Hold on,' said Baerwald in a jovial tone, 'I thought French was the language of poets.'

'No, it's the language of diplomats and lovers, which is much the same thing actually. It is especially well equipped for accepting terms of surrender.'

'There are times when you sound just like your father,' said Baerwald.

'God help me, I know it.'

Alan hoped to keep the conversation light-hearted, despite the tremendous odds against. He interjected with, 'How about puns? I imagine they give translators quite a headache.'

Hilda brightened at the question. 'Sometimes we can find an adequate substitute, close enough in meaning and still retaining the flavor of the original. I always hate it when I must sacrifice word play in a translation.' Her eyes wandered to the packet she had placed on the table beside her manuscript. 'Some things cannot be sacrificed,' she said in a lower voice. Then, changing tone yet again, she asked: 'How far did you get in your reading?'

'I've only just begun, but I'm fascinated with it so far. I must admit that the stuff on Burgundy is hard to believe. I knew that they were crazy but – '

'They are not insane,' Hilda interrupted. 'We would be better off if they were, uh, crazy. You, and your fellow Americans, have no inkling how nearly you came to total destruction.'

'Well, nuclear stalemate works. I haven't noticed any new world wars lately. Some say you helped maintain the balance at a critical juncture. I'm hoping you might go public.'

'Alan, I'm not talking about the Reich or its missiles. I'm talking about Burgundy and a worse weapon than all the hydrogen bombs in the world.' It was certainly turning into a day of surprises for the editor of *The American Mercury*. Visions of canceled subscriptions began to dance before his eyes, and he forgot to blink as Hilda continued: 'The data on genetics that I sold to scientists over here was not acquired cheaply. Until now, I've kept secret my information about an insidious conspiracy. The data was the only good thing that came of a scheme to commit the Final Crime. Now I have a document to support my accusation.'

'You're talking about the Burgundians?' asked Alan. 'A handful of religious fanatics who don't enjoy living in modern times . . .'

'To these people, any date with A.D. after it is modern times,' said Hilda. 'Despite that, they could tolerate progressive views up until the ninth century, when, according to their shamans and historians, everything went to hell. A few years ago, they decided to correct history's mistake. They were stopped. But they will try again. The next time, they must be defeated forever.'

Here was a strange turn of events, all right. Alan Whittmore was not happy. Could it be that this fabulous woman was herself suffering from a mental aberration? He suddenly felt guilty about neglecting his wife lately. At least she lived in the same universe as he. His brief

editorial career had been devoted to combating hysteria
and panic; and now Hilda Goebbels, daughter of the
Great Liar himself, was carrying on in so eccentric a
fashion that she cast doubt on her considerable virtues.
The situation was untenable.

No, he berated himself – he must not think that way.
Had he not been in the grip of fear because of an
unfriendly glare from a decrepit gentleman riding around
in an antique automobile? Who was he to judge this
woman for overheated rhetoric? He owed it to her to
suspend judgement until she'd made her case.

While these thoughts were racing through his mind,
Hilda was opening the package on the table. She brought
its contents over to him, a musty old volume of Houston
Stewart Chamberlain's *Foundations of the Nineteenth
Century*. Flipping open the cover, he saw that the inside
had been hollowed out, and reposing at the center was a
diary. He didn't have to open the book-within-a-book to
know its author. This was the reason he was here.

'If a ponderous, fat book had to be gutted,' said Hilda,
'I could think of none more deserving than a tract by an
Englishman that laid the basis for Nazi racial theories.'

'But why have you gone to such lengths?' asked Alan.

'After you've read it, you'll understand,' said Baerwald.
'But do you really want to know? Ignorance has its
compensations.'

'I get the impression you two are playing mind games
with me, and I don't like it.'

'Please believe me, Alan. We don't mean to annoy you.
We want you to know what you are getting yourself
involved with. Borrowing from your popular culture, it's
as if you have the *Necronomicon* in your hands.'

'The what?'

'Forgive me, I'm referring to an imaginary tome of evil
from the American fantasist H. P. Lovecraft. He was a

101

prewar writer, and there is quite an audience for his stories back home, among those who can get the books, of course.'

Alan shook his head. 'You know more about my own country's entertainers than I do. I'm afraid I have little time for fiction. I stick to facts.' As if on cue, three sets of eyes turned to the little diary. 'This is factual, right?' he asked.

'Unfortunately,' said Hilda. She disappeared into the bedroom and moved some furniture about before returning with another typed manuscript, her translation of the small volume Alan had opened. He had immediately recognized her father's handwriting, thanks to earlier research.

Dinner had not yet arrived. The appetizer would be a big lie or a disturbing truth from the inventor of modern propaganda. The Goebbels technique was practiced worldwide, selling everything from soap to the first space platform. Words from the source had to be treated with the greatest of caution. But if Alan Whittmore was to publish these words, it was about time he read them.

Chapter Eight

If you gaze long into an abyss, the abyss will gaze back into you.

– Friedrich Nietzsche,
Beyond Good and Evil

ENTRIES FROM THE DIARY OF DR PAUL JOSEPH GOEBBELS, NEW BERLIN APRIL 1965/TRANSLATED INTO ENGLISH BY HILDA GOEBBELS.

Today I attended the state funeral for Adolf Hitler. They asked me to give the eulogy. It wouldn't have been so bothersome except that Himmler pulled himself out of his thankful retirement at Wewelsburg to advise me on all the things I mustn't say. The old fool still believes that we are laying the foundation for a religion. Acquainted as he is with my natural skepticism, he never ceases to worry that I will say something in public not meant for the consumption of the masses. It is a pointless worry on his part; not even early senility should enable him to forget that I am the propaganda expert. Still, I do not question his insistence that he is in rapport with what the masses feel most deeply, with the caveat that such exercises in telepathy only produce results when both sides are apathetic.

I suppose that I was the last member of the entourage to see Hitler alive. Albert Speer had just left, openly anxious to get back to his work with the von Braun team. In his declining years he has taken to involving himself full time with the space program. This question of whether the Americans or we will reach the moon first seems a negligible concern. I am convinced by our military experts that the space program that really matters is in terms of orbiting platforms for the purpose of global intimidation. Such a measure seems entirely justified if we are to give the Fuehrer his thousand-year Reich (or something even close).

The Fuehrer had recently returned from his estate on the island of San Michele. When he was certain that the end was approaching, he wanted to finish his life either in Berchtesgaden or the city that so uniquely belonged to him . . . and to me. My heart leapt with joy when he chose the latter, and once again infused the capital with his presence.

We spoke of Himmler's plans to make him an SS saint. 'How many centuries will it be,' he asked in a surprisingly firm voice, 'before they forget I was a man of flesh and blood?'

'Can an Aryan be any other?' I responded dryly, and he smiled as he is wont to do at my more jestful moments.

'The spirit of Aryanism is another matter,' he said. 'The same as destiny or any other workable myth.'

'Himmler would ritualize these myths into a new reality,' I pointed out.

'Of course,' Hitler agreed. 'That has always been *his* purpose. You and I are realists. We make use of what is available.' He reflected for a moment and then continued: 'The war was a cultural one. If you ask the man in the street what I really stood for, he would not come near the truth. Nor should he!'

I smiled. I'm sure he took that as a sign of assent. This duality of Hitler's, with its concern for exact hierarchies to replace the old social order – and what is true for the *Völk* is not always true for us – seemed to me another workable myth, often contrary to our stated purposes. I

104

would never admit that to him. In his own way, he was quite the boneheaded philosopher.

'*Mein Führer*,' I began, entirely a formality under the circumstances, but I could tell that he was pleased I had used the address, 'the Americans love to make fun of your most famous statement about the Reich that will last one thousand years, as though what we've accomplished is an immutable status quo.'

He laughed. 'I love those Americans. I really do. They believe their own democratic propaganda . . . so obviously what we tell our people must be what we believe! American credulity is downright refreshing at times, especially after dealing with Russians.'

On the subject of Russians, Hitler and I did not always agree. I had thought there could be points of contact between us ideologically, and possibilities for a united front against the capitalist West. In short order I learned that Hitler was indistinguishable from Rosenberg when it came to fearing pan-Slavism, of which the USSR was the latest variant. Once again history proved the Fuehrer correct. Our officials in the east often complain that there is no Russian word for saying 'this minute.' The closest they come is *seichas*, for 'this hour.' These are the people who had intended to let the Russian winter defeat us, as it had Napoleon. They almost got away with it; but German dynamism prevailed, and our fire melted the ice. They suffered a worse Stalingrad than we had. Hitler had told me personally that the Russians did not deserve as great a leader as Stalin.

There was no point in resurrecting the old debate at this late date. Before he died, I desperately wished to ask him some questions that had been haunting me. I could see that his condition was deteriorating. This would be my last opportunity.

The conversation rambled on a bit, and we again

amused ourselves over how Franklin Delano Roosevelt had plagiarized National Socialism's Twenty-five Points when he issued his own list of economic rights for domestic consumption. Even more astounding was that a member of his class would issue to the world, as part of his 'Four Freedoms' nonsense, a socialist plank for freedom from want. How fortunate for us that when FDR borrowed other of our policies, he fell flat on his face. He didn't understand Keynes as well as we did! War will always be the most effective method for disposing of surplus production, although infinitely more hazardous in a nuclear age. In those blissful days before we lived under the shadow of the mushroom cloud, we counted on numerous battlefield opportunities to use up weapons. FDR understood this as well. No Party member was more surprised than I when a corrupt American plutocrat used our approach to armaments production, quickly outstripping us because of the unlimited resources he could draw on. It was our time of gravest peril, and all because FDR had figured out that the only way a capitalist democracy can achieve full employment is with the timely assistance of a war.

Taking stock of his enemies was a favorite pastime of Adolf Hitler's, and the entry under 'R' had never been closed; in fact, after the death of a foe, he redoubled his acquisition of embarrassing facts. Hitler and Roosevelt had come to power the same year – 1933. They both took their countries off the gold standard that year. They both prepared for a future that would demolish the old certitudes. But let's face it, Adolf Hitler was simply better at the game. As a special treat, I'd brought to the sickroom a clipping from a long-ago February, one month before the American leader took office, when the stodgy business magazine *Barron's* forgot itself and published a piece worthy of me. In fact, I have a copy of it in my desk, and upon returning home, I underlined the passage Hitler liked best: 'Of course we all realize that dictatorships and even semi-dictatorships are quite contrary to the spirit of American institutions and all that. And yet – well, a genial and light-hearted dictator might be a relief from the pompous futility of such a Congress as we have recently had.' Exactly my sentiments when writing about the timid Weimar politicians in the old Reichstag.

Hitler brightened at the clipping. 'Those were the days! I had some grudging respect for Roosevelt at first, but I never dreamed he'd become such a threat to us. Too bad we weren't in a position to put him on trial for his violation of international laws and treaties. Why, he nearly broke as many of them as I did!' We both laughed at that. 'The Lend-Lease Act! The Neutrality Act! One bad joke after another! And the old hypocrite telling his mongrel citizens they wouldn't have to send their boys to die in the war when he was already fighting us at sea.'

'Pearl Harbor was the culmination,' I said, 'his back door to reach us.'

Hitler summed up: 'Roosevelt fell under the influence of the madman Churchill, but that dated back to the correspondence between them when they were naval officials in the Great War, and they pulled their Lusitania stunt! The second time around, Churchill had Roosevelt sinking our ships to prove his neutrality. To that, I say, "Remember the Bismarck!"'

'Fortunately, our greatest enemy in America was impeached,' I said. The last thing we'd needed was a competing empire builder with the resources of the North American continent. I still fondly recalled the afternoon the American Congress was presented with evidence that FDR was a traitor on the Pearl Harbor question. The administration had done about what I would do in their shoes – find a scapegoat. Admiral Kimmel and General

Short were to be crucified, but the ploy backfired when, during the course of the war, Dewey revealed his information that the Japanese purple code had been broken antecedent to the attack; and this information, of more than casual interest to the men in command at Pearl Harbor, was not passed on. The public outcry had been furious. We could not fathom how Americans could be so upset over sacrificing the lives of servicemen to achieve a foreign policy objective (that is why you have a service in the first place), but their sentimentality was FDR's undoing.

'I've never understood why President Dewey didn't follow Roosevelt's lead, *domestically*,' Hitler went on. 'They remained in the war, after all. My God, the man even released Japanese-Americans from those concentration camps and insisted on restitution payments! And this during the worst fighting in the Pacific!'

The propaganda possibilities had not escaped me when FDR signed the order for the 'relocation camps' on February 19, 1942. Here was a man who adopted the pose of Christian self-righteousness when condemning us for doing the same kind of thing. His was the country that had helped forge the chains of Versailles and held us down with immigration barriers and tariffs, then bleated about free trade. Into the greatest plutocracy in the world – of the banks, for the banks, and by the banks – came a rich man's son astride his silver wheelchair, dedicated to socializing America through the means of our destruction. Then everything fell apart for him. Everything. 'The salvation of the Nisei was largely the influence of Vice President Taft,' I reminded Hitler. His remarkable memory had _ pses, but these were rare.

'When this Robert Taft became president,' he said, 'I ceased understanding American foreign policy altogether.

108

And when their two big parties lost so much power that they had to merge into one . . . what was it called?'

'The Bipartisan party was what remained of the coalition between Democrats and Republicans favoring an interventionist foreign policy.'

'Right, the ones who understood the world. After America had a virtual civil war in the fifties, and the two major parties became – I'll remember these – the America First group and the Liberty party, I lost all track of what they were doing over there.'

'There were some self-proclaimed National Socialists in the America First party, but they never amounted to much; and all the elections have been won by the Liberty party, which keeps receiving defections from America First.'

'Ridiculous. I've said again and again that National Socialism is not for export. That eccentric Mosley character in Britain thinks he's me! At least he has the proper racist views.'

'The Liberty party in America condemns all forms of racism. Combine that with their open borders today and – '

'Crazy Americans! They are the most unpredictable people on earth. They pay for their soft hearts with racial pollution.'

We moved into small talk, gossiping about various wives, when that old perceptiveness of the Fuehrer touched me once again. He could tell that I wasn't speaking my mind. 'Joseph, you and I were brothers in Munich,' he said. 'I am on my deathbed. Surely you can't be hesitant to ask *anything*. Let there be no secrets between us. And it's a funny thing about my age, but I find that at my advanced age, events from the early days are clear while more recent developments are foggy. You speak about anything you like. I would talk in my remaining hours.'

And how he could talk. I remember one dinner party for which an invitation was extended to my two eldest daughters, Helga and Hilda. Hitler entertained us with a brilliant monologue on why he hated modern architecture anywhere except factories. He illustrated many of his points about the dehumanizing aspect of industrial-style living compartments with references to the film *Metropolis*. Yet despite her fondness for the cinema, Hilda would not be brought out by his entreaties. I joked that she was mesmerized by the gorgeous chandelier Hitler had recently installed in that dining room, but the social strain was not diminished. Everyone else enjoyed the evening immensely.

On this solemn occasion, I asked if he had believed his last speech of encouragement in the final days of the war when it had seemed certain that we would be annihilated. Despite his words of stern optimism, there was quite literally no way of his knowing that our scientists had at that moment solved the shape-charge problem. Thanks to Otto Hahn and Werner Heisenberg working together, we had developed the atomic bomb first. Different departments had been stupidly fighting over limited supplies of uranium and heavy water. Speer took care of that, and then everything began moving in our direction. After the first plutonium came from a German atomic pile, it was a certain principle that we would win.

I shudder to think what the world might be like if we hadn't won the race. A series of fortuitous developments saved our bacon, from acquiring Norway's heavy water supply to persuading the SS to stay the hell out of it and stop throwing roadblocks in the way of 'Jewish physics.' Then there was the case of Carl von Weizsäcker. The first year of the war was also the year he had shown how stars generate energy by making helium from hydrogen fusion. He was a natural choice to work on the atomic bomb project, but it came out that he was keeping work from the Party and interfering with the morale of his team. Through a fluke, I was personally involved with putting a stop to that; and his work was reintegrated with the rest of the project.

Looking back, I view that period as miraculous. If Speer and I had not convinced the army and air force to cease their rivalry for funds, we never would have developed the V-3 in time to deliver those lovely new bombs. The marriage made in heaven was between the flying bomb and the rocket, and their progeny was larger and faster, with a guidance system worth the name. In the beginning, there had been so many problems with the V-1 that engineers began calling it the *Versager* weapon, for failure. The Party did not approve of humor of that sort, and the men were reminded that V-weapons meant *Vergeltungswaffe* for retaliation and final vengeance. They caught on.

Once the bombs had been used, the military problem of how to turn the chaos back into tactical advantages was handled by Otto Skorzeny and his newly formed Werewolf detachments. What mattered most of all was that we saved industrial production in the Ruhr, without which we might as well have begun learning Russian and English. My job was to downplay the effects of radiation and poison in the blighted areas. Pamphlets did the job pretty well, except for the poor wretches who went blind.

In the small hours of the morning, one cannot help but wonder how things might have been different. We'd been granted one reprieve when the cross-Channel invasion was delayed in 1943. But 1944 was the real turning point of the war. Hitler hesitated to actually use the nuclear devices, deeply fearful of radiation hazards to our side as well as the enemy. If it had not been for the assassination attempt of July 20, he might not have found the resolve to issue the all-important order: destroy Patton and his Third Army before they become operational, before they invade Europe like a cancer. What a glorious time that was for all of us, as well as my own career. (Helping to round up the conspirators and being assigned the highest post of my life was a personal Valhalla.) For the Russians, there were to be many bombs, and many German deaths among them. It was a small price to stop Marxism cold. Even our concentration camps in the east received a final termination order in the form of the by now familiar mushroom clouds.

If the damned Allies had agreed to negotiate, all that misery could have been avoided. Killing was dictated by history. Hitler fulfilled Destiny. He never forgave the West for forcing him into a two-front war, when he, the chosen one, was their best protection against the Slavic hordes.

How he'd wanted the British Empire on our side. How he'd punished them for their folly. A remaining V-3 had delivered the Bomb on London, fulfilling a political prophecy of the Fuehrer's, and incidentally solving the Rudolf Hess problem. He had regretted that; but the premier war criminal of our time, Winston Churchill, had left him no alternative. They started unrestricted bombing of civilians; well, we finished it. Besides, it made up for the failure of Operation Sea Lion. The operation that finally put the British in our hands was dubbed King's Crown.

Just in case the British didn't learn their lesson amidst the fallout and ashes, we augmented their education at the war crimes trials. This was a pretty piece of irony, as the Allies were first to announce their intention of putting on a show trial at the conclusion of hostilities. Of course they waited until Total Victory seemed a certainty before taking the moral high ground. I would have suggested that they had been corrupted by alliance with Stalin and his kangaroo courts, except that the world was not about to forget our exercise in Realpolitik for the 1939 pact. We beat the Allies to that particular association.

The trials provided an invaluable opportunity. All grown-ups knew that Russia, Great Britain, and Germany had played fast and loose with the rhetorical drivel about recognizing the rights of smaller countries. The prime example was that the English encouraged Poland to be intransigent while never intending to come to her defense. Stalin and Hitler obliged by partitioning the upstart country. The trials were a chance to doctor the record. Everything we said about the British and the Russians was more or less true. The fun came with absolving ourselves of guilt, a new spin on the Great Lie. What with our selecting the judges and announcing that the court would not be bound by technical rules of evidence, the outcome was never in doubt. Hitler boasted: 'These trials will be the extension of war by other means.' Peacetime has its compensations.

On the largest scale, the impact came from trying the Russians. We hardly brought up Soviet treatment of our POWs. The political aim was to have decisions of the court reinforce our policies in the east. For example, we were able to prove that the head of the NKVD, Yezhov, killed more people than Himmler (although the direct comparison could not be publicly drawn). Dredging up Stalin's mass murder of seven million Ukrainians and three million others of his countrymen helped divert attention from our own activities, while winning the tacit support of the very people we were returning to the status of serfs, where the Bolsheviks had put them originally! A good day's work. Hitler had enough respect for Stalin that he was pleased the Georgian tyrant had not lived to see trial. Unlike leaders of the West, the Iron Man of Russia was at least a fellow ideologue. This was the grand fellow who had said that the undesirable classes do not liquidate themselves. We envied his slave-labor camp system, the longest stretch of such progressive activity that had ever been constructed, but now unfortunately beyond our reach because the camps were east of the Urals in the area that had fallen outside the warm embrace of civilization.

The most enjoyable aspect of the trials was seeing Winston Churchill in the dock at Nuremberg, a pleasure we would have been denied had he been in London when the bomb dropped. He was a broken man, mumbling that the upper crust had let him down and wishing that he'd been at his lodgings when 'Jerry's banger' went off, as he put it. I was disappointed that he wouldn't give us his famous 'V' sign for posterity. He was never the statesman that Chamberlain was.

Hitler had made it abundantly clear that war would mean the end of the British Empire. Churchill promised his people blood, sweat, and tears . . . and that's what they got. But the Fuehrer had his magnanimous side. Broadcasting to the survivors, he said that as the BBC had had the uncommon decency to pay royalties whenever it used excerpts from *Mein Kampf* during the war, he'd take that into consideration when calculating reparations payments.

My ministry played an important role at the trials, thanks in part to cooperation by Gauleiter Hölz of Nuremberg. What a field day for dirty tricks! For one thing, we would read Russian defendants a document written in Russian, get them to verify its authenticity, and then with sleight of hand, present the court with an altered version in German that the defendants didn't understand.

It was a regular cabaret! One defiant fellow, about to join Churchill on the British execution block (segregation in all things), asked how we could accuse him of crimes against humanity when we had atomized his family; thus he demonstrated a fundamental inability to come to grips with the realities of the modern era. No one whom we executed was taught a lesson. That's old-fashioned, egotistical thinking. The lesson was for the survivors.

Conspiracy theorists continue to believe that perfidious Albion secretly runs the world, and I must admit that far too many members of the British ruling class survived to do business with unidealistic Germans. But when history gave us the opportunity, we struck a blow that will never be forgotten. And the power that made it possible was technology.

Standing in a heated room, where a sick man wiped his forehead with a handkerchief, I listened to Adolf Hitler, the man who had wielded the weapons of superscience, admit: 'I had reached the point where I said we would recover at the last second with a secret weapon of invincible might . . . *without believing it at all!* It was pure rhetoric. I had lost hope long ago. The timing on that last speech could not have been better. Fate *was* on our side.'

So at last I knew. Right doesn't guarantee might. How had Hitler found the courage to fill us all with hope when there was no reason for anything but despair? Could he really foretell the future? It was more congenial for me to conclude that he had bluffed us all again. As he had begun, so did he end: the living embodiment of *will*. There was a kind of energy emanating from those blue eyes of his that held millions of people in thrall. I couldn't help noticing that his bathrobe was the same shade of blue.

It was an honor to have been present at so many historic moments by his side. I remembered his exaltation at the films of nuclear destruction. He hadn't been that excited, I'm told, since he was convinced of the claim for von Braun's rockets at Kummersdorf. At each report of radiation dangers, he had the more feverishly buried himself in the *Führerbunker*, despite assurances by every expert that Berlin was safe from fallout. Never have I known a man more concerned for his health, more worried about the least bit of a sore throat after a grueling harangue of a speech. And the absurd lengths he went to for his diet, limited even by vegetarian standards. Yet his precautions had brought him to this date, to see himself master of all Europe, holding a glass of distilled water with which to drink his toast. Who was in a position to criticize *him*?

He had a way of making me feel like a giant. 'I should have listened to you so much earlier,' he now told me, 'when you called for totalization of war on the home front. I was too soft on Germany's womanhood. Why didn't I listen to you?' Once he complimented a subordinate, he was prone to continue, even referring to so ancient a matter as the work I had done to secure his German citizenship when he was still on the records as an Austrian. Then his sense of humor made a surprise appearance. 'It was an inspiration, the way you pushed that morale-boosting joke: "If you think the war is bad, wait until you see the peace, should we lose."' I remembered how I'd kept American hate propaganda against Germany read on the nightly broadcasts so the people would not consider surrender to enemies willing to exterminate them right down to baby-in-arms. But Hitler was already on to other things, such as my handling of the foreign press during *Kristallnacht*, and finally concluding with his favorite of all my gimmicks: 'Your idea to use the same railway carriage from the shameful surrender of 1918, to receive France's surrender in 1940, was the most splendid moment of the war.' His pleasure was contagious.

'You understand the power of symbols, Joseph. What is true is never as important as what people believe. Consider this: there is no European continent because Asia is part of the same land mass. Old Haushofer had a traitorous swine for a son, but his real child was the geopolitical theory he bequeathed to the Reich. *He drew our map.* I'm not talking about some puny, overintellectualized concept, but a picture that is real because we made it so. Today the Swastika flies from the summit of Mount Elbrus, the highest mountain in the Greater Reich, to the hundreds of fortresses at sea level that protect the Atlantic shoreline. But the soil is no different than if the Allies had won. What has been saved is our blood; and that gives the land its meaning. The last mind to shape this dumb, blind world was Napoleon; but he failed because he was not a German.

'Now consider this: before me, it was a commonplace for European statesmen to downplay figures on armaments production. The game was to keep the enemy in the dark about your strength. Do you remember before the war, when I announced that we had spent ninety thousand million marks on rearmament?' I nodded. 'Did you believe the figure when you were using it in your broadcasts?'

'I didn't give it much thought.'

'It was a lie. Between the time we took power, and up to 1938, we had spent that amount on everything, domestic and military expenditures combined. By March of 1939, the rearmament came to no more than forty thousand million marks. Why did I do this? While the British and the French were busily at work, violating the military requirements of the Versailles Treaty that applied to them, I was pretending that we had an unbeatable military machine when we had no such thing. After Munich, I was convinced we would achieve our aims with no more than a small war here and there. The saner heads in Great Britain followed a similar course in the beginning. I never doubted the Englishman's willingness to fight for Poland . . . right down to the last Pole. I did not believe we could win a full-scale war.'

This came as a considerable shock. Although pleased that he was confiding in me, I was also flustered. 'Then forgive my asking, but how did we survive?'

'Our enemies outnumbered us, and outproduced us, but I was counting on one other thing they had in great quantity: stupidity. At least the Russians had courage; which is more than I can say for Americans.' Back to FDR, always back to him. 'The only battles they won against our brave soldiers were when they outnumbered us two to one!'

'You said they had some good generals.'

'Yes. Patton was a great general, but what could he do with men like that? I respected him sufficiently to award him an iron cross . . . painted on the side of the nuclear bomb that ended his career.'

I was strangely disoriented, in large part because I had thought I could keep track of what was factual and what fanciful in my propaganda. Now I learned that I was mistaken. The personal excesses of Goering had galled me when I was calling for the public to make sacrifices; but to learn that austerity measures had never been what I thought they were was unsettling.

Hitler's head for figures churned out the answer: 'Our slogan was "*Guns before butter*," but I didn't dare implement what the people would never tolerate. At the close of the First World War, when I returned home to see a collapsing army, and society collapsing along with it, I knew that the future belonged to me.

'I had grasped my historic mission as long ago as 1909, when I was starving in Vienna. The war was a godsend, a golden opportunity to test myself. I survived the rigors of the trenches, volunteering for the dangerous duty of a messenger. Twenty thousand men died in one day. It was dirty and horrible and indecent. Even before the armistice, I suspected that we would be stabbed in the back; but I fought on. I had to be a messenger, so that I could climb out of the living grave and face death in the open. I was only alive then. Had Destiny really chosen me to build the future? If so, I would survive. It was in my stars.

'No-man's-land was to be preferred over days condemned to a prison made of vertical walls of stinking mud, with a few soakaways for the rain as a break in the monotony. We lived with rats. Years later, when I sent my enemies to concentration camps, I remembered the zombies of the trenches. Payment was made in full! I remember seeing a few shells shining wetly after a rain, and then my sight was stolen from me; I, the Leader of the future, was blinded by gas. While I suffered the agonies of the damned, I knew that providence would restore my sight.'

It occurred to me that war was Hitler's natural environment, because it offered him the perfect balance between chaos and order. I really didn't like war myself. It was better when enemies didn't put up a fight.

Hitler was breathing deeply, and he paused in his harangue long enough to take a deep draught of water at his bedside, before continuing: 'I tell you all this because I want you to understand that peace was worse.' His voice was rising, and his face was flushed, but I didn't want to call the nurse. 'The Great Inflation made me long for the trenches. What could be more disgusting than to see pure Aryan stock starving in the streets? You remember, I know. Before the war, the mark was trading at 4.2 to the

American dollar. The soldiers returned to a weakened mark, where the figure was several times greater, the "fortunes" of war. Now I ask you, what economist who wasn't dead drunk would dream that by 1923, the mark would be trading at the insane figure of 4.2 billion to the Versailles-stained American dollar? To think we Nazis were told we railed against imaginary enemies!'

'I remember.'

'The people could not be made to suffer more than they had already, not if we wanted their support! We couldn't free them of Jewish capital while their bellies were empty. National Socialism had to work from the start. I had seen the failures of Marxism. They socialized the factories and farms, but the people starved. In Germany, we socialized the people. Then we had *Völk* factories and *Völk* farms, and the people ate, but on our terms! Private ownership is just another symbol, Joseph. Feed the people, then tell them what to do; and eliminate the troublemakers. Speak to them in their thousands, but do so at night, when their bellies are full and their bodies are tired, and they'd rather be making love. You see, I had to fool the other countries about rearmament. The only way was to talk sacrifice but give bread.'

As had happened so many times in the past, his explanation was like a flood of light, illuminating the dark corners of my mind. He was right. He was our beacon. Propping himself up slightly in bed, a gleam of joy in his eyes, he looked like a little boy again. If he had been well, he would have been pacing by then. 'I'll tell you something about my thousand years. Himmler invests it with the mysticism you'd expect. Ever notice how Jews, Muslims, Christians, and our very own pagans have a predilection for millennia? The number works a magic spell on them.'

'Pundits in America observe that also. They say the

number is merely good psychology and point to the longevity of the ancient empires of China, Rome and Egypt for similar numerical records. They say that Germany will never hold out that long.'

'It won't,' said Hitler, matter-of-fact.

'What do you mean?' I asked, suddenly not sure of the direction in which he was moving. I suspected it had to do with the cultural theories, but of his grandest dreams for the future Hitler had always been reticent . . . even with me.

'It will take at least that long,' he said, 'for the New Culture to take root on earth. For the New Europe to be what I have foreseen.'

'If von Braun has his way, we'll be long gone from earth by then. At least he seems to plan passage for many Germans on his spaceships.'

'Germans!' spat out Hitler. 'What do I care about Germans or von Braun's space armada? Let the technical side of Europe spread its power in any direction it chooses. Speer will be *their* god. He is the best of that collection. But let the other side determine the values, man. The values, the spiritual essence. Let them move through the galaxy for all I care, so long as they look homeward to me for the guiding cultural principles. Europe will be the eternal monument to that vision. I speak of a Reich lasting a thousand years? It will take that long to finish the first phase; and then comes something that will last for the rest of eternity.'

The fire was returning. His voice was its old, strong, hypnotic self. His body quivered with the glory of his personal vision, externalized for the whole of mankind to touch, to worship . . . or to fear. I bowed my head in the presence of the greatest man in history.

He fell back for a minute, exhausted, lost in the phantasms behind his occluded eyes. Looking at the weary remains of this once human dynamo, I was sympathetic, almost sentimental, and said: 'Remember when we first met through our anti-Semitic activities? It was an immediate bond between us.'

He chuckled. 'Oh, for the early days of the Party again. At the beginning you thought me too bourgeois.'

He was dying in front of me, but his mind was as alert as ever. 'Few people understand why we singled out the Jew, even with all the Nazi literature available,' I continued.

He took a deep breath. 'I was going to turn all of Europe into a canvas on which I'd paint the future of humanity. The Jew would have been my severest and most obstinate critic.' The Fuehrer always had a gift for the apt metaphor. 'Your propaganda helped keep the populace inflamed. That anger was fuel for the task at hand.'

What more could be said about the Hebrew pestilence? We extracted some pleasure from contemplation of the Irgun, the sad and sorry attempt by Zionists to do a Jewish version of the Brown Shirts (or, some said, the model was Italy's Black Shirts). Whatever the cross-pollination, it was appropriate that the Irgun and the greatest failure of National Socialism should join one another in the void. (It remains a mystery how Ernst Röhm could have been such a *Dummkopf* as to think Hitler would replace the cream of the German army with a bunch of fuck-ups from the *Sturmabteilung*. Never did a man deserve death more than Röhm.)

'The Jews were useful in one regard,' said Hitler. 'They provided us with the means to demonstrate the hypocrisy of the so-called "Free World"! What year was the Evian Conference? It was just on the tip of my tongue.'

'Nineteen thirty-eight.'

'Correct. We couldn't give the precious Jews away at

that conference. The same countries that would later cry crocodile tears never raised a finger to take them.'

We had discussed on previous occasions the fundamental nature of the Judeao-Christian ethic, and how the Christian was a spiritual Semite (as any pope would observe, notwithstanding Alfred Rosenberg's weird Gnostic position, which nobody really understands). The Jew was an easy scapegoat. There was such a fine old tradition behind it. But once the Jew was for all practical purposes removed from Europe, there remained the vast mass of conventional Christians, many Germans among them. Hitler had promised strong measures in confidential statements to high officials of the SS. Martin Bormann had been the most ardent advocate of the *Kirchenkampf*, the campaign against the churches. In the ensuing years of peace and the nuclear stalemate with the United States, little had come of it. I brought up the subject again.

'It will take generations,' he answered. 'The Jew is only the first step. And please remember that Christianity will by no means be the last obstacle, either. Our ultimate enemy is an idea dominant in the United States. Their love of the individual is more dangerous to us than mystical egalitarianism. The decadent idea of complete freedom will be more difficult to handle than all the religions and other imperial governments put together.' He lapsed back into silence, but only for a moment. 'We are the last bastion of true Western civilization. Today's America is one step away from anarchy. They would sacrifice the state to the individual! But Soviet communism – despite an ideology – was little better. Its state was all muscles and no brain. It forbade them to get the optimum use from their best people. Ah, only in the German Empire, and especially here in New Berlin, do we see the ideal at work. The state uses most individuals as the stupid sheep they were meant to be. More important is that the superior individual is allowed to use the state.'

'Like most of the gauleiters?' I asked, again in a puckish mood.

His laugh was loud and healthy. 'Good God,' he said. 'Nothing's perfect . . . except the SS, and the work you did in Berlin.'

I did not have the heart to tell him that I thought he had been proved soundly mistaken on his predictions for the United States. How could this be, when he was right about everything else? With the nuclear stalemate and the end of the war – America having used its atomic bombs in the Orient, and demonstrating to the world a resolve to match ours – the isolationist forces had had a resurgence because of the incredible possibilities for defense represented by ownership of these weapons. In the blink of an eye, it seemed, they had moved the country back to the foreign policy it held before the Spanish–American War. Hitler had predicted grim consequences for that country's economy. The reverse unobligingly came true. This was in part because the new isolationists didn't believe in economic isolation by any means; they freed American corporations to protect their own interests.

The latest reports I had seen demonstrated that the American Republic was thriving, even as our economy was badly suffering from numerous entanglements that go hand in gauntlet with an imperial foreign policy. We had quite simply overextended ourselves. New Berlin, after all, is modeled on the old Rome to which all roads led . . . and like the Roman Empire, we were having trouble financing the operation and keeping the population amused. There are times when I miss our old slogan 'Gold or blood?'

Although as dedicated a National Socialist as ever, I

must admit that America does not have our problems. What it has is an abundance of goods, a willingness to do business in gold (our stockpile of which increased markedly after the war), and paper guarantees that we would not interfere in their hemisphere. Diplomats have to do something. All adults understand that Latin America is fair game, especially the US soft drink companies that put together fierce mercenary armies south of the border.

I preferred contemplation of the home front. There is, of course, no censorship for the upper strata of Nazi Germany. The friends and families of high Reich officialdom can openly read or see anything they can get their hands on. I still have trouble with this modification in our policy. At least I keep cherished memories of 1933, when I personally gave the order to burn the books at the Franz Joseph Platz outside Berlin University. I never enjoyed myself more than in the period when I perfected an acid rhetoric as editor of *Der Angriff*, which more often than not inspired the destruction of writings inimical to our point of view. It was a pleasure putting troublesome editors in the camps. Those days seem far away now in these becalmed days. Many enjoy *All Quiet on the Western Front* without the extra added attraction of rats in the aisles, a little stunt of mine when we didn't want the film undermining morale before the war. I miss the good old days and the rowdy boys who used to work with me. In these timid times, simple intimidation keeps most editors in line.

Hitler would not have minded a hearty exchange on the subject of censorship. He enjoys any topic that relates at some point to the arts. He would have certainly preferred such a discussion to arguing about capitalist policy in America. I didn't pursue either. I am satisfied to leave to these diary pages my conclusion that running an empire is more expensive than having a fat republic, sitting back, and collecting profits. The British used to understand. If they hadn't forgotten, we probably wouldn't be where we are today.

Ironically, Hitler has spent most of his retirement (although he holds the title of supreme leader for life and can overrule the bureaucracy when he chooses) neglecting the areas of his political and military genius and concentrating on his cultural theories. He became a correspondent with the woman who chairs the anthropology department at New Berlin University (no hearth and home for her) and behaved almost as though he were jealous of her job. Lucky for her that he didn't stage a Putsch! Besides, she was a fully accredited Nazi.

I think that Eva took it quite well. *Kinder, Küche, Kirche!*

As I stood in Hitler's sickroom, watching the man to whom I had devoted my life waning before me, I felt an odd ambivalence. On the one hand, I was sorry to see him go. On the other hand, I felt a kind of release. It was as though when he died, I would at last begin my true retirement. The other years of supposed resignation from public duties did not count. Truly, Adolf Hitler had been at the very center of my life.

There were tears in his eyes as he recalled the happiest moment of his life: 'To return to Linz in Austria where I had been nothing as a youth; to walk the streets and possess the power of the Hohenzollern kings, and look into the faces of the people who were entirely mine to do with as I pleased; to return to the Fatherland the treasure of the Hapsburg emperors and place the regalia in its sacred place in Nuremberg, where the symbols of German authority will rest for a thousand years, casting their light upon all judgements pronounced in that place . . . I experienced an ecstasy transcending the human dimension. The reoccupation of the Rhineland, the return of

Danzig, the conquest of France, the conquest of England, even the defeat of Stalin himself, all these were glories, but none to compare with that day.' It was apotheosis! I was complete and made to take my leave.

I wish that he had not made his parting comment. 'Herr Reichspropagandaminister,' he said, and the returned formality made me uncharacteristically adopt a military posture, 'I want to remind you of one thing. Shortly before his death, Goering agreed with me that our greatest coup was the secrecy with which we handled the Jewish policy. The atom bombing of camps was a bonus. Despite the passage of time, I believe this secret should be preserved. There may come a day when no official in the German government knows of it. Only the hierarchy of the SS will preserve the knowledge in their initiatory rites.'

'Our enemies continue to speak of it, *mein Führer*. Certain Jewish organizations throughout the unliberated world continue to mourn the lost millions every year. At least Stalin receives his share of blame.'

'Propaganda is one thing. Proof is another. You know this as well as anyone. I'd like your agreement that the program should remain a secret. As for Stalin's death camps, talk that up forever.'

I was taken aback that he would even speak of it. 'Without question, I agree.' I remembered how we had exploited in our propaganda the Russian massacre of Poles at Katyn. The evidence was solid . . . and there is such a thing as world opinion. I could see his point. At this late date there was little advantage in admitting our vigorous policy for the Jews. The world situation had changed since the war.

Nevertheless, his request seemed peculiar and unnecessary. In the light of later events I cannot help but wonder whether or not Hitler really was psychic. Could he have known of the personal disaster that would soon engulf members of my family?

(NOTE FROM HILDA: I would have been really surprised if Hitler didn't know that most of the finance capital he railed against all his life was controlled then, as it is now, largely by Anglo-Saxon Protestants.)

Chapter Nine

Without the Leader the whole National Socialist movement would be unthinkable.

> – Dr Joseph Goebbels,
> *My Part in Germany's Fight*

The conversation kept running through my mind on the way to the funeral. As we traveled under Speer's Arch of Triumph, I marveled for, I suppose, the hundredth time at his architectural genius. Germany would be paying for this city for the next fifty years, but it was worth it. Besides, we had to do something with all that Russian gold! What is gold, in the end, but a down payment on the future, be it the greatest city in the world or buying products from America?

The procession moved at a snail's pace, and considering the distance we had to cover I felt it might be the middle of the night by the time we arrived at the Great Hall. The day lasted long enough, as it turned out.

The streets were thronged with sobbing people, Hitler's beloved *Völk*. The Swastika flew from every window, and it was evident that many were homemade. When I thought to conceive a poetic image to describe the thousands of fluttering black shapes, all I could think of was a myriad of spiders. *Leave poetry to those more qualified*, I thought – *copywriting is never an ode*.

Finally we were moving down the great avenue between Goering's Palace and the Soldier's Hall. Unbidden, I remembered the day I spent taking Hilda on a tour of the final construction work. Despite her sarcasm, I could tell she was impressed. Who wouldn't be? The endless vertical lines of these towering structures remind me of Speer's ice cathedral lighting effects at Nuremberg. Nothing he has done in concrete has ever matched what he did with pure light.

God, what a lot of white marble! The glare hurts my eyes sometimes. When I think of how we denuded Italy of its marble to accomplish all this, I recognize Il Duce's one invaluable contribution to the Greater Reich.

Everywhere you turn in New Berlin, there are statues of heroes and horses, horses and heroes. And flags, flags, flags. Sometimes I become a little bored with our glorious Third Reich. Perhaps success must lead to excess. But it keeps beer and cheese on the table, as Magda would say. Speer was the architect, and Hitler the inspiration, but I too am an author of what towers about me. I helped to build New Berlin with my ideas as surely as the workmen did with the sweat of their brows and stones from the quarries. And Hitler, dear, sweet Hitler – he ate up inferior little countries and spat out the mortar of this metropolis. Never has a man been more the father of a city. 'We'll make buildings that haven't been seen in four thousand years,' he said before the war; and some wits suggest that the war was solely for the purpose of keeping his promise.

The automobiles had to drive slowly to keep pace with the horses in the lead, pulling the funeral caisson of the Fuehrer. I was thankful when we reached our destination.

It took a while to seat the officialdom. As I was in the lead group, and seated first, I had to wait interminably while everyone else ponderously filed in. The hall holds 150,000. Speer saw to that, complaining every step of the way. I had to sit still and watch what seemed like the whole German nation enter and take seats.

Many spoke ahead of me. After all, when I was finished with the official eulogy, there would be nothing left but to take him down and pop him in the vault. When Norway's grand old man, Vikdun Quisling, rose to say a few words, I was delighted that he only took a minute. Really amazing. He praised Hitler as the destroyer of the Versailles penalties, and that was pretty much it.

The only moment of interest came when a representative of the sovereign nation of Burgundy stood in full SS regalia. A hush fell over the audience. Most Germans have never felt overly secure at the thought of a nation given exclusively to the SS . . . and outside the jurisdiction of German law. I'm not very happy about it myself; but it was one of the wartime promises Hitler made that he kept to the letter. The country was carved out of France (which I'm sure never noticed – all they ever cared about was Paris, anyway).

The SS man spoke of blood and iron. He reminded us that the war had not ended all that long ago, although many Germans would like to forget that and merely wallow in the proceeds from the adventure. This feudalist was also the only speaker at the funeral to raise the old specter of the International Zionist Conspiracy, which I thought was a justifiable piece of nostalgia, considering the moment. As he droned on in a somewhat monotonous voice, I thought about Hitler's comment regarding secret death camps. Of course, there are still Jews in the world, and Jewish organizations across the Atlantic worth reckoning with, and a group trying to reestablish Israel – so far unsuccessfully – and understandably no people would rather see us destroyed. What I think is worth emphasizing is that the Jew is hardly the only enemy of the Nazi.

By the time he was finished, the crowd was seething in that old, pleasing, violent way . . . and I noticed that many of them restrained themselves with good Prussian discipline from cheering and applauding the speaker (not entirely proper at a funeral). We weren't holding an Irish wake! But if they had broken protocol, I would have gladly joined in.

Even eternity must end, and I had my turn standing at the microphone to make my oration. I was surrounded by television cameras. How things have changed since the relatively simple days of radio. I often miss sending out Party exhortations and edicts over the crackling static of the old *Völksempfanger*. The television picture is more intrusive, but paradoxically it is easier to ignore. The spoken word allows the listener to maintain the illusion of independent thought; but an endless stream of pictures tends to deaden the mind, thereby losing the real power of images – their immediacy. One newsreel in a public theater had more impact than ten television reports today.

My ardent supporters were probably disappointed that I did not give a more rousing speech. I was the greatest orator of them all, even better than Hitler (if I may say so). My radio speeches are universally acclaimed as having been the instrumental factor in upholding German morale. I was more than just the minister of propaganda. I was the soul of National Socialism.

Toward the end of the war, I made the greatest speech of my career at the Sportpalast, and this in the face of total disaster. I had no more believed that we could win than Hitler had when he made his final boast about a mysterious secret weapon still later in the darkest of dark hours. My friends were astonished that after such an emotional speech, I could sit back and dispassionately evaluate the effect I had had upon my listeners.

Alas for the nostalgia buffs, there was no fire and fury in my words that day. I was economical of phrase. I listed his most noteworthy achievements; I made an objective statement about his sure and certain place in history; I told the mourners that they were privileged to have lived in the time of this man. That sort of thing.

Finishing on a quiet note, and heeding what he had told me at our last meeting, I said: 'This man was a symbol. He was an inspiration. He took up a sword against the enemies of a noble ideal that had almost vanished. He fought small and mean notions of man's destiny. Adolf Hitler restored the beliefs of our strong ancestors. Adolf Hitler restored the sanctity of our' – and I used the loaded term – 'race.' (I could feel the stirring in the crowd. It works every time.) 'Adolf Hitler is gone. But what he accomplished will never die . . . *if*' – I gave them my best stare – 'you work to make sure that his world is your world.'

I was finished. The last echoes of my voice died, to be replaced by the strains of *Die Walküre* from the Berlin Philharmonic.

On the way to the vault, I found myself thinking about numerous matters, none of them having directly to do with Hitler. I thought of Speer and the space program; I philosophized that Jewry is an *idea*; I reveled in the undying pleasure that England had become the Reich's 'Ireland'; I briefly ran an inventory of my mistresses, my children, my wife; I wondered what it would be like to live in America, with a color television and bomb shelter in every home. (A recent piece in the *New Berlin Review of Books* convinced me that our enemy managed to put out a cheaper color set because they hadn't followed our line of research, vis-à-vis mass-produced microbes and X rays.)

The coffin was deposited in the vault, behind a bullet-proof sheet of glass. His waxen-skinned image would remain there indefinitely, preserved for the future. His last request had been that he be dressed in the military

133

jacket he had sworn not to remove until the war was won. As he had in life, so did he in death forbid smoking in his presence; even more important now that he was combustible. I went home, then blissfully to bed and sleep.

October 1965
Last night, I dreamed that I was eighteen years old again. I remembered a Jewish teacher I had at the time, a pleasant and competent fellow. What I remember best about him was his sardonic sense of humor.

Odd how after all this time I still think about Jews. I have written that they were the inventor of the lie. I used that device to powerful effect in my propaganda. (Hitler claimed to have made this historical 'discovery.')

My so-called retirement keeps me busier than ever. The number of books on which I'm currently engaged is monumental. I shudder to think of all the unfinished works I shall leave behind at my death. The publisher called the other day to tell me that the Goebbels war memoirs are going into their ninth printing. That is certainly gratifying. They sell quite well all over the world. Even enemies pick up phrases from my books, such as the term I used to describe Bolshevik might as 'the iron curtain.' This label is now applied to us! The imagination atrophies under representative government, and they have to steal ideas from me.

My daughter Hilda has wasted her studies to become a chemist. She won't have anything to do with industrial firms, but then she veered towards medical research originally. All that money down the drain!

(NOTE FROM HILDA: When it sunk in just how restricted National Socialist medicine was, I lost interest. Research was slanted toward the homeopathic school because Hitler was convinced that those kind of treatments were keeping him alive.

134

Surely I was the fluke of the Goebbels family, born with a Western outlook; and so my natural pragmatism led me in the direction of allopathic techniques. I just wasn't cut out to be a Nazi.)

Saints preserve us, as my old nursemaid used to say, Hilda wants to be a writer. Yet another person to sit around and play with words while neglecting the world of action. If her letters are any sign, I have no doubt that she might succeed on her own merits. There's the rub. The worst part is that her political views become more dangerous all the time, and I fear she would be in grave trouble by now were it not for her prominent name. The German Freedom League, of which she is a conspicuous member, is composed of sons and daughters of approved families and so enjoys immunity from prosecution. At least they are not rabble-rousers (not that I would mind if they had the correct ideology). We accommodate their iconoclasm for now, but we may be embracing a risk.

It was not too many years after victory before the charter was passed allowing 'freedom of thought' for the elite of our citizenry. I initially opposed the move. It was as if all the incendiary titles I had personally ordered reduced to bland ashes were to be resurrected, as the Phoenix flying home to roost. One title had been given a clean bill of health during the war, however – Einstein's *The Foundations of the General Theory of Relativity*. We had to admit a mistake there. Other books I never expected to see in the possession of Reich citizens (albeit the elite) were works by Tucholsky and Ossietzky, plays by Bertolt Brecht, novels by Thomas Mann and Jaroslav Hasek and Ernest Hemingway. We have a long way to go before achieving genuine socialism. As for the moment, only the masses are protected from cultural decadence.

Hitler was surprisingly indifferent to the measure. After

the war, he was a tired man, willing to leave administration to Party functionaries and the extension of ideology to the SS. He became frankly indolent in his new lifestyle. Censorship is a full-time job! It even wore me out. Anyway, it doesn't seem to matter now. 'Freedom of thought' for the properly indoctrinated Aryan appears harmless enough. So long as he benefits from the privilege of real personal power at a fairly early age, the zealous desire for reform is quickly sublimated into the necessities of intelligent and disciplined management. And we can always rely on the people's sense of taboos, a stronger force than state censorship when you get right down to it.

(NOTE FROM HILDA: It is just a little ludicrous that if Party officials and their families could read and see what they wanted – with myself as the prime example – Father took this as a lessening of censorship. As he wrote the above words, he was involved with trying to suppress, at all social levels, a play that made fun of the Party, and himself in the bargain: a satire by an anonymous author, about which more anon.)

Friday's *New Berlin Post* arrived with my letter in answer to a question frequently raised by the new crop of young Nazis, not the least of whom is my own son, Helmuth, currently under apprenticeship in Burgundy. I love him dearly, but what a bother he is sometimes. What a family! Those six kids were more trouble than the French underground. At least Harald, from Magda's previous marriage, is a placid bureaucrat . . . but I digress.

These youngsters ask why we didn't launch an A-bomb attack on New York City when we had the bomb first. If only they would read more! The explanation is self-evident to anyone acquainted with the facts. Today's youth has grown up surrounded by a phalanx of missiles tipped with H-bomb calling cards. They have no notion

of how close we were to defeat. The Allies had thorough
aerial reconnaissance of Peenemünde. The V-3 was only
finished in the nick of time. As for the rest, the physicists
were not able to provide us with a limitless supply of A-
bombs. There wasn't even time to test one. I explained
how we used all the bombs against the invading armies
except for one that we fired at London, praying that a
sympathetic Valkyrie would help guide it on its course so
that it would come somewhere near the target. The result
was more than we anticipated.

The letter covered all this and also went into considerable detail concerning the technical details prohibiting a
strike on New York. One notion had been to launch a
rocket from the mountains near Traunstein, but it didn't
come off, and new hopes were pinned on a long-range
bomber that had been developed. It was ready within a
month of our turning back the invasion. But there were
no more A-bombs to be deployed at that moment, curse
the luck! After we had suffered the Allied fire storms, it
had become Hitler's obsession to take revenge on New
York and turn its man-made canyons into Dante's
Inferno. He thought the new weapon was his opportunity,
but he had to be reminded by Speer (the usual recipient
of thankless tasks) that the atomic pantry was bare.
Besides, intelligence reported that America's Manhattan
Project was about to bear its fiery fruit. That's when the
negotiations began. We much preferred the Americans
teaching Japan (loyal ally though it had been) a lesson
rather than adding to the radiation and fallout levels on
our shores. We'd had enough of their obliteration bombing already, thank you very much, and had done enough
damage to the countryside with our own V-3s.

The war had reached a true stalemate, our U-boats
against their aircraft carriers; and each side's bombers
against the others. One plan was to deliver an atomic

rocket from a submarine against New York . . . but by then both sides were suing for peace, and the Citadel of Evil was spared. I still believe we made the best policy under the circumstances. We had so many spies in the woodwork, it's a wonder we got off as well as we did.

What would the young critics prefer? Nuclear annihilation? They may not appreciate that we live in an age of détente, but such are the cruel realities. The postwar policy is one of latent crisis. We never intended to subjugate decadent America anyway. Ours was a European vision. Dominating the world is fine, but actually trying to administer the entire planet would be clearly self-defeating. Nobody could be that crazy . . . except for a Bolshevik, perhaps.

Facts have a tendency to show through the haze of even the best propaganda, no matter how effectively the myth would screen off unpleasantries. So it is that my daughter, the idealist of the German Freedom League, is not critical of the Russian policy. Why should it be otherwise? She worries about freedom for citizens and gives the idea of freedom for a serf the same analysis the Russian serf gives it: which is to say, none at all. Here is one of the few areas where I heartily agree with the late Alfred Rosenberg.

(NOTE FROM HILDA: It is typical of my father to blacken my name by assuming the best about me, in his terms. By this point in my life, I'd come to doubt nearly everything I'd been taught about the Russians as a people. Emma Goldman's testimony had persuaded me that the Soviet system was, in essentials, our system wearing a different face. It was Hitler who learned from Lenin; and it was Lenin who said, 'It is nonsense to make any pretense of reconciling the State and liberty.' Father is honest in his diary pages, if nowhere else, and his hopeful comment about my sharing at least one of his prejudices may be taken at face value. Before he took me for the ride in Goering's helium plane for the purpose of threatening me with commitment to an asylum, I'd wised up about what I dared to say to him. When I was a naïve adolescent, I had stupidly thought I might reform Papa!!!!! Maybe I was insane.)

Once again *mein Führer* calls me. I was so certain all that was over. They want me at the official opening of the Hitler Memorial at the museum. His paintings will be there, along with his architectural sketches. (His most accomplished canvas depicts a field in which office buildings, before the Great War, have been stacked sideways as if so much cordwood. The color yellow pervades the picture. I particularly like the sketch he did of the Spear of Longinus, a key item of the Hapsburg imperial treasure. It is the earliest drawing.) They will display his stuffed shepherd dogs and complete collection of Busby Berkeley movies. Ah well, I will have to go.

Before departing, there is time to shower, have some tea, and listen to Beethoven's *Pastorale*.

December 1965

I loathe Christmas. I'm always stuck with doing the shopping! It is not that I mind being with my family, but the rest of it is so commercialized, or else syrupy with contemptible Christian sentiments. Now if they could restore the vigor of the original Roman holiday. Perhaps I should speak to Himmler . . . What am I saying? Never Himmler! Too bad Rosenberg isn't around.

Helga, my eldest daughter, visited us for a week. She is a geneticist, currently working on a paper to show the limitations of our eugenic policies and to demonstrate the possibilities opened up by genetic engineering. All this is over my head. DNA, RNA, microbiology, and *literal* supermen in the end? When Hitler said to let the technical side move in any direction it chooses, he was not saying much. There seems no way to stop it.

There is an old man in the neighborhood who belongs to the Nordic cult, body and soul. He and I spoke last week, all the time watching youngsters ice skating under a startlingly blue afternoon sky. There was an almost fairy-tale-like quality about the scene, as the old fellow told me in no uncertain terms that this science business is so much fertilizer. 'The only great scientist I've ever seen was Hörbiger,' he announced proudly. 'He was more than a scientist. He was of the true blood and held the true historical vision.' All this was said while he poked at me with a rolled up copy of the *Key to World Events* magazine.

I didn't have the heart to tell him that the manner in which Hanns Hörbiger was more than a scientist was in his mysticism. He was useful to us, in his day, as one of Himmler's prophets. But the man's cosmogony was utterly discredited by our scientists. Speer's technical Germany has a low tolerance for hoaxes.

This old man would hear none of it at any rate. He would believe every sacred pronouncement until his tottering frame decayed into a useful commodity. 'When I look up at the moon,' he told me in a confidential whisper, 'I know what I am seeing.' *Green cheese*, I thought to myself, but I was aware of what was coming next.

'You believe that the moon is made of ice?' I asked him.

'It is the truth,' he announced gravely, suddenly affronted as though my tone had given me away. Like all zealots, he was persistent, and before I could make good my escape, he had challenged me on the Articles of Faith – among which I recall such gems as that the Milky Way is a shroud of ice sustained in helium, and not a multitude of stars, no matter what the telescopes show; that sunspots are caused from blocks of ice impacting on the solar surface; and to bring it all home, that ice blocks falling

140

into the atmosphere are the cause of our worst hailstorms. 'Hörbiger proved his theory,' he said with finality.

Hörbiger said it, I thought to myself. So that's all you need for 'proof.' I left the eccentric to his idle speculations on the meaning of the universe, and his final cry of, 'Down with astronomical orthodoxy!' I had to get back to one of my books. It had been languishing in the typewriter far too long.

Frau Goebbels was in a sufficiently charitable mood come Christmas to invite the entire neighborhood over. I felt that I was about to live through another endless procession of representatives of the German nation – all the pomp of a funeral without any fun. The old eccentric was invited as well. I was just as happy that he did not come. Arguing with kooks is not my favorite pastime.

Magda put herself in a Party frame of mind, and there was nothing to be done about it except bite the bullet. My home was occupied by a ragtag folk band. They were off key. Worse, most of the selections were of their own composition, except that the lead song had been suggested by Magda herself and so was politically correct. It was in memory of the six million unemployed of 1932, the year before we took power and set things to rights. My wife throws around numbers with a vigor to match her husband! Symbols and numbers guide us, each and every one. She also coerced me into joining in with the Netherland Hymn of Thanksgiving, a blessedly traditional number, after which the singers stopped howling and started eating.

Speer and his wife dropped by. Who would have thought that an architect could become so effective a minister of armaments, a post he has never relinquished, although much of the work had to be delegated to competent subordinates, leaving him with the freedom to design the dream city of the Reich. His ministry is even more important in peace than it was during the war. This I consider to be an important innovation. Between industrial requirements on the one hand, and concentration camps on the other, National Socialism has no unemployment problem. Nor is the enemy imaginary. Our policies guarantee a steady supply of implacable foes. Eternal vigilance is the price of empire.

Mostly Speer wanted to talk about von Braun and the moon project. Since we had put up the first satellite, the Americans were working around the clock to beat us to Luna and restore their international prestige. As far as I was concerned, propaganda would play the deciding role on world opinion (as always). This was an area in which America had always struck me as deficient because of the absence of one clear position.

I listened politely to his worries, largely of a technical nature, and finally pointed out that the United States wouldn't be in the position it currently held if so many of our rocketry people hadn't defected. 'It seems to be a race between their German scientists and ours,' I said with a hearty chuckle.

Speer was not amused, but replied with surprising coldness that Germany would be better off if we hadn't lost so many Jewish geniuses when Hitler came to power. 'It was as if we cut away a lobe of the nation's brain,' he said. To my horror, he launched into a tirade, in my home, about how Hitler's policy for Italy had driven away those Jewish physicists who were at the cutting edge of developing an atomic bomb in the late 1930s, thereby losing us an atomic monopoly. After uttering an oath against the SS (and glancing over his shoulder, I noticed), he began dropping forbidden names in mixed company: Fermi, Segré, Rossi, and Pontecorvo. Was it up to me to remind Speer of Party discipline? The line was that Italians were anti-Semitic by nature, the same as the

French. All we did was to help them live up to their potential. I remembered that Hitler once told me the best way he handled the Reich's organizational genius was to bang his fist on the table and boom, 'Speer, don't you realize that . . .' followed by whatever was useful at the moment. But I wasn't the Fuehrer.

When I swallowed hard on my brandy, he must have seen the consternation on my face, because he was immediately trying to smooth things over. He is no idealist, but one hell of an expert in his field. I look upon him as a well-kept piece of machinery. I hope no harm ever comes to it, no matter how the tongue may wag. (And he will always have high marks in my book for turning down the honorary rank of SS Oberstgruppen-fuehrer. Anything to offend Himmler!)

Speer always seems to have up-to-date information on all sorts of interesting subjects. He had just learned that an investigation of many years had been dropped with regard to a missing German geneticist, Richard Dietrich. Since this reputedly brilliant scientist had vanished only a few years after the conclusion of the war, the authorities supposed he had either defected to the Americans in secret or been kidnapped. After two decades of fruitless inquiry, a department decides to cut off funds for the search. I'll wager that a few detectives had been making a lucrative career out of the job. Too bad for them.

Magda and I spent part of the holidays returning to my birthplace on the Rhineland. It's good to see the old homestead from time to time. I'm happy it hasn't been turned into a damned shrine, as happened with Hitler's childhood home. Looking at reminders of the past in a dry, flaky snowfall – brittle, yet seemingly endless, much as time itself – I couldn't help but wonder what the future holds. Space travel. Genetic engineering. Ah, I am an old man. I feel it in my bones.

Chapter Ten

But the state tells lies in all the tongues of good and
evil; and whatever it says it lies – and whatever it has
it has stolen. Everything about it is false; it bites
with stolen teeth, and bites easily.

– Friedrich Nietzsche,
Thus Spoke Zarathustra

March 1966

What kind of retirement is this, anyway? I'm on another
publicity junket. Go east, young man; go east. The son of
Otto Saur will meet me at the monument-on-treads, as
we call it, that stands against the remaining Slavic menace.
At the height of his surrealist period, Hitler ordered the
construction of a supertank. Poor Speer had only just
convinced the Fuehrer that a proposed 180-ton tank was
impractical because six Tiger tanks could be manufactured
for the same expenditure. I'd love to have seen Speer's
face when Hitler and Saur presented the supertank proposal: a 1,500-ton monster, armed with mortars having an
80-centimeter caliber, not to mention a couple of long-
barreled cannon; and to run the thing, an estimated
10,000-horsepower motor.

This mad dream was in 1943, the same year that Hitler
finally gave full support to the rocket program and other
state-of-the-art technology. I suspect that someone had
been feeding him on H. G. Wells again. After all,
Churchill was reputed to have originated the concept of
the tank; but Wells had written about it many years
earlier in a story entitled 'The Land Ironclads.' The

Fuehrer's logic was that if Wells predicted the first tank, and was proven right, then perhaps his predictions of supertanks would come true as well. Only this time, Hitler insisted, Germany would win the race. (When he was a journalist during the Great War, Wells had predicted that future tanks would weigh thousands of tons, running on caterpillar tracks that would permanently damage the soil.) Speer used his considerable powers of persuasion to veto the project, and he threw around budgets and timetables until the matter was shelved.

So the behemoth was not on the schedule for 1944. Instead, the monster was built in 1948, at the tail end of what some have called World War II and a half. We were going solo with the Russians, pushing deeper into their territory, astounded that Marxists kept popping up when we had expected a purely ethnic foe by then. Resource management was at an all-time high, and my propaganda hammered away at the theme. Conservation was so important that we were building *Monte Klamotten* in all our bombed cities, mountains formed of the debris. Waste not, want not. Yet while Germany was discovering new dimensions of frugality, Hitler built his supertank. It was transported in sections by train, and by the time it was assembled, the eastern battlefield in which it was to be deployed had been pacified. So there it stood, and stands, and will probably rust . . . unless we spend the outrageous sum necessary to bring it home for a war museum.

Magda seems pleased that I am leaving. I'll lay odds she has a tryst planned with Karl Hanke, the gauleiter of Silesia. I should complain? She's had the same boring affair for years and years, while I have sown my seed far and wide. Her peccadillo keeps her satisfied and out of my hair when the restless spirit moves me. If it had not been for Hitler forbidding it, we probably would have divorced; but now we are used to each other. She is a

145

most presentable wife and mother; while passion does not interfere with duty.

The children take after their mother when it comes to sex, all except Hilda that is. My stunning, redheaded daughter has my blood and a roving eye. When I saw her dressed in her first evening gown, and her bare shoulder was white against black velvet, I remember thinking at the time . . . no, that will be enough of that.

I go to see the iron leviathan.

Picking up where I left off, with the tank, Commissioner Koch and I contrived a number of photo opportunities. Actually, the monster is good for propaganda. Rumor has it that not even partisans wish to see it destroyed. The thing has never been used in battle, and it is something to show one's children.

Koch and I trust each other because of a number of past considerations. We spoke frankly about the Rosenberg affair. Officially, when Alfred (Koch prefers to use the informal 'Du' when speaking of fellow officials) was at the summit of his power as commissioner for the entire East European regions, he was assassinated by a Marxist revolutionary group. Everybody in the know draws the conclusion that Heinrich did his rival in, and that the reason had unsurprisingly to do with Burgundy. The incidental beneficiary was Koch, who was promoted from gauleiter for the Ukraine to Rosenberg's successor. Koch's record was first rate. He had made invaluable contributions in neutralizing trouble emanating from the North Caucusus and Volga Tartar areas; and he was gifted at handling our fool of a foreign minister, Ribbentrop.

'Over Christmas, Speer was telling me how Rosenberg helped smuggle Ukrainian quartz past the Ministry of Armaments to the SS, and in the middle of the war yet!' I said.

'Himmler isn't famous for gratitude,' was Koch's wry understatement. 'He's a hypocrite, too. I was shocked when I learned he was using several thousand Jews as slave labor in his SS factories when they were slated for termination. He said one thing in his Posen speech and then faltered in execution.'

We had returned to his office, and I was fingering the bishop of his ivory chess set. How much did our lives resemble those pieces restricted to sixty-four squares. Maneuver and outmaneuver; and one serious mistake took you off the board. Himmler was a serious rival. 'He's even worse when it comes to matters of faith,' I said with feeling. 'Rosenberg found that out the hard way. You're certainly right about his hypocrisy. It burns me up the way Himmler controls the best quartz mining in your area, uses his monopoly to stick his nose in the technological progress of the Reich, and then plows the profits into Burgundy where they sit around on their fat asses and bemoan modern life.'

'They've got the tourist trade, so what do they care? Heinrich is a rich man. He gets more than his fair share of manganese, lead, zinc, coal – '

'Stop, stop. It makes me sick just thinking about it.'

'That's the SS for you.' As soon as he said it, we glanced around. It's habit forming.

'Well, they provided me with excellent bodyguards during the war,' I said.

'They are the best bodyguards for sure,' he agreed. Order was restored.

Koch kept my tour brief. I owe him one. (Next winter I'm putting my foot down. Magda and I will vacation in Vienna, where Wagner so often took his ease.) An unusual sight he saved for last, the corpse of a Waffen soldier who had suffered a peculiar mutilation. Branded across the width of the man's considerable chest was a huge Swastika that had been altered to include a hammer at one point and a sickle at another. Koch was visibly bothered.

'Not all our difficulties are with Bolsheviks. They continually reduce their numbers by trying each other as Trotskyists, you know. The ethnic and nationalist identities reassert themselves and are the real problem.'

'They could be National Socialists in their own right,' I said with a smile, but Koch's face clouded over. Not everyone appreciates my sense of humor. Time to change the subject. 'Uh, who leaves this gruesome signature on our stalwart lads?'

The commissioner was a policeman at heart. 'We chased down several false leads. Our first surmise was a Baltic outfit that hates both socialisms; and I can't begin to calculate how many Ukrainians escaped east, cursing Bolsheviks and Nazis with equal passion. Now we are convinced it's a band of renegade Germans.'

'What!'

'The Wild East is to blame. Once a German has tasted freedom, watch out. A number of missing persons sneak across the border regularly, and they've all taken the name Schmidt. They're reported to have a leader named Neil, but as they're obviously a gang of deranged anarchists, that's probably untrue.'

'Have you caught any?'

'Yes, but they blow up.'

'Oh.'

The responsibilities of authority weigh heavily on all of us. That's why I would make one last stop, when I wished to head straight home instead.

I have seen the *Europa*. The captain graciously altered course to take me part of the way home. Too bad neither Roosevelt nor Churchill lived to see Hitler's poetic answer to their all too long mastery of the sea. The world's largest vessel of war is 2.5 kilometers in length, and everything but its atomic motor, engine room, bridge, and crew's quarters is made of ice. I understand that an American Admiral Heinlein wondered 'how an ice cube over a mile long will stay in one piece.' Funny. Those were my sentiments as well when I first heard about it. But as *mein Führer* so often said, where there is a *will*, there is a way.

Like the supertank, the supership was built in sections. The most important ingredient was sawdust added to the water in the molds. The ice blocks were rendered more stable in this fashion. Although its use is primarily restricted to the North Atlantic, water loss in warmer climates is minimal because of the impurities in the ice and the absurd size of a vessel that would have been christened the *Hörbiger* if there was any justice. Goering used his influence to have the greatest battleship of all time named the *Europa* and donated an excellent reproduction of the painting by the same name, a startling nude that was one of the prizes of his art collection. It's a wonder she doesn't catch cold.

Of course, it's warm enough where she is. But I caught a chill on deck that I'm certain will get worse. I hate northern climates. I was not meant to be a Viking! The captain was a tough old sea dog who probably never had a sick day in his life. He also had the virtues we cultivate in National Socialist man, with as firm a grasp of geopolitical theory as the latitude and longitude on his nautical charts. Every man should have a dream. His was the conquest of Canada. He was especially taken by the vision of the uranium and nickel such an enterprise would add to the Reich. He'd even worked out a tentative plan that involved landing in the Maritimes and sending the men up the St Lawrence River valley. As much as I hate to burst a good man's balloon, I reminded him of the nuclear realities, and how North America might talk a lot about peace and neutrality in foreign policy, but they did so under their nuclear hat with a brim wide enough to accommodate friends to the north. Splitting the atom has done more to dampen the high spirits of fighting men than anything else in memory.

It was beautiful on the *Europa*. I remember smart uniforms, black against the white expanse of the ship. Even our enemies must admit that we have the best uniforms. There was a bronze sunset right out of the *Eddas*. This quite remarkable ship has never been in a battle, another similarity to its spiritual cousin, the super-tank. Deterrence is better than war; and awe is a deterrent.

I shall open a medium's parlor. I predicted a cold, and now I have one. These words are being written with a pencil on a pad as I lie flat on my back. If I choke in my own fluids, let my last will and testament show that I am of sound mind and leave everything to neofascist movements abroad. We are the wave of the future, and every country that tries freedom will sooner or later learn its lesson. Even in lunatic America there are voices grown weary of the irrational life that denies the need for order. These voices call for 'getting tough' and 'cracking down' and 'ending permissiveness.' The irony is that some who upheld 'law and order' in the old United States also opposed the inevitable steps the country took toward socialism. When will they learn that 'law and order' and socialism are corollaries? Capitalism is the enemy of both.

The subject is on my mind because as I am stuck in bed, I've had the chance to catch up on correspondence. A number of letters from the states were waiting for me. The very freedom touted in America provides a chance for subversion that we dare not ignore. So far, we haven't made a dent, but we will keep trying.

When the Roosevelt administration ignored the Bill of Rights and launched its sedition trials, they were acting as realists. Now the Bill is used as a hammer to prevent a powerful executive from taking care of its enemies. Hitler said they had become more helpless than Weimar was at its worst. Still, a number of names came to my attention when John Rogge went after his list of fifth columnists. Alas, the ones who were genuinely sympathetic to us were hopeless boobs we couldn't use; and the able ones were staunch nationalists we couldn't turn to our purposes, although some did have fascistic ideas but of the home-grown variety. One such individual who interested me was Lawrence Dennis, who was later to run for president on the America First ticket, but who lost to a libertarian in that wild and woolly country.

Dennis would never respond to my letters. I wonder if George Viereck had still been in business if he might have made a difference. No matter. Dennis had done such an excellent job of indicting old-style American imperialism that I happily used his material. You can't copyright history, and we use anything we want from other countries without paying royalties anyway. There are reasons to be a socialist. The main sticking point with my anti-American propaganda used to be that we did all the same things. Today, there is even less reason to rail against American imperialism because they have given it up. Well, I never let details get in the way of a good campaign.

As soon as I recover, I will get to work on my hundredth anti-American program. This one won't require any lies, only a selective use of facts. The notion that only dictatorships start wars is so pervasive that even now we have trouble with it. And I can't write any more with this pencil.

* * *

I can breathe again. To work, to work!

Although the list Dennis compiled is common knowledge in his country, I like to give him credit. *Signal* magazine will carry a cover story on the wars in which peace-loving America has found itself embroiled. If it is so peace loving, how did it get in so many? It angers me that they got out of the Big War without their continent receiving so much as a scratch, just as they had in the previous world cataclysm.

Here is the Dennis list, from his international best-seller *The Dynamics of War and Revolution*, although maybe the first entry shouldn't be included, as it was their revolution. I have no problem including their domestic quarrels, however, as once the revolution was won, it was time to live the peace-loving stereotype they've been shoving down the throats of Europe ever since. And their Civil War led to what our historians refer to gaggingly as the Prussianization of America. Something else I like about the list is that a mere ceasefire does not indicate the end of hostilities when other military-political factors are taken into account.

War of the Revolution	1775 to 1784
Wyoming Valley Disturbances and Shays's Rebellion	1782 to 1787
Northwest Indian Wars and Whiskey Insurrection	1790 to 1795
War with France	1789 to 1800
War with Tripoli	1801 to 1805
Northwest Indian Wars	1811 to 1813
War with Great Britain	1812 to 1815
War with Algiers	1815
Seminole Indian Wars	1817 to 1818
Yellowstone Expedition	1819
Blackfeet Indian Wars	1823
LeFevre Indian War	1827
Sac and Fox War	1831
Black Hawk War	1832

Nullification Troubles in South Caribbean	1832 to 1833
Cherokee and Pawnee Disturbances	1833 to 1839
Seminole Indian War	1835 to 1842
War with Mexico	1846 to 1848
Indian Wars (Sioux, Comanche, Navaho, etc.)	1848 to 1861
Civil War	1861 to 1866
Indian Wars	1865 to 1890
Sioux Indian War	1890 to 1891
Apache and Bannock Indian Troubles	1892 to 1896
Spanish–American War	1898 to 1899
Philippine Insurrection	1899 to 1903
Boxer Expedition	1900 to 1901
Cuban Pacification	1906 to 1909
First Nicaragua Expedition	1912 to 1925
Vera Cruz Expedition	1914
First Haiti Expedition	1915
Punitive Expedition into Mexico	1916 to 1917
Dominican Expedition	1916
The World War	1917 to 1921
Second Haiti Expedition	1919 to 1920
Second Nicaragua Expedition	1926 to 1932

All this before they entered the Big One, for a second crack at us. No doubt their previous warfare was done to extend democracy and make the world safe for large investors everywhere. Of course, if *Signal* ran a chart like this about the Fatherland I'd have the editor's head. The issue is not war, or the grievances on either side. The issue is propaganda. I wish I had seen this data before Hitler died. I would have asked him if he had been familiar with it when he spoke of America's military unpreparedness and lack of martial will. Was he being disingenuous or did he really believe what he said? Apparently America has been the first warrior nation in history unwilling to admit what it is. And now it has finally given up direct warfare, settling instead for economic weapons when it wants something. But that means its actions are finally in line with its propaganda! All this is giving me a headache.

I'm sufficiently recovered to return to the office. First, I must attend to a matter that irritates the hell out of me. Young hoodlums have been spray painting the Star of David on the walls of my ministry. They probably think this vandalism very funny, but I'm not laughing. What's more, it's a sure bet that they are Aryan teenagers. When actual Jewish subversion takes place, it is always serious; not childish pranks.

The press is very good about handling sordid details of this kind. We have the most responsible reporters in the world. They follow orders. Any publicity would only encourage similar vandalism, so as the walls are wiped clean so are the memories of anyone in the vicinity.

Speer's comments about the Jews haunt me. How can someone as intelligent as he is continue to miss the point of our anti-Semitic policy? Destroying their power in Europe does not mean smooth sailing henceforth. Every step we take in the Middle East runs afoul of their schemes. Although we have some small Arab nations allied with us (and a few even attempting a modified National Socialism of their own, but not making a lot of progress because of religious objections inherent in Islam), the majority of Arabs don't like us. Hitler worked out a brilliant strategy for playing Arab factions against one another, when the Jewish wild card came into the picture.

A dozen of our soldiers were recently killed by an operation handled by Jews and Arabs working together! This is intolerable. Although publicly I have to defend our policy in all things, I feel that we have never taken a right step when it comes to the Middle East. One would think that between our synthetic fuels on the one hand,

and nuclear power on the other, we wouldn't need Arab oil in the first place. Let the region dry up and blow away! The curse of an industrial empire is that its appetite for energy is insatiable. We need everything, and then some.

Part of the Middle Eastern problem we brought on ourselves back in the 1930s, when we hadn't decided on a final solution to the Jewish problem and were floundering around with one hair-brained scheme after another. Nothing came of the Madagascar Plan, but we actually went through with the initial phase of the Palestine Plan. Very few citizens of the Reich are aware that we moved sixty thousand Jews and a sizable sum of money to Palestine, if the Zionists would provide a market for goods when the rest of the world was threatening us with a stringent boycott because of our Jewish policy! I didn't think it would work; our being in bed, so to speak, with Jewish Palestine. Today we spill German blood into the desert sands whenever the fruit of earlier policies chokes us. An industrial application of murder proved a far more expeditious approach. Go east, young man . . .

One lesson is clear as Hitler's moustache: the Third Reich was the only political force in the world that could drive Jews and Arabs into an alliance. Everybody hates us.

Chapter Eleven

The magnificent possibilities of the school as an
instrument of propaganda had been perceived very early;
Alexander Hamilton, who never missed the boat on a chance
of this kind, expounded them in 1800 . . . When the Church
became weak and the centralized, nationalist-imperialist
State grew strong, the State began to do its own dirty
work; and with the schools, press, cinema and radio under
its control, this work is now child's play.

> – Albert Jay Nock,
> *The Memoirs of a Superfluous Man*

Who knows in this crazy world?

> – Bela Lugosi as a Nazi plastic surgeon in
> *Black Dragons* (Monogram, 1942)

It was good to spend an entire day at the old office in the
Wilhelmplatz. Work keeps me fit. No more colds this
year! Restoration work on this fine, white palace goes on
steadily, and I don't even want to know which wall was
defaced. I have kept the office in its original condition,
mindful that they sell postcards in the kiosk out front
showing this most public of my inner sanctums, with its
marble writing desk next to the huge globe of the world;
and both overseen by a colorful portrait of Frederick the
Great, who seems to glare at a recent addition to the
desk: a terminal hooked up to the latest state-of-the-art
liquid-helium-cooled analog computer.

The Propaganda Ministry extends throughout the city,
and its departments have multiplied since the days I
managed press, film, radio, propaganda, and theater from

this one office. Television is a separate division. It receives the most direct control over content. We don't worry all that much about looser standards applied to the other media. The common sense of the *Völk* insures that dangerous ideas will not go unpunished. I think my primary task is to reinforce the people's habits – a reason to keep up the *Der Juden Verboten* signs in areas that have not seen a Jew in years. Elections serve the same purpose. Once the Party has selected its candidates, it is crucial to get out the vote.

Fresh flowers had been placed in the vase standing on my heavy walnut bookcase, and their petals were a vivid purple in the early morning sunlight. Feeling a decade younger, I was eager to write. Two editorials had been waiting for completion while I galavanted about the continent. Later in the day I was to have a visitor, so the Op Ed pieces had to be disposed of quickly. Here the word processor is a real help, although I refuse to use it for personal writing, or when I prepare a speech. (If I didn't use different-color inks for my speeches, setting off key words and phrases for emphasis, I wouldn't be able to rehearse properly.)

Sitting at the terminal, I finished off the vital plea for a tougher policy on the 'pirates,' my term for faceless cowards who use bombs against defenseless citizens of the Reich. Some of these vermin can be traced back to the Resistance, but the rest are young guerrillas, gifted in the arts of terror and largely financed with gold from hither and yon. Of late there has been a rash of bombs aboard passenger aircraft (shades of the Hindenburg). My suggestion for how to stop the problem is taken from America, whence many of the pirates originate. There private airlines employ stricter security measures than we do – right down to body searches. The customers voluntarily accept the inconvenience because they are paying for safety. Now if we can only persuade our prudish citizens to disrobe! Not even Leni Riefenstahl's films, reveling in naked young bodies, have made a dent in the taciturn German character. Today's Americans are more playful, and more casual about nudity, the lucky bastards.

More pleasurable was dashing off a piece on the admirable Otto Skorzeny. He has said that nothing but death will persuade him to retire. A recent close shave suggests that a real hero will be among us for some time to come. The information has been declassified, and I was the first to describe how Skorzeny landed a new kind of jet fighter in a dead-stick glide when it would have been safer for him, once the engine failed, to jettison the external fuel tanks. He was over New Berlin at the time and refused to put civilians at risk. What a pilot! I concluded the paean by reminding my loyal readers that Otto is the same daredevil today that he was back in the war, when he used a glider to rescue Mussolini from the supposedly impregnable fortress in which the Allies had imprisoned Il Duce. I kick myself because the first popular movie to depict that aerial feat was American, for God's sake; and they showed their own soldiers using Otto's method for an imaginary mission against Germans!!! What nerve.

With the writing out of the way, I was ready to greet my young guest, who appeared promptly at noon: a new movie director named Stefan Schellenberg. He has made a big splash with his movie *Pflichterfullung im Lichte des Heiligen Gral* (Fulfillment of Duty in the Light of the Holy Grail). The picture had taken in so much at the box office that he was planning a sequel with the same hero, the irrepressible Professor von Moltke (named after the World War I army chief who spent much of his free time on the Grail mystery). As preparations for the remake of Riefenstahl's *Triumph des Willens* (Triumph of the Will)

158

were nearly completed, all that was needed was the director, and I believed this man to be the one.

No sooner was the Holy Grail movie in release than I received a stormy letter from Himmler. It seems that arcane secrets of the Ahnenerbe, the SS occult bureau, had been splashed across the movie screens of Europe – and worse, that the Grail movie was becoming an international hit. This latter development surprised even me. The picture was being touted in America as a nonpolitical entertainment. They have to say that in Britain, but America??? After five viewings, and reading a cross-section of reviews, I had been forced to revise one of my theories of propaganda. Naturally, I sent for the cinema wunderkind who was responsible for the turmoil.

As for Himmler's nonsense, I am utterly fed up with the occult. When Hitler brought the Spear of Longinus to Nuremberg, along with the other Hapsburg treasures, our mystics went off the deep end. The debate between Rosenberg and Himmler flared to new heights in the Thule group. An adherent of Wagner's theory of the Aryan Christ, Rosenberg saw the Grail in a Gnostic light, and the spear that pierced the side of Christ as a totem for those of the pure blood, the same as the holy chalice would be. Himmler was of the old school. As a hard-nosed pagan, he believed the Grail legend to have been perverted by the Semitic superstition of Christianity; and that the spear wielded by the Germanic Longinus had a different significance, albeit possessing magical power for those of the pure blood still seeking the legendary Book of the Aryans or the Aryan Stone. This endless bickering over fantasy was serious business in Burgundy, but it must not be allowed to interfere with decisions of the Greater Reich. Stefan's film had been viewed as harmless, and even constructive, by some true believers; but what counted with me was that the certificate had been issued by inhabitants of the planet Earth.

Stefan was not overly articulate and I wondered if the most effective passages in his work were less a result of conscious design than a byproduct of his *Kultur*. Was this young man the end product of our state indoctrination in the classroom and cinema? He seemed unconcerned with my criticisms of inconsistencies and holes in the plot you could run a panzer division through. At first I mistakenly thought his behavior in my presence showed his mettle, but that wasn't it. His lack of fear was less a result of courage than an inability to face reality.

As my students are taught every day, the objective of propaganda is to repeat a message so often, and in such a variety of guises, that it becomes part and parcel of the common wisdom. Every prejudice of the people can be turned to the advantage of the Party, and a feeling of virtuousness is to be preferred over an honest conviction. The leitmotif of effective propaganda is to strip the enemy of humanity, so that the mere sight of his face, his accent, his symbols, will inspire immediate loathing. Love of country has limitations, but hatred of the enemy is sublime and forever.

The Grail movie employed the techniques of emotional engineering with sufficient aplomb to merit qualified praise from my ministry, and an invitation extended to its director. As per my request, he had brought a copy of the script so that I could go through it with him, pointing to the parts that worked, and the lapses as well.

First, we have the hero, a man who is an intellectual when teaching archaeology at New Berlin University. The rest of the year, he dons workingman's clothes and goes adventuring in the wilds on the lookout for archeological finds. While having these adventures, he suddenly becomes the ideal of the Workingman, a beer hall brawler able to hold his own with the best of them. The obliteration of class lines is especially to be commended. The fight scenes are carefully staged to maximize visceral responses from the audience at the same time that they overwhelm objections by the sheer speed with which everything transpires.

Stereotypes absolutely dominate the film. The setting is before the war, but after we have taken power. Our hero is looking for the Grail – the Aryan Stone in this story – reputed to be somewhere in Iceland. A troop of British soldiers has been dispatched to the same area by the king of England. The monarch hopes that by obtaining this stone, he will be invincible in war. The soldiers represent such a collection of dunderheads that they never manage to kill even one of the hero's sidekicks, much less impede his progress. They are mainly good at killing each other off through clumsiness. Another incredible touch is that although most of these soldiers would be recruited from the working class, Schellenberg has all of them speaking with upper-class accents. The audience hates them from the word go.

Whenever characters from different ethnic groups aid the hero, they are portrayed in a positive, proletarian light. When these same types aid the British, they become racial caricatures that appeal to every deep-seated feeling of disgust. So far, so good. But here the problem begins.

I pointed out to my young guest that films by Leni and myself handled matters with more finesse than was to be found in his work. For other examples of better filmmakers, I referred to three directors who work in Hollywood: Alfred Hitchcock, Orson Welles, and the traitor Fritz Lang. (I'll never forgive myself for letting Lang escape Germany with the first sound Mabuse film under his arm. To think he turned down my generous offer of the top job in the industry!) An adult thriller, I told Stefan, achieves its effect through a close study of human moods and a cumulative buildup of sinister detail. The Grail picture completely obliterates anything resembling human character. I was in the middle of complaining about his abdication of directorial control through cheap manipulations (as mummies are discovered in the Temple of Thor, a scream is dubbed on the soundtrack to cue the audience to yelp) when I noticed that he was sucking on a lollipop that he must have brought with him. I suddenly needed a drink.

Hoping that a compliment might facilitate communication, I praised the portrayal of the Jewish villain in the picture – as sadistic a torturer as the imagination can conceive, yet he never so much as musses the hair on the heroine's head. The plot won't allow him even temporary satisfactions. (If it had been a film submitted to me, as they all used to be excepting Leni's work, I'd have had the villain do one or two nasty things before the hero thwarts his schemes.)

Come to think of it, just why was this film such a success? If the hero is being chased by the British, the terrain magically alters so that his pursuers will drive off a cliff, even though we were in flat country a moment before. Should the good Herr Doktor Moltke hold on to the outside of an airplane – where the air pressure would sweep him off – the audience cannot be bothered with unfulfilled expectations. Hold on he does, for hours.

The climax is either too clever or too stupid for me to appreciate. A glowing figure rises from the magic stone. Is it the Spirit of Arya or the Gnostic Christ of Manichaeanism? 'SS,' as we call Stefan around the ministry, doesn't say. He at least has the sense to avoid that quarrel. It suffices that the supernatural visitation disintegrates the remaining British (traitors to their race) while the German hero and heroine not only emerge unscathed, but are even released of their bonds. (Once again, if it had been my story, I'd have had them escape under their own steam.)

Asking 'SS' if he didn't see the hidden agenda of his film only resulted in another blank stare and his crunching on the remains of his candy. He is not the only one who didn't see it. Were the hero an independent, egotistical type (suggested by the performance), he would keep the Aryan Stone hidden for his own uses; or, to simplify his life, he would bury it deep in the ground and deny having found it. At the beginning of the story, he denies the supernatural, but he can no longer hold to such comforting beliefs. He does the patriotic thing and turns the stone over to the Fuehrer. Was this a sly calculation on Schellenberg's part to avoid trouble with a certificate, in which case he must not be quite the dolt I see in my office? If 'SS' is implying that we won the war for reasons other than Hitler's military genius, then it is a harmless enough conceit in this childlike context. Nobody in the audience is thinking by the time the end credits roll.

When I had finished my analysis, 'SS' was completely unmoved. Curiously, he wanted to know if I believed in the Holy Grail, with a special emphasis placed on the Spear of Longinus (an item that doesn't appear in his movie). Dismissing his question with a scornful laugh, I moved the conversation back to business. Was this man to walk in Riefenstahl's footsteps or not?

Showing him that part of my private film collection kept at Wilhelmplatz, I offered to screen my favorite anti-Nazi picture, Hitchcock's *Foreign Correspondent*. Schellenberg had the right content, but he needed to work on technique. He declined my offer! 'You haven't mastered the tricks of plotting,' I told him. 'Your story doesn't show the villainy of Moltke's adversaries.'

At last he showed passion about his work: 'They're bad

163

guys. The audience knows who they are. I don't have to prove anything.'

His uncertainty unnerved me. It might even presage a shift in ministry policy. The crudest race-hate propaganda we had churned out in the old days, such as *The Eternal Jew*, had sought to win over opinion. One last time, I tried to make the case for subtlety. Back in 1941, I had had a brainstorm about one of our British internees we had taken when advancing into Belgium the year before: the famous P. G. Wodehouse. Now there was a nonpolitical entertainer. His quaint, Edwardian view of the world provided me with an opportunity to apply the theory of context management.

Other hard workers in the ministry wondered if I had gone off my head when I had Wodehouse moved to the Aldon Hotel in Berlin, where I offered him the opportunity to do uncensored broadcasts. I knew my man. His commentary was the same lightly humorous material it always was, including a good-natured jesting at the foibles of the powerful, and a jovial uncertainty about the outcome of the war. I had correctly gauged the response of my opposite number in London, who did the anonymous 'Cassandra' broadcasts, a more cowardly operation than I would stoop to. Soon all of Wodehouse's home country was howling for the blood of the collaborator. The same writer who had slightly kidded the privileged class was now served on a platter to the British public by members of that class . . . as an example of the privileged class! A double-twist with a back flip worth ten points out of ten. The furor served the purposes of *mein Führer*.

'Wodehouse's content didn't matter,' I told Schellenberg. 'Context was everything. Does this teach you something you can use?'

'SS' was having none of it. 'That's ancient history,' he said. 'What does it have to do with movies?'

I gave up trying to communicate with him after that. He was an overgrown child, product of Nazi schools and media. I made him. With a good scriptwriter to guide him, he could do the job I wanted, and that would be that. As Hitler's health had deteriorated, plans to recreate the Nuremberg rally and another film had waned. Riefenstahl's original was safe in that regard (although I'm considering the possibility of artificially adding color to her precious little masterpiece). The new picture would be more in the manner of a sequel, while using the same title. Schellenberg would have to travel the length and breadth of the Reich for years to get his film in the can. Whereas Riefenstahl used fifty cameras, I'd allot hundreds to this picture. Progress.

Meanwhile, my young technician had become entranced with lobby cards and stills I kept with my foreign film collection. When he casually passed over some excellent shots of the most glamorous actress of them all, Greta Garbo, it confirmed my worst suspicions about his lack of taste. Then my heart stopped as he began pawing at the film cans. 'You have a title I've never heard of,' he said petulantly. What kind of creature was he? The source of his irritation, instead of healthy curiosity, was an uncut copy of James Whale's *The Road Back*, a brilliant interpretation of yet another load of pacifistic drivel from the author of *All Quiet on the Western Front*.

'I keep trophies,' I told him. 'In 1936, our consul in Los Angeles threatened Universal Studios with a German boycott of all their films if they didn't reedit *Road* to suit us. Can you believe that the craven studio heads caved in? Whale was a good director, even if he was an Englishman, same as Hitchcock. He didn't do valuable work after that. To top it off, only a few years later they were grinding out the same war propaganda as all the other studios.'

'Like these?' asked Schellenberg, pointing to a tower of film cans from Warner Brothers, the studio that borrowed so many of my techniques.

'Especially those,' I answered. Wartime America was willing to learn from me. One of the movies suggested that Warner Brothers didn't mind the idea of a *Kristallnacht* if it was directed against Germans in New York instead of Jews in Berlin. Someday I'll make a film of that memorable evening, sparing no detail – the *ping, ping* of violin strings breaking as a music shop burned, and the broken glass from the store windows, glittering like ice under the stars. This kid could probably make a good movie about *Kristallnacht* that he wouldn't understand himself.

There was a certain charm about his childlike acquisitiveness as he hinted he'd like to have a memento or two for his collection, in return for which I could have whatever I desired in the way of props or stills from the Grail movie. I didn't mind indulging him, although I was surprised that he mainly wanted American stuff. He didn't gravitate to the Germans of Hollywood, but went after straight Americana. I let him have some Captain Midnight knickknacks. (I enjoyed finding out that this estimable hero of American radio commanded his own SS: the Secret Squadron.) In a fit of generosity, I threw in a one-sheet from *Enemy of Women*, a curiosity released by Monogram Studios that had undergone a sudden title change when the direction of the war shifted in our favor. It was now simply *The Goebbels Story*. I had shown a subtitled print to friends. It was quite hilarious in places, but I was rather taken with the performance by Paul Andor, a better version of me than the one turned out factory-style by Martin Kosleck in productions for the major studios. It was not surprising that I couldn't rouse interest in Stefan for low-budget productions of the Monogram sort, even when I mentioned a legendary secret weapon, or 'bomb,' they had produced starring the comic strip character Snuffy Smith that went by the improbable designation of *Hillbilly Blitzkrieg*. Stefan collected unusual *objets de nostalgie*, but my desire to track down this film was too much for him.

To get rid of him, in a manner of speaking, I let him have publicity shots from a sampling of American war films I had utilized to prove a degree of racism in their cinema equal to ours, albeit against different targets. But I would not surrender my copy of *Air Fighters Comics* where the cover depicts the intrepid Airboy exterminating a Japanese pilot who must have been a ghoul or vampire considering the size of his fangs, spattered with his own life's blood. (How ironic that our earlier ally – intrepid Samurai I had portrayed as *Herrenvölk* – is today a lackey of Western imperialism.) When Julius Streicher was publishing his gallery of monstrous faces to represent the Jews, he hadn't thought to give them fangs. Live and learn.

Schellenberg was so put out that I wouldn't part with my American comic book that I gave him a consolation prize: a good reproduction of the December 12, 1942, issue of *Collier's*, which presented the 'Japs' as a race of bats. Our former partner in the Axis has become so cooperative with their former enemies that I may employ the bat image myself if this keeps up.

True to form, 'SS' had no capacity for gratitude. I didn't expect otherwise. But as he was leaving, he had the impudence to ask, 'Herr Doktor Goebbels, do you share a dual citizenship between the Reich and Burgundy?'

'Certainly not!' I answered immediately. 'Why do you ask that?'

'Oh, just curious,' he said. 'Let's do lunch sometime and discuss the remake.'

He departed and I reflected on what is wrong with

167

today's youth. They have known too much peace. A year on the eastern front would have done wonders for this lad. And as for Burgundy, I was beginning to resent the very name. I longed for the good old days when the religious problem consisted of dueling with conventional Christians in the Centre party.

Chapter Twelve

No happiness without order, no order without authority, no authority without unity.

– Bulwer Lytton,
The Coming Race

May 1966

I have been invited to Burgundy. Helmuth has passed his initiation and is now a fully accredited member of the Death's Head SS, on his way to joining the inner circle of the Thule eccentrics. Oh, well. Naturally he is in a celebratory mood and wants his father to witness the victory. I am proud, of course, but just a little wary of what his future holds in store. I remain the convinced ideologue and critical of the bourgeois frame of mind. (Our revolution was against that sort of sentimentality.) But I don't mind some bourgeois comforts. My son will live a hard and austere life that I hope will not prove too much for him. Then again, he's not a decadent Schellenberg, and my boy ought to make me proud once he's been steeled in the furnace.

No sooner had I been sent the invitation than I also received a telegram from my daughter, Hilda, whom I had not seen since the Yuletide, when she stopped over for Christmas dinner. Who was it who once said to talk as a radical but dine with the establishment? Somehow she has learned of the invitation from Helmuth and insists that I must see her before leaving on the trip. She tells me that I am in danger! The message was clouded in mystery because she did not offer a hint of a reason.

Nevertheless I agreed to meet her at the proposed rendez-vous because it was conveniently on the way. And I am always worried that Hilda will find herself imprisoned or worse for going too far with her unrealistic views.

The same evening I was cleaning out a desk when I came across a letter she had written when she was seventeen years old – from the summer of 1952. I had the urge to read it again:

Dear Father,

I appreciated your last letter and its frankness, although I don't understand what you want me to do. Why have you not been able to think of anything to say to me for nearly a year? I know that you and Mother have found me to be your most difficult daughter. I remember when I was younger that Helga, Holde, and Hedda never gave Mother trouble about their clothes. I didn't object to the dresses she put on me, but could I help it if they tore when I played? I asked for more casual attire suited to climbing trees and hiking and playing soccer.

Ever since Heide died in that automobile accident, Mother has become very protective of her daughters. Only Helmuth escaped that sort of overwhelming protec-tiveness, and that's just because he's a boy.

At first I wasn't sure that I wanted to be sent to this private school, but a few weeks here convinced me that you had made the right decision. The mountains give you room to stretch your legs. The horses they let us ride are magnificent. Wolfgang is mine and he is the fastest.

Soon I will be ready to take my examinations for the university. Your concern that I do well runs through your entire letter. Now we have something to talk about again. It is too late to change anything. I'm sure I'll do fine. I've been studying chemistry every chance, and I love it.

My only complaint is that the library is much too small. My favorite book is the unexpurgated Nietzsche, where he talks about the things the Party forbade as subjects for public discussion. At first I was surprised to discover how pro-Jewish he was, not to mention pro-freedom. The more I read of him, the more I agree with what he has to say.

One lucky development was a box of new books that had been confiscated from unauthorized people (what you would call the wrong type for intellectual endeavor, Father). Suddenly I had in front of me an orgy of exciting reading material. I especially enjoyed the Kafka . . . but I'm not sure why. Have you read his story 'An Old Manuscript'? Wasn't it among the titles you burned? There is something very disturbing about it.

My biggest surprise is a book by that American writer of German background, H.L. Mencken. I've seen a few quotes from him before, but it was always his criticisms of, wait a minute while I look it up, Germanaphobia in the United States. I had no idea how many other things he'd written about. His book is very funny. They should teach us more about the Roaring Twenties and Prohibition and gangsters. What made me think of you, Papa, was that Herr Mencken wrote that folk art does not come from the people at all. How could anyone think that, even a famous man like he is? Do you think you should send him one of your books about the creative spirit of the *Völk*? He probably doesn't have the facts. He says that ballads do not come from a nation's community but from individual poets who did the songs originally for the royalty in castles, and that the songs sort of trickled down to the people afterward. Silly, isn't it?

Some students here want to form a club. They are in correspondence with others of our peer group who are allowed to read the old forbidden books. We have not decided on what we would call the organization. We are

171

playing with the idea of the German Reading League. Other names may occur to us later.

Another reason I like it better in the country than in the city is that there are not as many rules out here. Oh, the school has its curfews, but they don't really pay much attention, and we can do as we please most of the time. Only one of the teachers doesn't like me and she called me a little reprobate. I suspect she might make trouble for me except that everyone knows that you're my father. That always helps.

I was becoming interested in a boy named Franz, but it came to the dean's attention and she told me that he was not from a good enough family for me to pursue the friendship. We ignored the advice, but within a month Franz had left without saying a word. I know that you are against the old class boundaries, Father, but believe it when I say that they are still around. The people must not know that Hitler socialized them.

Now that I think about it, there are more rules out here than I first realized. Why must there be so many rules? Why can't I just be me without causing so much trouble?

I don't want to end this letter with a question. I hope that Mother and you are happy. You should probably take that vacation you keep telling everyone will be any year now. I want to get those postcards from Hong Kong! Love, Hilda

(NOTE FROM HILDA: It is a wonder that I have seen so many birthdays. How could I have been so dense as to write this letter to my father? I didn't have the brains of an eel after it's been in the soup. I suppose that he loved me in his own twisted way. It helped that I was still sufficiently brainwashed that I would believe his propaganda over a thinker of Mencken's caliber in a matter of historical fact.)

I sat at the desk in my den and thought about a red-haired little girl who had played in this very room when she was happy and content. I had to admit that she was my favorite and always had been. Where had I gone wrong? How had her healthy radicalism become channeled in such an unproductive direction? There was more to it than the books. It was something in her. I eagerly anticipated our reunion.

On a Wednesday morning I boarded a luxury train; the power of the rocket engines is deliberately held down so that passengers may enjoy the scenery instead of merely rushing through. Hilda would be waiting for me in a French hamlet directly in line with my final destination. I took along a manuscript – work, always work – this diary, and, for relaxation, a mystery novel by an Englishman. What is it about the British that makes this genre uniquely their own?

Speaking of books, I noticed a rotund gentleman – very much the Goering type – reading a copy of my prewar novel, *Michael*. I congratulated him on his excellent taste and he recognized me immediately. As I was autographing his copy, he asked if I was doing any new novels. I explained that I found plays and movie scripts a more comfortable form in which to work and suggested he catch my filmed sequel to *The Wanderer* when it was released. The director was no less than Leni Riefenstahl, irony of ironies.

Other Party leaders may grouch about the lack of privacy, but I've never minded that my name is a household word. It makes of me a toastmaster much in demand. The most requested lecture topic remains my best film, *Kolberg*, my answer to *Gone with the Wind*.

I contemplated the numerous ways in which my wife's social calendar would keep her occupied in my absence. Since the children have grown up and left home, she seems more active than before. It's amazing the number of things she can find to do in a day. I would have liked to attend the Richard Strauss concert, but duty calls.

The food on the train was quite good. The wine was only adequate, however. I had high hopes that the French hamlet live up to its reputation for prime vintages.

The porter looked Jewish and probably is. There are people of Jewish ancestry living in Europe. We couldn't get them all. It doesn't matter, so long as the practicing Jew is forever removed. God, we made the blood flow to cleanse this soil. Of course I'm speaking figuratively. But what could one *do* with Jews, Gypsies, partisans of all kinds, homosexuals, the feebleminded, race mixers, and all the rest? Sometimes when I'm at a dull party, I imagine various conceited people wearing the patches we used on internees: brown triangles for wine-guzzling Gypsies, pink triangles for prancing queers (the SA fags were the worst), and yellow stars for the supreme enemy, the children of Abraham. Next December I'll use the designs for Christmas ornaments.

We reached the station at dusk and my daughter was there. She is such a lovely child, except that she is no child any longer! I can see why she has so many admirers. Too many. I have spoken to her about this. She had the temerity to throw my own affairs back in my teeth. If it had been anyone other than Hilda, I would not have given in to the sensitive side of my nature.

Hedonism is bad enough, but her political activities (if they deserve such a label) are becoming dangerous. When an ambitious young assistant charged her with actual treason, and couldn't back up his ludicrous charge, I had him sent away for a long vacation. If I thought for a minute she was being pulled into the noxious underground, I would take steps. She has gone to the brink, but not taken the plunge.

174

(NOTE FROM HILDA: I was already a member of the underground. Only a highly professional organization could keep this a secret from the Nazi state. Any doubts I'd had about its efficacy were soon dispelled.)

Her folly has not made her any the less attractive. She has the classic features. On her thirtieth birthday I once again brought up the subject of why she had never married. I wouldn't mind her having lovers if there was a husband in the picture. That she may never reproduce vexes me greatly. As always her deep-throated laugh mocks my concern.

A few seconds after I disembarked she was pulling at my sleeve and rushing me to a cab. I had never seen her looking so agitated. We virtually ran through the lobby of the hotel, and I felt as though I were under some kind of house arrest as she bustled me up to my room and bolted the door behind us.

It was the most old-fashioned room I'd occupied in years, with quaint round mirrors and overstuffed furniture. The setting was inappropriate for the virulent exchange that began with: 'Father, I have terrible news.' The melodramatic derring-do was a trifle annoying, and she was gasping her words while she was out of breath. Leave intrigues to the young, I always say . . . suddenly remembering in that case my daughter qualified for numerous adventures. If only she would leave me out of it!

'Darling,' I said, 'I am worn out from my trip and in want of a bath. Surely your message can wait until I've changed. Over dinner we may –'

'No,' she announced sternly. 'It can't wait.'

'Very well,' I said, recognizing that my ploy had failed miserably and surrendering to her – shall we say – blitzkrieg. 'Tell me,' I said as I sat in a chair.

175

'You must not go to Burgundy,' she began, and then paused as though anticipating an outburst from me. I am a master at that game. I told her to get on with it.

'Father, you may think me mad, but I must tell you!' *A chip off the old block*, I thought. I nodded assent, if only to get it over. She was pacing as she spoke, and I thought it unfortunate that Hitler could not be with us to evaluate her performance. 'First of all, the German Freedom League has learned something that could have dire consequences for the future of our country.' It sounded like one of my press releases. 'Think whatever you will of the league, but facts are facts. We have uncovered the most diabolical secret.'

'Which is?' I prompted her, expecting something anticlimactic.

'I am sure that you have not the slightest inkling of this, but during the war millions of Jews were put to death in horrible ways. What we thought were concentration camps suffering from typhus infections and lacking supplies were in reality death camps at which was carried out a systematic program of *genocide*.' I could not believe that she had used Raphael Lemkin's smear word. The United Nations effort was long defunct, but we were saddled with the rhetorical baggage to this day.

The stunned expression on my face was no act. Hilda interpreted it as befitted her love for me – she took it, if you will, at face value.

'I can see that you're shocked,' she said. 'Even though you staged those public demonstrations against the Jews and made blood-curdling threats, I realize you meant to force the Party's emigration policy through. I detest that policy, but it wasn't murder.'

'Dear,' I said, keeping my voice as calm as possible, 'have you been reading philo-Semitic tracts? What you

176

are telling me is nothing more than thoroughly discredited Allied propaganda. We shot Jewish partisans, but there's no evidence of systematic – '

'There is now,' she said, and I believe that my jaw dropped at the revelation. She went on, oblivious to my horror: 'The records that were kept for those camps are forgeries. They must have thought the real records would all be destroyed by the atomic bombs, but a separate set of documents, detailing the genocide, has been uncovered by the league.'

What a damnably stupid German thing to do. To keep multiple copies of *everything*. This matter would have to be suppressed. The only positive side to this turn of events was that I could be certain Hilda was not in the underground. She would never bring the matter to my attention.

(NOTE FROM HILDA: We were both pawns in someone else's game, but he'd never be able to face that.)

Hope springs eternal, and I took a stab at shifting her attention from the latest obsession. 'Hilda, you persist in using the term *genocide*. Aren't you aware that Lemkin, the man who originated the word, meant it to describe any loss of national or ethnic identity as the result of a planned move? By that standard, genocide goes on in the United States on an almost daily basis, to the extent that people lose their cultural identity in the so-called melting pot. Likewise, anyone we allow to be Germanized, because we find them racially acceptable, is a victim of genocide if he loses his small, ethnic identification.'

'Father, you always do this to me. You change the subject, or you go off on a tangent. I don't care about the word. I'm talking about mass murder; the loss of identity through the loss of life, as a planned move.'

'Oh.' This definitely meant trouble. It was as if my daughter disappeared from the room at that second. I could see her, but she had become indistinct, unreal. A far more solid form came between us, the image of the man who had been my life. It was as if the ghost of Adolf Hitler stood before me then, in our common distress, in our common deed. I could hear his voice and remember my promise to him. Oh, God, was it to be Hilda who would provide the test? I really had not the least desire to see her eliminated. I liked her. There must be some alternative.

As she continued, I realized she was on at least one wrong track, and I eagerly grasped at that. She had gotten the idea that Field Marshal Erwin Rommel was persuaded to take his own life because he had come across evidence of the mass murders and intended to go public. It remains a state secret that the hero of the North African campaigns was implicated in the assassination attempt against the Fuehrer in the army bomb plot. After the fates decreed that the Leader of the Fatherland would survive the bombing of his headquarters at Wolfsschanze, we had our work cut out for us – and something to take our minds off the Allied invasion. Rommel was a reasonable man. He cared about his family. He took his poison like a good boy. The Rommel problem had absolutely nothing to do with the murder of Jews. Without going into details, I swore on our family honor that I knew Rommel's death to be in no way connected to the issue Hilda had raised. This gave her pause. I think she believed me.

(NOTE FROM HILDA: I did. But not until reading these pages have I known the truth about Rommel. That he would join in a plot to kill Hitler only raises him in my estimation.)

What I said next was not entirely in keeping with my feigned ignorance, and if she had been less upset she

178

might have noticed the implications of my question: 'Hilda, how many people have you informed?'

She answered without hesitation. 'Only members of the league, and now you.'

I heaved a sigh of relief and asked, 'Don't you think it would be a good idea to keep this extreme theory to yourself?'

'It's no theory. It's a fact. And I have no intention of taking out an advertisement. It would make me a target for those lunatics in the SS.'

So that was the Burgundy connection! I still didn't see why I should be in any danger during my trip. Even if I were innocent of the truth – which every relevant SS official knew to be absurd, since I was an architect of our policy – my sheer prominence would keep me safe from harm in Burgundy.

Testing the hypothesis, I asked Hilda what this fancy of hers had to do with my visit. 'Only everything,' she answered.

'Are you afraid that they will suspect I've learned of this so-called secret, which is nothing more than patent nonsense to begin with?'

She surprised me by answering, 'No.' There was an executioner's silence.

'What then?' I asked.

'It is not a crime of the past that endangers you,' came the sound of her voice in portentous tones, 'but a crime of the future.'

'You should have been the poet of the family.'

'If you go to Burgundy, you risk your life. They are planning an action so stupendous that it will make World War II and the concentration camps, on both the Allied and Axis sides, seem like nothing but a prelude. The Reich itself will be attacked, and you will be one of the first victims!'

Never have I felt more acutely the pain of a father for his offspring. I could not help but conclude that my youngest daughter's mind had only a tenuous connection to reality. Her reactionary politics must be to blame. On the other hand, I regarded Hilda with genuine affection. She seemed concerned for my welfare in a manner that I supposed would not apply to a stranger. The decadent creed she had embraced had not led to disaffection from her father.

I thought back to the grand old days of intrigue within the Party and the period in the war years when I referred most often to that wise advice of Machiavelli: 'Cruelties should be committed all at once, as in that way each separate one is less felt, and gives less offense.' We had come perilously close to *Götterdämmerung* then, but in the end our policy proved sound. I was beyond all that. The state was secure, Europe was secure . . . and the only conceivable threat to my safety would come from foreign sources. Yet here was Hilda, her face a mixture of concern and anger and – perhaps love? She was telling me to beware the Burgundians. I was no cheerleader in their camp, but the idea that they were plotting against the Reich itself was too fantastic to credit.

They had invited me to one of the conferences to decide the formation of the new nation. Those were hectic times in the postwar period. As gauleiter of Berlin (one of the Fuehrer's few appointments of a district leader with which I fully concurred), I had been primarily concerned with Speer's work to build New Berlin. The film industry was flowering under my personal supervision, I was busy writing my memoirs, and I was involved heavily with diplomatic projects. I hadn't really given Burgundy much thought. I knew that it had been a country in medieval times, and I had read a little about the Duchy of Burgundy. The country had traded in grain, wines, and finished wool.

They announced at the conference that the historical Burgundy would be restored, encompassing the area to the south of Champagne, east of Burbonais, and north and west of Savoy. There was some debate on whether or not to restore the original place-names or else borrow from Wagner to create a series of new ones. In the end, the latter camp won out. The capital was named Tarnhelm, after the magic helmet in the *Nibelungenlied* that could change the wearer into a variety of shapes.

Hitler did not officially single out any of the departments that made up the SS: Waffen, Death's Head, or the General SS. We in his entourage realized, however, that the gift was to those members of the inner circle who had been most intimately involved with both the ideological and practical side of the exterminations; which meant that, in practical fact, Burgundy was a country for the Death's Head SS, or Himmler's black order. The true believers! Given the Reich's policy of secrecy, there was no need to blatantly advertise the reasons for the gift. Himmler, as Reichsfuehrer of the SS and Hitler's adviser on racial matters, was naturally instrumental in this transfer of power to the new nation. His rival, Rosenberg, met his death . . . and this set a precedent for future fun and games. As far back as the nuclear destruction of the concentration camps, I believe that Himmler had been eliminating opposition within his own organization; although I haven't figured out how he managed to have his chosen elite safely away when the bombs dropped, and his least favorite SS men on duty.

The officials who would oversee the creation of Burgundy were carefully selected. Their mission was to make certain that Burgundy became a unique nation in all of Europe, devoted to certain chivalric values of the past, and the formation of pure Aryan specimens. It was nothing more than the logical extension of our propaganda, the secularizing of the myths and legends with which we kept the people fed during the dark days of lost hope. The final result was a picturesque fairy tale kingdom that made its money almost entirely out of the tourist trade. It takes a lot of money to run socialism. America boasts of its amusement parks, but it has nothing to match this.

(My first contact with the atmosphere of unreality pervading the make-believe country was when a minor official approached me with a request that I use my ministry to hoist the USA on its own petard. The scheme was that since Americans are committed to the sanctity of property rights, I should take steps to register the Swastika as a trademark. Then Burgundy and the Reich would split the loot. Wonderful. It would take another world war to collect the first pfennig. Still, there was a nutty appeal to the idea. The little man was half British, and that probably explains it.)

Hilda interrupted my reverie by asking in a voice that bordered on presumption, 'What are you going to do?'

'Unless you make sense, I will continue on my journey to Tarnhelm and see Helmuth.' He was living at the headquarters of the SS leaders, territory that was closed off to outsiders, even during the tourist season. Yet it was by no means unusual for occasional visitors from New Berlin to be invited there. My daughter's melodramatics had not yet given cause to worry. All I could think of was how I'd like to get my hands around the throat of whoever put these idiotic notions into her pretty head.

She was visibly distressed, but in control. She tossed her hair back and said, 'I am not sure that the proof I have to offer will be sufficient to convince you.'

'Aren't you getting ahead of yourself?' I asked. 'You

haven't made a concrete accusation about this plot. Drop the pose. Tell me what you think constitutes the danger.'

'They think you're a traitor,' she said.

'What?' I was astounded to hear such words from anyone for any reason. 'To Germany?'

'No,' she answered. 'To the true Nazi ideal.'

I laughed. 'That's the craziest thing I've ever heard. I'm one of the key – '

'You don't understand,' she interrupted. 'I'm talking about the religion.'

'Oh, Hilda, is that all? You and your group have stumbled upon some threatening comments from occultists, I take it.'

Now it was her turn to be surprised. She sat upon the bed. 'Yes,' she answered. 'But then you know?'

'Not the specifics. They change their game every few months. Who has time to keep up? Let me tell you something. The leaders of the SS have always had ties to an occult group called the Thule Society, but there is nothing surprising about that. It is a purely academic exercise in playing with the occult, dear girl, the same as the British equivalent – the Golden Dawn. Certainly you are aware that many prominent Englishmen belonged to that club!

'These people are harmless eccentrics. Our movement made use of the type without stepping on pet beliefs. It's the same as dealing with any religious person whom you want on your side. If you receive cooperation, it won't be through insulting his spiritual convictions.'

'What about the messages we intercepted?' she went on. 'The threatening tone, the almost deranged – '

'It's how they entertain themselves!' I insisted. 'Listen, you're familiar with Hörbiger, aren't you?' She nodded. 'Burgundians believe that stuff, even after the launching of von Braun's satellite, which in no way disturbed the

183

eternal ice, as that old fool predicted! His followers don't care about facts. They believe the moon in our sky is the fourth moon this planet has had, that it is made of ice like the other three, that all of the cosmos is an eternal struggle between fire and ice. To tell you the truth, our Fuehrer toyed with those ideas in the old days. The Burgundians no more want to give up their sacred ideas merely because modern science has exploded them than fundamentalist Baptists in America want to listen to Darwin.'

'I know,' she said. 'You are acting as though they aren't dangerous.'

'They're an irritation, but that's all.'

'Soon Helmuth will be accepted into the inner circle.'

'Why not? He's been working for that ever since he was a teenager.'

'But the inner circle,' she repeated with added emphasis.

'So he'll be a Hitler Youth for the rest of his life. He'll never grow up.'

'You don't understand.'

'I'm tired of this conversation,' I told her bluntly. 'Do you remember several years ago when your brother went on that pilgrimage to Lower Saxony to one of Himmler's shrines? You were terribly upset, but you didn't have a shred of reason why he shouldn't have gone. You had nightmares. Your mother and I wondered if it was because as a little girl you were frightened by Wagner.'

'Now I have reasons.'

'Mysterious, threatening messages! The Thule Society! It should be taken with a grain of salt. I saw Adolf Hitler once listen to a harangue from an especially realistic believer in the Nordic cult, bow solemnly when the man was finished, enter his private office – where I accompanied him – and break out in laughter that would wake the dead. He didn't want to offend the fellow. The man was a good Nazi, at least.'

My daughter was fishing around in her purse as I told her these things. She passed me a piece of paper when I was finished. I unfolded it and read:

JOSEPH GOEBBELS MUST ARRIVE ON SCHEDULE.
THE RITUAL CANNOT BE RESCHEDULED.
DEATH TO TRAITORS IN HIGH PLACES.

'What is this?' I asked. I was becoming angry.

'A member of the Freedom League intercepted a message from Burgundy to someone in New Berlin. It was coded, but we were able to break it.'

'To whom was the message addressed?'

'Heinrich Himmler.'

Suddenly I felt very, very cold. I had never trusted *der treue Heinrich*. Admittedly, I didn't trust anything that came from the German Freedom League, with an oxymoron for a title. Nevertheless something in me was clawing at the pit of my stomach, telling me that maybe, just maybe, there was danger. Crazy as Himmler had been during the war years, he had become worse in peacetime. At least he was competent regarding his industrial empire.

'How do I know that this message is genuine?' I asked.

'You don't,' she answered. 'It was a risk bringing you these, if that helps you to believe.'

'I was going to ask why the Burgundians haven't stopped you.'

'They don't know the league broke their code; and the league doesn't know I'm here either. They hate you as much as Himmler.'

I felt the blood rush to my face, and I jumped to my feet so abruptly that it put an insupportable strain on my club foot. I had to grab for a nearby lamp to keep from stumbling. 'Why,' I virtually hissed, 'do you belong to that despicable bunch of bums and poseurs?'

Standing also, and grabbing her purse, Hilda fended off my ire. 'Father, I am leaving. You may do with this information as you wish. I will offer one last suggestion. Why don't you take another comfortable passenger train back to New Berlin, and call Tarnhelm to say that you will be one day late? See what their reaction is. You didn't manage to attend my college graduation and I'm none the worse for it. Would it matter so much to my brother were you to help him celebrate after the ceremony?'

She turned to go. 'Wait,' I said. 'I'm sorry I spoke so harshly. You mean well, but you've been misled by this damnable league. I see now that we in the government have been too lenient with all of you. I'll call for an investigation at the first opportunity.'

Her laughter was not the response I had intended. There was no fear in it. 'So I'm to feel guilty over betraying my friends to you. Father, the league is the least of your problems.'

'Censorship is the answer. It always worked before, and it – '

'You're losing your touch.' She reached into her purse again, and I began seeing that black bag as a Pandora's box. Out came a folded booklet that I recognized. The sight of it made me want to throw up. 'You've been trying to ban this play all over the Reich. Thousands of copies are available on the black market, in at least a dozen languages. Every time you destroy one, two more take its place. I was a child on your knee when you told me the story of the Hydra.'

Shoving the cursed pages into my hands, she stormed out the door. I watched the closed door for several minutes, not moving, not really thinking. Then I remembered to take my bath. As I luxuriated in the hot water, I watched the crumpled wad of paper that had been the play lying beside the tub, surrounded by steam as if a boulder in the pit of hell. I reflected that a parent can't be too careful about the fairy tales he reads to his children.

Chapter Thirteen

I am a horse for single harness, not cut out for tandem or team work. I have never belonged wholeheartedly to country or state, to my circle of friends, or even to my own family. These ties have always been accompanied by a vague aloofness, and the wish to withdraw into myself increases with the years.

– Albert Einstein,
Living Philosophies

Last Act, Scene Two, from
LOOKING FOR THE JEWS
by
Anonymous

Forbidden for display or presentation in the Greater Reich, or its territories. English-language version by Hilda Goebbels; puns and slang adapted to colloquial American usage.

SCENE: the Reich Chancellery

The curtain rises on ADOLF HITLER *pacing in his office. He is highly agitated and keeps referring to documents on his desk. This desk is twice normal size and he has the appearance of a child in his father's study as he reaches across for papers. Sitting to the rear center is* MARTIN BORMANN, *busily taking notes. Three of Hitler's aides enter from stage left. They are* DR JOSEPH GOEBBELS, JULIUS STREICHER, *and* RUDOLF HESS.

STREICHER: *Mein Führer,* now that we've grabbed Germany, we are ready to implement some final solutions, you bet.

GOEBBELS: We'd like to begin with Berlin.

HESS: Why is Bormann staring at me? He gives me the creeps.

HITLER: You haven't saluted yet, and you have the creepiest eyebrows of anyone in the room.

(Everyone, including Bormann, who jumps to his feet, gives the Nazi salute)

HESS *(Grumbling)*: Speer never salutes, or hardly ever.

HITLER *(Shrieking at the top of his voice)*: He's an artist, an ahrrrrr-teeeeeeest, the same as myself! He's not to be judged by the philistine standards of the street rabble.

GOEBBELS: Very interesting that you should employ that particular biblical reference when one considers that –

HITLER: Shut up!

GOEBBELS: *Jawohl.*

(Streicher begins laughing at Goebbels, but a dirty look from Hitler puts an end to that)

HITLER: When I speak of street rabble, I'm talking about you *(He points to Streicher, who stands at attention)*; and you *(He turns around to address Bormann, who continues taking notes)*; but I'm not referring to the good doctor, who is my intellectual. *(Goebbels bows in appreciation)* But enough small talk.

HESS: What about me? You're always forgetting me.

HITLER: You're rabble, too.

HESS: Thank you, oh, thank you.

HITLER: What's the status report on rooting out 'the Chosen People'?

GOEBBELS: Chosen for what?

HITLER: Exactly.

STREICHER: Are you talking about the Jews, boss?

HITLER: Yeah, dose guys.

GOEBBELS: The Hebrews are an insidious lot, to be sure. But they won't hide for long. We will put a crown of thorns on their heads, but it will be fashioned from barbed wire. They have infested Berlin long enough, like rats.

HESS: I'll be rat back!

(Hess begins to exit)

HITLER: Halt! Where are you going? I haven't given you leave.

HESS: *Mein Führer*, we have a surprise for you.

(Goebbels and Streicher nod; Bormann takes notes)

HITLER: All right, then, but hurry back.

(Hess exits stage right)

BORMANN *(Half muttering)*: He's probably going to defecate.

HITLER: What's that? What's that? I haven't given him authorization to take such steps on his own. There could be international repercussions if Hess takes it on himself to –

GOEBBELS: He's not going to leave the building, *mein Führer*. We've been hoping you would clarify our policy about detecting the Jews; and the surprise has to do with that. Although I always know 'em when I see 'em, less expert National Socialists could do with some guidelines.

HITLER: I've been working on that for weeks, Doc. First,

we gotta introduce the public, bless their pointy little heads, to arithmetical reasoning.

STREICHER: Say what?

HITLER: The moral premise of our movement, you dummy cop! We National Socialists believe in what's good for the nation, right?

EVERYONE *(Including Hess from off stage)*: Right!

STREICHER: You've made Germany feel good about itself again.

HITLER: And that means the greatest good for the greatest number within the nation, right?

EVERYONE: Right!

HITLER: And that means it is all right to sacrifice a minority for the good of the majority, right?

EVERYONE: You said it!

GOEBBELS: It's kosher. *(Withering in dirty looks from the rest)* Sorry about that, chief.

HITLER: If we accept the premise that the good of the majority takes precedence, then the next step is to select a proper minority to sacrifice. Here the Jew is perfect for the role.

GOEBBELS: The people are getting the drift, but guidelines would still be a real help.

HITLER: Very well. It is crucially important to recognize that there is no such thing as the individual Jew. When I was fourteen years old, I met my first Jew at the *Real-schule*, a fellow schoolmate. I was only mildly suspicious of him at first, but I felt a disagreeable sensation that could not be ignored. It was not until I was a young man, bumming around Vienna, that I understood the Jew at last.

(The others exchange glances; they have heard it all before)

HITLER: I was already indignant at the Viennese press for its weak-kneed cosmopolitanism when I encountered the germ that had so infected the city that the press could be nothing other than rotten. The boy in Linz had looked nothing like this: a dark creature in a long caftan, with a long nose and black curls, and giving off a most peculiar odor. Then and there I knew the enemy I would fight forevermore.

GOEBBELS: They are not always so obliging as to appear in costume.

HITLER: That is unimportant. The creature I saw was but one tentacle on the octopus. The Jew has no individual ego. He is only part of a whole. He is the Displaced Person of the Universe. He has no soul. He's a real meanie, I'm telling you.

GOEBBELS: But isn't that the virtue we encourage in our own *Völk*, to submit the ego to the greater whole, the 'I' to the 'thou'? Oops. *(Goebbels realizes that he's gone too far)*

HITLER *(Jumping up and down)*: Doesn't count! Doesn't count! Besides, I said the Jew has no ego *to* submit. The German has an ego that we have to beat out of him.

GOEBBELS: But some of the trouble I've had has been with Jewish individualists. Oops. *(Goebbels ducks as Hitler throws papers)*

HITLER *(Jumping up and down)*: There is no Jewish individual! He doesn't exist!

GOEBBELS: May I ask a hypothetical question? It's purely hypothetical. Would the Jew be tolerable if he had his own land? Zionism is a kind of *Völk* conception, and I'm wondering – in terms of an intellectual problem – if the Jews could be lived with if they were segregated on their own soil instead of in ghettos. I bring this up as an academic . . . uh . . . what I mean to say is . . .

(There is dead silence for several beats as Hitler stares at Goebbels)

HITLER: What's up your fundament, Doc? Don't you like your job? You've got good pay, plenty of perks. You are one of the most ardent anti-Semites I know, so why provoke me with these decadent musings?

GOEBBELS: The problem is purely technical, *mein Führer*. We need guidelines to find the Jews, and then we'll kill 'em.

(Hess enters stage right, waving a copy of Julius Streicher's newspaper, Der Stürmer, *and followed by a tall, young blond man)*

HESS: Oh, savior of Germany, we received thousands of applications for an advertisement we ran –

STREICHER: It was my idea!

HESS: – to find an official Heroic Hebrew Hunter. Here stands the winner before you, a real *Mensch* named Olaf Mann.

MANN *(Saluting Hitler)*: *Sieg Heil.*

STREICHER: He awaits your command.

HITLER: Get out there and round up those children of Abraham, *mach schnell!* Never forget that they can't be

193

baptized out of their natural condition, which is to be born three ways.

MANN: Three ways?

HITLER: Religiously, ethnically, and *(Shouts)* racially.

MANN: Does every Jew have these characteristics?

STREICHER: He wants to avoid error, *mein Führer*. He couldn't find anyone who looks like the cartoons I publish in my paper.

HITLER *(Ignoring Streicher)*: Yes, they have all three, especially the ones who deny it. You must be a fanatic to seek them out and penetrate any disguise. Have you any experience for the job?

MANN *(Pulling out a long list that falls to the floor)*: On the first day of the contest, I went to a synagogue. It was easy to find one by following a trail of burning books and broken glass.

BORMANN *(From the back)*: Further proof that the Jew is sloppy and slovenly.

GOEBBELS: You can take the ghetto out of the Jew, but you can't make him a German.

HITLER: Silence! *(There is silence)* Speak! *(They all begin to chatter)* No, no, no, no, no, no, no, no, no . . . or, *Nein!* Only Mann is to speak. The rest of you shut up!

(From off stage a VOICE *begins declaiming)*: 'There must be a chemistry of the immaterial, there must be combinations of the insubstantial, out of which sprang the material – '

HITLER: Not Thomas Mann!

GOEBBELS: We destroy the words, but they echo in the vaulted chambers of our despair.

BORMANN: Please don't repeat that.

HITLER *(Testily)*: Is everybody finished? I will hear Olaf.

MANN: So I entered the synagogue, and some were dressed in funny costumes, and some were dressed as Germans. I asked, 'Are there any Jews in here?' The rabbi said, 'Maybe.' So I asked how I could tell, and the rabbi said I should find out if they live by the Talmud, because being Jewish means being religious. So I started to take down the names of everyone in the synagogue and a young man dressed in the same street clothes I was wearing –

HESS: How did you both fit in one suit? *(Laughs idiotically)*

MANN *(Ignoring the interruption)*: – came over and said not to include him because he didn't believe in God. 'Being Jewish is cultural,' he said. He was there for the music.

HITLER: Don't be deceived. The Jews are a race.

MANN: How do I find the Jews when they're not in costume?

HITLER: By descent, and the first wisecrack will lead straight to a concentration camp. A single grandparent marks a person with the star of David. *(He calls off stage)* At ntion! Play some Wagner. I need inspiration.

(The music begins)

STREICHER: Didn't Richard Wagner have a Jewish relation somewhere?

HITLER: Doesn't count, doesn't count! He has special dispensation. He's the soul of Germany. He's dead. And most important, he was anti-Semitic.

STREICHER: I meant to say: wasn't Wagner a genius?

MANN: One drop of Jewish blood makes a Jew, then?

HITLER: By Odin, you've got it, I think you've really got it . . .

STREICHER: One drop, unless he's the leader of the Aryans.

HITLER: What did you say?

STREICHER *(Nervously)*: Unless he can escape the leader of the Aryans.

MANN: Is a Jew always swarthy?

HITLER: Not always.

MANN: Does he always have a long nose?

HITLER: No.

MANN: Does he always have shifty eyes?

HITLER: No.

MANN: The same color hair?

HITLER: No.

MANN: The same bone structure?

HITLER: No.

MANN: *Then how do I tell?*

HESS: He's good at making money.

MANN: Are all rich people Jews?

HITLER: Certainly not. We socialists have many millionaire friends who are true-blue Aryans.

(Goebbels, Hess, Streicher, and Bormann rise, begin to chant, and do a choreographed dance step)

EVERYONE: Give us K and R and U and P and P. Waddaya got? Krupp. Three cheers for Krupp! Give us F and A and R and B and E and N. Waddaya got? Farben. Three cheers for Farben!

GOEBBELS: And let's not forget our friends on Wall Street. Oops.

(Silence)

HITLER: You are too enlightened, Herr Doktor Goebbels. *(Hitler walks over and puts his arm around Goebbels)* But I love this guy.

MANN: Excuse me, *mein Führer*, but you answered all my questions in the negative. If the Jews are a race, how am I to find them?

HITLER: If? Did you say if?

MANN: I do not mean to give offense, but I need a method by which to find the Jewish race.

HITLER: It's very simple. You have to trust to the blood. Over a period of many years, I have developed an invaluable method. I *sense* the presence of Jews. Once I was eating in a restaurant that served good, honest German food; and yet, I felt a strange disquiet.

STREICHLR. Quiet! He wants us to be quiet! *(No one pays him any attention)*

HITLER: The waitress was a blond girl with a voluptuous figure and soft, rounded features, and full, pouting lips –

GOEBBELS: Yeah, yeah.

HITLER: – but despite the gorgeous appearance of Aryan womanhood, my sixth sense tingled at her approach. Even the wallpaper bothered me. It was necessary to use the power of my will!

BORMANN: Oy vey.

HITLER *(Addressing the back of the room)*: What was that?

BORMANN: OK, as they say in America.

HITLER: I stared at that wallpaper, waiting, waiting, waiting . . .

GOEBBELS: Waiting for the Jews! That would be a good title for a play.

HITLER: I'm staring at the wallpaper, see, and I realized what was pissing me off. The design was a variation on the Star of David! I'd thought they were meaningless triangles at first.

GOEBBELS: Were there eyes in them?

HITLER: You're cruisin' for a bruisin', Doc. After I penetrated the secret of the wallpaper, I invaded the kitchen and found the waitress eating a bowl of matzoh ball soup.

(Everyone gasps)

STREICHER: What a man!

MANN: How can I, a mere German, match your powers?

GOEBBELS: You could start by being born Austrian. Oops.

HITLER *(Ignoring Goebbels)*: You must develop your faculties. You must act without thinking. When your blood tingles, you will be in the presence of the enemy, the corrupter of Aryan womanhood, the defiler of Aryan children.

MANN: What are the signs?

HITLER: You will feel that something unclean is near, a hater of the Natural Man. All that is honest in you will be repelled by the scheming mentality of the profiteer on human misery. When everything in you cries out that you are in the presence of Evil, it is then that you must do your duty and strike down the vermin.

MANN: I obey. *(So saying, Olaf Mann pulls out a nine-millimeter pistol and shoots Adolf Hitler dead. The others are aghast. Bormann throws down his notepad and joins the others at front center)*

GOEBBELS *(Shouting)*: He has stopped the heart of Germany. Strike him down! Strike him down! *(Streicher raises a fist against Mann)*

MANN *(Leveling his gun on the others)*: I was only following orders. I will now look for more Jews, and I will do my duty. Are any of you Jewish? *(Streicher lowers his fist)*

(Goebbels, Bormann, Streicher, and Hess are as rigid as statues. Silence. Mann exits, stage anywhere)

CURTAIN

Chapter Fourteen

I have seen the man of the future; he is cruel; I am frightened by him.

– Adolf Hitler to Hermann Rauschning,
Table Talk

THE DIARY OF DR GOEBBELS

I felt better after the bath, and still better after destroying the copy of *Looking for the Jews* page by insidious page. My anger against Hilda was so intense that it burned itself out. The rational part of my mind had set up a persistent whispering: So what if your daughter is seriously disturbed, if there is the slightest possibility of danger to you? Survival must be paramount at all times. There were grounds for an investigation of more than just the German Freedom League.

A half hour later I was back at the railroad station, boarding an even slower passenger train back to New Berlin. I love this sort of travel. The rocket engines were held down to their minimum output. The straining hum they made only accentuated the fact of the violent power at our command. Trains are the most human form of mass transportation.

With my state of mind in such turmoil I could not do any serious work. I decided to relax and resumed reading the English mystery novel. I had narrowed it down to three suspects, members of the aristocracy, naturally – all highly offensive people. The servant I had ruled out as much too obvious. As is typical of the form, a few key sentences give up the solution if you know what they are. I had just passed over what I took to be such a phrase and returned to it. Looking up from my book to contemplate the puzzle, I noticed that the woman sitting across from me was also reading a book, a French title that seemed vaguely familiar: *Le Théosophisme, histoire d'une pseudo-religion* by René Guénon.

Returning to the mystery, I suddenly noticed that the train was slowing down. There was no reason for it, as we were far from the next stop. Glancing out the window, I saw nothing but wooded landscape under a starry night sky. A tall man up the aisle was addressing the porter. His rather lengthy monologue boiled down to an elementary question: Why was there a delay? The poor official was shaking his head in bewilderment and indicated that he would move forward to make inquiries. That's when I noticed the gas.

It was yellow. It was seeping in from the air conditioning system. Like everyone else, I started to rise in hope of finding a means of egress. Already I was coughing. As I turned to the window, with the idea of releasing the emergency lock, I slipped down into the cushions. I seemed to be falling as consciousness fled. The last thing I remember was seriously regretting that I had not sampled a glass of wine from that hamlet.

I must have dreamed. I was standing alone in the middle of a great lake, frozen over in the dead of winter. I was not dressed for the weather but had on only my Party uniform. As I looked down at the icy expanse at my feet, I noticed that my boots were freshly shined, the luster already becoming covered by flakes of snow.

A drumming comes from within the black shroud of night and it has a fearful rhythm. I heard the sound of hoofbeats echoing hollowly on the ice and saw emerging from the darkness a small army on horseback. I recognized them. They were the Teutonic Knights. The dark armor, the stern faces, the great, black horses, the bright lances and swords and shields – they could be nothing else.

They did not appear to be friendly. I started walking away from them. The sound of their approach was a thunder pounding at my brain. I cursed my lameness, cursed my inability to fly, suddenly found myself suspended in the air, and then I had fallen on the ice, skinning my knees. Struggling to turn over, I heard a blood-curdling yell and they were all around me. There was a whooshing of blades in the still, icy air. I was screaming. Then I was trying to reason with them.

'I helped Germany win the war . . . I believe in the Aryan race . . . I helped destroy the Jews . . .' But it was to no avail. They were killing me. The swords plunged in deeply.

I awakened aboard a small jet flying in the early dawn. For a moment I thought I was tied to my seat. When I glanced to see what kind of cords bound my arms, I saw that I was mistaken. The feeling of constriction I attributed to the effects of the gas. Painfully I lifted a hand . . . then with increased anguish I raised my head, noticing that the compartment was empty except for me. The door to the cockpit was closed.

The most difficult task that confronted me next was turning my head to the left so that I could have a better view of our location. A dozen tiny needles pricked at the muscles in my neck, but I succeeded. I was placed near the wing and could see a good portion of the countryside unfolding like a map beneath it. We were over a run-down railroad station. One last bit of track snaked on beyond it for about half a mile – we seemed to be flying parallel to it – when it suddenly stopped, blocked off by a tremendous oak tree, the size of which was noticeable from even a great height.

I knew where we were immediately. We had just flown over the eastern border of Burgundy.

Attempting to relax my muscles, I leaned back, very slowly, into the seat, but met with little success. I'd never been so sore in all my life. I was terribly thirsty. Assuming that I'd have a serious dizzy spell if I stood, I called out instead: 'Steward!' No sooner was the word out of my mouth than a young, blond man in a spotless white jacket appeared. He passed me a small, fancy menu.

'What would you like?'

'An explanation.'

'I'm afraid that is not on this menu. I'm sure you will find what you seek when we reach our destination. In the meantime, would you care to dine?'

'No,' I said, relapsing into the depths of my seat, terribly tired again.

'Some coffee?' asked the persistent steward.

I assented to this. It was very good coffee and I was soon feeling better. Looking out the window again, I observed that we were over a lake. There was a long ship plying the clear, blue water – its brightly painted dragon's head glaring at the horizon. My son had written me about the Viking Club when he first took up residence in Burgundy. This had to be one of their outings.

Thirty minutes and two cups of coffee later, the intercom announced that we would be landing at Tarnhelm. From the air the view was excellent: several monasteries – now devoted to SS training camps – were situated near the village that housed the Russian serfs. Beyond that was another lake, and then came the imposing castle in which I knew I would find my son.

There was a narrow landing strip within the castle grounds, and the pilot was every bit the professional. We hadn't been down longer than five minutes when who should enter the plane but Helmuth! But something was wrong. He had blond hair and blue eyes. The only trouble was that my son did not have blond hair and blue eyes! Of course I knew that hair could be dyed, but somehow it appeared to be quite authentic. As for the eyes, I could think of no explanation but contact lenses. Helmuth had also lost weight and never appeared more muscular or healthy than he did now.

There I was, trapped within an enigma – angry, bewildered, unsettled. And yet my first words were 'Helmuth, what's happened to you?'

'This is real blond hair,' he said proudly. 'The eye color is real as well. I regret that I am not of the true genotype, any more than you are. I was given a hormone treatment to change the color of my hair. A special radiation treatment took care of the eyes.'

As he was saying this, he was helping me to my feet, as I was still groggy. 'Why?' I asked him. He would say no more about it.

The sun hurt my eyes as we exited down the ramp from the plane. Two tall young men – also blond haired and blue eyed – joined my son and helped to usher me inside the castle. They were dressed in Bavarian hunting gear, with large knives strapped on at their waists. Their clothes had the smell of freshest leather.

We had entered from the courtyard of the inner bailey. The hall we traversed was covered in plush red carpet and was illuminated by torches burning in the walls; this cast a weird lighting effect over the numerous suits of armour standing here. I could not help but think of the medieval castles Speer drew for his children every Christmas.

It was a long trek before we reached a stone staircase that I was not happy about ascending. I was not completely recovered from the effects of the gas and wished we could pause. My club foot was giving me considerable difficulty. I did not want to show weakness to these men, and I had not forgotten that my sturdy son was right behind me. I took those steps without slowing down the pace.

We finally emerged on a floor that was awash in light from fluorescent tubes. A closed-circuit television console dominated the center of the room, with pictures of all the other floors of the castle, from the keep to the highest tower. There was also a portrait of Meister Eckhart. I hated everything I'd learned about this bald fanatic who thought himself a German Aleister Crowley. The only good he ever did was to introduce Rosenberg and Hess to Hitler. The evil, little eyes of the portrait regarded me with equal disdain, and added to the sordid effect was a third eye painted on his forehead.

'Wait here,' Helmuth announced, and before I could make any protestations he and the other two had left the way we had come, with the door locked behind them. The room seemed to be a kind of museum for ornate Bavarian pipes and the most elaborate beer steins of Europe. Someone was living well.

I went over to a large picture window and surveyed my position from the new vantage point. Below was another courtyard. In one corner was what could be nothing else but an unused funeral pyre! Its height was staggering. There was nobody upon it. Along the wall that ran from the pyre to the other end of the compound were letters inscribed of a size easy to read even from such a distance. It was a familiar quotation: ANY DESCRIPTION OF ORGANIZ- ATION, MISSION, AND STRUCTURE OF THE SS CANNOT BE UNDERSTOOD UNLESS ONE TRIES TO CONCEIVE IT INWARDLY WITH ONE'S BLOOD AND HEART. IT CANNOT BE EXPLAINED WHY WE CONTAIN SO MUCH STRENGTH THOUGH WE NUMBER

SO FEW. Underneath the tirade in equally large letters was the name of its author: HEINRICH HIMMLER.

'A statement that you know well,' came a low voice behind me, and I turned to face Kurt Kaufmann, the most important man in Burgundy. I had met him a few times socially in New Berlin.

Smiling in as engaging a manner as I could (under the circumstances), I said, 'Kurt,' employing the informal mode of address, 'I haven't a clue why you have seemingly kidnapped me, but there will be hell to pay.'

He bowed. 'What you fail to appreciate, Herr Doktor Goebbels, is that I will receive that payment.'

I studied his face – the bushy blond hair and beard, and of course the bright blue eyes. The monocle he wore over one of them seemed quite superfluous. I knew that he had 20/20 vision.

'I have no idea what you are talking about.'

'You lack ideas, it is true,' he answered. 'Of facts you do not lack. We knew your daughter contacted you.'

Even at the time this dialogue seemed overly melodramatic. Nevertheless it was happening *to me*. At the mention of Hilda, I failed to mask my feelings. Kaufmann must have noticed an expression of consternation on my face. There are occasions I wish we could wear masks every day of our lives. This whole affair was turning into a hideous game that I feared I was losing.

I parried with: 'My daughter's association with a degenerate aesthetic group is well known.' There was no reason to mince words with him. 'I was attempting to dissuade her from a suicidal course, but I resent your spying on a personal family matter that in no way concerns you.'

The ploy failed miserably. 'We bugged the room,' he said softly.

'How dare you spy on *me*, you parasite. Have you any idea of the danger?'

'Yes,' he said. 'You don't.'

I made to comment, but he raised a hand to silence me. 'Do not continue. Soon you will have more answers than you desire. Now I suggest you follow me.'

The room had many doors. We exited through one at the opposite end from my original point of entry. I was walking down another hall. This one, however, was lit by electricity. We entered a large room that didn't have a stick of furniture, but in which a number of young men (where were the women?) sat in a semicircle on rugs. They wore simple robes made of some coarse fabric. Their heads were shaved.

Kaufmann held a finger to his lips, but he needn't have bothered. I wasn't about to say anything in there. Not a muscle moved or eye flickered as we passed the boys. I noticed that they were entranced by a single apple that had been cut in half and set out before them. I had a hunch that this was not a cafeteria. As we reentered the hallway, Kaufmann anticipated my question. 'They're initiates recently returned from India,' he volunteered.

'Did Helmuth do this? He didn't answer letters from home for several months.'

'I can't tell you that.'

'Can you tell me what they are doing, or is that a state secret, too?'

His smile was unfriendly. 'It won't hurt to tell you that. They are contemplating Vril power.'

'Thanks for clearing it up, Kurt.'

We returned to civilization-as-I-know-it and entered an elevator. The contrast between modern technology and Burgundian simplicity was becoming more jarring all the time. Like most Germans who had visited the country, I had only experienced it as a tourist. The reports I had received on their training operations were not as detailed as I would have liked but certainly gave no hint of dire conspiracy against the Fatherland. The thought was too fantastic to credit. Even now I hoped for a denouement more in keeping with the known facts. Could the entire thing be an elaborate practical joke? Who would run the risk of such folly?

The elevator doors opened and we were looking out onto the battlements of the castle. Following Kaufmann onto the walk, I noticed that the view was utterly magnificent. To the left I saw imported Russian serfs working in the fields; to the right I saw young Burgundians doing calisthenics in the warm morning air. At last there were some girls, but there was another item that gave me pause. I was used to observing many blond heads in the SS. Yet suddenly there was nothing but that predictable homogeneity. Something was going on in Burgundy.

We observed the young bodies gyrating and perspiring in the bright sunlight. Beyond them, a group of young men were outfitted in chain mail shirts and helmets. They were having at one another with the most intensive swordplay I had ever witnessed.

'Isn't that a bit dangerous?' I asked Kaufmann, gesturing at the fencing.

'What do you mean?' he replied, as one of the men ran his sword through the chest of another. The blood spurted out in a fountain as the body slumped to the ground. I was aghast, and Kaufmann's voice seemed far away as I dimly heard it say: 'Did you notice that the loser did not scream? We teach discipline here.' It occurred to me that the fellow might have simply died too quickly to express an opinion; it also was worth considering that if the Burgundians were this wasteful of men, the Reich proper had nothing to worry about.

Kaufmann was probably a sadist. He was certainly amused by my sickened reaction. 'Dr Goebbels, do you remember the *Kirchenkampf*?'

I recovered my composure. 'The campaign against the churches? What about it?'

'Martin Bormann was disappointed in its failure,' he said.

'No more than I. The war years allowed little time for less important matters. You should know that the economic policies we established after the war helped to undermine the strength of the churches. They have never been weaker. European cinema constantly makes fun of them.'

'That's not good enough,' said Kaufmann evenly. 'They exist. The gods of the Germanic tribes are not fools – their indignation is as severe as ever.' I stared at this man with amazement as he continued to preach: 'The gods watched Roman missionaries build early Christian churches on the sacred sites in the hope that the common people would continue climbing the same hills they had always used for worship . . . only now the people would pay homage to a false god!'

'The masses are not easily cured of the addiction,' I pointed out.

'You compare religion to a drug?'

'It was one of the few wise statements of Marx,' I said, with a deliberate edge to my voice. Kaufmann's face quickly darkened into a scowl. 'Not all religions are the same,' I concluded in an ameliorative tone. I had no desire to argue with him about the two faiths of Burgundy. So far as I was concerned, the remnants of Rosenberg's Gnostics and Himmler's majority of pagans could hold hands and jump down the nearest live volcano.

'Words are toys to you,' he said. 'Let me tell you a story about yourself, Herr Goebbels. You have always prided yourself on being the true radical of the Nazi Party. You hammered that home at every opportunity. Nobody hated the bourgeoise more than Goebbels.

209

Nobody was more ardent about burning books than Goebbels. As Reichspropagandaminister you brilliantly staged the demonstrations against the Jews.'

Now the man was making sense. I volunteered another item to his admirable list: 'I hear some young men humming the Horst Wessel song down there.' They were even in key. Manufacturing a martyr to give the Party its anthem was still one of my favorites. My influence remained on the Germanic world, including Burgundy. But how quickly they forget.

Kaufmann had been surveying rows of men doing pushups . . . as well as the removal of the corpse from the tourney field. Now his stony face turned in my direction, breaking into an unpleasant smile. I preferred his frown. 'You misunderstand the direction of my comments, Herr Doktor. I will clarify. I was told a story about you once. I was only a simple soldier at the time, freezing my ass off on the Russian front, but the story made an indelible impression. You were at a party, showing off for your friends by making four brief political speeches: the first presented the case for the restoration of the monarchy; the second sung the praises of the Weimar Republic; the third proved how communism could be successfully adopted by the German Reich; the fourth was in favor of National Socialism, at last. How relieved they were. How tempted they had been to agree with each of the other three speeches.'

I could not believe what I was hearing. How could this dull oaf be in charge of anything but a petty bureaucratic department? Had he no sense of humor, no irony? 'I was demonstrating the power of propaganda,' I told him.

'If you're so wonderful at propaganda, then why does the rest of the world believe decades after our victory that we were the sole cause of World War II? They seem to think that Europe was Little Red Riding Hood, happily minding her own business, when the German wolf pounced on the innocent Fraulein and dragged her into the black forest, where he devoured her piece by piece.'

As he went into meticulous detail about the failings of my control over newspapers, magazines, television, cabaret shows, and apparently his own son's term papers, I had the sinking feeling I only suffer when confronted by an unpleasant fact. There is nothing worse than when a religious fanatic makes sense. You know it's only temporary. Bereft of rational coordinates, he sails on a sea of confusion where the only safe haven is supernatural revelation. I had never approved of the attempt to justify our prejudices on mystical grounds when the best course of action lay in scientific research. Burgundians gave racism a bad name. Hitler in this, as so many other things, was willing to let everyone follow their own stars, so long as conclusions corresponded to the pronouncements of *Mein Kampf*. That was politics.

My failure to shift world opinion was cause for distress. When America turned against FDR, I had thought we had a chance to win favorable opinion there, despite our incompetent bunds of the 1930s. I misjudged the American character. They condemned us more than ever. The collapsing prospects of the New Deal did nothing to help our image; it merely implicated us along with all the other wartime leaders. What was needed was a whitewash, which I did my best to provide. The outcome was never in doubt: only the Reich and its satellites accept the Party outlook. Independent historians across the Atlantic remain my curse, especially a bastard named Barnes.

Believing that one should always give the Devil his due, I granted Kaufmann a fraction of his complaint, to which he answered: 'When Schopenhauer said that human life must be some kind of mistake, he pointed the way for our mission: to correct the error with Aryan magick!' I lost

my self-control. Kaufmann was exactly what Schopenhauer had in mind when he cried his lamentations into the
void. I laughed in my kidnapper's face.

'In what do you believe, if not the race?' he asked
sharply.

'This is preposterous,' I nearly shouted. 'Are you
impugning – '

'It is not necessary to answer,' he said consolingly. 'I'm
aware that you have only believed in one thing in your
life: a man, not an idea. With Hitler dead, what is left for
you?'

'This is insane,' I replied, not liking the shrill sound of
my own voice in my ears. 'When I was made Reich
Director for Total War, I demonstrated my genius for
understanding and operating the mechanisms of a dictatorship. I was crucial to the war effort then. Hitler chose
me, damn you.'

'Yes, he did. We have never forgotten. But what you
are incapable of appreciating, because your spirit eye is
forever closed, is that Hitler was more than a man. He
was a living part of an idea. He did not always recognize
his own importance. He was chosen by the Vril Society,
chosen, damn *you*, by the sacred order of the Luminous
Lodge, the purest, finest product of the believers in the
Thule. Adolf Hitler was the medium. The society used
him accordingly. He was the focal point. Behind him were
powerful magicians. He used words of power to control a
nation, and then more, much more. The great work has
only begun. Soon it will be time for the second step. Only
the true man deserves *Lebensraum*.'

Kaufmann was working himself up, I could see that.
He stood close to me and said, 'You are a political animal,
Goebbels. You believe that politics is an end in itself. The
truth is that governments are nothing in the face of
destiny. We are near the cleansing of the world. You

should be proud. Your son will play an important part. The finest jest is that modern scientific method will also have a role, as will traitors from the big city.'

One last time I appealed to reason: 'If there is a traitor to National Socialism, my friend, it's you. The movement is political. What do you think geopolitics means? You wouldn't be playing these games if the Reich couldn't afford to indulge you, and after my report, you'll be on an austerity budget.'

A flash of metal in his hand caused me to jump, but it wasn't a weapon. He held a coin under my nose. 'This is one of the German gold coins minted before 1914. They are all in our possession now. Burgundy has never been off the gold standard, and we have other sources of income. Soon money won't matter to the Reich anyway.'

'What do you mean by that?'

'You'll find out. Your movement may be political, but ours has never been. No one in Burgundy is accepted until he has been in touch with the Race Memory in the Akashic Record and has been initiated into the secrets of the Eternal Man. This we call being "twice born"!'

'Why tell me? I don't care.'

'Soon that won't matter either.' He turned to go. I had no recourse but to follow him. There was nowhere else but straight down to sudden death. As we reentered the elevator, he spat out, 'Don't try anything. One kick in the knee can be an initiation all by itself.'

Adrenaline pumping through me, thanks to his stupidity of putting me on guard, I forced another question: 'Have I been brought here to witness an honor bestowed on my so. ?'

'In part. But we will bestow an even greater honor on you, one you won't live to regret. You saw the decoded message.'

That was enough. There could no longer be any doubt.

I was trapped amidst madmen. Having determined a course of action, I feigned an attack of pain in my club foot and crouched at the same time. When Kaufmann instinctively made to offer aid, I struck wildly, almost blindly. I tried to knee him in the groin but – failing that – brought my fist down on the back of his neck. The fool went out like a light, falling hard on his face. I congratulated myself on such prowess for an old man.

No sooner had the body slumped to the floor than the elevator came to a stop and the doors opened automatically. I jumped out into the hall. Standing there was a naked seven-foot giant who reached down and lifted me into the air. He was laughing. His voice sounded like a tuba.

'They call me Thor,' he said. I struggled. He held.

Then I heard the voice of my son: 'That, Father, is what we call a true Aryan.'

I was carried like so much baggage down the hall, hearing voices distantly talking about Kaufmann. I was tossed onto the hard floor of a brightly lit room and the door was slammed behind me. A muscle had been pulled in my back and I lay there, gasping in pain like a fish out of water. I could see that I was in some sort of laboratory. In a corner was a wildly humming machine, the purpose of which I could not begin to guess. A young woman was standing over me, wearing a white lab smock. I could not help but notice two things about her straight away: she was a brunette, and she was holding a sword at my throat.

Chapter Fifteen

MAGNET, n. Something acted upon by magnetism.
MAGNETISM, n. Something acting upon a magnet.
The two definitions immediately foregoing are condensed from the works of one thousand eminent scientists, who have illuminated the subject with a great white light, to the inexpressible advancement of human knowledge.

– Ambrose Bierce,
The Devil's Dictionary

As I look back, the entire affair has an air of unreality about it. Events were becoming more unlikely in direct proportion to the speed with which they occurred. It had all the logic of a dream.

The room in which I had been unceremoniously dumped had an antiseptic hospital smell that reintroduced a modicum of reality to my beleaguered senses. As I lay on the floor, under the sword held by such an unlikely guardian (I had always supported military service for women, but when encountering the real thing I found it a bit difficult to take seriously), I took an inventory of my pains. The backache was subsiding so long as I did not move . . . but I was becoming aware that the hand with which I had dispatched Kaufmann felt like a hot balloon of agony, expanding without an upper limit. My vision was blurred and I shook my head trying to clear it. Dimly I heard voices in the background, and then a particularly resonant one was near at hand, speaking with complete authority: 'Oh, don't be ridiculous. Help him up.'

The woman put down the sword and was suddenly

assisted by a young Japanese girl gingerly lifting me off the floor and propelling me in the direction of a nearby chair. Still I did not see the author of that powerful voice.

Then I was sitting down and the females were moving away. He was standing there, his hands on his hips, looking at me with the sort of analytical probing I always respect. At first I didn't recognize him, but had instead the eerie feeling that I was in one of my own movies. No, that wasn't it exactly. It was someone else's movie.

The face made me think of something too ridiculous to credit, and then I knew who it really was: Professor Dietrich, the missing geneticist. I examined him more closely. The first impression had been more correct than I thought. The man hardly resembled the photographs of his youth. His hair had turned white and he had let it grow. Seeing him in person, I could not help noticing how angular were his features . . . how much like the face of the late actor Rudolf Klein-Rogge in the role of Dr Mabuse, Fritz Lang's character, who had become the symbol of a superscientific, scheming Germany to the rest of the world. Although the later films were banned for the average German, the American-made series (Mabuse's second life, you could say) had become so popular throughout the world that Reich officials considered it a mark of distinction to own copies of all twenty. We still preferred the original series where Mabuse was obviously Jewish, and screenwriter Thea von Harbou wrote in the spirit of that perception; but Fritz Lang had not seen it that way when he refused to alter *The Testament of Dr Mabuse* to depict a Fuehrer hero defeating the mastermind in the last reel. Lang thought Mabuse a perfect symbol for Hitler himself! Artists live in a dream world. But I digress from the living fantasy that breathed in the laboratory of a Burgundian castle.

Since the death of Klein-Rogge (so many are gone),

216

other actors had taken over the part, but always the producers looked for that same startling visage. This man Dietrich was meant for the role, but he was most certainly not interested in auditioning for photoplays when he was already the star of something real.

'What are you staring at?' he asked. I told him. He nodded. 'You chose the right profession,' he continued. 'You have a cinematic imagination. I am flattered by the comparison.'

'May I ask you what exactly is happening here?'

'Much. Not all of it is necessary. This show they are putting on for your benefit is pointless.'

I was becoming comfortable in the chair, and my back had momentarily ceased to annoy me. I hoped that I would not have to move for yet another guided tour of something I wasn't sure I wanted to see. My curiosity had no physical component at present. To my relief, Dietrich pulled up a chair, sat down across from me, and set me at ease with:

'I expect that Kaufmann meant to introduce you to Thor when the doors to the lift opened, and then enjoy your startled expression as you were escorted down the hall to my humble quarters. They didn't think you'd improvise on the set. They're amateurs and you are the professional when it comes to lights-camera-action. Bravo!'

'Thor . . .' I began lamely, but could think of nothing to say.

'He's not overly intelligent. I'm impressed that he finished his scene with such dispatch. I apologize for my assistant. She had been watching on one of our monitors – where would we be without television, eh? – and must have come to the conclusion that you are a dangerous fellow. In person, I mean. We are all acquainted with what you can do in an official capacity.'

217

It was a relief to talk to such an obviously cultured man. As a sense of ease returned, I took in my surroundings. The size of the laboratory was tremendous. It was like being in a scientific warehouse. Although lacking technical training myself, it seemed to my layman's eye that there was a lack of systematic arrangement: materials were jumbled together in a downright sloppy fashion, even assuming a good reason for the close proximity of totally different apparatuses. Nevertheless I realized that I was out of my depth and might be having nothing more than an aesthetic response.

'They closed the file on you,' I said. 'They think you've been kidnapped by American agents.'

'That was the cover story.'

'Then you were kidnapped by Burgundians?'

'A reasonable deduction, but wrong. I volunteered.'

'For what?'

'Dr Goebbels, I said that you have a cinematic imagination. That's good. It may help you to appreciate the teacher.' He snapped his fingers and the Japanese girl was by his side so swiftly that I didn't see where she had come from. She was holding a small plastic box. Opening it, he showed me the interior: two cylinders resided there, each with a tiny suction cup on the end. He took one out. 'Examine this,' he said, passing it to me.

'One of your inventions?' I asked, noticing that it was as light in my palm as if it were made of tissue paper. But I could tell that whatever the material was, it was sturdy.

'A colleague came up with that. It's an application of one of my discoveries. He was a good man, but he's dead now. Politics.' He retrieved the cylinder, did something with the untipped end, then stood. 'It doesn't hurt,' he said. 'If you will cooperate, I promise a cinematic experience unlike anything you've sampled before.'

There was no point in resisting. They had me. Whatever

their purpose, I was in no position to oppose it. Nor is there any denying that my curiosity was aroused by this seeming toy.

Dietrich leaned forward, saying, 'Allow me to connect this to your brain and you will enjoy a unique production of the Burgundian Propaganda Ministry, if you will – the story of my life.'

Without further ado, he pressed the delicate suction cup against the center of my forehead. There was a tingling sensation and then my sight began to dim! I knew that my eyes were still open and I had not lost consciousness. For a moment I feared that I was going blind.

There were new images. I began to dream while wide awake, except that these were not my dreams. They were someone else's.

I was someone else!

I was Dietrich . . . as a child.

I was buttoning my collar on a cold day in February before going to school. The face that looked back from the mirror held a cherubic – almost beautiful – aspect. I was happy.

As I skipped down cobbled German streets it suddenly struck me with solemn force that I was a Sephardic Jew.

My parents had been strict, Orthodox, and humorless. An industrial accident had taken them from me. I was not to be alone for long. An uncle in Spain sent for me and I became part of his household. He was living as a Gentile (not without difficulty) but was able to take a child from a practicing Jewish family into his home.

It did not take more than a few days at school for the beatings to begin, whereupon they increased in ferocity. There was a bubbling fountain within easy distance of the schoolyard where I could wash away the blood.

One day I watched the water turn crimson over the rippling reflection of my scarred visage. I decided that whatever it was a Jew was supposed to be, I didn't qualify. I had the same color blood as my classmates, after all. Therefore I could not be a real Jew.

Announcing this revelation at school the next day nearly got me killed for my trouble. One particularly stupid lad was so distressed by my logic that he expressed his displeasure with a critique made up of a two-by-four. Yet somehow in all this pain and anguish – as I fled for my life – I did not think to condemn the attackers. I concluded that surely the Jew must be a monstrous creature indeed to inspire such a display. Cursing the memory of my parents, I felt certain that through a happy fluke I was not really of their flesh and blood.

Amazingly, I became an anti-Semite. I took a Star of David to the playground and in full view of my classmates destroyed it. A picture of a rabbi I also burned. Some were not impressed by this display, but others restrained them from resuming the beatings. For the first time I knew security in that schoolyard. None of them became any friendlier; they did not know how to take it.

Suddenly the pictures of Dietrich's early life disappeared into a swirling darkness. I was confused, disoriented.

Time had passed. Now I was Dietrich as a young man back in Germany, dedicating myself to a life's work in genetic research. With a meticulously worked out family background, fraudulent in every detail, I joined the Nazi Party on the eve of its coming to power – I did this not so much out of vanity as from a pragmatic reading of the zeitgeist. I entertained my new 'friends' with a little-known quotation from the canon of Karl Marx, circa 1844: 'On e society has succeeded in abolishing the empir-ical essence of Judaism – huckstering and its preconditions – the Jew will have become impossible.'

The National Socialists were developing their biological theories at the time. To say the basis of their programs was at best pseudo-scientific would be to compliment it. At best, the only science involved was terminology borrowed from the field of eugenics.

I was doing real research, however, despite the limitations I faced due to Party funding and propaganda requirements. My work involved negative eugenics, the study of how to eliminate defective genes from the gene pool through selective breeding. Assuming an entire society could be turned into a laboratory, defective genes could be eliminated in one generation, although the problem might still crop up from time to time because of recessive genes (easily handled).

In deciding to breed something out of the population, the door was opened as to what to breed *for*, or positive eugenics. Now, so long as we were restricting ourselves to a question of one genetic disease, we could do something. But even then there were limitations. What if some invaluable genius had a genetic disability? Would you dismiss the possibility of his having intelligent offspring because of one risk?

It wasn't until 1943 that Hitler began releasing sufficient funds for all the scientific projects. If the A-bomb failed, a biological weapon was to be the fallback; and I was assigned to lead a team working in that area. In a rare moment of clarity, Hitler insisted that we fly in separate planes to avoid losing all of us in one accident. It would have been easier to disappear if my plane had gone down, but I didn't think of departure until I was interrogated about samples of my work that were being smuggled out of Germany by a spy, a Jew who would soon be sent to a concentration camp. The thought that I shouldn't have to put up with the inconvenience (they had the temerity to send Gestapo men who wouldn't even be allowed inside an SS camp) grew over the years until it flowered into a mania with me. I would go into business for myself.

Whenever I was engaged in a fruitful line of inquiry, the deranged, mystical ideas of the Nazis would intrude, and complications would set in. They wanted to breed for qualities that in many cases fell outside the province of real genetics – because they fell outside reality in the first place. An example was the request, passed on by Himmler himself, that we develop a revenge weapon to deploy if Germany lost the war. They wanted a virus that would be spread sexually, but only applying to miscegenation!

During this period in my life, I made another discovery. I was no longer a racist. My anti-Semitism vanished as in a vagrant breeze. I had learned that there was no scientific basis for it. The sincere Nazi belief that the Jew is a creature outside of nature was so much rot. As for the cultural-mystical ideas revolving around the Jew, the more I learned of how my patrons perceived these matters, the more convinced I became that Hitler's movement appealed to the irrational. (An ironic note was that many European Jews were not Semitic, but that is beside the point. The Nazis had little concern with, say, Arabs. It was the European Jew they were after, for whatever reasons were handy.)

Although I had come full circle on the question of racism, something else had happened to me in the interim. My hatred for one group of humanity had *not* vanished. My view of the common heritage of Homo sapiens led me to despise all of the human race. The implications escaped me at the time, but this was the pivotal moment of my life.

E n at the peak of their popularity, the world of genetics was only slightly influenced by Nazi thinking. Scientists are scientists first, ideologues second, if at all. To the extent that most scientists have a philosophy, it is a general sort of positive humanism: so it was with my teacher in genetics, a brilliant man – who happened to fit the Aryan stereotype coincidentally – and his collaborator, a Jew who was open about his family background, unlike me.

They were the first to discover the structure of DNA. No, they are not in the history books. By then Hitler had come to power. The Nazis destroyed many of their papers when they were adjudged enemies of the state – for political improprieties having nothing to do with the research. But I was never found guilty of harboring traitorous notions; and my Gentile pedigree continued to withstand the scrutiny of morons.

Long before the world heard of it, I continued this work with DNA. Publishing my findings was the last thing I wanted to do. I had other ideas. By giving the Nazis gobbledygook to make their fanciful policies sound good, I remained unmolested. There would be a place for me in the New Order. I remembered when Einstein said that should his theory of relativity prove untrue, the French would declare him a German, and the Germans call him a Jew. At least I was certain of my place in advance.

The National Socialists and their Third Reich gave me what I needed: unlimited human material. What good is a theory if you can't test it? What I needed most was the supply of pregnant women in a steady stream from the concentration camps. I injected a clone of naughty genes into the livers of the fetuses. The data on synthetic viruses was invaluable and the monster children provided amusement for the more decadent members of the SS.

(NOTE FROM HILDA: So here is the one responsible for the twisted forms of the wretched children that have haunted my every night since first seeing the photographs in Burgundy.)

And yet, all my progress left me curiously unsatisfied. It was as if I had the largest jigsaw puzzle in the world, with the central piece missing. And then one day I realized that that piece was not to be found in biology.

Through the haze of Dietrich's memories, I retained my identity; I could reflect on what I was assimilating directly from a pattern taken from another mind. I was impressed that such a man existed, working in secret for decades on what had only recently riveted the world's attention. Only last year had a news story dealt with microbiologists doing gene splicing. Yet he had done the same sort of experimentation years earlier. Even while respecting his achievements, the relish with which he described the unsavory aspects made me a little ill. And then . . .

What had been a trickle suddenly turned into a torrent of concepts and formulae beyond my comprehension. I felt the strain. With quivering fingers I reached for the cylinder and . . . the images stopped; the words stopped; the kaleidoscope exploding inside my head stopped; the pressure stopped . . .

'You have not finished the program, Dr Goebbels,' said Dietrich. 'It was at least another ten minutes before the "reel change."' He was holding the other cylinder in his hand, tossing it lightly into the air and catching it as though it were of no importance.

'It's too much,' I gasped, 'to take in all at once. Hold on, I've remembered something: Thor in the hallway. Is it possible?' I thought back over what I had experienced. Dietrich had left simple eugenic breeding programs far behind. His search was for the chemical mysteries of life itself, like some sort of mad alchemist seeking the knowledge of a Frankenstein. 'Did you . . .' I paused, hardly knowing how to phrase it. 'Did you create Thor?'

'Don't I wish,' he said, almost playfully. 'Have you the slightest understanding of what that would entail? To find the genetic formula for human beings would require a language I do not possess.'

224

'A language?'

'You'd have to break the code, be able to read the hieroglyphic wonders of not just one, but millions of genes. It's all there, in the chromosomes, but I haven't been able to find it yet. No one has.' He put his face near to mine, grinning, eyes wide and staring. 'But I will be the first. Nobody can beat me to it, because only I can do it; and I'm almost there!'

For a moment I thought I was again in the presence of Hitler. This man was certainly a visionary. Moreover, he was dangerous in a fashion beyond any politician. Having caught his breath, he wiped his head with a red handkerchief and said, 'I'll admit I did something for that young man, or to him, but it's peripheral to what we really do here. Thor used to be a mere six feet tall. I injected a growth hormone extracted from the pituitary gland in corpses, of which articles we have no shortage in Burgundy.'

'Why are you here?' I asked.

'They finance me well. See the requirements,' he said, pointing at what he told me was an atmosphere chamber. 'The work is expensive. Do you know how to invade the hidden territory of life itself? With radiation and poison to break down the structures and begin anew. To build! I can never live long enough, never receive enough sponsorship. It is the work of many lifetimes. If only I had more subtle tools . . .'

Before I lost him to a scientist's reverie, I changed the subject: 'My son's hair and eyes have changed.'

'That's nothing but cosmetics,' he said disdainfully.

'The SS wants you to do that?'

'It is considered a mark of distinction. My beautician there' – he pointed at the pretty Japanese girl – 'provides this minor and unimportant service.'

Only a few blond-haired, blue-eyed people were working in the laboratory. I asked why everyone had not undergone the treatment. The reason was because the few I had just seen were authentic members of that genotype. Dietrich was blunt: 'We don't play SS games in here.'

Although I did not want to leave my chair, he insisted on taking me on a guided tour of his workshop, treating the technicians as no more than expensive equipment. I wondered how Speer would react to all this. The place was even larger than I had first thought. I wondered what Helga would make of it all, cramped in her small cubbyhole at the university.

The seemingly endless stroll activated my pains again. He noticed my distress and suggested we sit down again. 'Did I really share in your memories?' I asked him when I had regained my composure.

'A carefully edited production, but yes.'

'How is it done?'

'Electromagnetic waves can cause hallucinations. These I control by a process that is tedious but highly effective.'

'I thought your area was genetics.'

'Molecular biology, Goebbels, is the marriage of earthly salts with the blood of the *Völk*. It is not my field; it is only a means to an end. I have no field. Listen, little man, the arbitrary divisions thrown up between mathematics and science and engineering are devices by which to create specialized fools who wouldn't know the truth if it swallowed them whole. Western science doesn't believe in anything unless it is explained in terms of the atom; National Socialist science doesn't believe in anything unless it is traced to the cell. Yet despite these mental straitjackets, both sides depend on both atom and cell for their very survival. We've reached a day when physicists can't talk to chemists, mathematicians won't talk to anyone, and engineers are deaf. Unlike them, I am interested in the Truth . . . because I have a use for it.'

This was all Greek to me, but he spoke so forcefully that he made a deep impression on my admittedly phenomenal memory. Anger over my abduction shrank in this man's presence. Kaufmann was merely an enemy, but Dietrich was a creature from another world. He had my full attention as he described the workings of the remarkable information tube. The device was a propagandist's dream come true. He told how the idea traced back to an inventor named Tesla, a contemporary of Edison's, who had constructed huge coils for storing electromagnetic energy. When he stuck his head in one of them, he'd seen strange lights and colors; he concluded that the coil's field was interfering with his own brain's energy. Dietrich's teaching devices had been developed along these lines, augmented by his own discoveries. Then and there, I decided if I got out alive from Burgundy, I would steal at least one of the micro-Tesla coils.

The politics of Burgundy took on a new meaning. 'Despite what you've told me about your, I suppose it could be called a sinecure,' I said, 'I don't see how a man like you can function in Burgundy.'

He did not take offense. 'They are innocents in search of an imaginary past. I'm good with children. They think that state-of-the-art science is the discovery of the four elements: fire, earth, air, and water. I simply told them that my genetic work is based on the four bases of life: adenine, cytosine, guanine, and thymine. I'm a wizard to them.'

'You said that you'd almost discovered the secret of life. I'm not trained in medicine, but I could try to understand.' My curiosity was reborn with a passion.

'There you go again, compartmentalizing your thinking. Haven't you been paying attention? My work with electromagnetism had a more important application than motion picture toys. There is a uniform force. Magnetism, electricity, and gravity are manifestations of this one force! My breakthrough came on the day I discovered that nucleic acids are magnetic. Think of RNA as a gauleiter, passing orders from a Fuehrer nucleus to the peasant ribosomes. Can you grasp that?'

'Yes.'

'Good. To break into this process is the next step. The body is a battlefield anyway, so there is room for an interloper to take the high ground. If I can demagnetize and then remagnetize a human being, I can eliminate disease by ordering the diseased cells to become normal cells. Or I can do the reverse. Once again, the difficulty lies with instrumentalities. Imagine that you erase a magnetic tape and begin tabula rasa. You could record anything, Goebbels . . . anything! The future of computers does not lie with dead matter but with organisms I will breed myself . . . for company.'

It was all very interesting as he described the myriad possibilities of the Superman. I found it more congenial to picture gods and monsters than to think through the meaning of his favorite topic, to which he returned repeatedly: 'Einstein gave physicists a fourth dimension to play with after what he did with time,' he said. 'More recently, a mathematician living in Königsberg, the city of Immanuel Kant, came up with a fifth dimension, the equations for which make gravity look like . . . guess what?'

I could catch on to a popular term: 'Electromagnetism?'

'Exactly! You may understand what I am doing, in the limited time remaining to you.' It was the sort of offhand comment to freeze the blood of Surtur, but he paid no heed and continued explaining his weltanschauung – he even had a kind word for the SS project during the war

228

that had done research on whether positively and negatively charged ions in the atmosphere could affect morale; the finding was that positive ions made people irritable and depressed. 'Not everything they did was insane, like looking for entrances to the hollow earth,' he said, 'but most of the time they accomplish nothing of value. What can you expect when they run off to monasteries in Tibet and Druidic sites in Ireland and buried caves in Iceland, searching for archaeological evidence of the origins of the Aryan race. Boys will be boys.'

Then he was back on track with science. He claimed that people had no justification to live unless they advanced the cause of knowledge. He scorned the conservative Babbitts – that invaluable American phrase – who exhausted themselves worrying that their children might not turn out to be perfect reproductions of their useless, bloodless selves. 'I've never believed in Natural Rights,' he said, 'and I know you don't either, if your propaganda against the republic across the sea is any indication.' I nodded vigorously, as if I were back in school. 'What is a right? Can you weigh it, measure it, taste it?'

'It's probably not even electromagnetic,' I added.

'Very good! Why should anyone respect the rights of others if they don't exist? It's another religion, and I don't believe in spooks. Americans wallow in ethical abstractions and it impedes their scientific progress. Soon that won't matter anymore, nothing will; but I'm getting ahead of myself.' No sooner were these words out of his mouth than he began spinning around as if a whirling dervish. He came to a stop before a most startled guest. 'I made a pun. You see, I have a doppelgänger, but it's only in my mind.' He suddenly grinned, and I noticed that one of his teeth was pointed.

'Pardon, what did you say?'

'Oh, nothing important. It's only that my mind is so powerful that it projects another me on an external wavelength.'

This was one day I should have stayed in bed. 'I thought you didn't believe in spooks,' I said.

'I don't.'

'Does anyone else see this other . . . you?'

'Sometimes.'

'That sounds like a spook.'

'Energy is not supernatural,' he said, then changed the subject . . . in a manner of speaking. 'Dr Goebbels, if I were to live forever, would that make me God in a nonsupernatural sense?'

'Why are you making fun of me?'

'If I can perform miracles, I'll achieve immortality. Now a second question: If I were the only living ego, would that make me God?'

I was no longer at ease in his company, not the least little bit. I wished that I'd listened to Hilda. Was there no way out? I had to play for time. 'Are you sure you're not religious?' I asked.

'You answer my questions with questions of your own, thus demonstrating an unacceptable independence of mind. Perhaps you'd like to sample the contents of the other cylinder?' He'd slyly kept it on his person. As one who had served Adolf Hitler, I recognized a command when it came in the guise of a query. I agreed.

Chapter Sixteen

Again ye come, ye hovering Forms!
I find you as early to my clouded sight ye shone!
Shall I attempt, this once, to seize and bind you?
Still o'er my heart is that illusion thrown?
Ye crowd more near! Well then, be power assigned you
To sway me from your misty, shadowy zone!
My bosom thrills, by youthful passion shaken
That magic breezes round your march awaken.

– Goethe,
Faust

I attached this cylinder by myself and . . .

I did not know who I was.

In vain I searched for the identity into which I had been plunged. What there was of me seemed to be a disembodied consciousness floating high above the European continent. It was like seeing in all directions at once. The moon above was very large, very near the earth – it was made of ice.

Hörbiger's *Welteislehre*! It was a projection of one of his prophecies, when the moon would fall toward the earth, causing great upheavals in the crust – and working bizarre mutations on the life of the planet. The oceans would rise and there would be a new Flood, but the *Übermenschen* would survive, reveling in their giant bodies, which could become lighter than air at will. Finally, the descending moon would disintegrate, leaving an ice ring of immense proportions surrounding the planet. Then the True Reich would flourish, bathed in the godly light of cosmic rays. Yet all this was not merely a

231

vision of the future; it was also a vision into the antediluvian past. Ours was the fourth moon.

There was a panorama unfolding like the worm Ouroboros: ancient epochs and the far future were melded together in an unbreakable circle. The world and civilization I knew were nothing but passing aberrations in the history of the globe.

Mankind was fifteen million years old. It had achieved triumphs in the past and degenerated since. Modern man was engaging in the worst kind of self-flattery when he saw himself as a risen ape. He was a dreadfully Fallen Being, but not in the Christian sense believed by Catholics and Protestants; nor in the more outré interpretation of the murdered and martyred Cathars and Albigensians whose travails in European history had contributed to Alfred Rosenberg's Nazi version of Gnosticism. None of these beliefs were drawn from the racial template that could only be divined by the spirit eye of the awakened Aryan. This same spirit sight revealed that astrology was a pathetic remnant of the Great Truth: WHAT OCCURS IN THE SKY DETERMINES LIFE ON EARTH.

I saw ancient Atlantis, not the one spoken of by Plato, but from a time before Homo sapiens. The first Atlantis was inhabited by great giants who preceded man and taught the human race all its important knowledge: I beheld Prometheus as real. Then did I see that the pantheon of Nordic gods had a basis in this revelation. Fabled Asgard was not a myth, but a legend – a vague race memory of the giant cities that once thrived on a terrifyingly ancient earth. And the most powerful of these was Thule, almost forgotten when the first Atlantis was young.

The capital of the first Atlantis had a library the size of New Berlin. Many kilometers of books were devoted to the study of the mysteries of Thule. In the first building that had existed on the planet earth, long before the first ice age drove more advanced hominids south, where they defeated lesser hominids, there stood a calendar that was the Vril Time Lens. It did not record time. It created time. From this came Destiny. The Atlantidean library had pictures of this first building on the island of Thule. Viewed from above, it had six sections, and each was a polygon. One five-sided structure was attached to a larger six-sided structure, which in turn was attached to another six-sided structure a farther distance away. Below, the pattern was repeated with the remaining three structures. Strange lights and gossamer threads connected these structures to one another, but there was a shifting, shimmering quality. Then I intuited what I was seeing, and the words of Dietrich echoed somewhere that I could hear. I was looking at the four bases of life; below glistened the adenine-thymine and guanine-cytosine base pairs of DNA. From this came the double helix. Were the lights and threads the hydrogen bonds? Knowledge flowed into my mind's eye. The Thule beings had planned the future down to the smallest detail. They had written it upon the structure of life, and in the glowing symbols of their calendar.

Man first came into existence because of the descent of an ice moon. Without such events, all life would be puny and weak. An ice moon created the gigantic, rainbow-hued dinosaurs; and another gave birth to the King of Fear, with his many-colored fingers and burning eyes.

When Atlantis sank beneath the waves, the survivors sailed to the Himalayas. At that time, Tibet was at sea level. The cataclysm that reduced Atlantis to a legend – and changed the rotation of the earth in the process – raised Tibet 13,000 feet above sea level. So that untold generations later, earnest young men of the SS could make pilgrimages to lonely monasteries in search of lost Arya.

Most startling of all was the tapestry flickering in myriad

colors to depict the final destiny of the Aryan race. There would be a period before the giants, when all of Homo sapiens would perish but for the Aryans. Most of these idealized Viking types would happily prepare, not for their transformation, but for their extermination at the hands of the fortunate few to undergo the godding passage. The ultimate *Übermensch* was not 'human' other than for superficial appearance. The human race – as I knew it – was only a means to an end. The Aryan was closest to True Men, but when mutations caused by the descending moon brought back the giants (not merely creation, but a rebirth of specific consciousnesses), then the remaining Aryans could join all the other races of man in their proper place: oblivion. The masters, the gods, would have returned. They would cherish this new world, which was also the old world; and they would perform the rites on the way to the next apocalypse, the *Ragnarök*, when the cycle would start again – for the ice ring would fall, and the earth would be torn.

These images burned into my brain: gargantuan cities with spires threatening the stars; science utterly replaced by a functional magick that was the central power of these psychokinetic supermen who needed little else; everything vast, endless, bright . . . so bright that it blinded my sight and mind and filled my soul with the terror of infinity.

Suddenly I had a body. It was a very old one. I was the senior Druid of my tribe. They were depending on me to acquire enlightenment through attainment of the Holy Grail and a means for combating the pale new religion sweeping the world.

Before me was the Well of Kunneware. Above the well was a globe. This represented the sun, and in its center burned the Swastika. Fire will melt the ice. Coiled on top of the globe was the Dragon Father from which all lesser dragons are the shadows: Nidhögg, Fafnir, Midgardsörmr. The only parts of the earth-serpent that weren't dark green consisted of the red spots of its eyes and mouth, yellow projections of its teeth and claws, and a mud-brown underskin that was visible as it lifted its unbearably long neck to reach down where it could gnaw at the vitals of the world, eating from the roots of Yggdrasil, the tree of life.

As I neared the Dragon, the heat increased, and it became so humid that my white robes felt as if they were a second layer of skin on my wrinkled body. My brain was turned into a ball of cloying cotton and my eyes were two raw oysters, stinging as if they were full of sand that would never turn to pearls.

Fire and ice. Everything is fire and ice. Only a pact with the fire can withstand the blind forces of the ice.

When I was at the limit of my endurance, and felt the last of my strength draining into the Druid staff I carried, the Dragon consented to produce the Book of the Aryans, written on scrolls made from the hides of monsters that lived beyond the stars. Two secrets were revealed to me.

The first was that not all the giants produced by the moons of ice were on the side of True Man. During the deluges, races were corrupted, and the Anti-Man was spawned. They had their giants as well. The enemy came in all sizes, and some were terrible monsters; but every last one of them, from the most common to the most frightening, shared one power in common. They could create nothing of their own, but only drain strength from the Aryan race. In the future, the enemy would become so populous as to threaten Aryan man with destruction before he fulfilled his earthly destiny. Yet armed with knowledge, Aryan heroes could defeat the enemy.

The second secret was the means to control reincarnation. The Aryans would have to draw upon heroes of the past in times of dire peril. The parasites challenged the nobility of the dust; so the dust would be raised against them.

Looking to my staff, I saw a pale oval begin to form at the top. The oval became a skull and then was clothed in flesh. The Dragon's eyes were glowing from within the sockets of the skull, and then the flesh took on features, solidifying into the face of the blond giant who had held in his powerful arms some other version of myself in a place I could only dimly glimpse in the far future.

The whole man appeared where my staff had been. He was proud and strong in the glare of the Swastika sun. He climbed up high, reaching the back of the Dragon. Suddenly he was holding something bright in his hand: Siegfried's sword. Then the Dragon Father unfolded his wings and rose into the air. The shadow of the sword held aloft and the leviathan's wings outspread made a three-taloned claw racing along the ground. Cities of normal men and women were waiting, like so much wheat in the wind. Rituals had to be performed.

They flew through space and time, and I was disembodied again, a witness to the wreck and ruin of a modern metropolis. It was New Berlin.

I was screaming. I was screaming. I was screaming.

Dietrich had ripped the device from my perspiring forehead. 'This is madness,' I said, putting my head in my hands. 'It can't be really true. The SS religion . . . no!'

'*Es walten die Übel!*' was his reply.

'I deny these phantoms,' I choked out. 'I don't believe that the evils hold sway, except in fever dreams.'

Much to my surprise, he put a comforting hand on my shoulder. 'Of course it is not true,' he said. There were tears in my eyes, the pearls from my hallucination, and my expression must have been a mask of confusion. He went on: 'What you have seen is no more true than one of your motion pictures, or a typical release from the

236

Ministry of Propaganda. It is more convincing, I'll grant you. Just as the first micro-Tesla coil allowed you to peer into the contents of one mind, this other has provided you with a composite picture of what a certain group believes; a collaborative effort, you could say.'

'Religious fanatics of the SS,' I muttered. 'And it's full of contradictions.'

'You recognize that, do you? I expected you to be an intelligent man.'

'It's wrong from the start. Hörbiger's cosmogony isn't accepted by any educated person.'

'I quite agree about that, but it's not with the peculiar astral theories that the vision contradicts itself, but the predestined racialism.'

'Well, yes, but if you reject Hörbiger, the rest falls apart. Wernher von Braun did a devastating piece against the cosmic ice beliefs in an issue of *Signal* magazine that I cherish. Imagine anyone believing in four moons of ice, or that space is full of hydrogen.'

Dietrich smiled. 'Actually, there is a goodly amount of hydrogen in outer space,' he said. 'It's not a perfect vacuum by any means. This discovery in no way supports the Hörbigerians, who made so many wild guesses that some were bound to come true. On the other hand, the scientific establishment hasn't exactly fallen over itself giving credit to their opponents for getting something right. Scientists are only human; all too human.'

This mild rebuke taught me one lesson: don't try to show off a layman's knowledge of popular science around the genuine article.

'Hörbiger is a crackpot, though,' said Dietrich. 'Small wonder he is popular in a place like this. As for the SS fantasy in toto, you should be the last person to forget the theatrical side. They have a colorful prediction and a hypothetical history. Their faith draws on deep, imaginative sources – a well from which you have drawn yourself,

237

if I recall samples of your work with any degree of accuracy. Now I admit that the SS cylinder is not as worthwhile as my autobiography. Still, there is something I've been wondering, and you might be able to help. You knew Hitler intimately. Did he believe this stuff?'

The question took me completely off guard. Unconsciously, I had been wrestling with that very conjecture. 'Hitler told different people what they wanted to hear,' I began. 'When he was with laborers, he talked socialism. When he was with bankers, it was money. Put him with a philosopher and he could quote Kant. But he preferred being with the military because he carried so much relevant information in his head that he could always beat them to the facts at hand. He spent less time with the occult crowd as the years wore on, but he could quote chapter and verse when he wanted to. In his youth, I think he believed parts of this vision to which I've been subjected. I would guess that skepticism increased with age and experience. At least one part of his faith received a hammer blow at Stalingrad. Hörbiger had predicted a mild winter, the feebleminded old goat. No, in the end Hitler only trusted in blood and iron.'

'And anti-Semitism.'

'That goes without saying. When his friend Henriette von Schirach committed the blunder of defending the Jews in his presence, she was asked to leave the Berghof, never to return. To this day, I'm involved with finding ways to penalize upper-class families that allowed their daughters to marry the money lenders to extricate themselves from debt. The Fuehrer never compromised on that.

'You mentioned friends. I didn't think Hitler had friends.'

The man had a point. 'To the extent that he did, I was a friend. So was Speer.'

'You say that as a boast. Please remember this conversation of ours when you learn what they have planned for you.'

'You won't tell me?'

'That's not my department.'

'May I ask what they plan for you?'

Richard Dietrich stood and put his hands behind his back. He was appearing to be more like Dr Mabuse all the time. His voice sounded different somehow, as though he were addressing a large audience: 'They have hired me to perform a genetic task. While I'm working on their project, I have the means to finish a job of my own. An ideal arrangement. Which do you want to hear about first?'

'You can tell me?'

'Dr Goebbels, I will tell you anything you'd like to know that doesn't touch on the surprise they've planned for you. I gave my word on that.'

'What is the personal project?'

'I would have expected you to ask for the other first, but even I am not always right. Very simply, I intend to make myself immortal. I thought I'd already suggested as much to you. At the very least, I'd like to live, oh, a thousand years. Can't remember where I picked up that number, but I got it somewhere close to home.'

'You're joking.'

'The punch line is real.'

'What about the other project?'

'A minor operation, really. In this laboratory a virus is being developed that will spare only blond, blue-eyed men and women. Yes, Dr Goebbels, the virus would kill you – with your dark hair and brown eyes – and myself, as readily as, say, my Japanese assistant. It means that your son would die also, because his current appearance is, after all, only skin deep. It means that most members of the Nazi Party would perish as not being "racially" fit by this standard.

'I am speaking of the most comprehensive mass murder of all time. A large proportion of the population in Sweden and Denmark and Iceland will survive. Too bad for the SS that virtually all those people think that extermination of the human condition, or most of it at any rate, is evil. You are aware that much of the world's folk have rather strict ethical systems built into their quaint little cultures. They probably believe in Natural Rights, too. That sort of thing gave the Nazis a difficult time at first, didn't it?'

It was becoming more difficult to understand him because someone was giggling in the room. But I made out that he had considered using sexual transmission as a mechanism for spreading the Final Plague and had referred back to earlier research done during the war on the biological revenge weapon. 'Sex would take too long, but that's what they say makes for the best relationships, isn't it? Mustn't rush the orgasm. The mass murder must be hurried through, however. And we can't let the celibate people have a free ride to life and liberty. So I've decided that an airborne virus is best; and it's even quicker than dumping the bug in the water supply. We'll explode virus bombs in ten strategic places across the planet, and even get the Eskimos, because this little critter survives just fine in the cold.'

The giggling was getting on my nerves. Dietrich continued: 'It will take about one more week to get the bugs out of the thing. Right now it's harmless. Think of that – harmless, and in one place. If only the world knew, eh? Well, that's life . . . in a manner of speaking.'

Yes, he was Mabuse, all right. That's who he was. But it was so blasted difficult making out what he was saying over that giggling; only now it had become a deranged laughing. Then I recognized the voice.

I was hysterical. I'd never had the experience before. Part of me wanted to analyze the disturbance, but the rest of me was too occupied with screaming laughter to cooperate. What was left of my concentration was directed at trying to stop the crazy sounds coming out of my chest and throat and mouth.

Suddenly I was surprised to find myself on the floor. Hands were pulling me down and the professor was putting a hypodermic needle in my arm. As the darkness claimed me, I wondered why there were no accompanying pictures. Didn't this cylinder touching my flesh have a story to tell?

Chapter Seventeen

'Sentence first – verdict afterwards.'

– Lewis Carroll,
Alice's Adventures in Wonderland

'Treason!' shouted his Majesty King Pest the First.
'Treason!' said the little man with the gout.
'Treason!' screamed the Arch Duchess Ana-Pest.
'Treason!' muttered the gentleman with his jaws tied up.
'Treason!' growled he of the coffin.
'Treason! Treason!' shrieked her Majesty of the mouth.

– Edgar Allan Poe,
King Pest

It felt as though I had been asleep for many days, but I came to my wits a few minutes later, according to my watch at least. I was lying on a cot and *he* was standing over me. I doubted that there had ever been a man named Richard Dietrich. 'Goebbels, I thought you were made of sterner stuff,' came the grim voice of Dr Mabuse.

'You are . . . evil,' I told him hoarsely.

'That's unfair. What in my conduct strikes you as unseemly?'

'You said you had been anti-Semitic. Then you told me that you had rejected racism. Now you are part of a plot that takes racism farther than anything I've ever heard of!'

'You've been out of touch.'

'The whole mess is a shambles of contradictions.'

'No, if you are talking about the SS beliefs, that's one thing; but my position is perfectly consistent. I expected more from a thoughtful Nazi. My sponsors want a project carried out for racist reasons. I do not believe in their theories, religion, or pride. This pure blond race they worship has never existed, in fact; it was a climatological adaptation in northern Europe, never as widely distributed as Nazis think. It was a trait in a larger population group. I don't believe in SS myths about lost colonies from Atlantis or spirit guidance from Thule. Blond hair is blond hair, that's all. My involvement in the project is for other reasons.'

A voice in my head was telling me that a man of ability should not do such things. Desperately, I appealed to his mind: 'There can be no other reason, Herr Doktor.'

'You forget what you have learned. Remember that I came to hate the human race. This does not mean that I gave up reason or started engaging in wishful thinking. If the Burgundians enable me to wipe out most of humanity, with themselves exempt from the holocaust, I'll go along with it. The piper calls the tune.'

'You couldn't carry on your work. How will you be immortal if you're dead?'

Sometimes one has the certainty of having been led down a primrose path, with the gate being locked against any hope of retreat, only *after* the graveyard sound of the latch snapping shut. Knowledge has a habit of arriving too late. Such was the emotion that held me in an iron grip as soon as those words escaped my lips. Dr Mabuse could never be a fool. It was impossible. Even as he spoke, I could anticipate the words: 'Oh, I *am* sorry. I forgot to tell you that a few people outside the fortunate category may be saved. I can make them immune. In this sense, I'll be a Noah, collecting specimens for a specialist's ark. Anyone I consider worthy I will claim.'

'Why do you hate the human race?' I asked him.

'To think that a Nazi has the gall to ask that question. Why do you hate the Jews?' he shot back. 'They think

243

they are the Chosen People. You fellows think you are the Chosen People. My Japanese assistant over there believes herself to be of the Chosen People. Find the group, any group, and I'll show you a majority within that group saying the same. Tribes in Africa believe only themselves to be human. The British were born to rule; only the French have culture; the Chinese live in the only civilization, and everyone else is a barbarian. The American Indian, what's left of him, is the dying ember of the Chosen People. I ask myself why this is the case. I think back to my own flirtation with racism. Can it be that human beings are born racist, that racial prejudice is in the genes? If this is so, why do we babble about improving the lot of man? Why do the most racist people in the world howl about their love of democracy and drool over the nobility of the Common Man? Humans are killer apes. The only equality they accept is to be found in the grave. Very well. I am God. I am going to correct my mistake and give the people equality. World socialism at last! The fraternity of ghosts. They expect no less of their deity. The religions of man only worship a being with the power and the will to slaughter man. My virus will be the Flood of the twentieth century. Of course, God is supposed to create life as well as destroy it; but I will be doing that too.'

Never have I experienced such dread as I felt at that moment. It just wasn't fair. I could not think, I could barely breathe, as he continued: 'I know what you advocated during World War II, Goebbels. The difference between us is that I've set my sights higher. So what if Germany and the Greater Reich is annihilated? By what right can a Nazi criticize me? And we have agreed that human beings do not have rights.'

In desperation, I tried again: 'Why do it at all? You won't have destroyed all mankind. Burgundy will remain.'

'Then Burgundy and I will play a game with each other,' he said.

In a moment of careless familiarity, I asked, 'What in God's name are you talking about?'

Another voice entered the conversation: 'In Odin's name . . .' It was Kurt Kaufmann walking over to join us. I was pleased that he had a bandage on his head, and his face was drained of color. I wanted to strike him again! He made me think of Himmler at his worst. Looking back, I wonder why at no time I ever thought to use violence against Dr Mabuse. I was afraid of him, as a child is afraid of the dark.

It is certainly understandable that expedient agreement is possible between two parties having nothing in common but one equally desired objective. There was the pact between Germany and Russia early in the war, for instance. The current case was different in one important respect: I doubted this particular alliance would last long enough to satisfy either party. I was certain that this was the Achilles' heel.

A comic opera kingdom with a mad scientist! If Hilda had known the details, why had she not told me more? I suspect she was guessing at much of the terrible truth herself. The knight in armor and the man in the laboratory: the two simply didn't mix. Since the founding of Burgundy, there had been an antiscience, antitechnology attitude at work.

Even French critics, who never had good things to say about the Reich, managed to praise Burgundy for its lack of modern technique. (The French could never be made to shut up altogether, so we allowed them to talk about nearly everything except practical politics. The skeptics and cynics among them could be counted on to come up with a rationale for their place in postwar Europe, stinging though it was to their pride. What else could they do but make sauces?)

245

Here was the most advanced geneticist in the world making common cause with a nation devoted to the destruction of science, and nearly everything else. That the Burgundians trusted his motives was peculiar; that he could go along with them was even more bizarre.

I had never met a scientist remotely like this man. The ones who had any philosophy at all belonged to the humanist tradition and believed that genetic engineering would improve the life of human beings. They were naïve healers, but indispensable to the Reich – as they are indispensable to modern civilization everywhere.

To what universe did Mabuse belong? And what was this game he intended to play with Burgundy? Apparently, he would use the building blocks of life to create something nonhuman. Despite his jeers at the SS religion, he was counting on it in at least one respect: his creatures might very well be mistaken by a good Burgundian as the New Men or *Übermenschen*, and viewed as an object of worship. He already had blueprints from which to design new life, as witness the images from the SS dream. Where the rest of mankind would oppose these new beings, the Burgundians – trained from birth in religious acceptance of superior beings in human form – would present no obstacle. By the time he succeeded, Europe would belong to Burgundy. And as for men like Kaufmann, they had to believe that wicked science had produced at least one genius who was the vehicle of higher mysteries: a puppet of Destiny. Mabuse could play along with this, because in his solipsistic mania, it didn't matter. Furthermore, his creations would probably not have minds of their own. His would be the only ego when the game was finished.

I looked into the faces of these two men, such different faces, such different minds. There was something familiar there – a fervor, a wild devotion to the Cause, and a lust to practice sacrificial rites. As minister of propaganda, it had been the look I had sought to inculcate in the population with regard to the Jews.

It was evident that I had not been made privy to their machinations carelessly. Either I would be allowed to join them or I would die. As for the possibility of the former, I did not consider it likely. Perhaps the forebodings engendered in me by Hilda were partly to blame, but in fact I knew that I could not be party to such a scheme against the Fatherland. Could I convince them that I would be loyal? No, I didn't believe it. Could I have persuaded them if I had inured myself against shock and displayed naught but enthusiasm for their enterprise? I doubted it. And I was too worn out to try.

The question remained why I had been chosen for dubious honors. The message that Hilda had shown me was rife with unpleasant implications. I took a gamble by sitting up, pointing at Mabuse, and shouting to Kaufmann: 'This man is a Jew!'

I could tell that that was a mistake by the exchange of expressions between the two. Of course they had to know. No one could keep a secret in the SS's own country. If they overlooked Dr Mabuse's ideas and profession, they could overlook anything. This was one occasion when traditional Jew-baiting would not help a Nazi! I didn't like the situation. I didn't want to be on the receiving end.

The voice of Mabuse spoke to me, but the words appeared to be for Kaufmann's benefit: 'As I'm not supposed to have a soul, I choose to live forever. You see, Goebbels, everything fits. It's too bad that you will not be around to work with the new entertainment technology. I was hoping we could transfer your memories of the affair with Lida Barova. As she was your most famous scandal, it would have made for a good show. We could have sold the first ticket to your wife. I do know a lot about you, more than you dream. I know that your favourite offspring is not the right genotype to survive.

Poor Hilda. How's this for a magnanimous offer: we'll have the last act of your career put on film by Stefan Schellenberg, then transferred to one of our little cylinders. Oh, I forgot; he's making a documentary about Hamburg right now, and he's not slated to survive the virus.'

Each word had the force of a blow. Why should Mabuse hate me? Kaufmann grinned stupidly and nodded so vigorously that I half expected to see his head fall to the ground trailing bandages.

Hatred tends to trigger my political instincts, and I struck with: 'So even Heinrich Himmler doesn't receive any respect from you, not to mention the insult to the Fuehrer.'

For a brief, blessed moment I saw that Kaufmann was discomfited, but Mabuse came to his rescue: 'Hitler is beyond Burgundian reproaches; and Himmler's day is long past. This is for your benefit.'

Kaufmann was back in control of himself. 'It is time to face your Destiny, Paul Joseph Goebbels. Don't keep your son waiting.'

I had enough wit to say, 'It is a son's duty to wait for his father.'

Kaufmann was oblivious: 'He is with the honor guard. Come.' Mabuse helped me off the cot, and then we were marching down the corridor. I was dizzy on my feet, my hand hurt, and my head was thick with pain. So many random thoughts swirling in my mind, easily displaced by immediate concern for my future welfare . . .

Efficiency was not the hallmark of my captors. After Kaufmann's experience in the elevator, I expected that he would not take my acquiescence for granted, and yet he had not unholstered his gun, and there were no extra men with him. If he thought my spirit was broken, I would disabuse him of the notion.

Otto Skorzeny probably wouldn't have been overly

impressed with my making a break for stairs leading down into a basement. The off chance that going below might lead me to an exit instead of a cul-de-sac seemed worth taking at the time. I should have realized it was a bad idea when Kaufmann made no immediate motions to prevent me.

As I reached bottom, the footsteps of the scientist and the knight were audible at the top of the stairs, coming slowly and deliberately. I was blocked by an ugly green door limned in the light of one dirty bulb hanging above. It was locked, but there was a key hanging in plain view on the wall; not exactly a maximum security arrangement.

'I wouldn't advise opening the door,' Mabuse's voice languidly drifted down, as I did precisely that. Taking two steps inside, I realized that the room had no light but the dim illumination streaming in from behind, throwing my shadow across a completely empty cubicle apparently constructed of plastic. I was standing at the edge of a step. The floor was lower. As I leaned over, the hair on my arms and head began to stand up and my skin tingled all over, as if receiving a charge of static electricity.

Human instincts do exist. Without evidence, I was aware that something was alive in that seemingly empty room. There was no sound, no movement, no odor – not a solitary stimulus but the creeping electrical current. But the fear that began as a bad taste was not electrical, it was horrible; it drove any semblance of rationality from me. I dropped the key, but it made no sound when it struck the floor. Kaufmann's beefy hand was on my shoulder, pulling me roughly backward, as the floor ate the key.

For the first time, I heard the edge of panic in Mabuse's voice as he said, 'Get that door shut.' A blue-green mass ballooned up in dreadful silence as the door blocked it from my view.

'The cell is a difficult study,' said Mabuse as we returned to the laboratory. 'The best electron microscopes

249

have limitations. Using magnetic fields to reduce the effect of gravity – all the same thing, remember? – I grew a mutated cell to a size where even the twelve blind men could gather useful data. I'll have to make a new key, though.'

My spirit to resist had received another crushing blow. Predictably, it was then, when it was no longer necessary, that Kaufmann leveled his Pistole .08 (the nine-millimeter Luger) at my midsection. I anticipated his warning, word for word: 'No more tricks, Goebbels.' At least some portion of the universe continued to make sense.

It was late afternoon as we entered the courtyard I had noticed earlier from Kaufmann's office. The large funeral pyre was still there, unused. Except that now there was a bier next to it. We were too far away to see whose body was on it, but with every step, we drew nearer to death.

A door beside the pyre opened and a line of young men emerged, dressed in black SS regalia. In the lead was my son. They proceeded remorselessly in our direction. Helmuth gave Kaufmann the Nazi salute. He answered with the same. Quite obviously, I was in no mood to reciprocate.

'Father,' said Helmuth gravely, 'I have been granted the privilege of guiding you to repentance.' Had he no feelings for me any longer? Was this the lad I had taken to the Bayreuth Festival and whose eyes had mirrored the firelight? He had loved me once. I searched for a break in his emotionless demeanor through which might peek the little boy I'd reared to manhood. I prayed for a sign that he did not hate me, or at the very least that he was ill at ease with his treatment of his father. Perhaps I make too much of it now, but he had acquired a nervous tic that was out of character. Although it was a temperate day and Helmuth was tolerant of a wide range of temperatures, he would take off his jacket as if he were too hot, and then, a moment later, he would put it on again as if he had felt a chill. A disapproving glance from his squad leader put an end to my son's audition to be a quick-change artist. With the cold eye of scrutiny upon him, as the Pole Star gazes down on lonely mariners, he became implacable once again. Magda and I had trained our children to show no mercy where duty was concerned.

Helmuth shoved me, the cruelest blow of all. He was performing for the audience. 'You will approach the body,' he said. Such was the formality of his tone that I hesitated to intercede with a fatherly appeal. His expression was blank to my humanity. I did as ordered.

Not for a moment did I suspect the identity of the body. Yet as I gazed at that familiar, waxen face, I knew that it fit the Burgundian pattern. It had to be his body. Once more I stood before Adolf Hitler!

'It was an outrage,' said Kaufmann, 'to preserve his body as though he were Lenin. His soul belongs in Valhalla. We intend to send it there today.' My mouth was open with a question that would not be voiced as I turned to Kaufmann. He bowed solemnly. 'Yes, Herr Goebbels. You were one of his most loyal deputies. You will accompany him.'

There are occasions when no amount of resolve to be honorable and brave will suffice; I made to run yet again, but many strong hands were on me in an instant. Helmuth placed his hand on my shoulder. 'Don't make it worse,' he whispered. 'This must be. Preserve your dignity. I want to be proud of you.' Well, that was something.

There was nothing to do; nothing but contemplate a terrible death. I struggled in vain, doing my best to ignore the existence of Helmuth. It was no surprise that he had been selected. It made perfect sense in the demented scheme of things.

Other men began to appear, and it was all I could do to keep from laughing. They were decked out as if performers in a Wagnerian opera. They must have gotten the attire from the Burgundian Museum. Some of the huskiest representatives of the Age of Heroes brought out an entirely modern aluminum ramp. Two of these began to carry Hitler's body up the incline, while Helmuth remained behind, no doubt with the intention of escorting me up that unwelcome path.

One of the antiquarians seemed as old as his costume, a Methuselah with a long white beard (the spitting image of Hörbiger, or the Druid I had imagined myself to be in the vision). He tottered over to us, carrying a spear in his gnarled hands. I recognized the artifact immediately: it was the Spear of Longinus that Hitler had placed at Nuremberg to cast an aura of ancient authority over the political trials we held there. I couldn't imagine how they had spirited Hitler's body away from one city and the spear from another, when both were on public display! The two possessions of the German people were reunited as a young SS man took the spear to the top of the pyre and laid it across Hitler's cadaver.

'The manner of your death will remain a state secret of Burgundy,' said Kaufmann. 'We received good publicity from your ministry when we executed those two French snoopers for trespassing: Louis Pauwels and Jacques Bergier. This is different. It wouldn't go over nearly so well, and . . .' he stared off into space. 'I keep forgetting that soon publicity won't matter any more. The true Aryans who survive the virus will be given one chance to join us. If they refuse, they die.'

'All this talk of death is depressing our guest,' said Mabuse. 'Let's cheer him up, shall we?'

'Don't do me any favors!' I nearly shrieked.

'A last request, eh? But there I go again. You may be amused to learn that they gave you a trial along the lines of the people's courts you so ardently defend in your propaganda. As the verdict was known in advance, it wasn't necessary for you to attend.'

My options were being reduced to nothing. Even facing death, I could not entirely surrender. The years I had spent perfecting the art of propaganda had taught me that no situation is so hopeless that nothing may be salvaged from it. I reviewed the facts: despite their temporary agreement, Kaufmann and Mabuse were really working at cross-purposes. Nothing had altered my earlier resolve to exploit those differences and sow dissension in their ranks. Mabuse held the trump card, so I directed the ploy at Kaufmann.

'I suppose I'm free to talk,' I said to Kaufmann's back as he watched the red ball of the sun beyond the castle walls. The sky was streaked with orange and gold, the thin strands of cumulus clouds that seemed so reassuringly distant. There were a million other places I could have been at that moment, but for a vile twist of fate. There had to be some way to escape!

No one answered my query and I continued: 'You're not a geneticist, are you Kaufmann? How would you know if you can trust Dietrich?' He was Dietrich to them, but to me he would always be Mabuse. 'What if he was lying? What if his process can't be made specific enough to exclude any group from the virus?'

Mabuse smiled as Kaufmann, not bothering to turn around, answered: 'For insurance's sake, he will immunize everyone in Burgundy as well as his assistants. If something goes wrong, it will be a shame to lose all those excellent Aryan specimens elsewhere in the world.'

'Nothing will go wrong,' said Mabuse.

I wouldn't give up that easily: 'What if he injects you with poison when the time comes? It would be like a repetition of the Black Plague that ravaged Burgundy in 1348.'

'I applaud your inventive suggestion and admirable interest in history,' said Mabuse.

'We have faith,' was Kaufmann's astounding reply.

'A faith I will reward,' boomed out Mabuse's monster voice. 'They are not stupid, Goebbels. Some true believers have medical training adequate to detect the wrong stuff in the hypodermic. And I play fair.'

One last time I appealed to my son: 'Do you trust this?'

'I am here,' he answered in a low voice. 'I have taken the oath.'

'It's no good,' taunted Mabuse. 'Stop trying to save yourself.'

This plan of mine to sow dissension was getting nowhere fast. I even tried to resurrect the old travails between Rosenberg's splinter group and Himmler's pagan mainstream. Kaufmann said, 'We've forgiven the Gnostics. They were misled. It's a tragedy that a great man like Rosenberg had to die. His book *Der Mythus des 20. Jahrhunderts* remains our racial bible. We ignore the silly parts.'

They had Hitler's body at the top of the ramp. The SS men stood at attention. Everyone was waiting. The sun seemed to pause in its descent. Time itself was waiting. What had been written for me on the calendar of Thule? I was delirious.

'Father,' said Helmuth, 'Germany has become decadent. It has forgotten its ideals. That my sister Hilda is allowed to live is proof enough. Look at you. You're not the man you were in the good old days.'

'Son,' I said, my voice trembling, 'what is happening in Burgundy is not the same thing.'

'Oh, yes, it is,' said Dr Mabuse.

Kaufmann strolled over to where I was standing and craned his neck for a better view of the men at the top of the ramp with the worldly remains of Adolf Hitler. He said, 'We in the Death's Head SS were reliable killers during the war. Jews, Gypsies, Serbs, Czechs, Poles, and so many others fell by the sword, even when it exacted a heavy price from other elements of the war program.

Speer always wanting his slave labor for industrial requirements. Accountants always counting pfennigs. The mass murder was for its own sake, a promise of better things to come!

'After the war, only Burgundy seemed to care any longer. Rulings that came out of New Berlin were despicable, weakening the censorship laws and not strictly enforcing the racial standards. Do you know that a taint of Jewishness is considered to be sexually arousing in Germany's more decadent cabarets of today? Hamburg is the worst. *Ent judeng* is a joke. Even the euthanasia policy for old and unfit citizens was never more than words on paper after the Catholics and Lutherans interfered. The Party was corrupted from within. It let the dream die.'

The kind of hatred motivating this Burgundian leader was no stranger to me. Never in my worst nightmares did it occur to me that I could be a victim of this kind of thinking.

The men who had placed Hitler's body on top of the ramp had returned to the ground. All eyes were on me. My life hung on the moment. Talk, I thought, talk like you never have before.

'Germany is not as bad as all that! At least we defend our colonies, which is more than the British ever did with theirs.' They weren't buying it. I tried something else: 'We still have guts. Look at how the Reich kidnaps British war criminals from Australia. The Aussies yammer about how we are violating their territorial sovereignty, but that doesn't stop brave German commandos.' One guard warmed to me a bit, but the rest were statues. Think, Goebbels, think! 'We haven't lost our nerve. When Hitler came to power with the *Machtübernahme* he laid out the plans for our future, and we have kept faith with that.'

'You've grown soft,' said Kaufmann. 'Why did you stop

showing the executions of the traitors in the army bomb plot?'

'Wait a minute! I was the one who first suggested we put those films in public theaters. But Hitler said it was a bad idea after we won to subject the public to material as gruesome as that. When the Allies were endangering the soil of the Fatherland, showing a wavering German a shot of a general strangling to death on a piano wire had justification. We were scaring the masses into standing firm. But why show that in peacetime?'

'We have always been at war,' said Kaufmann.

'Peace ended with the First World War,' added Mabuse helpfully.

'There are alive in Europe today Germans who surrendered with the Sixth Army at Stalingrad,' said Kaufmann. 'Why are they allowed to live?'

'You should have asked Hitler that! The amnesty was his idea, not mine. He said we'd made enough object lessons by the time he signed the order. Why are you putting all this on me?'

'You are here,' said Mabuse. 'Some fun, eh?'

Kaufmann made a chopping motion with his hand. 'It is time,' mourned Helmuth's voice in my ear. Other young SS men surrounded me, Helmuth holding my arm. We began to walk.

Kaufmann's last words to me were: 'The Reich is so softhearted that it allows Protestants to have *Busstag*, their Day of Repentance. I offer the same favor to you.'

SS men had appeared around the dry pyramid of kindling wood and straw. They were holding burning torches. Kaufmann gestured and they set the pyre aflame. The crackling and popping sounds plucked at my nerves as whitish smoke slowly rose. It would take few minutes before the flame reached the apex to consume Hitler's body . . . and whatever else was near. My only consolation was that they had not used lighter fluid – dreadful modern stuff – to hasten the inferno.

Somewhere in the blazing doom Odin and Thor and Freyja were waiting. I was in no hurry to greet them.

For the first time in my life, I wondered at how the SA must have felt when the SS burst in on them, barking guns ripping out their lives in bloody ruins. Perhaps I should have thought of Magda, but I did not. Instead all my whimsies were directed to miracles and last-minute salvations. How I had preached hope in the final hours of the war before our luck had turned. I had fed Hitler on stories of Frederick the Great's diplomatic coup in the face of a military debacle. I compared our acquisition of the atomic bomb to the remarkable change in fortunes for the House of Brandenburg. Now I found myself pleading with the cruel fates for a personal victory of the same sort.

I was at the top of the ramp. Helmuth's hands were set firmly against my back. To him had fallen the task of consigning his father's living body to the flames. They must have considered him an adept pupil to entrust him with so severe a task. As his muscles tensed, he leaned close enough to whisper in my ear: 'Now you can serve Adolf Hitler for eternity. You always loved him best.'

Chapter Eighteen

If Governments, as Mr Burke asserts, are not founded on the
Rights of Man, and are founded on any rights at all, they
consequently must be founded on the right of something that is
not man. What then is that something?

– Thomas Paine,
The Rights of Man

What Was Meant to Be the Last Day of My Life

So completely absorbed was I in thoughts of a sudden
reprieve that I barely noticed the distant explosion. Someone behind me said, 'What was that?' I heard Kaufmann
calling from the ground, but his words were lost in a
louder explosion that occurred nearby. Then Mabuse was
shouting that he was feeling a reduction in his personal
magnetic charge, and this would only occur if a large
number of enemies were near.

A manic voice called out: 'We must finish the rite!' It
was Helmuth. He pushed me into empty space. I fell on
Hitler's corpse and grabbed at the torso to keep from
falling into an opening beneath which raged the impersonal executioner.

'Too soon,' said one of the refugees from the opera.
'The fire isn't high enough, Helmuth. You'll have to shoot
him or . . .'

Already I was rolling onto the other side of Hitler's
body as I heard a gunshot. Out of the corner of my eye I
could see my son clutching his stomach as he fell into the
red flames.

Shouts. Gunfire. More explosions. An army was clambering over the wall of the courtyard. A helicopter was zooming in overhead. My first thought was that it must be the German army come to save me. I was too delighted to care how that was possible.

The conflagration below was growing hotly near. Smoke filling my eyes and lungs was about to choke me to death. I was contemplating a jump from the top – a risky proposition at best – when I was given a better chance by a break in the billowing fumes. The men had cleared the ramp for being ill protected against artillery.

Once again I threw myself over Hitler's body and hit the metal ramp with a thud. What kept me from falling off was the body of a dead SS man, whose leg I was able to grasp as I started to bounce back. Then I lifted myself and ran as swiftly as I could, tripping a quarter of the way from the ground and rolling bruisedly the rest of the way. The whizzing bullets missed me. I lay hugging the dirt for fear of being shot if I rose.

Even from that limited position I could evaluate certain aspects of the encounter. The Burgundians had temporarily given up their penchant for fighting with swords and were making do with machine guns instead. (The one exception was Thor, who ran forward in a berserker rage, wielding an axe. The bullets tore him to ribbons.) The battle was going badly for them.

Although I searched the grounds for Mabuse, I saw him nowhere. I did have the pleasure of watching Kaufmann's head explode like a rotten apple. I trust that he appreciated the release of Vril power.

Then I heard the greatest explosion of my life. It was as if the castle had been converted into one of von Braun's rockets as a sheet of flame erupted from underneath it and the whole building quaked with the vibrations. The laboratory must have been destroyed instantly.

'It's Goebbels,' a voice sang out. 'Is he alive?'

'If he is, we'll soon remedy that.'

'No,' said the first voice. 'Let's find out.'

Rough hands turned me over . . . and I expected to look once more into faces of SS men. These were young men, all right, but there was something disturbingly familiar about them. I realized that they might be Jews! The thought, even then, that my life had been saved by Jews was too much to bear. But those faces were like the faces that I've thought about too many times to count.

'Blindfold him,' one said. It was done, and I was being pushed through the courtyard blind, the noises of battle echoing all around. Once we stopped and crouched behind something. There was an exchange of shots. Then we were running and I was pulled into a conveyance of some sort. The whirring sound identified it instantly as a helicopter revving up; and we were off the ground, and we were flying away from that damned castle. A thin, high whistling sound went by – someone must have still been firing at us. And then the fighting faded away in the distance.

Within the hour we had landed. I was still blindfolded. Low voices were speaking in German. Suddenly I heard a scrap of Russian. This in turn was followed by a comment in Yiddish; and there was a sentence in what I took to be Hebrew. The different conversations were interrupted by a deep voice speaking in French announcing the arrival of an important person. After a few more whisperings – in German again – my blindfold was removed.

Standing in front of me was Hilda, dressed in battle fatigues that fit her very snugly. 'Tell me what has happened,' I said, adding as an afterthought, 'if you will.'

'Father, you have been rescued from Burgundy by a military operation of combined forces.'

'You were incidental,' added a lean, dark-haired man by her side.

'Allow me to introduce this officer,' she said, putting

her hand on his arm. 'We won't use names, but this man is with the Zionist Liberation Army. My involvement was sponsored by the guerrilla arm of the German Freedom League. Since your abduction, the rest of the organization has gone underground. We are also receiving an influx of Russians into our ranks.'

If everything else that had happened seemed improbable, the latest was sufficient to convince me that I was enmeshed in the impossible. 'There is no Zionist Liberation Army,' I said. 'I would have heard of it.'

'You're not the only one privy to secrets,' was her smug reply.

'Are you a Zionist now?' I asked my daughter, thinking that nothing else would astound me. I was wrong again.

'No,' she answered. 'I don't support statism of any kind. I'm an anarchist.'

'But, Hilda,' came a voice from the rear. There was no reason not to use her name. 'You admitted the possibility of anarcho-Zionism.'

'Yes,' she said without losing a beat, 'theoretically. But you have admitted it is by no means the mainstream.'

'When I suggested it to my mother,' said a pretty young woman to my left, 'she threatened to sit *shiva* for me. She thinks all anarchists are crazy bomb throwers and can't imagine that sort of violence in the Zionist movement.'

The serious-faced young man standing next to Hilda held up a hand and said: 'Be glad you still have a mother to make threats.' Several nodded at this.

As they began to discuss the ramifications of applying pacifism to anarchy, I wondered if Mabuse was playing another trick on me. Had he injected me with an hallucinogenic drug? I certainly didn't have a cylinder attached to my head to account for these fantasies involving my daughter. I returned to reality with a shock: I had not pocketed one of the micro-Tesla coils when I had the opportunity. Damn it!

A large Negro with a beard took it on himself to edify me: 'There is only one requirement to be in this army, Nazi. You must oppose National Socialism, German or Burgundian. As for myself, I'd be satisfied to have a European government that respected rights, the same as they have in America.' He had a French accent, wouldn't you know it?

Hilda took it from there. 'After growing up in your family, Father, I don't trust any government not to become a tyranny; but I respect the American Dream.'

If I had to listen to much more of this, I would regret not having joined Hitler in the flames. Flesh of my flesh, blood of my blood, Hilda had her ruthless side. Next, she told me: 'We have Marxists here. We don't trust them, but we will not turn them away. If we are victorious, we won't give them the chance to do to us what they did to the anarchists in Spain, or what Lenin did to his own radicals.'

'Don't forget the anarcho-Marxists,' came the exact same voice that had mentioned anarcho-Zionism. Did he do nothing but hyphenate words? What was next? Anarcho-Nazism? I couldn't take it.

'You and your dirty Party are responsible for everything,' my daughter said. 'The small wars Hitler kept waging well into the 1950s, always pushing deeper into Russia, made more converts to Marx than you realize.'

'But you hate communism, daughter. You've told me so ever since you were a teenager and began thinking about politics.' In retrospect, it was not prudent for me to say this in such company, but I no longer cared. I was emotionally exhausted, numb, empty.

She took the bait, but I was unable to reel her in. 'I hate all dictatorships,' she said, a breeze stirring her hair on cue, and every male eye admiring her convictions. 'In the battle of the moment, I must take what *comrades* I can get. You taught me that.'

I could not stop myself from trying to reach her. I had lost Helmuth, and it was in the cards that Hilda was next. 'The Bolsheviks were worse statists than we ever were. Surely the war crimes trials we held at the end of hostilities taught you that, even if you wouldn't learn it from your own father.'

She raised her voice: 'I know the evil that was done. What else would you expect from your darling princess than I can still recite the names of the Russian death camps: Vorkuta, Karaganda, Dalstroi, Magadan, Norilsk, Bamlag, and Solovki. But it has only lately dawned on me that there is something hypocritical about the victors trying the vanquished. You didn't even try to find judges from neutral countries.'

'What do you expect from Nazis?' added the Negro.

My daughter reminded me of myself, as she continued to lecture all of us, captors and captives alike: 'The first step on the road to anarchy is to realize that all war is a crime, and that the cause is statism.' Before I could get a word in edgewise, other members of the group began arguing among themselves. I was in the hands of real radicals, all right. The early days of the Party were like this. And whether Hilda was an anarchist or not, it was clear that the leader of this ad-hoc army – enough of a state for me – was the thin, dark-haired Jew.

He leaned into my face and vomited up the following: 'Your daughter's personal loyalty prevents her from accepting the evidence we have gathered about your involvement in the mass murder of Jews. You're as bad as Stalin.'

I don't remember the other words he spoke. Perhaps the tape recorder I carried in my head had become demagnetized because of Mabuse. But I do remember the pain that came off my captor like a wave. He had known nothing but violence his entire life. His parents had died at Auschwitz. He had become a 'pirate' while still a child.

He had seen most of his friends killed or driven mad, some quiet as the grave, some chattering like a machine gun, before they threw themselves to their deaths before the steel treads of the Reich. He had been forged in a hundred night missions where the flashing lights of artillery fire, like strobe lights in a nightclub, had hypnotized him and made him an automaton of a killer. I had never thought a Jew could have the qualities we worked so hard to program into our soldiers.

I do remember him saying, 'You know what you are, Reichsminister Goebbels? You're the pig who complained about how ghetto Jews were unclean, and then helped to put them in the most unsanitary conditions imaginable. You're a conductor of hatred. You *are* hatred!'

My dear sweet daughter couldn't believe the worst of me. Not she! Reaching out to embrace her and to escape my accuser, I not only caused several guns to be leveled on my person, but received a rebuff from her. She slapped me! Her words were acid as she said, 'Fealty only goes so far. Whatever your part in the killing of innocent civilians, the rest of your career is an open book. You are an evil man. I can't lie to myself about it any longer.'

So it was over between us. I regarded my new enemy, who had just risked her life to rescue me. There was no room for anger. No room left for anything but a hunger for security. I was ready to happily consign my entire family to Hitler's funeral pyre, if by so doing I could return home to New Berlin. The demeanor of these freelance terrorists suggested that they bore me no will that was good. Having just escaped death, it was a less exciting prospect the second time.

Hilda must have read my thoughts. 'They are going to release you for now, as a favor to me. We agreed in advance that Burgundy was the priority. Everything else had to take a back seat, including waking up about my . . . parents.'

'When may I leave?'

'We're near the Burgundian border. My friends will disappear, until a later date when you *may* see them again. I don't care what happens. As for me, I'm leaving Europe for good.'

'Where will you go?' I didn't expect an answer.

'To the American Republic. My radical credentials are an asset over there.'

'America,' I said listlessly. 'Why?'

'Just make believe you are concocting another of your ideological speeches. Do this one about individual rights and you'll have your answer. They may not be an anarchist utopia, but they are paradise compared to your Europe.'

'Daughter, they have a terrible society. Don't you realize that you can legally will your body to a necrophiliac to raise money for your family? There has never been a country so monstrous in history as to allow that.'

'In other words, they have the first free society. The only crimes are force and fraud, murder and theft, kidnapping and rape . . . crimes where you have a victim. And you, one of the supreme criminals of history, choose one unsavory example of what it means to live free and . . . oh, why do I bother? Fuck you.'

So that was that. I was blindfolded again. Despite mixed feelings, I was grateful to be alive. The last I saw my daughter was her angry face in the twilight, surrounded by other young faces, all of them impractical and naïve; none of them mature enough to live by Bismarck's profound insight that politics is only the science of the possible. Civilization cannot survive without hypocrisy; and to whatever extent possible, murder and kidnapping and all those other activities must be a monopoly of the state.

They released me at the great oak tree I had observed when flying into Burgundy. As I removed the blindfold, I heard the helicopter take off. My eyes focused on the plaque nailed to the tree that showed how SS men had ripped up the railway and transplanted this tremendous oak to block that evidence of the modern world. It had taken a lot of manpower.

How easily manpower can be reduced to dead flesh.

Turning around, I saw the flowing green hills of a world I had never fully understood stretching to the horizon. With a shudder, I looked away, walked around the tree, and began following the rusty track on the other side. It would lead to the old station where I would put in a call to home . . . to what I thought was home.

Postscript by Hilda Goebbels

January 1975

In a few months, I will place these pages in the hands of an American editor. But, first, I will enjoy the most exquisite pleasure of my life and type the following words:

PAUL JOSEPH GOEBBELS
BORN OCTOBER 29, 1897
DIED MARCH 15, 1970

For half a decade I tried to get my hands on the final entries. I didn't know for certain that they existed until a few years ago. But I'd had my suspicions that Father recorded everything. He was a remarkable diarist. It was the only place where he could allow himself to be honest.

He must have recorded his Burgundian experiences shortly after returning to New Berlin. I make this deduction because all entries dated past this point are incoherent. He had a mental breakdown, a most convenient development for Reich officials. It must have been galling to Father when they assigned psychiatric help.

Hypocrisy was their watchword as much as it was his. Even while treating him as a lunatic, they sent in a full strike force to clean out Burgundy. I doubt they got them all. The top Burgundians who survived the attack to which I made my contribution had more than enough time to regroup. The real issue boils down to one man: Richard Dietrich.

I saw white-coated lab technicians escaping from the castle before the explosives went off, sending the virus and Dietrich's other monsters to kingdom come. If they could get away, surely the greatest genius in the world could have escaped. I never saw the man in person, but there were photographs. I knew the danger he posed before reading my father's account. But after translating these pages, Dietrich seems to have taken on new life for me. Until I know that he's dead, I live in dread. One man could eliminate mankind. If he survived, why is the world still around? Was he injured? Did he run out of funds? Or did he simply lose interest? If the latter, what new project could engage his attention? Mother of Jesus, I do not want to think about this.

The Greater Reich also came down hard on the underground. The concentration camp population needed an infusion of new blood, I suppose. No more favoritism for the children of the well-to-do. That was the policy for a little while at least. It appears that nothing stays the same in this mad world. Only yesterday I heard that the Reich intends to liberalize itself and set prisoners free, so as to curry favor with the West over some new business enterprise involving Africa. I don't want to think about this either.

Sometimes I try to decode Father's final entries, scrawled out in the last year of his life. He was a broken man in 1970, unhinged by the Burgundian affair, afraid of reprisals from the underground (which never happened), and to the bitter end unable to fathom why his favorite child hated him so. His last comment about me suggests that he was suffering senility on top of everything else. He goes into a rage about what a cruel and faithless daughter I am because of something I did as a child that I can't even remember. It seems that Hitler had given

Father an ornate Swastika that was made of fine, hand-blown Austrian crystal. While playing in the study, I had accidentally broken this symbol of Hitler's high regard for a subordinate. Despite everything else that happened, I didn't believe Father was so petty as to harbor a grudge over something like that.

There is a consistent pattern in his last writings, and it is that his recurring nightmare of the Teutonic Knights had been displaced by a Jewish terror: an army of Golems concocted by Dietrich. Father was also convinced that the doppelgänger visited him late at night. The manner in which he determined that it was the double instead of the man who had 'entertained' him in the laboratory was because this white-haired phantom entered and exited through the walls.

Yet even in his madness, Father never questioned the wicked beliefs that had twisted his life; and that is part of the madness. Not until I read the diary did I realize what a moral lesson Father could have learned in Burgundy. If he is to be believed, he even had a brief moment in which he could recognize Dietrich's evil. Why could he not see the black heart in himself?

His cynical and murderous outlook never softened. He remained what he was. Fortunately, he was in such a decrepit state, and his influence so eroded, that he was in no position to cause any more harm in the world. His talents in this regard could have added more suffering very easily. According to his final scribblings, he regretted not being able to finish a work he'd been doing to foment unrest in the Middle East, as if that tragic region didn't have more than its fair share of sorrow already. He had intended to foist off on the public a forgery of his entitled *The Protocols of the Elders of Islam*. Thank God he wasn't able to do to the Arabs what he did to the Jews.

Images that crop up in these sad pages include a landscape of broken buildings, empty mausoleums, bones, and other wreckage that shows he never got over his obsession with the war. As for Mother leaving him at long last, he makes no comment but *das Nichts*. To the end he retained the habits of a literary German.

Mother's last criticism of him had nothing to do with his philandering. It was a charge that could be laid against me, but not with as much justification. She felt that Father's tendencies to self-dramatize had been given undue reinforcement by his work with the film industry. In effect, she disbelieved his recounting of the Burgundian affair because she said it was too much like a movie! She was reminded of how he used to inspire his listeners by suggesting they were starring in an imaginary Technicolor film, and if they showed cowardice in the face of the enemy, an equally imaginary audience would boo. He had simply imagined the events in Burgundy. And as I was no longer available to corroborate the story, and Helmuth had died in a 'hunting accident,' there was little he could do on that front.

What probably was the straw breaking Mother's back was when he made a scene in front of Hitler's tomb, demanding to be let inside where he would prove that the body behind the glass was a double that had been substituted for the real Fuehrer. It didn't help his case that he wasn't confusing film and real life, when later he asked Magda to accompany him to Nuremberg, where he could make a public spectacle of himself again by proving that the Spear of Longinus had also been replaced. When he told her that he suspected Stefan Schellenberg was involved, *a movie director*, Mother had all the evidence she needed that he was beyond recovery. If there had been any real love between them, she would have stayed. But their marriage had been more a matter of politics than anything else, a favor to Hitler; and ghosts of the past no longer had a claim on her.

The examples of my father's alienation are drawn from

an almost infinite supply. How did he get through the day? One moment he takes pleasure from the 'heart attack' suffered by Himmler on the eve of Father's return – and there are comments here about how Rosenberg has finally been avenged, the 'unluckiest Nazi of them all,' to quote directly. This material is interspersed with grocery bills from the days of the Great Inflation, problems he had with raising money for the Party in the mid-thirties, and a tirade against Hörbiger. Before I can make heads or tails of this, he's off on a tangent about Nazis who believed in the hollow earth, and pages of minute details about Hitler's diet.

I am a woman of the world, and I know that what I am placing before the world will be subjected to the most intense scrutiny. The only hard evidence I have about Richard Dietrich has been in the hands of American scientists these past five years. Yet it's only a small part of what was to be found in that laboratory; and it is a wonder I was able to lay my hands on one of the complete genetics files. They do not prove the rest, but if the only way to prove it all was to destroy the world, then I'll live with readers having doubts.

As for the critics who will heap abuse on my head, some will operate from sincere motives; but many will take a page from Hitler's own book. It was well known in 1943 and 1944 that the Fuehrer punished the bearers of bad news. Many were the clever manipulations to avoid the personal dishonor of telling him what he did not want to hear. As one who has survived in the blast furnace of Hitler himself, I will be little bothered by the slings and arrows of historians and critics who will question everything up to, and including, the ink used by my father when he penned these mind-numbing pages.

The world must be told the truth, no matter what the cost!

Chapter Nineteen

I believe that all government is evil, in that all government must necessarily make war upon liberty; and that the democratic form is at least as bad as any of the other forms.

> – H. L. Mencken,
> *Living Philosophies*

New York

Alan Whittmore's hands were trembling as he put down the pages he had been reading with such intense concentration that he had a crimp in his neck. Hilda and Baerwald were talking. He leaned back and listened, not to the content of their words, but to the sound. They were two brave and happy people. They were free. Life was a challenge to them instead of a nightmare.

How, how could a majority of Germans have supported the government of Adolf Hitler? But this wasn't the real question. Before this day, Alan had wondered why the majority of people at all times in history had advocated tyranny. The Founding Fathers of the American Republic had feared the mob as much as the return of a king. Nobody said that freedom was going to be a picnic. But who would choose hell over freedom? The statists throughout history promised security, but didn't deliver it. Well, freedom didn't deliver it either . . . because there was no such thing as security in the first place. What mattered was that in America they couldn't shoot your rights down, and they couldn't vote them away. If Alan had any religion, it was to be found in those two words of Jefferson: 'inalienable rights.'

The first time he'd seen Hilda Goebbels on television, she was standing in front of an American flag (she wasn't fetishistic about her anarchy), and she was saying bright, clean words for the camera: 'Private property to the people!' The circumlocutions and obliquities of an unfriendly television interviewer had done nothing but make her look better and better. She would not be tarnished by her family name; but neither would she give in to blackmail by people who believed in Voodoo. She would not change her name.

Sure, he'd had a moment of unease when he first saw the name GOEBBELS on a letterhead addressed to him. But inside was a fan letter from an already famous woman who had read his article on how the first recipients of the Roosevelt administration's socialized largesse had been filthy-rich tycoons. The idea that capitalism was the best hope for the poor had almost been wiped out during the red decade of the 1930s. But the truth could not be buried forever, and the very magazine that Alan so proudly edited had been one of the first voices saying that governments had caused the Depression, just as governments created monopolies and almost every other ill except, maybe, Dutch elm blight. Hilda had about a million footnotes to add, taken from her inside view of what happens when nationalism and socialism get together.

Before he could say negative financing, they were engaged in an enriching correspondence. They talked about how Woodrow Wilson tried to export freedom when liberty was endangered at home. They talked about Bismarck and the first modern welfare state. They talked about what kind of world it might be if the primary threat to freedom were communism instead of fascism, and the rhetoric of collectivism relied on class instead of race. And he learned from her about alternate histories and a peculiar genre of entertainment called science fiction (which he had thought was restricted to invasions-from-outer-space stories).

It was to be a fulfillment, his coming here today and reading her manuscripts. He had expected yet another ringing denunciation of the Nazi system, and this she had given him in spades. What he had in no way been prepared for was the rest of it: his sense of reality and logic was shaken to the core. He wasn't sure that he wanted to live in a world that had a Richard Dietrich in it.

The morbid contemplation kept him occupied until he realized that Hilda had been watching him for an indeterminate length of time. Baerwald was in the bathroom. 'I'm sorry,' said Alan, 'I've been in never-never land.'

'You've finished,' she said. 'Thank you for reading it straight through without asking questions.'

'I wouldn't know what to ask.'

'Would you like something more to drink?'

'No thanks. I've had enough.'

Night had fallen, and the city had become an insect hive of lights drifting to and fro, traffic flowing beneath the penthouse window in the busiest part of town. Alan watched the flickering lights – a medley of traffic signals and automobile headlights turning off here, turning on there. He'd heard that lightning bugs were used in genetic research because the on/off mechanism of their illumination was one of nature's more generous clues for those who would penetrate her mysteries.

Baerwald was returning to his seat when someone knocked on the door. Hilda tensed slightly, and Alan felt his heart stop. Harry Baerwald remained nonchalant as he opened the door and let in the young Russian waiter who had brought them their dinner. Hilda and the waiter knew each other and exchanged pleasantries in Russian, before she gave him a good tip and sent him on his way.

'You probably think I'm being ridiculous with all these

precautions,' she said. 'I only want to eat food prepared by people I know personally, at least for the immediate future.'

'I don't question it at all, Hilda, after reading your father's diary. And there is something I have to tell you. I couldn't let myself believe it at first, but as I read the manuscript I became convinced I'd have to share my experience with you.'

He told them about the man in the Horch limousine. He described the face in detail . . . and admitted why Baerwald had startled him at first. Neither of his listeners seemed surprised or skeptical, a very bad sign for someone wanting to be put at ease. He even mentioned the mysterious phone call.

'It's not possible, is it?' asked Alan Whittmore. 'This Dietrich person couldn't still be alive, and following you?'

The young editor might not want a refill, but Hilda poured herself a stiff one before resuming her seat and answering him. Their dinners remained untouched under the steam covers on the cart the Russian had wheeled into the room. 'As you read in my postscript, I have doubts about whether or not he perished in the explosion. Toward the end, my father referred alternately to Dietrich's doppelgänger and to an immortal "Mabuse." He had it all mixed together, and I doubt that he really saw him again.'

'What about the man I saw?'

'It could be a coincidence. It could be someone playing a joke on us.'

'With the diary a secret, who would know enough about Dietrich to be able to fool us?'

'Burgundians,' said Baerwald in the tone of voice one uses for expletives. 'They'd be more likely to harass us with stupid phone calls. That's not Dietrich's style.'

'I wouldn't worry too much about the phone call,' said Hilda. 'There's a science fiction convention going on downstairs. Quite a remarkable phenomenon, really. There's nothing like it in the Reich. They'd be arrested for the jokes they're telling if this were back home. The call may have been a prank or a wrong number.'

'You don't seem very concerned that we might be under surveillance from the scientist,' said Alan, a bit let down.

'To tell you the truth, Alan, my precautions have been against the Burgundians. The Death's Head SS has been reduced in power and wealth, but it still has what is left of a whole country as a base of operations. They will give us trouble when we bring out the book. If nothing else, they will see to it that the final testament of my father is banned in Europe. Any Reich official who is foolhardy enough to give the book a certificate of approval will be in hot water with them.'

'You're not worried about Dietrich?' asked Alan in confusion.

'There are limits to what we can do,' said Baerwald. 'During the war, I was frightened by what I learned concerning biological weapons being developed by the Reich. When I arrived in America, I met a man to whom I'd been sending intelligence. I learned that of the data I'd provided, all of it that was of any value came from one man – this Dietrich. I thought it was the result of a whole team of researchers.'

Hilda was ruthlessly logical: 'If he lived, he's had time to improve on his virus, or find something else. What if the means to destroy humanity could be had for the price of a few chemicals and some secondhand equipment? What if he's gotten it down to where he can afford to finish the project on his own?'

No one spoke for several minutes. Any doubts he might have had concerning the authenticity of what he'd read were long gone. Alan understood the rumors of Hilda stopping World War III. She had been involved with preventing something compared to which a world war was a sane enterprise. 'So the fact we are still here,' said Alan, 'proves that either Dietrich is dead, or he is out there somewhere, still working on the virus.'

'There is a third possibility,' said Baerwald. 'He may be alive, but no longer interested. Kaufmann died. No one may have offered him a renewal of the contract.' Hilda and Alan stared with horror at the survivor of a concentration camp. 'You must bear in mind that this man is completely mad. Although a genius, he thinks like a petulant child. He took the words of Adolf Hitler literally and extrapolated from there. Unlike the usual demented follower, the rank and file of the Nazi Party, this man was in a position to do something about the odious principles of the *Übermensch*.'

'I don't agree with you,' said Hilda. 'Nietzsche's Overman is a noble ideal that was completely twisted by the Nazis, and by Dietrich as well. The superior man would have no reason to enslave anyone. He would be a creator, not a destroyer. The Nazis put uniforms and shiny boots on street thugs and called that the Superman. Nietzsche warned against German nationalism. He condemned Wagner for racism.'

'All very true,' said Baerwald, 'but you must also consider – '

'How can you sit there and debate history?' Alan cried out. 'Our lives may be endangered at this very moment.'

'Young man,' answered Baerwald in a kindly voice, 'nobody gets out of here alive. I learned that in the camp. I wouldn't let the Nazis degrade me in my own mind. I refused to feel shame. But there was a price: I became philosophical about death. Modern man has been very quick to give up religion, but he hasn't put anything in its place to help him face the truth. Man is mortal.'

'What about the religions of the SS?' asked Alan, still

reeling from his journey through a mental landscape he could hardly credit.

'A perversion, Mr Whittmore. The religions of antiquity were not a concoction of mad ravings. Wise old pagans would be as horrified by what goes on in Burgundy as the rabbi who instructed me.'

'Or the pope. Or any minister of the gospel,' said Hilda.

'OK, OK, but what about Dietrich? Isn't there some way to find out what happened to him?'

'Let's say he's dead,' said Baerwald. 'We dance around his grave. But his discoveries are not secret. Science gives its fruit to anyone who plucks the vine. Others will learn what he learned. How would that be different from living under the threat of nuclear annihilation? You seem able to live with that.'

Hilda came to the rescue. 'Don't pick on Alan. I am especially bothered by Dietrich and would take personal offense to die at his hand.'

'Yes, but no death is preferable. If he crosses our path again, we will fight him. I would kill him if I could. But I will not waste my life thinking about him. There are limits. Vengeance is mine, saith the Lord. An "eye for an eye" was an accounting for God, not for man.'

'I envy your faith,' said Alan.

'Mine is not an exceptional case. I choose not to live as if I were a Nazi. I prefer the hard path of love to the easy path of hatred.'

Hilda leaned over and kissed Baerwald on the cheek. Alan embarrassed himself by remembering he had intended to ask her frankly impertinent questions about her sex life. The answers to those questions seemed irrelevant now.

'I have a splendid idea,' said Hilda. 'Let's eat our dinners before they get cold.'

And they did. The food was unexceptional, but with

every bite, Alan felt a lessening of tension. He couldn't help noticing the almost painful formality with which Hilda dined, her back straight, the silverware used with a studied correctness. At first, no one spoke, and there was only the sound of cutlery tapping and scraping on the plates, and the labored breathing of Baerwald, who was old, but still strong beneath his weathered frame. Raising his gray head from contemplation of a brussels sprout, the man known to the world as H. Freedman said, 'I dread someday to learn that Total Evil and innocence are one and the same, but a man such as Dietrich cannot be innocent, can he?'

Catching Hilda's glance, Alan could see that she was as perplexed as himself. There was tenderness in her voice. 'Harry, what are you saying?'

'My brief experience of Nazi hospitality is something that stays with me, spoils little things for me. There is a point where physical horror crosses over into the spiritual. The flesh takes on new meanings. I never eat a meal that I don't recall the hungry faces of the other internees, who had been there longer, so much longer than I, even in what was officially a temporary holding area. I saw a man I knew from before, but I didn't recognize him until he spoke. He'd changed that much. He was very thin. I think that he was a Lutheran, but I'm not sure. He was a Berliner, though. He'd been quite cosmopolitan before.'

Alan and Hilda looked to each other once again. Baerwald was drifting in memory, his words coming farther apart, eyes focused on the wall that was a blank screen for the past. Alan felt a spark jump the distance between Hilda and himself – a sudden empathy seeming to suggest that all the facts and theories with which they had been wrestling were nothing in the face of existential experience. A man like Baerwald was shaped by his suffering, but he had refused to relinquish his identity to that suffering.

The sad witness continued: 'I think they selected certain recalcitrant individuals to starve to death. What did your father say, Hilda? Wasn't it that the disruption of transport by Allied bombing was why so many starved? Yet some ate. I ate. I shared, but I was caught and punished. Still, they fed me. They made up categories, you know, and we couldn't change their rules for them. Only they could make the changes. They didn't seem very scientific, not these men. I only remember cruelty. But, then, Dietrich was both scientific and cruel, wasn't he? We only have our memories in the end. I remember the face of that young man. I held him in my arms and saw that he was beyond anger and hatred. That may be why his words stay with me. He said a phrase I'd always abhorred when he whispered, "Forgive them, Father, for they know not what they do." I answered him too quickly, in a voice much too loud for that place: "Do *not* forgive them, for they know what they do." With a last tired smile, he spoke in a voice much firmer than before: "But evil *never* knows." And he died. I wanted to embrace him, but I also wanted to cast him away. I'd have called him a fool, but he was no longer with me. Then another internee told me that I should not draw attention to myself and quickly moved away to demonstrate that he was himself an apt pupil of these hard lessons. But I sat on the floor, next to the corpse, until the ones who never knew about anything came to take us away.'

There were tears when he finished, but they weren't from his solemn eyes still transfixed on the wall. Hilda was crying. And Alan, looking at her the whole time, began to cry as well. 'Oh, what have I done?' asked Baerwald, his voice completely different and attention returned to the Isabel Paterson Hotel. 'You must forgive an old man,' he said.

'It's as if I've lived a whole year in the course of one evening,' said Alan, passing a handkerchief to Hilda.

'I think that I should leave and let you two talk business,' said Baerwald.

'Not tonight,' said Hilda. 'As far as business is concerned, I have a headache.'

Inopportunely and irritatingly, the phone rang. 'I hope it's not the convention downstairs,' said Hilda, 'asking us to keep the weeping down.'

'Puts a real damper on parties,' chimed in Alan.

Baerwald said something in German, and while Alan was working out its meaning about the penalties awaiting punsters in hell, Hilda took care of the call. She had returned the phone to its cradle for some moments before Alan noticed that she was just standing there, a statue.

'Hilda, what's the matter?' he asked.

'Someone just asked if my name was Goebbels. When I said it was, he said the phrase *Yom Hashoah*, then hung up.'

Baerwald half shouted, 'That's Yiddish for "the Night of Fire"!'

'I know,' said Hilda, as Alan was already running for the door. She called after him but he was already in the hallway, headed for the elevator. It had to be him! The white-haired man he'd confused with Baerwald earlier! Could it really be Richard Dietrich? He was certain that the man had been following him. Maybe he had called from the lobby.

The elevator doors were closing as he rounded the corner, and without even looking pressed the OPEN button and slid between the doors before they reversed direction. He bumped into a woman standing dead center and she fell against the wall. 'Hey,' she began, but her outrage lacked conviction. With her beehive hairdo and red leotard, she was in the regulation outfit of an 'elevator operator.'

'Excuse me,' he said, already pushing LOBBY and trying to mentally speed them on their way.

280

'I wasn't sure there was anybody on this floor, it's so dead up here.'

'You're not supposed to be here, are you?'

'You're kind of cute,' was her entirely professional response. 'Besides, I've paid the hotel dick for the rest of the week, and I do mean pay.'

He had no time for this. But the special elevator, with no stops on the way, was still taking forever and then some to descend. 'I guess this isn't your night,' he replied.

'Oh, jeez, you're not with that convention are you? They're all kids, and nobody pays. The old guys have these young girls hanging around them for free. Don't they know that free enterprise built this great country?'

'Old? How old?' He was finally looking at her, and she wasn't half bad. She must have retired from the street trade before it was too late.

'Search me, puh-leeeeze. One really old gootch seemed to be giving me the once over, and I was charitable enough to make contact, but he had such a crazy grin that it gave me the creeps and I moved on. Now you – '

'How old?' Alan had her by the arm, but the funny thing was that he didn't remember reaching for her.

'Ancient.'

'Where?'

'Toward the bar up by the phones but . . . oh, jeez, now you're running away. Don't you like my perfume?' They had arrived.

Alan was sprinting across the lobby, driven to reach the man sidling over to the revolving door that led to the street, the man from the Horch limousine. Adrenaline rushing through his system, Alan's body became one uninterrupted motion – all his violence channeled into reaching the target. The grinning-skull face maddened him with its awful sneer.

He could kill the mysterious old man if he weren't careful. This is what brought him up short. Here was not

281

the body of the Superman. Why, if Joseph Goebbels had been prescient in his worst imaginings, then Richard Dietrich would appear younger today than he was at the time of the Burgundian affair. He wouldn't be this tottering wreck of a man shaking in front of him. None of these infirmities had been evident from the window of the car.

But the damned sneer was still there on the huge head with the shock of white hair, and the malign intelligence must still be reckoned with. If final proof of his guilt were required, he was attempting to escape. 'Hold it right there,' said Alan, and as the man paid no heed, the young embraced the old, one strong arm behind a stooped back, the other in front of a fallen chest. The elderly body was trembling as Alan released the pressure. 'You've got some explaining to do,' said Alan, himself out of breath. 'Why have you been following me? Why did you make that call?' Even now, with the quarry firmly in hand, he couldn't bring himself to ask what was really on his mind: *Who are you?*

It was a relatively simple matter to move his prisoner back toward the elevator. The man was offering no resistance. Alan's immediate concern was to think of a semiplausible explanation should someone inquire as to why he had kidnapped a seemingly harmless old man. He was certainly not prepared for the booming voice of Harold Baerwald emanating from the elevator that had since ascended and returned with its new passenger: 'Oh, my God, I don't believe what I'm seeing. It can't be, and yet it is, it is. I'd know that face anywhere.'

'Dietrich?' asked Alan, heedless of the curious onlookers.

'No,' said Baerwald, in a softer voice. 'He's my brother.'

Back in the penthouse apartment, old affections were rekindled as best they could be, and small mysteries were solved. Hilda had ordered coffee brought up, and she complimented Alan on his quick, diplomatic recovery. As an agitated hotel manager approached them, Alan's hold on the old man had transformed into a friendly patting on the back. The lost brother would not speak at first, which provided some difficulties, but at least he didn't contradict anyone.

Poor, long-lost Herman, the older brother of Harold, not seen since the war. It did not take long to ascertain that he was to some degree demented. Baerwald was so thrilled over finding his absent sibling that he could not be put off by the eccentric circumstances of the reunion; or, as he wisely observed to Alan, 'Don't fret, my boy. It's all for the best. And one does expect a certain lassitude from the elderly, rather than high-spirited skullduggery.'

It was such a close thing. Alan was still concerned that he might have done serious damage to his prisoner. His right hand shook when he thought about it and spilled coffee in his saucer. Hilda watched his every move.

Encouraging Herman to speak was a bit like extracting gold from an unstable mine. But Harold was persistent. It was learned that the Horch limousine and chauffeur had been rented for the day. Herman seemed to find it difficult to speak, even after he accepted that this was indeed his brother and that he could trust him. A contributing factor to the man's unease was physical. The sneer that had so inflamed Alan was a permanent scar from the war. It was a sobering experience to confuse two Baerwalds with the ghostly presence of Dr Dietrich, and this in one day. No need for doppelgängers around here.

But how could such a family separation have lasted for so many decades, especially when Harold had become world famous? The pseudonym was not the explanation, as biographical material was in all the Freedman books and his photograph was well publicized. The answer seemed to be amnesia. In that great human wake of wartime refugees, the addled Herman had been swept up and deposited in an institution where he was all too common a case. And so he had adjusted. Hitler had stolen his past.

The flood of newspaper reports about Baerwald and Goebbels and the *American Mercury* had triggered something in the deeper currents of memory that had driven half-mad Herman to make contact with these people. He sat near the window, trying desperately to communicate something of this. When asked questions, he would adopt the mannerisms and gestures of response, moving his shoulders, nodding his head, but the words rarely came except in spurts. He had not seen the name Baerwald since the war, according to him; although it was more likely that he had and simply failed to recognize it.

'What name have you been using?' asked Alan, the first to wonder.

'I'm . . . I've been Raymond.'

'I'm sorry that I attacked you, Raymond.'

'You did?'

For a very long time, the Baerwalds spoke together, and pieces of the past were reconstructed, or invented to fill in the spaces. Hilda and Alan observed the past come alive. Then, at length, the night passed into memory. Outside, the dawn began to paint the sky with a mixture of pink and dark blue. A bird was singing somewhere below their window, but still high above the soon to be crowded streets.

Alan felt stiff in every joint and was delighted when Hilda – too wound up to sleep – suggested that they go out to breakfast. As they took a last glance at the disheveled form being embraced by Harold Baerwald, Hilda whispered, 'I was ready to believe he was our mad scientist as well.' They shared in equal portions of relief.

'There won't be time for you to sleep before the

television interview we've arranged,' he reminded her as they hit the street.

'I'll be fine. Just slap some makeup on me so I won't dissolve under the lights.'

He reached out for her hand. She held it tightly.

They met in dark places but they brought their own light. They were banished from their own country and left muttering curses at the sallow-faced youngsters who now sat on their old thrones of power, humbly following orders from New Berlin. But these last of the true Burgundians were not beaten. Not while old ideas bubbled just below complacent surfaces. Not while the young eagerly sought out the old for guidance. These angry ones would not let the flame of vengeance be extinguished.

There had been no word from Herr Doktor Dietrich, but neither had they found his body. If he rejoined them, all the better; but if his services were forever denied them, they would simply have to improvise. There was still a good crop of Hitler youth waiting to be harvested – and their numbers would grow, the longer the secret masters bided their time.

Each month brought reports of new outrages, as self-proclaimed Nazis discovered the practical benefits of compromise and expediency. This was not the Das Tausendjährige Reich *that Hitler had intended. To strike now would be futile, and so the Burgundians camouflaged themselves, pretending conformity to that which they most despised; but only in the daylight were they bourgeoise New Europeans. Under cover of darkness they came alive.*

A crisis had arisen in their diminished ranks when the initial space missions did not disturb the Eternal Ice. But the orthodox may always be relied on to explain away discrepancies when the Sacred Articles of Faith do not quite fulfill expectations. It was suggested that there would be a cumulative effect. Too much activity in outer space would bring down the wrath of the gods, later if not sooner. They would wait out the years.

The miserable failure of an attempt to sabotage a German rocket launching taught them the strategy of patience, and the tactical necessity of a more significant target. Against the audacious plans for industrialization in space must be brought the most daring attack, and to win the favor of the gods, the sin must be large and complete before it was punished. Only then would the Burgundian schemers believe that they might win the favor of all the gods, who were known to quarrel among themselves. What the gods really needed was a proper Fuehrer, a role that Odin did not completely satisfy.

And so they planned for the future, as did their enemies. A decisive blow must be struck against the false dream of progress. To achieve this lofty purpose, hundreds must be prepared, tested, screened, and distilled into one special individual. He would have a technical aptitude unhampered by any convictions about the skills he would acquire. They would train him and condition him and lie to him. And when the time drew near, they would take him out under the night sky of Burgundy and point out the star he must destroy.

Their ceremonies always ended at dawn.

Chapter Twenty

The dead can be more dangerous than the living.

> – H. R. Trevor-Roper,
> quoted in *Imagining Hitler*

Mein Führer, I can walk.

> – Peter Sellers in
> *Dr Strangelove, or: How I Learned to Stop*
> *Worrying and Love the Bomb*

Alan and Hilda's first week in New York had been a hectic one. There is nothing quite like an American audience, composed as it is of volatile contradictions – Puritanism colliding against hedonism, while self-absorption vies with rhetorical high-mindedness. Hilda was a magnet to draw the expected guest but also the peculiar, the sincere alongside the antagonistic and the ignorant. She had thrived in the electric atmosphere at first. With a woman's eye for detail, she found delight in the *outré* costumes parading in front of her that seemed to be playfully mocking her old-world tastes. New York was the first place she'd ever seen a zoot suit, which Alan helpfully explained was making a comeback among the literati. She signed hundreds of autographs and wore unusual hats. She made new friends; but there was also the requisite number of enemies.

Hilda had been surprised by the abuse she received in some quarters. It was one thing to face an honorable opponent who challenged her assumptions, but quite another to be roundly denounced by a total stranger employing the sort of personal terms she didn't expect to hear outside a family circle. But always Alan was there to help. 'This is America,' he told her. 'Remember that we threw out the libel laws for running contrary to the spirit of the First Amendment. In this country, the only opinions that matter are the ones you choose to accept. It's not nearly so easy to destroy a reputation as it used to be. For every fool, there is an intelligent person who makes up his own mind.'

After the life she'd led, Hilda was nothing if not adaptable. Although she was committed to theoretical anarchy, the American Republic was still the freest society she had ever experienced. She even picked up the uniquely American trait of making light of impertinence. 'It's just that under National Socialism,' she recalled, 'character assassination is performed at the institutional level . . . with literal results.'

'We do a lot of forgiving over here,' said Alan. 'We have to.'

He enjoyed coaching her. Where she would answer difficult questions at considerable length, he advised the succinct response. A few grillings on television and radio brought her around to his persuasion. The decisive encounter was on Alexei Tierni's aptly named show 'The Inquisition Box.' This former Bible salesman had a national audience, but most of his subscribers were in what he himself called the boondocks. Guests were warned to expect a hard-hitting interview on the 'Box,' which weekly ordeal Tierni quite predictably touted as a family program. But when a guest struck his fancy, he could be nice.

'So, Hilda Goebbels,' he began in the tone of voice he reserved for passing judgement, 'why should we believe this little book of yours?' Sitting in the green room, watching her on the monitor, Alan could see Hilda brace herself. Until that moment, neither of them had known if they'd be in for the hard or soft treatment. If Tierni was going to be a bastard about it, Alan could only hope that the practice sessions he'd insisted on would pay off. He was spending more time on Hilda than on his wife or the magazine.

'What would you like documented?' she asked without allowing the pause that is deathly in broadcasting.

'You speak English well, I'll give you that.' When all else failed, Alexei relied on the non sequitur.

Her eyes kept drifting to the quite remarkable wig the host carried on his head, a black spread of oil that seemed in danger of sliding off at any moment. Also the lights were too bright. Was this a plot to make her squint into the camera? At least the studio audience seemed divided in its sympathies.

Tierni appealed to the disenchanted who wanted the return to a more vigorous nation-state. Even so, his religious zealotry limited his practical influence within this group. And a large part of his audience simply enjoyed the circus. Alan had warned Hilda of the problems, but she insisted on going after the publicity anyway. She'd be a good American, yet.

'I don't know what's worse,' intoned Alexei, 'our libertine liberty lovers here – and I do mean lovers – or the Nazis over there who at least show a little public decorum.'

'I've lived there and I know what's worse,' Hilda shot back. She garnered a few random bits of applause for that. So far, so good.

Alexei made the mistake of returning to her facility with languages, an unsubtle way of reminding the viewers not to trust a damned foreigner. She remembered that Baerwald had told her of how Jews who had come to America to escape persecution in Germany all too often found themselves the victims of prejudice for being Germans! Times had changed a lot since then, and the kind of demagoguery she was experiencing was no longer the norm. In some ways, she found the Yankee style of hate mongering almost quaint, compared to the Nazi variety.

'Do you want to know if I'm grammatical in every language I speak?' Smiling sweetly, she continued: 'How about you? I understand that you lapse into "Tongues" when you worship. When yours is the voice, does the Holy Ghost speak grammatically or not?'

'How the hell would you know about that?' he shouted, unaware that the research was courtesy of Mencken's good old magazine, ever vigilant. Tierni didn't want to play up his religion currently (despite the oath to witness for the faith). The Lord's Laborers, the sect to which he belonged, was currently in hot water because some of its most vocal members were being prosecuted for violating two of the laws that the libertarian republic actually enforced. The leader had mistakenly thought that decentralization of powers meant that the Bill of Rights did not apply to local matters, such as the regulation of sin. The right reverend gentleman was duly informed that the Fourteenth Amendment was still on the books, much to the dismay of a constabulary made up almost entirely of members of the Lord's Laborers who had imprisoned pornographers and burned a bookstore. These officials were themselves now up on criminal charges. Property rights were taken seriously in the republic.

'Well, Hilda Goebbels,' stammered Alexei, 'if you're going to get personal, I ain't . . . I'm not going to stoop to your level.' Alan silently applauded as the interview moved on and noted that the audience was laughing with Hilda.

The flustered host went back on the offensive: 'If you're a repentant Nazi, like you say, then why haven't you changed your name?'

'First, I never joined the Party. Contrary to popular belief, you're not born into it. Oddly enough, Father never insisted. I turned down an invitation to join the

Reichsschrifttumskammer, their writers' organization. I wanted no part of it. Second, I don't believe in Voodoo.'

'Huh?'

'Guilt by association is bad enough. Guilt by name is so primitive an idea that I'm shocked it has seeped into our civilization. In fact, there is no reason why the greatest enemy of Hitler couldn't be named Hitler himself!'

Shifting in his seat, leaning toward her menacingly, the host lamented, 'Obviously you don't care about the feelings of the people.'

'Are we concerned with form or substance?' she asked. 'The feelings that matter are not isolated from thought, for heaven's sake. From the earliest age, German children are taught that there is no injustice so great that it cannot be cured by more injustice. The Nazis are very concerned with the people's feelings, take it from me. The only way to fight that is with clear thought.' This won her murmurs of approval out there beyond the stage lights, and Alan marveled at how the cadences of her speech were adjusting to TV talk. In private, she spoke slowly, accumulating pauses with the unconscious certainty that her listeners would bear with her. She wasted no seconds now. She finished her hymn to reason by suggesting that if the Allies had been reasonable at Versailles, the world would have been spared the worst monstrosities of the century.

When sensing a sea change in the studio audience's prejudices, Alexei Tierni could always be relied on to plumb the depths. 'Well, Miss Goebbels, isn't it true that the SS is full of homosexuals?'

'I can't believe you'd ask a question like that in America!'

'Hey, we have free speech here. Maybe you don't appreciate how much inquiring minds want to know.'

She shrugged. 'You're confusing the SA with the SS. National Socialist Germany is homophobic, in case your inquiring mind missed that detail.' Tiring of the boor sitting across from her, Hilda wondered if she shouldn't have heeded Alan's suggestion to pass on this one. But if her new home was to be the country devoted to the teachings of the Profits, then she did not want to pass up a potential market, even one so unsophisticated as the subscribers to this benighted program. Rather than discuss her views on sex, she preferred putting the inquisitor on the defensive. 'Why are you so interested in . . .' She committed her first pregnant pause as she struggled to recall her American slang, confused for a moment by the British slang for cigarette. '. . . the fags, Mr Tierni? Is it from tender concern over some of Hitler's victims?'

He used his down-home, simple-boy voice: 'I just want Mom and Pop to know that Nazis are all sexual degenerates and Europe is perverted.'

It was becoming a worse spectacle than Alan had anticipated. In his self-adopted role as Hilda's manager, he wanted to reach out and pull her off the stage. His admiration for her grew as she weathered the storm, a woman of the old world with elegant vices and staunch virtues. While she wanted to tell America how Germany was pursuing the siren call of empire, and turning its people into dupes and corpses in the bargain, this amateurish demagogue with the phony hair was less interested in what came out of a leader's head than his loins. Alexei Tierni seemed a whole lot less quaint all of a sudden.

Having caught his drift, she made it abundantly clear that she would not answer questions about her sex life, or her father's or mother's, or Hitler's, or even Hitler's dog. Chuckles from the audience reminded her how silly it all was. There was no point in losing her temper, apparently the only reason this man had guests. He'd probe and prod and insult until he struck angst. The trick was to make yourself calm and avoid the traps.

At which moment, the man in the 'Box' became the first interviewer to raise the specter: 'What about this

292

Dietrich feeb, this lunatic in the lab, huh? You can't expect Mom and Pop to believe someone like that really exists.'

Oh, hell, thought Alan.

The mere mention of the dreaded name was like a trickle of cold water dampening Hilda's high spirits of the earlier moment. To her it was as if Tierni had asked for proof that there had been an Isaac Newton. She explained: 'Someone did the work that's led to the new vaccines, hormones, and drugs. And that's only the tip of the recombinant DNA iceberg. However, these facts don't mean that Dietrich is still living. We have the fruits of his brilliant mind, but hopefully he has taken his evil soul with him to the grave.'

'Pretty poetic. Sounds like you're quoting from your book. But how do we know that a whole bunch of guys didn't do this work you claim is Dietrich's.'

This segued nicely into a plug, which opportunity she was not about to miss. 'For the answer to that, you should read my book!'

Before the time ran out, Alexei had one last inanity he'd been saving. He actually asked if there shouldn't be limits on technology. Without missing a beat, she suggested that any medical technology that might prolong the life of rude television hosts should be withheld by all means. The studio audience liked her, a good indication of how she was received by the home viewers. The thunderous applause caught Tierni by surprise. Every now and then this happened, but he couldn't let that discourage him. He was all set to torment his next guest: a Nordic cult believer who was planning an expedition to reach the hollow interior of the earth. This was one of his theme programs.

Alan had planned their escape route beforehand, and a limo was waiting for them. (He'd made sure it wasn't a Horch!) Hilda was laughing as they sped off into the night. She wanted to be angry, but she couldn't quite manage it. There are limitations to righteous indignation when the inquisitor is a clown. Alan began rattling off a list of advantages and disadvantages to accrue from the broadcast, but she didn't want to hear it. 'My good friend,' she said, 'you have a tendency toward an over-bearing solicitude that is fortunately offset by a paranoia to match my own.'

'Hilda Goebbels,' he replied, mimicking the style of the unlamented program, 'you sure are a writer, and you use English real good.'

'You warned me that this "gentleman" with the living wig has the right to, what was the term, bleep me?'

'Yeah, he'll bleep the word *fag*, for instance.'

'That's terrible. Didn't I use the right word?'

'It fit.'

'Why am I to be . . . bleeped?'

'It offends the morality of the show, says he.'

'I'm surprised that kind of censorship can happen in America.'

'He's not the government, Hilda. Don't forget you signed his contract, and when he says "family program," he means *his* family. Alexei is the kind of guy who is afraid of his own imagination. Your other interviews didn't allow any bleeps. Contracts are sacred.'

'Let's not do any more shows like "The Inquisition Box." I've learned my lesson. To tell the truth, I'd just as soon not make any more appearances for a while. I need a rest.'

He moved closer to her, and she pleased him by putting her head on his shoulder. Now was the time to ask if she'd let him show her the town. She nodded. He gave instructions to the driver.

'Alan, where do you find so much time for me?'

'I manufacture it.'

'You'll have to teach me how to do that.'

He'd never seen her vulnerable before, or so relaxed. They parked just outside a pedestrian zone and went to a Bohemian restaurant that specialized in soft lighting and good wine. When they had finished, he suggested that they once again face the hazards of motorized traffic so as to reach an entertainment ghetto and take in a show. This they did, and the chauffeur, waiting for them a second time, thanked Alan for the generosity of his tips.

Perhaps the Teutonic gods were in a capricious mood, because the first notable entertainment that caught their attention was a Sturm und Drang concert, the vibrations of which could be felt for blocks . . . and the musicians were only warming up. She was drawn to find out what this could be and Alan had a morbid fascination as well. His music reviewer on the *American Mercury* had referred to this stuff as the secret weapon of German *Kultur*. The only musical taste he was certain he shared with Hilda was a fondness for the German Richards: Strauss and Wagner. (But theirs was reputed to be quiet music next to an S&D concert.)

As if they were two children, accepting each other's dares, they waded into the steam pouring out the doors, money held out in front of them as if to propitiate demons. They never made it to seats. The sound was a physical force blocking them in the aisles, but judging from the collection of frenzied Townies (probably looped on Speck) in the auditorium, standing was an appealing proposition. It was impossible to understand what language was being sung, but each word had the force of a blow to the head.

Alan saw Hilda's lips move, but no smaller sounds could be heard over the cacophony. Realizing this, she pointed with some amusement to the lead singer, whose attire was nothing to talk about. He was shaved bare all over, covered in neon paint, and his sole attire consisted of shiny black boots that came up to his knees. While

295

marveling at his various bodily imperfections, Alan and Hilda were rewarded by the incomparable sight of a Townie in the front row throwing an entire mug of beer on the lead singer.

This was not a smart move. Having successfully avoided electrocution from his electric violin, the singer-screamer silenced the fellow members of his band and began shouting at the Townie in a most recognizable American idiom: 'Hey, this piece of slime in the front row threw a beer on me. Do you hear me, loyal fans? He could've killed me. Now why don't you take this slime outside and turn him into ashes, man. *Kill him for me!*'

They went for him. They held up in the air this one Townie begging for mercy over the fever throbbing of the mob, and suddenly Alan felt Hilda trembling up against him, and she was dry heaving. There was no rush for the exits. The rush was in the other direction, down toward the stage where they could get a better view. The security guards were shouting into their walkie-talkies and trying to figure out what they could do.

Alan got Hilda out of there fast, and when they were back on the street she threw up. He hustled her back to the limo as fast as he could, and the driver, who was good, didn't talk but knew a quiet place to go when Alan asked.

They took a walk, not far from the car but far enough. 'I can't stand it, Alan. I'm in the concert, hating it, sensing how much it's like a Party rally, but telling myself it's not really the same thing, not really. And then *that* happens. And it comes back, it all comes back. I don't want to listen to the filthy rhetoric here, not here. I don't want to hear about killing slime and ashes and . . . not here, not here. And then to see them, that killing fury. First the chaos, then impose order. That is how Hitler did it.'

She sat on the ground exhausted. He joined her, arm

at her waist. They rocked together like that until she was ready to go home.

The publication of Hilda's books changed Alan Whittmore's life. There were rough times in the beginning, but the rewards made it all worthwhile. Dr Evans came out of the woodwork long enough to try proving that the diaries were fake, but the Bipartisan party provided him with less than adequate experts. The general public bought the book in droves. And then they bought the books arguing about the book. As Alan said to Evans on the occasion of their last meeting, 'The most money you've ever made was from debunking the Goebbels Diary.' Evans couldn't argue with that. The public preferred reading about Nazis over the definitive study of the New Deal.

The kooks had a field day. Hundreds of phone calls and letters and telegrams purported to be threats from 'Doctor Mabuse.' It got to the point where Hilda and Alan agreed that the real mad scientist would need to provide his bona fides before anyone would take the next end-of-the-world threat seriously.

The SS behaved in Europe as Hilda had predicted. They ignored the book. Within a few months of the diaries being published, Baerwald sent one of his best bottles of wine to Hilda in celebration of the fact that no acts of terror had been committed against them for her exposé. They all hoped that SS bravado had been dealt a mortal blow. (Baerwald wasn't about to miss the diary bandwagon. He wrote an introduction and helped with the considerable documentation. Hilda said that he was invaluable; and to repay the compliment he used his real name.)

Harold Baerwald died in 1984, and Hilda and Alan attended the funeral in New York, where the author of the Freedman books had finished his life. The next day,

Alan introduced Hilda to Oscar, who now had a chain of restaurants; and an autographing party ensued for Hilda, on condition that a complete set of Harry's works be auctioned off to raise money for his family.

'So when are you going to give me your autobiography to publish?' asked Alan.

'You were pushy when you were solely an editor. Now that you've become your own publisher, you're in danger of terminal megalomania.'

'Got bills to pay.'

'You don't need more money, do you?' she asked cheerfully. 'Success has gone to your head.' She pointed to the golden dollar sign he wore on his cheek. 'You used to abhor tattoos and face illustration.'

'They like it for the talk shows,' he said apologetically. 'But why are you wasting a talent like yours on translating German science fiction when you're famous? Any political book with your name on it will sell a million copies right off the bat.'

'It's the fault of our mad scientist, Dietrich. I've come to see that we live in a science fiction world. Nothing is certain. There have been more changes in the last century than, oh, God, how many millennia before? The First World War finished off the old world and left humanity high and dry, without purpose or direction. Then World War II created a new world, an incredible world that we don't really understand, but we must embrace. We've unlocked powers that will either send us to the stars or turn the whole planet into a death trap where everyone is a victim. We have no guarantee that there won't be another Hitler, with a man like my father orchestrating his followers, and a Dietrich giving him new weapons of destruction. Let's spread out and make ourselves a more difficult target.'

'Go to space, young man; go to space,' said Oscar, ever the eavesdropper in his own establishment. 'That's what I told my son when he graduated. He's up there on temporary, but he's signed up for permanent residence when a berth is available. He sent me back to school. I wouldn't have done it for anyone but my son.'

'Business has been good?' asked Alan.

'The best with my chain opened up, and with my son's winning a choice contract on the station, I didn't have any excuse not to go to college. He wants me to move spaceward eventually, but I don't know about that.'

'I'm going,' said Hilda.

'You are?' asked Alan. 'But what about – '

'Writing is allowed in space, Alan. They haven't outlawed it. I only regret that Harry won't be coming with me.'

As they parted at the curb, Alan thought back to a rainy day when he and a sour old man had exchanged words on the same piece of pavement, and Alan was about to enter the Isabel Paterson Hotel and a new life. 'I'll make you a deal,' said Hilda. 'I'll give you a finished copy of the autobiography, for what it's worth, if you come to a convention at which I'll be a guest next month.'

'I'm game.'

'Here.' She passed him a flyer. 'The Free Tribes of South Africa are hosting the World Science Fiction Convention at the Laissez-Faire Center in Capetown. This will be the first convention where artists from the Reich will attend in company with us lucky stiffs from the Free World.'

'I'm surprised the Reich will let them attend.'

'It's the latest attempt at good public relations. We'll be on the outlook for Gestapo agents shadowing the German guests. Want to bet there will be defections? The writers with subversive tendencies gravitate to science fiction. The Reich is not exactly the utopia they've been promising their wretched populace year after year. And the authorities didn't predict the future of Africa with any success.'

'Maybe the Reich is disappointed over its attempt to forge the tribes into miniature National Socialisms. When apartheid collapsed, the last hope for the Nazis to colonize that region collapsed.'

'They're stuck, and they know it. Without American and African capital, they'll never finish the world's largest autobahn. Let them learn the limitations of empire! Let them learn that racism doesn't work!'

'You've mapped out quite an educational program there.'

'You said it. *Ciao*, honey.' He continued talking to her in his mind long after the cab was gone. It was a long month to wait.

On the flight to Africa, Alan considered the postcard Hilda had mailed. The picture was of the partially completed space habitat that she intended to make her home. The mineral resources of South Africa would contribute significantly to the celestial city. She wrote about how important it was to mine the moon for the many future environments that were planned. She started to say a few words about the resources of terrestrial oceans, but she ran out of space.

During the trip, he watched the moon grow brighter with the fall of night, as if it fed upon the day to become an unblinking eye to guide the plane. The hours passed peacefully. He slept. When he opened his eyes again, they were coming in at a low altitude, and the city was spread out like ladies' fine jewelry on black velvet. There were stars above and stars below. A young black man was waiting for him at the gate. 'Hello, Mr Whittmore. I'm David.'

'Oscar's boy! Welcome back to Earth. I've always wanted to meet you.'

'Hilda asked if I'd take you to the hotel.'

'How long have you known each other?'

'Since yesterday, but she comes highly recommended by my father. And there is the little matter that I'm a fan of her books.'

'The science fiction?'

'And your book, Alan. May I call you Alan?'

'If you want me for company, you better!'

She was waiting for them in the bar, the center of attention for well-groomed young men, self-conscious in their formal attire, escorting very proper, willowy ladies in white evening gowns. The waitresses were every bit as elegant as the guests. He'd never experienced an atmosphere so full of grace and etiquette, a small, polished, discreet echo of the old colonialism that had been preserved by the New Africa. Hilda took his arm and walked him out onto a spotlessly clean veranda overlooking a waterfall.

'Won't you miss Earth?' he asked.

'I will see all of it every day,' she answered. 'From space.'

'Will you be harder to pester about deadlines up there?'

'Not if you're nice about it. Why don't we discuss the matter at PAXCON tomorrow?'

'What's that?'

'The name of this year's world science fiction convention, of course. If we're going to have world peace, this is a good place to begin.'

He got her to admit that the seed of her complicated plot went back to the choice of hotel where they had first met. She must have had her eye on the teenage eccentrics and their fantasies all the time, but Africa was a safer place to meet than the Wild East. Yes, it was all a vast conspiracy to bring him halfway around the world to watch her deliver a prospace speech to Martians and monsters, as if he didn't have enough troubles.

Twenty-four hours later, he understood. She had done

this so he would better appreciate her impending change of address. And he enjoyed himself immensely at PAXCON.

Where but a convention like this, in a country recently torn by civil war but now enjoying the prosperity and camaraderie that only comes from the profit motive, where else, he asked himself, could be found on the same stage, in 1984, as co-guests of honor, the aged figures of Fritz Lang and Thea von Harbou? Lang, who had declined the odious offer from Joseph Goebbels to join in the symphony of hate and instead taken his directorial skills to Hollywood; von Harbou, who had remained loyal to the Third Reich but without a degeneration in her talent as a writer and scenarist – the husband-and-wife team who had presented the world with *Metropolis*, *Frau im Mond* (Woman in the Moon), *Die Nibelungen* (based on *The Ring of the Nibelungen*) . . . and introduced a sinister character to the cinema screens in *Dr Mabuse der Spieler*! Futuristic medical technologies they had dreamed in their fiction came true for them. Advanced eye surgery had returned to Lang his precious sight after he'd suffered the dark night of blindness; other medical advances had kept von Harbou alive.

Through the auspices of an American science fiction enthusiast named Forrest J Ackerman, the impossible had been accomplished. The couple had been reunited at PAXCON. (An earlier convention in Los Angeles had used the name in reference to the Pacific Ocean, but the title had been resuscitated for the first SF convention to capitalize on détente and hopes for world peace.) Lang's most recent film was premiered, finished since the recovery of his vision: *Tomorrow*, shown on a double bill with the H. G. Wells picture of 1936 that predicted World War II, *Things to Come*. The prediction of *Tomorrow* was: *No more war!*

Hilda introduced Alan to virtually everyone, and he was pleased that the Dietrich matter was not broached in

302

Lang's presence. He had the impression that the venerable director had not read the final entries of Joseph Goebbels's diaries, and this was just as well. No real Mabuse hovered over the shoulder of this man.

Alan enjoyed meeting Ackerman and his wife, Wendayne Mondelle. The high point of the convention was when Ackerman led a toast, first in English, then in Esperanto, in honor of departed writers of fantasy and science fiction. There was a special remembrance for H. G. Wells and C. S. Lewis, who both died in the nuclear destruction of London. Nothing better illustrated the waste and stupidity of war than the loss of these two inventive and imaginative minds. (Afterward, Alan learned that Lewis had come down from Oxford to debate with Wells on the day that became a holocaust. The subject: Is There an Afterlife? The Christian apologist and atheist lecturer found out the answer, all right, but the world was denied future works by two of the century's finest writers. The loss in talent and ability would never be calculated from Hitler's revenge on the British.)

When Alan got his autographed copy from Thea von Harbou of her *Erdtunnel Nr. 1 Antwortet Nicht* (Earth-Tube No. 1 Does Not Reply), there was a *Jugend Spräche* band in the background, playing music banned in the Greater Reich. He wondered how a talented artist, no matter what her political beliefs, could live in a country that stifled creativity and enslaved the mind. He mentioned Baerwald to her, but got no response. Was that a Gestapo man watching them over by the bar? Alan thanked liberty that civilization did not belong entirely to the killers and slavers. The hope for world peace lay in the dignity of man.

He couldn't sleep that night. The convention was showing a movie series until dawn. He didn't know what to expect until he was comfortably in his seat and watching an all-night Mabuse retrospective. A Mexican version was playing, and the first closeup he saw was of an actor who was the spitting image of Herman, who had frightened him so badly. Alan's Spanish was only rudimentary at best, but the subtitles were in English. 'Nothing in the world will save you from my vengeance,' the villain was telling an unseen victim. 'I will kill you, kill you, kill you.' The hair was white, the face a skull.

For the first time since the man in the Horch limousine stared with mad eyes in his direction. Alan could laugh about it. A young boy sitting in front turned around and hissed out a long 'Shhhhhhhhhhhhhhh.' He smiled to the boy and nodded.

If a lone madman was threatening the world, the guy was certainly taking his own sweet time about letting the axe fall. It was corny, actually. And what was the worst that could happen? Alan wouldn't have to put up with any more Townies. Meanwhile, he had his life to live, and Hilda Goebbels's autobiography to publish.

Chapter Twenty-One

Under a tyranny, most friends are a liability. One quarter of them turn 'reasonable' and become your enemies, one quarter are afraid to stop and speak and one quarter are killed and you die with them. But the blessed final quarter keep you alive.

– Sinclair Lewis,
It Can't Happen Here

LETTER TO ALAN WHITTMORE FROM HILDA GOEBBELS

The Charles A. Lindbergh Experimental Orbital Community, September 1, 2000

Dear Alan:

Don't send the marines. This is not Nicaragua. Seriously, we are all right up here. Nobody died. But it was a close call, I'm not about to deny that. The reports of my heroism are greatly exaggerated, I regret to say. But I did perceive the danger first, my only gift I sometimes think.

Will we never be free of Burgundy? The new computer technicians had arrived, and it was only by a fluke that I even saw Fritz – that's his name. There were plenty of other Germans in the crew, but there was something about him that bothered me. Next you'll be saying I have telepathy!

He had undergone security clearance, but when you believe in freedom, you only take a probe so far. Fritz was on the Greiman System team. You know that's how our weather is controlled. We live inside a cylinder that if Father had lived to see, he would certainly compare to one of those micro-Tesla coils. The solar collectors do look a bit like suction cups, now that I notice. At least the German colony is being developed along similar lines instead of a Swastika! But you want to hear about Fritz.

He was working on the code for the system that governs the climate-control unit. The Greiman system, in case you're not familiar with it, is a method by which the length of the day is controlled by large mirrors on the outside of the colony. The mirrors reflect the sun onto the landscape. They are rotated about a pivot attached to the end of our habitat. This is how, by a clever reflection, we have the impression of the sun crossing our sky once a day. But when anyone feels like being a space cadet, there are many viewing areas allowing unobstructed communion with the earth and the moon and the stars.

The Greiman system regulates the colony's environment. It is a giant air conditioning unit. Through solar power, the air can be heated or cooled according to taste. Most of the time we have temperate climate, but on special holidays arrangements are made for changes. We have snow for Christmas.

The climate-control device is huge, and it makes use of an endless flow of information. That's one of the reasons we have room for more computer people. Now, when someone like Fritz is hired, the main concern is that he be familiar with the solid-state digital computers we use instead of the unwieldy liquid-helium-cooled analog computers on which the Reich has wasted so much effort. He did fine on the tests. There was no reason to suspect he was a Burgundian. Why would one of them even come up here, in direct violation of their religious tenets?

Anyway, part of the weather system controls air circulation – what I used to call the wind before I started reading technical manuals in place of poetry. The wind blows because of energy from the sunlight that is reflected by the mirrors into the *Lindbergh*. Heated air rises here, the same as anywhere else, and we are subject to the 'coriolis force.' This is a real place, you know. A moving parcel of air is affected by the rotation of the colony.

The security officers blame themselves for not recognizing the degree of danger that could come from this quarter. Too many years on earth gave them what you might call a 'bomb mentality.' We almost lost our lives because of a thin wafer of software, but we would have entered eternity secure in the knowledge that no explosives were detonated inside our home.

Fritz had been well prepared for his assignment. The accelerated air currents resulting from the heated air move toward or away from the axis of rotation. The nearer to the axis, the slower is the air parcel's velocity. New streams of air enter the system at about 100 mph, where they encounter slower masses of air. But as the parcel retains its inertia, it cannot help but pass the slower-moving air; and there are no traffic cops to pull it over. The result, as Fritz knew, is that air spirals toward the center.

After interrogation, it was evident that Fritz wasn't smart enough to make the calculations he used. But he was a good soldier. The calculations had been made beforehand by his masters, who had all the data they needed from our own press releases. The plot was to alter the angles of solar collection so as to direct a concentration of energy inside the *Lindbergh*. The air would be superheated, and the resulting turbulence would create a hurricane of ever-increasing magnitude until that moment when our correspondence would of necessity be terminated.

I don't mean to make light (is that a pun?) about what almost happened, but I'm the sort who would rather laugh than cry. The changes were gradual, and that gave us time to act . . . but there would have come that moment when there was no turning back. Fritz was prepared to sacrifice his life, and he had other programs to seal off the computer section and prevent overrides in the short run. Nobody died, and I will take credit for sounding the alarm.

What gave Fritz away? I saw him in one of the *Lindbergh*'s nightclubs. And to think Mother looked down her nose at cabarets. The Lazy Fairy employs the full spectrum of light in its floor shows, including a touch of infrared. Oscar's boy, David, is invariably outgoing with new people who come to work here. He's always trying to get them to immigrate. There's nothing like closed borders here to people with skills who want to work. And as for the land question, we keep making more of it; and new colonies are flowering in the sky. Well, David can be very inspiring. So we were talking to Fritz when the infrared bathed his forehead for a brief moment.

The letters and diagrams had been washed from his forehead, but they had been written in something that left its signature, a concoction of blood and ink, I suspect. I recognized the five- and six-sided polygons; I recognized what the SS purports to be the lost letters of Arya. This in itself did not prove him to be a poor, deluded Hörbigerian. And even if he was, that's not the same as evidence we had a Burgundian saboteur in our midst.

I respect other people's rights even when my life is in danger. I'm not a Gandhi, but I also don't jump the gun. The evidence justified a thorough investigation of his work, and that's how the scheme was uncovered. The hard-core members of security suggested that Fritz be summarily executed by spacing him out an airlock, as had been done with our last murderer; but I defended him on the grounds that, thanks to my timely intervention, he had not managed to kill anyone, himself included. I'm a softy in my old age. I was also curious.

Obviously Fritz had been brainwashed. The first step was to communicate with the part of him that didn't

308

belong to Burgundy. He was earnest and amusing. Often, he would interrupt himself to comment on his comments, a sort of metaconversation. But when he would comment on the comment on the comment, an oral footnoting, he risked sliding into an uncomputable recursive function. Just about the time he'd put David to sleep, and bored our friends from security right out of their violent impulses, I found the key I needed. He had the ideal personality to be sucked into a cult. His mind was a series of disparate subjects linked together, but without a discriminator to tell him what was important and what was trivial. Because he had no true beliefs of his own, he was the perfect zombie for an evil master. I broke the chain. He had been programmed to come up here and destroy the colony. My death was to be a bonus, but not the main object of the mission. I knew the Burgundian mantra, and I could ask him in a fashion he could not ignore the question of why he had been sent to destroy us. As I suspected, his answer was that our habitat violated the Eternal Ice. I asked why the Eternal Ice had not destroyed us itself. He'd never thought of that. I asked him how the mechanics of his scheme against us made any sense if Hörbiger was correct. He hadn't thought of that either. Like all cultists, he only echoed the beliefs of others, but had no beliefs of his own. His mind was so compartmentalized that the orders he was following had no referent to the data he would pick up on the mission, the very facts of physics and meteorology he would have to employ to finish his task.

They'd used drugs on him, too. At least he wasn't suffering from that poison the Townies of New York use. Speck is applied natural selection, but let each man go to hell in his own way. Fritz didn't mind being rescued, so he was worth the trouble. The physiological side of his problem was easier to fight than the psychological. Only he could do something about the latter if we weren't to brainwash him all over again. Because he wasn't sent to his grave in the vacuum, he had the opportunity to learn a few facts about space.

Cynics think Fritz is exploiting my kindness, and that his reform is not genuine. As I have no intention of reforming him, I don't care about that. I'm introducing him to the universe. He has no argument against the nonaggression principle, which is the contract and bond between free men. He is not committed to force. When his façade collapsed, and he was crying in my arms, he told how they conditioned him in Burgundy. He recounted every detail of the last night of his training. They whipped him. They used Dietrich's dreadful mind-control cylinders on him. That is why I do not regret that we haven't been able to recreate the technology of those coils. I'm convinced they do more than inform or entertain; I think they alter the structure of the brain. I wouldn't be at all surprised to learn that exposure to two of the coils in quick succession contributed to Father's mental breakdown. Another reason to find this Burgundian cult – as if we need it – is to get our hands on those coils and take them out of circulation.

Yes, Alan, I will cover all this in the second volume of the autobiography, but after I submit the manuscript you must agree that whatever remains of my life is private. Deal?

Fritz also provided an opportunity to find out if Dietrich is still involved with Burgundy. You will be relieved to learn that our amateur in the art of sabotage never encountered anyone with Mabuse-like characteristics during his time with the enemy. This does not prove that Dietrich is dead, but it increases my conviction that the alliance between electromagnetic biology and the SS feudalists is at an end. Alan, let us agree that Dietrich died in the explosion. Say it with me. Believe it with me.

David wants me to ask you if you'd consider a book from him contrasting the difference in the German and

American space programs. This is a case of blowing our own horn, as the Reich is shifting its approach. They are probably envious of the new hydrogen-fueled hypersonic spaceplane traveling at twenty-five times the speed of sound. This will certainly facilitate travel between the colonies and Earth. Consider how much quicker it will be to get from Earth to the intermediary stations en route to the celestial cities. Everything tried in this line by the Reich was a flat bust. Maybe they'll learn.

Where would we be without leaks from the sieve of New Berlin? The impetus behind David's suggestion is the information smuggled out about the incredible stupidity of the German side in the moon race. Typical! Did you know they wiped out their entire ground crew at liftoff? Then again, this might not have been accidental. The ground crew was largely Hungarian, and some creep in authority might have decided that in the name of national security, the men should be told to move to shelters only half the distance from actual safety. When considering the Nazis, one must always be suspicious.

The only benefit of the doubt I'm willing to extend is because of the nature of the *Hitler*, their appropriately named boondoggle. Despite protests from Wernher von Braun, they did not follow the approach America used: multistage chemical rockets, and a space platform from which to launch for massive savings in payload to gladden a capitalist's heart. No, they insisted on building a colosseum-sized disk, with a diameter of half a kilometer, and powered by hundreds of small atomic bombs. The shielding for the ship alone could bankrupt most countries. What's your gut instinct about the blast area? Was it a miscalculation, or did they really put the bunkers within the destructive radius? However you slice it, this was an entirely characteristic Nazi project. Well, at least they had the sense to confront the Hörbigerians with the facts about what the moon is made of when they got back home.

I will always delight in the fact that without leaving a trail of bodies in its wake, the American Republic got to the moon first. You're a good minarchist, Alan, and you believe in a limited government; but as an anarchist, I'm pleased that the businessmen who first set foot on Luna did not erect a flag, but declared it an open range, for the use and development of whoever gets there. Nobody owns the moon. Wouldn't you know it that when their turn came, the National Socialists claimed the entire satellite as theirs? But of course that is common knowledge. There are twice as many non-Reich explorers on the moon right now as Teutonic imperialists; but it annoys me to see the Swastika in the German zones. Am I the only person to notice that socialists were the first to try and turn a new frontier into, well, a private preserve of their own, a monopoly?

Now, about your question. I don't see what more I can add to my father's diaries, even with the new editions. Will you make it available to the micronet? I have one of the carry-all books with me currently. It's strange to open a plastic box in the shape of a book and see a display screen that can bring up any text available in the library to which it is keyed. I'm a traditionalist at heart; I like the smell of glue and paper.

You are so insistent when you want something! You won't let me forget my father, will you? After all these years, it is a strange feeling to look at the diary pages again. He accurately described me as the young and headstrong girl I was, although I wonder if he realized that I was firmly in the underground by the time I was warning him about Burgundy. In one sense we were using him; but in another sense I hoped to save his life . . . then. What finally pushed me over the edge I can't rightly say. It was cumulative. I wonder what my father, my

312

enemy, would say if he could see the crotchety old woman I have become.

I regret not speaking to him on his deathbed, as he did with Hitler. The question I would have asked would be how he thought Reich officials would ever allow his diaries, from 1965 on, to appear in Europe? The early, famous entries, from 1933 to 1963, had been published as part of the official German record. The entries beginning with 1965 would have to be buried, and buried *deep*, by any dictatorship. Father's idea that no censorship applied to the privileged class – of his supposedly classless society – did not take into account sensitive state documents, such as his record of the Burgundy affair, or his highly sensitive discussion with Hitler. If the real *Final Entries* had not been smuggled out of Europe as one of the last acts of the underground, and delivered to me, I would never have been in a position to come to terms with memories of my father. Nor would I have had the book that secured my reputation. I'm honest enough to admit it. Americans love hearing about Nazi secrets.

As I begin a new life of semiretirement in America's first space city, haunted by equal portions of earthlight and moonlight, I'm willing to reconsider this period of history, but I would like to find something new to say. Yesterday, they had me speak to an audience of five hundred about my life as a writer. Only one questioner had a morbid curiosity about the details of my tenure as a soldier. Who was it who said that hell hath no fury like a noncombatant?

Most of them wanted to know how much research I had put into the series about postwar Japan and China. They wanted to know how I deal with writer's block. But most of all, they wanted to hear about Nazis, Nazis, Nazis.

A handsome young Japanese man saved me by asking what I considered the greatest moment of my life. I told him it was that I had been a successful thief. Once the audience of dedicated free-enterprisers had stopped gasping like fish out of water, I explained. The specter of cancer was put to rest because of work derived from original research by our old friend Richard Dietrich. There's no denying it. But why should we? The most pleasant irony I've ever tasted was that his final achievement was for life instead of death. I made it possible. It was I who brought his papers to human beings. If a flesh-and-blood Dietrich, or a ghost, intends to punish me for this good deed, it has yet to happen. Farewell to shadows, I say.

As the presentation was entirely in English, I wrapped it up with a pun that I think most of the Japanese had sufficient command of the language to appreciate, but they are so unfailingly polite that you can't help but wonder if there would be the slightest difference no matter what was said. The matter of German philosophy had been brought up, not without cause, and I was expected to give my opinion on the Big Names. I hit them with: 'Nietzsche sustains my interest but Immanuel Kant!' My pleasant young man's groan seemed real enough.

I must take repeated breaks in dictating this addendum. My back gives nothing but trouble, and I spend at least three times a day in zero-g therapy. How Hitler would have loved that. After the last bomb attempt on him, his central concern became the damage to his *Sieg Heiling* arm, and his most characteristic feature – his ass. To think my father virtually worshiped that man! I guess if Napoleon had succeeded in unifying Europe, he'd be just as popular.

Now I'm reclining on a yellow couch in Observation 10A. There is a breathtaking view of Europe spread out to my right, although I can't make out Germany. The Fatherland is hidden beneath a patch of clouds. What I can see of the continent is cleaner than any map. Do you know what is missing? You can't see any borders. You

314

can't see any districts. All there is is land and lakes and enough *Lebensraum* for everyone.

I have to think what sort of person I might have become if I had been a good little girl and done my duty. One of my prides is that I never betrayed a friend. My hope is to live to see Europe free once more. I'm not holding my breath, but I see small signs, small hopes. I am the last person in the world to suffer from wishful thinking, Alan, so you can take any optimism on my part as carefully considered.

How did it feel in the old days when I lived in the bowels of Hitler's monster, and will I ever forget when engaging in contemporary analysis? The bitter taste will never leave. There were more victims of the Nazis than only those who wore the patches. For me, it was as if I existed in a glass hothouse for the care of sickly plants in which I was the primary specimen. Instead of the refreshing aroma of sweet flowers, there was the cloying odor that comes from ripeness and decay. And the soil, although having the darkness associated with fertile earth, was a carpet of blood. I spent the empty hours listening to the howling of the wind outside those thin glass walls.

I do not miss the dangerous people, guarded conversations, and nameless dread. If a gauleiter failed to return a phone call, that was ample cause for the Asphalt Man to prowl the landscape of my dreams. No matter how high on the ladder, there was never a sense of the morrow assured. In fact, the greater the altitude, the more painful was the nibbling fear, for high above the ground is no good place to hide.

Every social engagement was cause for anxiety. If not the inexplicable frown, then the smile withheld would do the trick. Those who imagine Nazi Germany to have been an unsubtle place are right for the open victims of its policy; but for the rest of us, there were other infiltrations of the soul.

315

Can I put all this in context when attempting honest analysis today? My answer is that Harry Baerwald could. The emotional scars I wear from the Goebbels family cannot compare to his physical scars. He is my inspiration. I will be as objective as humanly possible. You have helped free me of my past as much as anyone could, Alan, and I will always be grateful.

Who could have predicted the ultimate consequences of Hitler's war? Certainly not myself. I recognized what Nazi Germany was because I grew up there, but that's not the same as seeing to the heart of things. It was an organization in the most modern meaning of the word. It was a conveyor belt. Hitler's ideology was the excuse for operating the controls, but the mechanism had a life of its own. Horrors were born of that machine, but so were fruits. Medals and barbed wire, diplomas and death sentences – they were all the same to the machine. The monster seemed unstoppable. In the belly of such a state, it was easy to become an anarchist. The next step was obvious: join a gang of your own, to fight the gang you hate. None of us on any side – not the Burgundians, not the underground, not the Reich itself – could see what was really happening. Only a few pacifists grasped the point.

Adolf Hitler achieved the exact opposite of all his long-term goals, and he did this by winning World War II. Economic reality subverted National Socialism.

The average German used to defend Hitler by saying that he got us out of the Depression, without bothering to note that the way the glorious Fuehrer paid off all the classes of Germany was by looting foreigners. This was not the friendliest method for undoing the harm of Versailles. But as Europe began to remove age-old barriers to commerce, economic benefits began to spread. A thriving black market insured that all would benefit from the new plenty, and ideology be damned. While the

Burgundians actually tried to implement Hitlerian ideals, the rest of Europe began to enjoy a new prosperity.

Father was intelligent enough to notice this trend, but he avoided drawing the obvious conclusion: Nazi Germany was becoming less National Socialist with every passing decade. For all the talk of Race Destiny, it was the technical mind of Albert Speer and his successors at the controls of the German Empire. Ideology would surface long enough to slow down the machine, or cause it problems, but in the end technical management would reassert itself.

The side-show bigots provided decoration. Their rationale was not the class fantasies of Marx or dreams of the Common Man during the most fascistic period of the democracies, but the myth of race. Whatever bleak form the rituals of self-delusion may take, the motivation remains to build an illusion of personal power in the age of impersonal bureaucracy.

Adolf Hitler was going to achieve permanent race segregation when it's not even clear what constitutes a race. He couldn't be bothered by details. His New Order lasted only long enough to knock down the barriers of ethnic and national separation. Economics did the rest. Today there is more racial intermarriage than ever, thanks to Adolf Hitler. The theories of Isabel Paterson rise over the wreckage of *Mein Kampf*. She had told us all along that it is through the mixing of cultures that the long circuit of economic energy is maintained. But I doubt that any Nazis have read her book *The God of the Machine*, even though it explains what is happening to them.

Judging from your last letter, you accept the Great Man theory of history. I know you have moved back and forth on this. As for me, I believe in the Inexorable Event. Is it my age speaking? But what really matters is the outcome, the world we live in. That is what should concern us.

Another cause for hope is that today we see an outbreak of historical revisionists within Germany itself. Although they choose their words with care, the message comes through: they show Hitler's feet of clay. They are asking why Germany used a nuclear weapon against a civilian population, while President Dewey restricted his atomic bombs to Japanese military targets in the open sea. Even a thickheaded German may get the point after a while. The Reich's youth protests against the treatment of Russians by the Rosenberg Cultural Bureaus, and they are no longer shot, no longer arrested . . . and who knows but that they may accomplish something. If this keeps up, maybe my books, including *Final Entries of Dr Joseph Goebbels*, will become available in the open market, instead of merely being black-market best-sellers already. America is still the only completely uncensored society.

More than anything else, I am encouraged by what happens when German and American scientists and engineers work together. The autobahns of Africa are finally finished, and they have the trade to justify it. But nothing is more beautiful than the space colonies: the American and German complexes, the Japanese one (only half finished but potentially the most efficient), and finally, Israel.

When I was extended an invitation by President Levi ben Sherot to attend, I asked if I could bring Fritz along. The last stage of the lad's cure should be to walk among hundreds of Jews and discover that he has nothing to fear. The noxious fantasies that were poured into his head are almost gone, but this should be the litmus test.

Personally, I look forward to setting foot inside a colony that proves *Der Jude* could not be stopped by a mere Fuehrer. I'm promised a full tour, including the smaller attached colonies, or *kibbutzim*, in which most of the farming is done. I understand that bananas grow very well in space. The most notable feature is the location of the

Israeli colony. They have returned to their Holy Land, but at an unexpected altitude.

What would Father make of this sane new world? His final testament was the torment of a soul that has seen his victory become something alien and unconcerned with its architects. His life was melodrama, but his death a cheap farce. They didn't even know what to say at his funeral, he, the great orator of National Socialism. Without his guiding hand, they could not give him a Wagnerian exit.

The final joke was on him, and its practitioner was a man in a laboratory. Father sincerely believed that, in Adolf Hitler, the long-awaited Zarathustra, the New Man, had descended from the mountain. This, above all the rest, was the greatest lie of Paul Joseph Goebbels's life.

The New Man will ascend from the test tube. Nothing can stop his coming. I pray that he will be wiser than his parents.